THE LILY OF THE WEST

THE LILY OF THE WEST

KATHLEEN MORRIS

FIVE STAR

A part of Gale, Cengage Learning

GALE
CENGAGE Learning

Farmington Hills, Mich • San Francisco • New York • Waterville, Maine
Meriden, Conn • Mason, Ohio • Chicago

GALE
CENGAGE Learning®

Copyright © 2019 by Kathleen Morris.
Five Star Publishing, a part of Gale, a Cengage Company.

LIBRARY OF CONGRESS CATALOGING-IN-PUBLICATION DATA

Names: Morris, Kathleen, 1944– author.
Title: The Lily of the West / Kathleen Morris.
Description: First edition. | Farmington Hills, Mich. : Five Star, 2019. | Identifiers: LCCN 2018025318 (print) | LCCN 2018027298 (ebook) | ISBN 9781432847357 (ebook) | ISBN 9781432847340 (ebook) | ISBN 9781432847333 (hardcover)
Subjects: LCSH: Elder, Kate, 1850–1940—Fiction. | GSAFD: Western stories. | Biographical fiction.
Classification: LCC PS3613.O77335 (ebook) | LCC PS3613.O77335 L55 2019 (print) | DDC 813/.6—dc23
LC record available at https://lccn.loc.gov/2018025318

First Edition. First Printing: January 2019
Find us on Facebook—https://www.facebook.com/FiveStarCengage
Visit our website—http://www.gale.cengage.com/fivestar/
Contact Five Star Publishing at FiveStar@cengage.com

JAN 2 9 2019

Printed in Mexico
1 2 3 4 5 6 7 23 22 21 20 19

The Lily of the West

PROLOGUE

1881

Strident voices drifted through the open window.

"I'll kill them sonsabitches this time, Ike, I swear to God I will. They won't get away with treating us like dogs no more."

"Frank, you got to calm down. I don't even have a gun. Them bastards took it."

As I leaned over and peered out the window, the book I'd been reading when I dozed off tumbled to the floor. Five men stood below with a couple of horses, and I recognized all of them—Cowboys.

Movement up the street caught my eye. Three men dressed in black strode purposefully towards the corral, their boots kicking up little puffs of dust. I dropped the curtain and fumbled through some of the buttons on my dress.

When I pulled back the curtain again, a fourth man—one I knew well—came around the corner, his long black duster doing little to disguise the shotgun in his right hand. He stood beside the other three, a silent choir of dark avenging angels.

"Throw up your hands, boys. I've come to disarm you." Virgil's voice was clear and steady.

Hell had come to Tombstone, and I was riding on its coattails.

CHAPTER 1

Mexico City, October 1864

Sometimes a thing as simple as darkness makes all the difference between ease and pain.

"Your chocolate, Miss Katherine."

I opened my eyes and promptly shut them again. Luisa deposited the silver tray with its wonderful-smelling contents on the small table beside my bed. She'd already pulled back the curtains, and the bright morning of a new day beamed into my bedroom.

I rose up on my elbows and then fell back on the lace pillows. My head was pounding like the bass drum in the orchestra last night. The emperor's ball. All of them, out of place and out of time, preening and pandering as though this could last forever. I had enjoyed my first glasses of champagne and from what I felt like this morning, my last.

The delectable smell of cinnamon roused me as much as the chocolate, and I sat up again, ignoring the drumbeat in my temples. I took a sip of chocolate, and as the warm, dark liquid slid down my throat, I sighed with pleasure. It helped. Before I knew it, I'd finished the first cup, along with the cinnamon-and-sugar coated pastries, and had poured another cup from the silver pot. Luisa bustled about the room, picking up my white, lacy ball gown from the floor where I'd thrown it off the night before. Getting to my bed was all I'd cared about then.

The bedroom door opened, and my mother rushed in.

9

"Katherine, you darling girl!"

I loved my mother dearly, but she was a silly woman who thought of nothing but clothes, prestige, and our place in society. She bored me.

"Mother."

"You made such an impression on the marquis last night! It was positively amazing, sweeting. Even in this godforsaken place, there may be hope of an advantageous marriage." She was impeccably dressed (as always) in a gray taffeta morning dress, her carefully arranged coiffure bouncing beneath a lace cap. Her smile was dazzling, and I couldn't help but wince.

"Mother, I'm fourteen. Even the Virgin was older than that when she got a visitation."

She stopped, auburn curls and peacock feathers vibrating. How does anyone manage to get peacock feathers in their hair this early in the morning? The woman was a wonder.

"Katherine." She frowned. "Your attitude does you no credit. You have to think about your future. Don't be obstreperous."

I sighed and took another sip of chocolate. She was as much a product of her environment as the rest of society. That I was an anomaly wasn't her fault. "I'm just a child, Mother, studying my Latin and history in the schoolroom. I'm hardly ready for the marriage market."

She sniffed and sat on the edge of my bed.

"Do not play games with me, miss. You are of marriageable age and look at least sixteen. Your father will answer for this attitude. I told him education for young girls was dangerous nonsense, and look what it's come to. Latin, indeed."

"Indeed," I muttered, from deep in the chocolate cup. She had no inkling about French, English, Greek, history, or biological sciences and wouldn't have grasped their dangers, anyway. The mistakes of Heraclitus were always repeated.

She grabbed the cup and set it on the tray. Her nose was

inches from mine as she glared at me. "That is enough. This evening we are dining at the Marquis de Montfort's villa."

She directed her attention at Luisa, the shy maid hovering nearby. "See that she's ready, girl. Choose the blue dress, and arrange her hair over the shoulders, as befits a maid."

First champagne and now this. I buried my head under the covers. Tonight was many hours away. Maybe I'd be dead of a headache by then.

"Shut the curtains," I mumbled when I heard the door slam.

Luisa complied, and I tried to go back to sleep. Instead, I thought about my future. Ha. What sort of future could a girl have in the court of Emperor Maximilian, trying to survive in Mexico City? My father had brought us here when he was appointed the emperor's personal physician, and so far, it had been not exactly what he'd hoped. I longed for the green hills of our estate in Hungary, left behind when he'd brought us to America, following his dreams and the wishes of the royal family. Mexico was beautiful, especially Chapultepec Palace, where we lodged close to the emperor and his family, but it was so different from the pine forests I'd grown up with in Europe. Here, lush tropical flowers twined upwards on the balconies outside my window, and every afternoon sweet breezes blew the scent of cinnamon and gardenias. But the beauty was accompanied by the sounds of violence on the streets far below, where the native Republicans and Imperial troops of the emperor fought continually, providing a constant reminder that this was not our place. The Europeans here would soon be gone, if history was any judge, and even I, with my limited studies, had learned that usually it was.

For me, the best thing here was still being able to attend the lessons offered by the royal tutor. My father had always thought education of any kind was beneficial, even to girls. This was a novel attitude and one I loved him for, whatever his other faults.

My younger sister, Wilhelmina, was not of my persuasion. She was a sweet girl, Mina, but typical of her sex. I knew I was what was politely called "precocious" in some circles, although I preferred "intelligent." Phrased either way, it was not a particularly marketable marriage quality in women. I had been an avid reader since age four, and my father delighted in my prowess, supplying me as many books as I could digest, much to the dismay of my mother, who thought girls should only study needlework, housekeeping, and readying themselves for a husband. It was an ongoing battle but one I kept fighting, despite her attempts to make me, as she put it, "a gentlewoman with traits suitable to a good wife" rather than the wild-eyed termagant she feared.

Here in this microcosm of a European court, so out of place on this wild side of the Atlantic, Mother was determined to secure for me an advantageous, even noble, marriage, due to the scarcity of suitable women available to the aristocratic hangers-on of the emperor. She'd settled on the Marquis de Montfort, an aging roué with a taste for young flesh, especially mine. I didn't think he had marriage in mind, but only a romp, although convincing my mother of this was beyond my skills at this point.

She was not a worldly woman, and she was easily shocked by the evils of sophistication. She was blinded by the sumptuousness of the court and didn't see that Emperor Maximilian's faux world was crumbling around him. The utter ridiculousness of a European royal coming to the New World to style himself an emperor over a country as foreign and fractious as this one never occurred to her and apparently hadn't occurred to Maximilian and his backers, either. I knew my father saw it, and his increasing dependence on the emperor's excellent port, after dinner and well into the night, hadn't escaped me. The man felt helpless, well beyond concerned, and rightly so.

While statecraft had not been expressly taught by my tutors, I hadn't wasted my powers of observation in the last ten years. I'd been brought up in the courts of the Hapsburgs and had seen politics and intrigue swirl around the household and palace, their tentacles reaching even into the schoolrooms I'd shared with young princes and dukes. I'd witnessed more intrigue and falsehoods under the guise of smiling faces and gentle hands than most, and I'd learned a thing or two about trickery.

"Miss Katherine."

The maid's soft voice roused me from my slumbers. Usually I never slept well during the daylight hours, and I turned over, throwing off the bedclothes, the late afternoon sun faint through the gap in the curtains.

"I've had a bath brought," Luisa said. I blinked, pushing my hair away from my face. The copper tub sat beside the tiled fireplace, steam rising from its depths, and rose petals floating on the surface of the water. I stepped in and found it was just what I needed, the water enveloping me in its warmth.

An hour later, I was resplendent—clad in the desired blue taffeta, golden bronze ringlets around my face and satin slippers on my feet, ready for an evening of festivities with the court of Emperor Maximilian and his divine Empress Carlotta, not to mention the lascivious Marquis de Montfort and my grasping mother. The face that looked back at me from the mirror was not what anyone would term conventionally pretty. My chin was strong and my nose a bit too long to be called pert, but given a tilt to the mouth and a sidelong look of green eyes under long lashes, it was a face that definitely intrigued and attracted, and I knew it. At least the headache was gone, and my skin felt soft under the corset that pinched rather tightly, thrusting my still-burgeoning breasts some inches higher than they had a natural whim to be. Still, what a wasted day I'd had. The last week we had been studying Catullus, and I'd missed his journey to Capua, as I'd been drowsing in a stupor. Never again, I vowed. The more I learned, the better equipped I was to avoid a vapid, stifling life as someone's wife, stuck in a country manor breeding children and doing nothing more complicated than ordering foodstuffs and planning dinners for visiting courtiers. That was something I vowed would never happen.

The latch clicked, and my father entered, shooing Luisa and the undermaids away, their skirts fluttering in their haste. They were confounded by the gentle manner that belied his strong words and took every opportunity to hie themselves to other regions of the palace when he arrived.

"Kate," he said, kissing my cheek and standing back to observe my magnificence. He frowned, obviously unimpressed, and began to pace back and forth from the window to the dressing table, hands clasped behind his back. The illustrious Dr. Haroney was dressed conservatively, as always—black waistcoat and trousers, stiffly starched shirtfront, beard trimmed neatly. His brown eyes were deep in thought, but he was clearly agitated by more than my appearance.

"What is it, Father?"

He continued pacing, but shook his head. "All of it, dear girl, all of it."

I waited, knowing there was more to come.

"This place. These people. The emperor. Foolishness that has led to disaster. Not yet come, but it will."

He gazed at me under brows newly frosted with gray. "It is not safe for us here anymore. I know you understand that, even if no one else does, Kate."

He was right; I did. Mexico City was a hotbed of unrest, from Benito Juarez and his rebels to the recalcitrant nobles, some of whom danced in the evening with the emperor and nervously booked passage on trains leaving the next morning. It

was a powder keg waiting to explode—not a place that gave
ease to those who saw through the façade.

"Perhaps that is true. But where are we to go, Father? Back
to Hungary? Vienna? Paris?"

All my life, we had lived at the whim of the Hapsburgs. My
father had been court physician to archdukes and kings, and
now the emperor. Life had been elegant, comfortable, and
prosperous for the Haroney family—my mother, sisters, brothers, and I went wherever Father had been bid by his noble
masters. Until now, no threat or harm had touched us, but this
was a different world with different rules, and it was proving to
be a different brew altogether.

"I've been thinking about that, my dear, and I've been hearing a lot about the United States. They don't have kings there;
it's a place where a man is made by his own merits. I could
start my own medical practice. It would be different from the
life we've known, but I believe it would be beneficial to us all.
We could send for the other children once I've established
myself, and we'd all be together again."

He resumed pacing, but I was intrigued in spite of myself.
Only Wilhelmina, Alexander, and I had journeyed to Mexico,
while my younger siblings had stayed with relatives. I did miss
them, and I knew he did, too. "I've heard about it," I said,
watching him carefully. "It's a wild place, at least in the West, so
they say, but more civilized farther north and east. But there's a
war going on there, isn't there? Between slave owners and
northern businessmen?"

"That doesn't concern us, Daughter. I met a man from a
place called Iowa the other day. Good families, decent farming
folk, just the sort of place a gentleman of breeding could make
a home and a profession, and somewhat removed from this war
they're so concerned with. Besides, the war will be over soon,
and that'll only be to the good for a doctor who's knowledge-

able with injuries and such as the soldiers return home. It may even be just the place for a doctor's daughter who's entirely too smart for her own good."

My father was nothing if not pragmatic when thinking about his earning capabilities, but I wondered if years of royal support had blinded him to the practicalities of everyday living. I was irritated, both by his short-sightedness and by the fact that he was discussing this with me. I needed him to be strong, not asking for advice. Even so, the whole situation had frightened me for some time, and hearing his summation of the situation we were in, I was scared to the tips of my toes. Having been raised at court had taught me not to show emotion. When I was frightened, however, I tended to be unpleasant. I stood up and brushed my blue taffeta free of wrinkles.

"Perhaps. At any rate, it doesn't concern me."

He stared at me, clearly disconcerted. "Why is that, miss?"

"I'm likely marrying the Marquis de Montfort within two months, and we'll take house in his chateau at LeBrun," I said, watching my father's face pale. He deserved that and more for this mess he'd embroiled us in. I smiled brilliantly, brushing my skirts past his shoes as I swept out the door to the evening's entertainment.

CHAPTER 2

Davenport, Iowa, March 1865

"Next stop, Daaavenpooort, Ioway!" crowed the conductor.

I peered blearily out the window, wincing at his cheery voice. We'd left behind Maximilian and his court of fools, but I hoped whatever new frontier our small family was headed to was a benevolent one. For the last two weeks, we'd passed through the emptiest, bleakest countryside the world had to offer, and I held little optimism for any place named so drearily as Davenport.

Since leaving Mexico City on the heels of the Republican army, we'd traveled steadily for a month, my mother crying at the slightest annoyance, my little brother Alexander whining, my sister Wilhelmina sniveling, and my father snarling at us while struggling to maintain some shreds of paternal dignity. All of this transpired in a country that may have welcomed immigrants at one time, but whose inhabitants were clearly in the grip of their own troubles as a civil war raged. Only my ability to speak English had gotten us this far, and my skills were rudimentary at best. I'd been tutoring my family, but my father and Wilhelmina had been the only students I'd managed to inspire, my mother and six-year-old brother oblivious to my talents. In my opinion, taking a ship to any port on the other side of the Atlantic would have been a wiser choice, but my father was following his dream, or at least his hope, of a life in America, where a man could make his fortune. My personal

17

hope was that my mother had pocketed some of the Emperor's serving silver, because we would have need of it.

Our final evening in Mexico City had been one of fire and bullets disrupting the emperor's ball and dinner party, and that night was the last my father was willing to subject his family's wellbeing to, royalty or no. I'd said good-bye to the unbetrothed Marquis and his roving hands with little regret. The next morning had seen us on the road to Texas, a place I'd mostly slept through after a quick perusal of its paltry charms, while we'd journeyed north to more civilized climes. Civilization had so far eluded us, but north we'd gone, towards my father's promised land. From the villages and plains we'd seen so far, I had little hope we would find it here.

"Pass the biscuits, please, miss."

I placed the platter into the waiting hands of my table companion and watched it make its passage to the end of the table. Mrs. Hudginson's boardinghouse, the very best in Davenport, provided a hearty breakfast before sending its inhabitants out into the wintry dawn, and it was a meal I never missed. Not only was the food good, as Mrs. Hudginson was a wonderful cook, but I also got firsthand news of all that was going on in Davenport as well as the wider world, and plenty of gossip as well. This morning, in fact, I learned the Union army was reputed to be winning the war between the American states, and the South was headed for defeat. I knew little about their conflict, although I admired the Southern states for their sense of tradition and gentility against the businesslike cold competence of the Northerners and their Union. Although slavery was a filthy institution, Europe had plenty of people whose status was not far above it, and except for France, no one had ever seemed to care enough to go to war over it.

Iowa was a Union state, and while no battles had taken place this far west, they had supplied their share of troops and equipment to the cause. Davenport, a bustling town of some ten thousand souls on the Mississippi River, was still doing so, and its mud-churned streets were busy with commerce from the riverboats and railroads. A week after we'd arrived in Davenport, my father had found adequate if somewhat Spartan lodgings at Mrs. Hudginson's and gainful employment with the Union army as a physician who ministered to their Confederate prisoners in the prison camp at Rock Island. The stories he'd told me of the gentle nature of the patients he treated had touched my heart, and I'd spent many snowy afternoons assisting him and helping some of the young men write letters to their loved ones as they lay wounded and in some cases dying, in the cold winter of Iowa.

"Grant's going to kick their asses out of Vicksburg," crowed the black-bearded man across the table from me. "Them Southern boys will be going home in pieces just like they deserve."

I winced and put my fork down. Many of the gentlemen here had either avoided military service altogether, in search of profits, or were soldiers recuperating from dire wounds. After witnessing the carnage in the hospital wards my father attended, I couldn't delight in this misguided opinion.

"What company were you with, Mr. Nesbit?" I asked. I'd watched him for weeks and knew him for a blowhard ass.

Discomfited, he briefly cast his eyes towards his plate but recovered quickly. "I have great value to the war office, as you all know," he said. "I volunteered for the First Iowa regiment, missy, but I was more valuable as their first cavalry wrangler right here in Davenport, and I've fulfilled my duties. No man is more dedicated to the Union. Coming from some sauerkraut country, you wouldn't know anything about that."

Another opportunist. Polite coughs were heard around the

table. In the short time I'd been here, even I knew there hadn't been decent horses available for anything at all, let alone military use, in Davenport for three years. Nesbit glared at me, and I knew I'd made an enemy, but I didn't care. Everybody knew Nesbit spent most of his time hanging around saloons these days, gambling and enjoying the charms of whores and dancing girls.

I shrugged and excused myself but felt Nesbit's eyes following me as I left the dining room. I had other concerns. My mother hadn't been able to get out of bed this morning, and I wasn't sure what to do. My father had been out at Rock Island for days but should be home tonight. I was hoping he'd be able to get her up and about again.

Wilhelmina opened the door to our rooms, her face pale. I strode quickly to my mother's bedside and was frightened to see the sweat beading on her forehead and hear her labored breathing. She'd ever been a fragile soul, but this was more than just female humors. In just the last day, she'd become deathly ill.

I turned to Wilhelmina and grasped her hand. "Listen to me, Mina. I'm going to get Papa. He'll know what to do. Stay with her." I looked into my sister's eyes. "Make sure she has whatever she asks for. Fetch Mrs. Hudginson if she gets any worse. I'll be back soon."

She nodded, frightened. I kissed my mother's damp forehead, but she never stirred. I threw on my heavy cloak and boots and made my way to the livery stables down the street. I'd befriended the hostelry boy some weeks ago, and he was happy to give me the gentle mare I'd ridden before. I headed towards Rock Island, blinking the snowflakes out of my eyes as I rode east into the storm and across the railroad bridge.

The sentry stopped me at the gates, even though he'd seen me many times before.

"Password, miss."

"I don't know the password today, sergeant. My father's been here all night and has had no chance to tell me. You know me; I'm here to see my father, Dr. Haroney."

He looked at me blankly. "Password."

The snow continued to fall between us, and my temper was rising as quickly as the snowflakes were falling.

"I have to see my father. Now."

He held his bayoneted rifle towards me. "Sorry, I have to hear the password."

I dug my heels into the horse's side and galloped towards the compound beyond, ignoring his shouts. Patience against stupidity has never been my forte. I jumped off the horse, pushed open the door of the hospital, and ran towards my father's office, only to find it empty. When I turned back to the hallway, I was met by the strong arms of Major McPherson, my father's adjutant.

"Whoa, Miss Haroney. Whatever has you in such a fluster?" He was, as usual, correct but concerned, his brown eyes kind.

"Fluster, Major?" I disengaged myself, brushing off snowflakes and military intention. "Hardly. I am, however, in need of my father's counsel immediately. Where is he?"

"I regret to say he's indisposed at the moment, Miss Haroney," he said and his eyes slid away from mine. He stood stolid and erect in his blue uniform, gold braid gleaming in the gaslight.

My heart sank. Was this an epidemic then? Some sort of disease my father had caught from his prisoners and brought to my mother and who knows else? I had feared thus, and perhaps it had come to pass.

"Take me to him immediately," I said, not expecting to be obeyed, but the major, his eyes troubled, led me down the hall to a room. Obviously, he hadn't been alerted by the guards.

My father lay on a narrow bed, covered with clean white linen, his eyes closed. I approached cautiously and touched his cheek.

"Papa," I said and his eyes flew open, fixing me with his gaze. "Kate."

I could tell it took enormous effort for him to even utter my name. His hand grasped mine. Major McPherson stood nearby.

"What is it, Major? Tell me the truth," I said.

He looked at me and shook his head. "You have to leave; you shouldn't have come. I can't say anymore."

"You don't have to. Is it typhus or diphtheria? I'd say typhus."

He stared at me in astonishment. "How would you know that?"

"I'm a doctor's daughter, Major, and I'm not stupid. You don't have to worry; I'll not say anything to them back in Davenport." I turned away from him in disgust, and my father squeezed my hand, an effort that took all his strength.

"Go home, my darling. Take care of your mother, sister, and brother. You've always been the strongest of us. I will be with you soon."

What could I do but smooth his brow and nod as though I believed him, and with an escort, a young sergeant and two enlisted men, return plodding through the snow to Davenport.

I arrived late, missing Mrs. Hodginson's ample dinner but in time to watch my mother die of typhus, my siblings sobbing at her bedside. She would wear peacock feathers no more. We may have been better off in Mexico. At least she would have died in an elegant bed with the satin curtains and perfumed pillows she so loved. America was not serving us well.

Daffodils were emerging in front of Mrs. Hodginson's porch that early spring, the patches of snow melting around their eager trumpets. My father didn't give them a glance as he waved good-bye to us and mounted his horse for the journey to Rock Island. I took Alexander's hand and mounted the stairs to our rooms for the morning lessons. I missed my mother and regretted my childish attitudes toward her. Foolish as she had been, she gave loving support to all of us, and no one more so than my father. He had recovered somewhat physically, but his face was grim these days, and no hopeful optimism shone in his eyes. Blaming himself for Mother's death, he was despondent and sorry he had brought us to this place where so far only death had thrived, both at Rock Island and for his beloved wife. His dreams had tarnished here. When this war in the States was over, he told me, we would return to Hungary and our estates there, and I longed for the manners and gentility of our homeland. Daffodils did little to civilize Davenport, Iowa.

"Morning, Miss Haroney." Ned Hudginson left off sweeping the porch as we passed him, smiling at me. He was a sweet lad, a gangly and awkward seventeen year old, a shock of brown hair spilling across his forehead, always ready to help with anything his mother needed, and she kept him busy indeed. I knew he fancied me. He was always popping up when I least expected it, but I rather liked it. I smiled back.

"Good morning, Ned. It promises to be a lovely day, I think."

He nodded eagerly. "Maybe we could walk down to the river later?"

"Perhaps we could," I said. Ned blushed and returned to his sweeping.

Wilhelmina, Alexander, and I spent the morning working on English for the most part, with a smattering of mathematics and whatever piqued my interest. I felt my life was in a holding pattern. I knew not what would happen next, but, at least, I could help my sister and brother better equip themselves for whatever might come, either a return to Europe or a life forged in this new country. To my surprise, I discovered that I learned by

23

teaching them, and knowledge was something I'd always found to be a solace.

Wilhelmina was woefully slow, and she'd really never been one for academics, preferring needlework and music. Alexander, however, surprised me. Since our mother's death, he'd become quite serious and kept close, making every effort to please me. Not only was his English improving rapidly, he showed an aptitude for learning and had an avid curiosity about our new surroundings, of which I knew very little myself. It reminded me of all the happy hours I had spent with the tutors of the princes and with my father, soaking up every scrap of knowledge like a thirsty sponge. The hours flew by each day, and before I knew it, it was time for the noon meal. I stretched, eager to be out of the cramped bedroom I'd turned into our erstwhile school, and we set off downstairs.

As we entered the dining room with its long table, already mostly occupied, I felt a gentle hand on my arm. I turned as Wilhelmina and Alexander went forward and took their places at the table, and I met Ned's Hudginson's bashful blue eyes.

"Miss Haroney, I have here a picnic, if you're so inclined," he whispered, lifting a small wicker basket for emphasis. He looked away quickly, cheeks flushed, and I couldn't resist. He was a pretty boy, no question about that.

"What a grand idea, Ned," I whispered back, smiling. "Just let me tell Wilhelmina."

It was a lovely day and a welcome one after the long winter. Ned and I sat on the new grass that covered the riverbank, watching the boats on the Mississippi—from small fishing dinghys to large steamboats that they said went all the way to New Orleans, their great paddle wheels churning the sparkling water while strains of banjo music drifted across the waves. For the first time since we'd arrived in Davenport, I found it bearable.

We'd polished off the fried chicken, biscuits, and apple

pandowdy Ned's mother was famous for, accompanied by a fresh breeze off the river and the song of the robins that had arrived back from their southern sojourns. It was warm, and I had unbuttoned a few of the tiny top buttons of my shirtwaist. Ned had taken off his vest and done the same, and somehow the casualness of the afternoon had unloosed our tongues as well. He had dreams, did Ned, and they didn't include staying in Davenport.

"I'm heading West—that's where the future of this country lies," he confided, brushing his hair from his forehead. "There's land to be had, and I mean to have some. My mother wants me to apprentice to the blacksmith, but I plan to leave Davenport before the summer's out."

I nodded, and he expanded on his plans as I listened and watched the riverboats passing by. I leaned back, nearly drowsing in the sun until he clutched my hand.

"What about you, Miss . . . Kate?" His face was close, and the earnestness of his question caught me off guard. I sat up abruptly and tightened my grip on his hand. I stared into his eyes and thought about just what I wanted for myself. I'd never done so before, not really. It had always been about my father and mother, and aside from vacuous flirting with members of the court, I had never thought about my future, and surely not about one that was independent of my family.

"I don't know, Ned. I really don't," I said truthfully. This was a new time in a new land, and there were possibilities that had never occurred to me before. Perhaps being an educated female might be worth something to me after all. I felt a fluttering in my stomach, and it wasn't just the closeness of Ned's face, although that was part of the whole feeling, that maybe I could do whatever I wanted to.

Ned leaned closer. "Would you ever . . . I mean, could you possibly think . . . that we might . . ."

He kissed me then, the sweetest kiss, so unlike the rapacious Marquis or the soft pecks of the schoolroom boys, that I was astounded and didn't draw away as I should have. He took that for acceptance and pressed me down on the soft grass and took another. It was nice, and I returned it, my lips on his, my arms curling around his neck. His breath was sweet, and his mouth soft, with the promise of something more.

"I think Mrs. Hudginson would be interested to hear what her lazy son's got up to with some uppity foreign baggage," drawled a voice, accompanied by a spit of tobacco that landed close by our heads. "Although it's no surprise to me."

We jerked apart as though scalded and leapt to our feet. Darren Nesbit stood nearby, a smirk on his bearded face that I longed to smack off.

"This is no concern of yours," Ned managed, his fists clenching. "Leave us alone, Nesbit."

Nesbit shrugged and strolled away, but as he reached the top of the bank he turned back and looked at me. I shivered, as I hastened to button up my dress. I'd done nothing wrong, but his gaze made me feel dirty. For the first time in my life, I felt shame, and I didn't like it. He vanished from view, and Ned grabbed my hand.

"He's nothing, Kate; don't let him ruin this. My mother knows him for a wastrel, and it doesn't matter what he says."

"I know, Ned. It's all right." I smiled and kissed his cheek. He put his arm around my waist with one hand and picked up the basket with the other. "Thank you for a lovely day."

We walked slowly back to the boardinghouse, my hand clasped in his, but some of the magic had gone, and no more words passed between us that day.

The Americans ended their war on April ninth, word reaching Davenport swiftly via telegraph. Celebrations erupted in the streets, with people cheering, shooting off guns, riding horses crazily around the town, and celebrating with parties for many nights thereafter. Meals at the boardinghouse were sparsely attended, no matter what Mrs. Hudginson was serving. My father was especially busy, tending to his patients and readying them as best he could for the journey home to their families, those who were able to make the trip. Many of them were determined to go no matter what, and while some were too weak, he knew from the desperation in their eyes, as I did, that nothing would stop them from leaving this hateful place where they'd been imprisoned. When Father had the time to come back to Davenport, he was exhausted, and he went to his room silently after a quick pat on our heads. When I would check on him later, he was usually in a sleep so deep he never heard me enter the room. One evening in late May, when spring was settling into Iowa and the trees had burst into full leaf, he didn't come home at all.

Major McPherson tied up his horse on the railing of the boardinghouse and stepped onto the front porch, where I had been waiting for my father. His bearing was stiffly erect as always, but his eyes gave him away.

"Good evening, Miss Haroney." He came closer and took my hand. I tried to pull away, knowing what he was going to say and not wanting to hear, but the words poured out quickly, a small torrent unleashed by his own uneasiness. "Miss Haroney, I'm afraid I have some bad news. Your father's passed."

My breath stopped somewhere between my throat and my stomach. I squeezed his hand in mine, and all I could manage was a whisper. "Don't say this to me, Major."

His military bearing crumbled, and he pulled me to his chest, the brass buttons of his uniform cold on my cheek. "I wish I didn't have to, Miss . . . Kate." I felt him take a deep breath. "He was so tired. He just lay down for a few minutes, and when

I went to wake him . . ."

My arms clutched his chest and seemed to stop the words, at least for a moment. It was all I could do. My father was my constant—a ship that plunged on, carrying me, carrying all of us, through every storm. The freedom I had flirted with, dreamed about, with the Marquis, with Ned, was always cocooned within the safety of knowing my father would always be there. Now the dream was a nightmare, and one I was ill prepared to live with.

CHAPTER 3

1867

"Hop to it, Kate. Mr. Smith can't wait all day for his breakfast, you lazy chit."

Mrs. Smith stood before me, her graying sausage curls framing her plump cheeks, eyes bright with malice as I struggled with the heavy tray. I wove around her voluminous skirts and up the servants' stairs to the second floor. I took a backward glance at Wilhelmina, who sat at the table, eyes averted from my travails as she nibbled a piece of toast, and I nearly stumbled on my skirts.

I entered the narrow hallway of the second floor and proceeded to the set of double doors that marked the bedroom of the master of this house, knocking with the edge of the burdened silver tray and pushing down the handle with my elbow.

Otto Smith, Esquire, lay back on his down pillows, watching as I entered and set the tray on the table before the fireplace, cold now in the July heat.

"Good morning, sir. Your breakfast, if you please." I'd learned to say exactly this phrase very well, considering the consequences. I watched in disgust, face impassive, as he threw back the bed linens and strode forward, his nightgown flapping around his calves. Otto was not a stately man, nor an attractive one. Even the bed-gown did little to disguise the rolls of flesh that strained the edges of the cotton garment as he sat heavily

29

in the armchair next to the table. Porcine eyes gazed at me above his pudgy cheeks, and the nightcap fell sideways to reveal the thin strands of graying hair that failed to cover his glistening scalp. I shuddered as his fingers trailed down my arm before they grasped a piece of bacon from the laden plate.

"Looking at you always starts my day well, Kate."

I took a step back, my arms clasped behind me. It pained me to take this servant's stance, but it was a good thing, because it stopped me from smacking his face as he stuffed it with food he scarcely needed.

He stuffed a honey roll into his mouth as his eyes looked me up and down. I took another step backward. The man made my skin crawl.

"If that's all, sir, I'll be needed downstairs."

He smiled. "You're needed in many ways, Kate." The sight of the honey roll in his mouth made my stomach churn. "But I concede your talents below stairs." He smiled, pieces of the roll stuck in his teeth. "I'll see you in the course of the day."

I made a hasty exit, shutting the door behind me. For a few moments I leaned back against it, before I returned to the kitchen below. God, how I hated this place. Of all the people in Davenport worthy of trust, we orphaned Haroneys had ended up with those who most betrayed it.

My poor father had made what he thought was provision for us, in the event something happened to him. He'd enlisted the services of a lawyer, one Otto Smith, a distinguished citizen of Davenport, so all declared, and had written a will naming Mr. Smith as the guardian of his children until they reached the age of consent, depositing his modest fortune in the Iowa State Bank in trust of Mr. Smith. Since that dreadful day well over two years ago, Wilhelmina, Alexander, and I had become the wards of the Smiths, those scions of Davenport society. In truth, we'd become their servants, while the Smiths had made free with my father's money. By the time I reached the age of eighteen, to say nothing of my poor sister and brother, there wouldn't be a penny left. In the last twelve months, the Smiths had twice visited Chicago, bought a handsome carriage and four, and were building a new house with a view of the river. Every Sunday morning we attended the First Baptist Church in the company of Mr. and Mrs. Smith, who received blessings and praise for their Christian charity and compassion. In the eyes of Davenport society, the Smiths were saints. I had already learned that any complaints to the contrary were dismissed as the whining of a spoiled and willful child who was unused to any discipline. Wilhelmina and Alexander fared better, perhaps because their English was limited, but I had always found it difficult to contain my frustrations and disdain. Besides, now everyone knew me for an ungrateful girl with loose morals.

Last October, Ned Hudginson and I had been apprehended by the sheriff of Scott County, Iowa, whose posse included Mr. Otto Smith, his Baptist faithful, and Mrs. Hudginson, not anxious to lose her dog of all work. We had been twenty miles outside of town, astride two horses and leading a pack mule, supplied with the meager tools to start a homestead. Our ill-prepared flight had been scuttled by my sister's ill-timed confession, and we were returned to the grasping arms of god-fearing Davenport. Come spring, Ned absconded for parts unknown, while I remained, my reputation in ruins, a helpful if recalcitrant fixture of the forgiving Smith household.

If there was a bright side to this, Wilhelmina and Alexander had become favorites of the Smiths, taking well to church and lessons, respectively, while I took on the role of scapegoat for all transgressions, real or imagined. They felt I had abandoned them, and I couldn't deny that. I had been foolish, wild with the flush of first love, and had felt like a lost thing since my father had died. Now, I felt shame at being so quick to divest myself of my siblings, and guilt was the glue that kept me here.

I sighed and made my way back to the kitchen. A longing for both my parents coursed through me, so sharp it was almost painful. A newfound respect for my mother had surfaced over the months she'd been gone. How loving my parents had been with us all and accepting of the responsibility of children in a world so unpredictable. I wasn't sure I'd ever be like that.

"There you are, finally," Mrs. Smith said. She waved a piece of paper in my face. "Here. When you're done with the dishes, get yourself to the market, then kill three chickens. We have guests tonight."

I took the grocery list from her, and she flounced out of the room without a backward glance, knowing I'd do what had to be done, as I always did.

The face in the hall mirror was hardly the saucy one I'd grown to recognize most of my life. No hairdresser or shampoo had touched my strawberry blonde locks in some time, and my hair was now pulled back from my face and held with a strip of cloth. My green eyes stared back at me, and I gave the reflection a smile, arching one eyebrow. *Not exactly court material anymore, Kate,* the mirror seemed to say, and I had to agree, although there was something comely still, I thought. Not that anyone, even in Iowa, much noticed the kitchen help.

I strode briskly down River Street to the market, basket in arm. I liked doing the shopping because it got me out of the house, and I could see what was going on in Davenport. My favorite place was the docks and the riverfront, maybe because it was the place where people left Iowa, something I longed to do. So much activity, so much life—barges, fishing trawlers, packet boats, steamboats, and the queens of the water, the huge paddle wheelers. Hundreds of barrels and crates were being loaded and unloaded, carried on strong shoulders, to be sold up and down the river, all the way to New Orleans, a place I dreamed about seeing one day. There was even a showboat, festooned with streamers, and I could hear music as I approached the mercantile. I'd love to see one of their performances, but the Smiths said it was "devil's work" and stayed away.

"Why, good morning, Miss Haroney," smiled Jack Rafferty, elegant in a black embroidered waistcoat, lounging in front of his saloon. Somebody was playing Mozart on the piano, and it was the first time I'd heard it in Davenport. "A pretty day for a pretty girl."

I smiled back. "Morning to you, Mr. Rafferty." I probably shouldn't, but I couldn't help but like him. He was handsome and friendly, and even though the Smiths said he was a "gambling whoremonger," he'd always been polite to me, and his greeting brightened my day.

I entered the mercantile and handed my list to Mr. Benson, who nodded and began filling my basket. I drifted over to the doorway just as two ladies from the Baptist church came in.

They glanced over at me, and one of them sniffed audibly. Within two seconds, their heads were close together, whispering, and I stepped outside, cheeks flaming. Would I ever be accepted in this town as anything other than a girl who was shamed? I wished at that moment that I had, at least, had the enjoyment of doing what they all thought I had and that I was as far away from here as possible.

"Girl." Another staunch Baptist, the man didn't even have the courtesy that Jack Rafferty had shown, to call me by my name, which he knew full well. "Your order's ready. Don't dawdle; Mrs. Smith will be waiting. Get along now."

Basket full, I ambled back along River Street, enjoying the sunshine and the bustle of the waterfront. I loved the feel of the sun on my skin, and I rolled up my sleeves and smoothed back my wayward hair, basking in the warmth.

"How you doin', Miss Kate?" Molly, the fishwife, called. She had fresh catfish hanging from strings on her tent.

"Mighty fine, Molly. How you?"

"Gettin' by." She laughed and waved her apron. I waved back. I'd picked up the dialect of the river folk quickly, and it came almost naturally to me now. As I continued back down River Street, I waved hello and chatted with many of the vendors I'd come to know and count as friends.

Just before my turnoff to the Smiths' house, I saw two fine gentlemen dressed in the dark blue suits and shiny brass buttons of riverboat captains coming my way. I smiled at them as they passed, and they returned the favor along with quick bows. One stopped and looked back at me, but I paid him no mind. Men often did that to me in the street, but I'd learned to keep on walking. Ladies should pay no heed to such glances, especially ladies with a reputation as shredded as mine.

Back at the Smiths', I unloaded my purchases in the kitchen and made my way to the chicken coop, making short work of three plump hens, dowsing them in a pot of boiling water, cleaning, and plucking them. A year or two ago I never thought I'd have to cook dinner, much less kill it, but I'd learned. I opened the recipe book and started the long process of cooking chicken fricassee.

Voices rose and fell from the front parlor as the Smiths entertained their guests. Wilhelmina had grudgingly been put into service. She delivered trays of appetizers full of deviled eggs, pickles, and olives that I'd arranged, as well as ice and glasses for the drinks, which, as could be gathered from the occasional burst of laughter, were being consumed at a fast pace. Baptists or no, the Smiths liked their whiskey just as well as their guests did.

The dining room was set with lace tablecloths and napkins, china, and silver, and the chocolate cake I'd baked was sitting on the sideboard. Wilhelmina had taken the vegetables, bread, and butter to the table, and I was spooning the chicken fricassee into a serving tureen when Mrs. Smith appeared in the doorway.

"Kate, wait until we're all seated before you bring in the chicken. Then you can serve it to each person individually, like they do in Europe and those fancy places, not like you'd know."

She peered at me sharply. "You'll be a sorry girl, if you splatter one drop, you hear me?"

"Yes, ma'am."

"Tie back your hair, wash your hands, and wipe the sweat from your face. You look a slattern, but you'll have to do." She sighed and left the kitchen.

Wilhelmina caught my eye, but even as strained as our relationship had been lately, we broke into laughter. "Europe and those fancy places? Oh, Kate, will we ever return to the place we belong?"

At her last words, the laughter died, and I hugged her close. "Some day, Mina. Davenport is just a stop on the way, remember that."

She stepped back, her hands gently pushing strands of my hair away from my face. "I think about Mama and Papa every day, you know. I even think about the emperor. Life was so much nicer then, wasn't it, Kate?"

"Yes, Mina, it was."

From the dining room, I could hear chairs scraping. "Bring the ladles, sweetie. I'll hold and you dip."

I picked up the heavy tureen, pushing open the swinging door with my backside. It was the brass buttons that first caught my eye, glinting in the light of the chandelier. To my surprise, the two riverboat captains I'd seen on River Street sat at the table, flanked by the Smiths and Mr. Smith's associate, Denton Peterson, and his wife. They glanced up as we entered, and the distinguished older captain who'd turned to look at me in the street smiled, his eyes twinkling. Straight-faced, Wilhelmina and I made the rounds of the diners, filling their plates with chicken fricassee, the only thanks coming from the two gentlemen in blue. We retired to the kitchen to wait for a second round or the next order from Mrs. Smith, and from time to time I peeked through the slit between the door and the frame.

Wilhelmina, Alexander, and I had eaten earlier, and a good thing, too. After a second serving, there was hardly a scrap of food left. Wilhelmina returned to the dining room to serve dessert, and I heard Mr. Smith introduce her and Alexander to the guests while I began washing the dishes.

When the kitchen door opened, I nearly dropped the pot I was scrubbing, my hands deep in the soapy water. The older riverboat captain stood there, smiling.

"Good evening, Miss Haroney. Thank you for a wonderful dinner."

"Ah . . . you're very welcome, sir." Mr. Smith stood behind him, scowling.

"My name's Joshua Fisher. I know you are busy, but perhaps you could take a moment and join us?"

Smith's scowl deepened, and I couldn't let an opportunity to discomfit him pass me by. I wiped my hands on my apron and untied it, throwing it on the back of a chair. What could Captain Fisher possibly want with my company?

I smiled. "Sir, I'd be delighted."

"So you see, Miss Haroney, I'm quite invested in seeing how you and your siblings are getting on here in Davenport. I regret it has taken me so long to do so." The captain leaned back in his chair, his eyes staring into mine.

I smiled politely, but my thoughts were whirling. Joshua Fisher had just expounded quite fully upon how he'd met my father and how that well-loved and wise personage had directed him to look in upon his children should anything untoward befall him in this foreign place. The Smiths looked as though they'd both sucked on lemons, and Captain Fisher raised his eyebrows quizzically.

"Well, sir, let me say how delighted I am to know you knew my father," I said, "and that you have had the happy circumstance to look in on us. I know he would be grateful, as we are."

I glanced towards the Smiths, both of whom smiled briefly before they went back to their lemons, Mrs. Smith glaring at me in warning. "As you can see, we are quite well here. Wilhelmina and Alexander are studying and doing well, and I am learning housewifely arts at Mrs. Smith's kind direction."

Joshua Fisher gazed into my eyes for a few seconds and then turned to the Smiths.

"You are to be commended, good people. I'm sure Mr. Haroney is resting easy."

He stood up abruptly and gestured to his young companion. "Come, Mr. Westerly. The hour grows late, and we must return to our berths. We leave at dawn, south to New Orleans." He bowed and took Mrs. Smith's hand, much to her simpering delight. "Such is the life of a riverman, I regret to say. Here one evening, gone the next. I'll be sure to look in on you and the children when next we come upriver. Thank you for a lovely evening and a most wonderful meal." He nodded at me at this, and I couldn't help but feel pleased. I was turning into quite a good cook, if nothing else.

He looked back at me as the company made their way towards the door, and I saw the concern in his eyes, but there was nothing to be said, especially with the Smiths standing guard. I looked away and made my way back to the kitchen.

There was a lot to be done before I went to my bed.

By the time I finished cleaning the kitchen, I was afire with determination. This was not the life my father would have wished for me, Wilhelmina, or Alexander, and I was the only one who could change it. Waiting would only make it harder— more condemnation, more drudgery, more spending by the Smiths—until there was no dignity or means left for us to begin anew.

After putting all to rights in the dining room, I thought a great deal about all that had been said by the good captain. I sat outside on the back porch for hours after the others were in their beds and the house was quiet. I left a note for Wilhelmina, this time not putting it under her pillow but in her clothes drawer, where she'd find it in a day or two. I'd no desire for another inglorious return to Davenport, this time hailed as a thief.

I crept through the deserted streets to the docks and had no trouble finding Captain Fisher's *Delta Queen,* the most magnificent riverboat there. Her railings and superstructure gleamed in the ghostly light from lanterns hung from the decks, like an iced wedding cake only waiting for the party to begin. The gangplank was down, invitingly so. I watched from the shadows until the sailor on sentry duty strolled down to the tavern to refill his mug and then, my heart pounding in my chest, quickly ran aboard. Now all I had to do was remain undiscovered until we were far downriver.

I sneezed and jerked awake from where I lay in the bottom of the lifeboat, my head touching the top of the moldy tarpaulin that covered my hiding place. I couldn't see much in the dawn light seeping through the lacings I'd undone to creep into the boat, but I could hear the thunderous pounding of the paddle wheel that reverberated up through the deck. So we were away, down the Mississippi.

My hands clutched tightly onto the carpetbag I'd stuffed with enough clothes to stop the clanking of a goodly portion of the Smiths' sterling flatware and a pair of silver candlesticks I'd appropriated from the dining room in the dark of night. To my mind, it was only a small fraction of what they'd taken from us and I'd need it to start my new life. Just thinking about it, I smiled in satisfaction. Then I gasped, blinking owlishly as the canvas cover was flung back, exposing my hideaway.

"Miss Haroney." Captain Joshua Fisher held out his hand. "Perhaps you might care for some breakfast?"

CHAPTER 4

St. Louis, Missouri, May 1869

Spring was beautiful in St. Louis. I watched the play of sunlight
and leaves on the white ceiling and walls of my tiny room, enjoying the peace and quiet before the day started at St. Joseph's
Academy. The good sisters of Carondelet despised sloth, and I
was certain daydreaming in bed qualified for that heinous sin. I
stretched my arms over my head and closed my eyes, the soft
white cotton of my nightgown stretching over my full breasts
and hips. I was a woman grown, and, fittingly, this would be my
last day here. Today was graduation day, a milestone I'd longed
for, but one that was tinged with anxiety as well. Now I would
make my way in the world, armed with a stellar education from
two continents but little else—except the goodwill and charity
of Captain Joshua Fisher. He and his wife, Emily, had taken me
in and provided everything for me, especially guidance and affection, ever since that morning I'd climbed out of the lifeboat
on the *Delta Queen*. I would be eternally grateful for their kindness.

As well as taking me under their wings, they had kept in
regular correspondence with the Smiths and made visits to
Davenport, bearing my small gifts and letters to Wilhelmina and
Alexander. Twice last summer I had accompanied Captain
Fisher on the *Delta Queen* and seen for myself that my siblings
were fit and well, and all three of us had rejoiced in our reunion.
The Smiths were civil to me, and nary a word was said of the

40

missing silver, one thing to their credit. Said silver now rested in a grave below a grassy mound on the Smiths' property overlooking the Mississippi, sleeping soundly until I might have need of it. Not even Joshua Fisher was aware of its existence.

What a piece of work is a man, I thought. Hamlet was right, to my mind. In my nineteen years I had glimpsed a fair bit of the best and worst of humanity, and little surprised me—although I had no doubt the world was waiting for me to discover more, and discover it I would. A shiver of anticipation ran through me, and I hugged myself, my skin cool and covered with goosebumps in the morning chill.

Three quick knocks in succession sounded against the wall and interrupted my reveries. I heard my name through the thin plaster.

"Kate? Are you awake?"

I knocked back three times, and within seconds, my door creaked open, and Rose Melvin scurried across the cold floor, her long white nightgown an exact copy of my own, the sisters' godly choice. I held out the bedcovers, and she nestled in, her bare feet cold against my warm ones. She hugged me, her brown eyes gleaming with excitement, her tangled dark hair mingling with my own blonde curls on the pillow.

"This is going to be the best day, ever. No more lessons, no more sisters, no more chapel, chapel, chapel. I will be a society lady, and you'll be right there beside me, my dearest friend. That will never change."

I hugged her back and smiled. "Never, my dear."

Rose sat up on one elbow and looked at me, mischief evident in her lovely, heart-shaped face. "I have a surprise, Kate. Guess who's coming to graduation? My brother, Silas. He's just back from New York, now finished with dentistry school. I've told him all about you."

"Oh, have you?" She was relentless. I'd been hearing about

this paragon of a brother for two years now, and Rose had plans for us, regardless of the fact we'd never met and most likely would disappoint each other when we did. In fact, young men were the furthest thing from my mind, and at St. Joseph's they were kept that way, mentally as well as physically. This was a convent school for young ladies, and only twice a year were we allowed to mingle with the opposite sex at two rigidly prescribed dances, when the boys from Sacred Heart were allowed inside our saintly halls. Although the dance was highly anticipated by most of the girls, I was one of the few uninterested in pimply chins, sweaty palms, and stumbling feet, and only too happy to resume my acquaintance with besieged MacBeth, heroic Hamlet, and even the swaggering cowboys and outlaws in the smuggled-in Western romances we avidly read by candlelight. The fantasy was preferable to the reality.

However, when it came to her brother, Rose was convinced he was the most handsome and charming young gentleman in the world and that I would think so, too. I had stopped protesting long ago, since he wasn't even in St. Louis, not wanting to dash her hopes. I would never tell her of the aristocratic and dashing princes I'd grown up with, a life now long behind me.

"Yes, indeed, Miss Haroney. He will be at the ceremony and dinner this evening, so there."

Enthused, she threw back the covers and pulled me out of bed. "The day awaits; come on, Kate!"

Together we stood by the window in the warm sunlight, watching workmen set up white chairs on the lawn. This was going to be a day to remember.

Twenty-four of us, dressed in our white gowns, stood on the dais behind the Mother Superior, Sister Josephus Maria. We faced rows of our teachers, peers, parents, and friends, arrayed in a vast semicircle, all sitting expectantly on their white wooden chairs on the green lawn of St. Joseph's Academy. It was a perfect day, sunny and not too warm, with birds singing in the trees and the buzz of bees in the blossoms of the apple trees in the sisters' nearby orchard a constant thrum. Sister Andrea, sitting at a piano the workmen had wheeled out beside the dais earlier in the day, played solemn Bach as we filed past Mother Superior, each receiving a ribbon-wrapped roll of parchment and her accolade. When it came my turn, I was ready. I walked firmly towards her, the smile on my face threatening to burst into a full-fledged grin.

"Miss Katherine Haroney. Miss Haroney has come to us from across the sea and has the distinction of being first in our graduating class this year. Congratulations, Katherine," Sister Josephus Maria said, as I bowed prettily and took the diploma from her hand. I looked out over the crowd. Captain Fisher and Emily waved back at me, and I broke with gentility and waved the scroll over my head, the grin winning out. Sister Josephus Maria's eyes twinkled, and she waved me on my way to a seat on the front row of chairs with the other girls. When Rose's time came, I waved at her, but she smiled demurely and stepped down to her seat behind me, poking me and giggling as she did.

In a few more moments the ceremony was over, and we all broke ranks, heading for our families and loved ones. Captain Fisher picked me up in a bear hug and swung me around, the late afternoon sun glinting on his brass buttons.

"Kate, I'm so proud of you," he said and kissed me heartily on the cheek. "I knew you could do anything you set your mind to since the first time I saw you carry in that chicken fricassee."

Emily Fisher hugged me close, her lemon verbena perfume a familiar delight. "Darling girl, you are such a treasure to us."

I hugged her back. Emily was a tiny woman, her head barely reaching my shoulder, but she was the engine that drove Joshua Fisher, their family, and their world, and masterfully so. Their two sons, Sam and Adam, aged ten and twelve respectively, tugged at my sleeve.

"Kate, Kate, you look beautiful," Sam said fervently, and I kissed him on his forehead.

"Thank you, kind sir," I said. "That is precisely what a lady wants to hear on important days." He blushed while Adam shook my hand.

"Congratulations on your graduation, Kate," he said solemnly in his most grown-up manner. I inclined my head and then pulled him to me for a hug, and Sam as well, all of us laughing, even their parents. I kissed the boys and watched with amusement as Adam's cheeks turned as red as his jaunty tie.

The boys had become like brothers to me during my times home from school in the last two years, and they were wonderful children. We'd made snowmen, fished in the river, and run like wild things on the grounds of the Fishers' house overlooking the Mississippi. I'd taught them how to dance and do math, and they'd taught me how to catch frogs, make a slingshot, kindle a fire, and ride horses without a saddle, among many other things.

"We've got a celebration dinner planned at the River Palace Hotel," Emily said, putting her arm through mine, the white ostrich feathers bobbing on her elegant hat, "with a few of the other families and graduates."

We set off across the lawn, amid the excited voices of a hundred other people, and before I knew it, we'd stopped beside the Melvins, where Rose gave a shriek and hugged me, her cheeks pink with excitement.

"Kate! We're graduates! Can you believe it?"

Her parents, the sedate Richard and Katherine Melvin, nodded and said hello to Captain Fisher and Emily. A tall young man stood beside them, his body turned back towards the chattering crowd, his gray waistcoat an admirable fit.

"Silas, I want to introduce you to my best friend, Kate," Rose said, grinning in great satisfaction. "She's been dying to meet you."

I wanted to kick her in the shins, but then the man turned around, smiled, and took my hand. My heart stuttered so in my chest I thought everyone could hear, but no one seemed to notice.

He had the same lively brown eyes as his sister, the beauty tempered by a masculine chin and strong nose, and when he smiled down at me, his longish hair fell across his forehead.

His smile faded as his gaze intensified, and it seemed we were the only two people on that vast lawn, the voices stilled and the shadowed sunlight glowing only for us. I don't remember dropping his hand or what anyone said for a while, but the next thing I do remember clearly is sitting at a white-linen–covered table at the River Palace Hotel—across the table from Silas Melvin. Amid the laughter and chatter of twenty other people and the discreet clamor of china and silver, it was the look in Silas Melvin's eyes that captured my attention.

"So, Kate, what plans have you made for the future, young lady?"

Richard Melvin's voice boomed down the table and effectively brought me into the moment—one of those ill-timed and awkward moments when it seemed all conversation had halted. I gazed back at Rose and Silas's father, his eyes inquisitive in his well-fed face.

"Teaching, sir. I believe I have something to offer in that regard." I have no idea what made me say that. I hadn't had a thought about teaching anyone, but I didn't think "I don't know" or "adventuress" would have been quite the right response.

He nodded thoughtfully, and conversation resumed. Joshua Fisher caught my eye and winked, and Emily smiled, eyes on her Yorkshire pudding.

Rose, sitting beside me, nudged me with her elbow. "Don't mind Daddy, Kate. He sees how captivated Silas is with you, and he's just trying to find out more about you. He's a peach, really."

I sincerely doubted that, and from the disdainful looks the tautly corseted Mrs. Melvin was casting at me, she was of the same mind as her husband.

"Miss Haroney, I must say teaching is a most respected profession, well suited to an educated young lady." Silas Melvin's deep tone carried well, and heads nodded in agreement. His eyes met mine across the table, and I could see the laughter in them, while Rose squeezed my hand.

"So I have been told, Mr. Melvin," I murmured, "so I have been told."

"Cannonball!"

Adam was true to his word as he careened into the water, causing Sam's face to be obscured by the splashing water, and some drops even reached me on the shore.

"No fair," Sam managed, tossing back his hair and making for dry land so he could have a chance to retaliate.

The quiet cove on the river was perfect for swimming, a serene idyll in the fast-flowing rush of the Mississippi, and the huge old elm that reached out over the water sported equally perfect low-hanging limbs for jumping into the water. We had been coming down here every summer since I'd been with the Fishers, and I'd always taken as much advantage as the boys when it came to swimming. Officially their chaperone and swimming teacher, I'd always shuck down to my drawers and camisole and jump in with them. After all, you can't teach people how to swim unless you're in the water with them, and Emily had never said a word about modesty or proper behavior, as I knew she wouldn't.

The St. Louis spring had passed into summer, and the rising temperatures and opening leaves had been a bellwether of my own emotions. Every time I thought about Silas Melvin, things seemed to warm up. I thought about him day and night, and even now, watching the boys play, he wound through every conscious thought like a wisp of silk threading its way through a ribbon. He had come to call almost every day. We had sat in the parlor, walked through the gardens, rode horses in the afternoon, taken tea in myriad locations, and even had dinner at a few of St. Louis's most elegant restaurants, all very proper and in keeping with the rules of society. But each time his hand brushed mine, or he looked down at me as he pulled out my chair, I felt myself wanting more, and I knew from the way his eyes darkened, he did, too.

He was coming to take me to the St. Louis Summer Cotillion this evening, and I was trying not to think about it, since the anticipation was almost more than I could bear. Emily and I had worked tirelessly on my ball gown, a confection of pale-yellow silk embroidered with tiny blue flowers and off-the-shoulder sleeves. I felt like a princess wearing it and couldn't wait to see Silas's reaction. Tonight would be different. For the first time, we would be truly alone, just the two of us.

Silas was a firm hand with the two matched bays that trotted smartly down the river road to the Fishers' house. Even at this late hour, the air held a lingering warmth from the day, and the breeze felt good on my face, still flushed from the dancing. My dress had elicited exactly the response I had hoped for, and it had been a magical evening. It was nearing midnight, I thought, as I glanced over at him, his profile etched in the moonlight. He turned, and his lips curved in a smile.

"Enjoyed the ball, Miss Haroney?"

I smiled back. "Indeed, Mr. Melvin." I boldly positioned my gloved hand on his thigh. "And the company."

"For a fact, it was most delightful." He pulled back on the reins and turned the horses into a lane dappled with moonlight by the overhanging tree boughs. We slowed and came to a stop, and he turned to me.

"It's too fine an evening to end, don't you think?" He stepped down from the carriage and held out his hand, which I quickly grasped. I jumped down from the seat, my voluminous skirts aswirl.

He spoke softly to the horses and tied the reins to a tree trunk, then spread a carriage robe on the soft grass under the trees. We sank down upon it, scarcely noticing its comfort as we were too absorbed in each other. He kissed me then, and I knew this was just the beginning. Our hands moved swiftly, eager to find the secrets hidden within each other's clothing. Buttons popped free, and my skirts flew. He loomed over me, blocking the moonlight and pressing a warm and welcome weight against my body.

"Kate, are you sure?"

"Ah, Silas." It felt as though every inch of my body was on fire and in him the only quenching. I arched my back and kissed him thoroughly. "I've never been so sure."

So it was done. A perfect summer night—the moon overhead, virginity lost, real life begun, and no regrets.

Summer played itself out—hot humid days and nights that afforded a cooling breeze across the river. Sickness descended on St. Louis, as it always did during these months, but we were immune, as were most. Dinners were prepared outside in the cookhouses, ice was at a premium and eagerly awaited by restaurants and housewives alike, and life went on, as always. For me, it was different. I was in love.

Silas and I spent every moment together we could, snatching our intimate moments after dinners and parties, during the afternoons when most sensible people were taking a rest from the midday heat, and even once early in the morning after sleepless nights for both of us, wracked with longing. We became fearless and careless, consumed by each other.

Silas's father was setting up a dental practice for him, and I had talked with several people about a position as governess or teacher, but the future held little interest for either of us, entwined in an immediate enchantment of our own weaving.

On a crisp but sunny morning in late September, Emily Fisher took my hand and led me outside to the gardens, her skirts brushing softly against the flagstones.

"Kate, talk to me now." Her eyes held only the most kindly concern, and I couldn't hide from them any longer. Emily never dissembled, her soft exterior masking an iron will. There had been too many mornings lately when I had tried to hide the fact that my breakfast came back up almost as soon as I'd eaten it.

"Will he marry you?"

Defiance and shame formed a retort on my lips, but my emotions betrayed me, and I burst into tears, clinging to her comforting arms.

"I haven't told him." I felt Emily sigh as she held me close. She patted my back, and I felt, for the first time in months, a peace of a sort.

"That, my darling, is something we shall have to remedy very soon indeed," she murmured.

October rain spattered the windows of St. Joseph's Cathedral, where I had sat not long ago as a schoolgirl and listened to Mass every morning. The flickering light of the candles barely held back the dark of the approaching autumn night, unseasonably cold for St. Louis. The warmth of the candles and that of the assembled guests released the tangy scent of the chrysanthemums and late asters that bloomed around the altar, scenting our rites. The pews were not full, only the first two rows on the groom's side filled and a scant three on the bride's—river captains and their families, long-time friends of the Fishers. My brother and sister had opted to stay in Davenport with their guardians, and, while I was hurt by their absence, I understood somewhat their obvious complacence in their comfortable lives, and besides, the Smiths were not likely to absorb the costs of an outing on my account. Silas gripped my cold hand in his and gently pushed the ivory veil from my face. His smile was as warm as his hand, and he kissed me soundly on the lips.

"I love you, Mrs. Melvin," he said softly, and the block of ice in my stomach began to melt at his words. We turned and faced the back of the church and made our way down the aisle bedecked with rosebuds thrown enthusiastically by Sam and Adam Fisher, my erstwhile knights.

"Congratulations, my darling," Emily Fisher said and hugged us both, as did her husband, following behind us. Captain Fisher had given me away, standing in for my late father, and his usually solemn face was bright with his smile. Not so the Melvins, on the other side of the aisle, their perfunctory words of congratulations accompanied by gritted teeth and lips drawn in a parody of goodwill for the benefit of the few business associates and their wives who had attended. The Melvins had not widely announced their son's upcoming hasty nuptials, perhaps in hopes they would never happen. My Silas, however, remained steadfast, despite his parents' hostility, and my love for him was intensified by his loyalty.

The reception dinner in the church hall was lavish, if some of the guests were recalcitrant. The Fishers had spared no expense, even engaging a string quartet whose renderings of Vivaldi, Mozart, and Hayden equaled the Austrian court, although only

I had the experience to compare them. We dined on succulent roast beef, stuffed partridge, late summer vegetables, and enough French champagne to float Captain Fisher's *Delta Queen*. And, judging from the laughter and jostling at the tables, the champagne was having its desired effect, even on the surly Melvin seniors. During the cutting of the six-tiered cake, properly crowned by a porcelain bride and groom who resembled neither Silas nor me, I stuffed creamy frosting and vanilla cake into Silas's laughing mouth and promptly kissed off the excess, to the lusty cheers of the assembled well-wishers.

Leaving the guests absorbed in their dessert, I hurried away to see the Fishers and rescue my bouquet. I hugged Emily, the woman who had been mother and confidante to me, more so than my own sadly departed mother had ever been. "I cannot thank you enough for everything you have done," I said. "Without you, this wonderful day . . ." I gestured behind me into the hall full of laughing guests. ". . . would never have happened, and I would be just another disgraced girl with no future."

She took my face in her hands. "Kate, my dear. You underestimate yourself, but I thank you for your faith in me. Go and make a happy life." She kissed me, and I was loath to leave the comfort of her arms. I turned to Captain Fisher, and his eyes fixed on mine, full of the same mixture of compassion and knowledge they had always held. He knew me, this man.

"I should never be surprised at any turn your life takes, little one," he said. He swept me up as though I weighed less than a river bird. "Go and make a strong family with your Silas. I know you can do anything you set your mind to, Kate Haroney Melvin, and I've been fortunate to be a small part of making that happen."

I choked back tears and kissed his cheeks soundly, clinging to his shoulders so tightly the lace of my veil left patterns on my hands. Had it not been for him, I could still be in Davenport, plucking chickens for the Smiths. I tore myself away and, grabbing my bouquet with one hand and Silas with another, ran to the front of the hall.

"Is the carriage ready?" I asked, breathless from the corset, laced tightly as befits a virgin bride.

Darling Silas swept me up in his arms and hurried me outside. "Of course, my sweet wife. What sort of a husband do you take me for?"

"The most beloved of all husbands," I said, and he stopped, his face an inch from mine.

"And the most beloved of all wives," he said, smoothing the veil from my face. "Forever."

I threw the bouquet and saw Rose catch it, her face aglow, her arms elbowing aside any eager takers. We hustled into the carriage and drove away into a new life.

Chapter 5

1870

The loose hairs on the back of my neck stirred in the faint breeze off the river. The Mississippi was some distance away, blocked by the teeming streets of the waterfront and the tangle of clapboard houses built on them higgledy-piggledy in an attempt to catch a water view from the second- or third-story windows. We were not so fortunate at our house, but I did love the front porch with its waist-high railing and just enough room for two rocking chairs, where I sat watching the darkening evening sky.

Joshua whimpered, and I pushed my feet against the boards, moving the chair in its soothing rhythm. Concerned he was still so warm, I pressed the curls from his forehead as his eyes fluttered shut once again. He'd been slightly feverish since midafternoon, and I was exhausted from consoling him, of little good in the fierce heat and humidity of a St. Louis summer. I'd heard rumors of influenza and worse at the market yesterday, and my heart caught at the very words, images of my poor mother and father still imprinted in my mind. People around here said the river itself brought the sickness, some years in torrents and in others merely a trickle, but death floated in on humid winds just the same, taking those blissfully unaware as easily as the cautious. I glanced down at Joshua and caught my breath at the wave of love and protectiveness that washed over me. Not *my* son, never him.

53

"Kate, my Hungarian rose!"

Ah God, he'd been at the whiskey again. I watched Silas stagger up the path to the porch, his hair sticking to his cheek with sweat, his fine white suit spotted with dirt and stains of other origins, which I'd have to scrub out as usual. He collapsed at my side, clutching my knees and waking the baby.

Joshua gave a hiccup and wailed, and Silas's face darkened at the sound. I rocked harder and put the baby on my shoulder, patting his back and murmuring soft shushes.

"Can you not have the brat in his crib when I come home to you, Kate? You know I need my solace. A man has a right to his solace, wouldn't you agree?" He leered at me, eyes glassy and hands probing. "Those teats were mine first, remember that."

I twisted in revulsion and made myself smile. "Silas, there's beef stew on the stove, and biscuits too. Go have some dinner while I put Joshua to bed. I'll join you soon. How'd things go today?"

He pushed himself up, his hands on the porch floor, and yanked open the door, turning back to me. "That bastard Rosell took all my patients again. But fuck him. Billy Cassidy came by, and I'll meet him again tonight. We have plans. Dentistry is not for me, Kate. I'm getting into the beer brewing business. That's where the money is." The screen door slammed behind him, and my heart sank.

Dr. Steve Rosell was Silas's partner in the dentistry practice his father had set up for him right after we married. Rosell was an experienced dentist, and at first Silas, fresh out of school, had been an apt pupil to the older man. Silas's skills, however, hadn't improved, and Rosell's patience was growing thin, particularly so since Silas was taking half the profits and doing little of the work, thanks to his father's shrewd contract. He'd left by noon nearly all the days in the last eight months. He'd go out for lunch and return drunk after two hours or more, doing damage that Rosell had to repair for the unlucky patients that showed up in the afternoon. At the close of business at five o'clock, Silas made for the taverns again before returning home, tonight being the usual.

The only time I saw my husband sober was in the mornings, and half the time he retched up his breakfast. It was taking a toll not only on our marriage but on Silas himself. His flawless face was now etched with red veins, his eyes were constantly bloodshot, and his belly rather than his chest filled out his waistcoats. Some nights he stank so of the liquor of the day I could hardly bear to lie beside him in our bed, and I aired out the linens the minute he stepped out the door in the morning. Many evenings lately he'd left the house in a rage at my inability to sympathize with his rants against Rosell, and I was suspicious that drink was not the only vice he'd entangled himself with. Opium dens were rampant on the waterfront, and the smell was quite specific. I was, after all, Joshua Fisher's ward, and had learned well the trials the riverboat captains had with their sailors.

I got up from the rocker very carefully and entered the house. As I crept down the hall, I saw Silas at the kitchen table, devouring a plate of stew. I carried Joshua upstairs, laying him in his crib. I put only a light cotton blanket over his legs, the heat still so oppressive, but made sure the window was open so the night breeze would cool the room. I stood there for a moment, watching him sleep. I had never thought I could feel love like this for any living being. I had loved my parents and loved my siblings, those in Davenport and those still in Austria. I loved Silas, no matter our troubles, and I had thought that to be the zenith of what love could be. But until I birthed this child and took him in my arms, I had never known what love truly meant.

It was like a blizzard that encompassed you completely, whirling over you and consuming you in its intensity. I would die for my child in an instant, and gladly kill any threat that came near him, attacking like a screaming Amazon brandishing a spear fashioned with the passion and intensity that only a mother could know. When I thought about Joshua, I sometimes had to stop and take a breath or two just to compose myself into what the world thought a normal human being was supposed to be. Perhaps all mothers were like this, or perhaps not. I only knew that now Joshua's mother was who I was and who I was meant to be. I kissed his forehead and tiptoed out of the room, leaving the door ajar lest he cry out in the night.

Silas was slumped over the table when I entered the kitchen, his arm resting in the plate mostly empty of stew. I gently slid the dish out from under his arm and went about setting the kitchen to rights, putting the pot of stew on ice in the pantry for tomorrow and cleaning the dishes. Just as I finished, he jerked upright and stared at me.

"Kate, my sweet Kate. C'mere." He slid the chair out and gestured at his lap. I rinsed the last cup, dried my hands, and stepped towards him. He grasped me about the waist and pulled me down into his lap. I slid my arm around his neck, partially for balance and partially out of a desire to be what we once were. He kissed my neck, and his hand grasped my breast over the plain calico housedress I wore. I pushed his hair back from his forehead and pressed my lips to his cheek.

"Jesus, woman." He smiled up at me, his face so handsome still. "Have you no perfume? You smell like the boy's diapers and sweat. Amaya always smells like jasmine. I'll ask her for some. You'd like it."

My body went rigid. I couldn't believe what he'd just said. I blinked in astonishment, not knowing what to say. Had I heard correctly? Surely not. This must be a joke, he couldn't . . .

I pushed off his lap and stood up.

"What did you say?" My voice sounded weak and thready,

and I hated it. He shook his head and stood up as well, grasping my shoulders.

"My Hungarian rose smells like no rose in memory, lady wife. I think I'll go out."

Something snapped in me, and I grabbed the lapels of his coat. "What did you say, Silas?" My voice was near a scream. "Tell me, what did you say?"

He shook me off, shoving me against the stove, and I fell to the floor.

"Never mind what I said. Get back to your precious baby, nursemaid. I have business to tend to."

He brushed his hands against his coat and pants and smoothed his hair back from his face as I scrambled up from the floor. I launched myself at him, fists flying, and saw the shock register on his face before he recovered and punched me full in the face. Never had I thought to lay a hand on my husband and never had he to me; I will think that until my last breath.

I heard the screen door slam as I staunched my bleeding nose with my skirt, the salt of my tears stinging almost as sharply as my pride.

It wasn't so much the marriage that failed, it was the people who failed each other, and that outcome should have been obvious from the outset. It didn't take long after the wedding for the veil to lift on our own foolishness. In fact, it was only two weeks later that I found Silas throwing crockery in the kitchen. Broken china littered the floor.

"Stop this nonsense immediately!"

He turned to me in surprise, setting down a cup like an unruly child.

"What is the matter with you, Silas?"

He sat at the kitchen table and put his head in his hands.

"I'm sorry, Kate. It's just that the great Richard Melvin has refused to advance me another penny unless I sign his damned contract."

"For what?" I said, pulling out a chair and sitting myself. I was pretty sure I knew.

"For a dentistry practice with Dr. Rosell. I'll be like an apprentice, no say of my own, no decent money." His voice rose in anger. "My father doesn't trust me; he says my judgment is flawed, and I'm not thinking straight." He looked pointedly at me and at least had the grace to flush as he lowered his eyes.

"We'll barely have enough money to live on." Silas's chair scraped back, and he stood abruptly. "No extras, no fancy living, no gewgaws for you, sweet wife. I hope you can cook as well as you fuck."

I stared at him, stunned. In truth, for the last month, I'd not been as dewy-eyed with love as I had been, and I had come to see Silas with new eyes. For a week before the wedding, stowing away again on the *Delta Queen* had sounded like a good thing to do, even as I knew how silly that was. Emily had laughed and said it was pre-wedding jitters along with pregnancy nerves, but I knew in my heart it was more than that. Still, I had few choices, in fact only one, so I had made what I thought was the best of a bad situation. I may have been wrong.

"I'm going down to Mackey's. I expect dinner when I get back," he said.

"Cooking is one thing, plates to eat from are another. Perhaps you might get some to replace the ones you just smashed, after you've indulged in your whiskey," I said. "Unless we've already sunk so low we should just eat from the pot with spoons."

He picked up the last cup from the table and hurled it to the floor in front of my feet, shards flying into my skirts. I stared up at his handsome, smiling face and didn't give him the satisfaction of so much as a twitched finger or a blinked eye. He turned on his heel, and that was the last I saw of him that night. In the morning he woke me with a red rose in his hand, murmuring apologies and unbuttoning my nightshift, making promises he wouldn't keep.

That had begun the pattern of our days—scornful rages followed by loving contrition, and each time a little piece of my love for Silas crumbled away. My life had become a waiting game until the stormy March day when Joshua was born, a sea change for both of us. I had not thought to be a mother so young and had not been happily anticipating what I thought of as a hindrance to my life rather than a joyous arrival. However, as many new mothers are, I was obsessed with my child. His downy skull, the bones so fragile under my fingers, the unfocused blue eyes—everything about him was endlessly fascinating to me. I would count his tiny toes and fingers over and over, and I'd whisper into his shell-like little ear as he sucked hungrily on my breasts.

Silas seemed happy with Joshua, but his interest waned rapidly between the baby's cries and constant need for attention from me. Joshua had to come first, and Silas grew steadily more impatient and aggravated, seemingly jealous of the child. His temper worsened as spring came, and by mid-summer, just a year from when we had been so happy, he hardly came home at all. I knew about the drinking and the opium but never suspected he had been unfaithful. Now, in August, I realized in an instant how blind and foolish I had been. We couldn't go on like this anymore.

I set the portmanteau near the front door and ran back up the staircase to gather the small trunk of Joshua's clothes and diapers. I glanced at the crib and saw that he was still sleeping, but turning restlessly in the noonday heat. I had taken advantage of his morning nap to pack our belongings and to send Billy

Samuels, the neighbor boy, to the Fishers' with a note asking for asylum. Emily had written back quickly, and the lad breathlessly handed me the note on his return, his cheeks red from the long run. *Come immediately,* she had written in her fine copperplate. That was all, but all I had wanted.

"Miz Fisher says I'm to help carry if you need it, ma'am," he announced proudly. "I'm very strong for my age. She said to hurry, and she paid me a dollar."

The smile died on his face as Silas staggered up the walk, looking even more disheveled than when he'd left the night before. His face was pale, his eyes bloodshot. He shoved the boy out of his path and looked to do the same to me until I sidestepped beyond the doorway. He hadn't taken three steps before he swayed and fell to the floor unconscious, his head narrowly missing the bottom stair.

"Quickly, now." I grabbed Billy's arm as he made to run. "I'll take his head, you grab his feet, and we'll put him on the sofa in the parlor." He didn't look happy but did as I ordered, and with supreme effort we dragged most of Silas's two-hundred-pound weight onto the green brocade seat, his booted feet dangling over the end.

"We still leavin'?" Billy asked, eyeing Silas warily.

I put a pillow under Silas's head, shocked at the heat that radiated from his skin. I felt for a pulse on his wrist, and it was weak but steady. His eyes fluttered, and he focused glassily on my face.

I sighed. "Not today. Go on home now."

"Kate, help me." Silas heaved himself up on his elbows and vomited profusely onto the carpet. Then he lay back, exhausted by his efforts. Billy, lip curled in disgust, lost no time in running out the front door.

The next three hours passed in a blur, between rocking a fussing baby and nursing a sick husband, both with fevers that

climbed steadily higher in spite of the cloths soaked in cold
water and vinegar that I kept pressing on both their foreheads.
Silas was clearly suffering from more than a hangover, and
Joshua from more than teething or the humidity. My store of
nursing knowledge was little more than what I'd gleaned from
helping my father in the Confederate camp, and I knew I was
out of my depth when Silas vomited up even the sips of water
I'd forced down his throat. Eyes glassy, he clutched my arm.

"God, Kate, I'm dying here." His eyes rolled up, only the
whites showing, and he lost consciousness. I'm not the sort to
panic easily, but I knew this was more than I could cope with.
Setting Joshua down on the rug, I rushed out the front door
and over to the Samuelses' house next door.

Mabel Samuels opened the screen, wiping her hands on her
apron. It was obvious from the look on my face, as well as what
Billy must have imparted earlier, that she was expecting me. My
stomach growled at the smell of baking bread, but there was
little time for that, nor had there been earlier this day.

"Kate. Needin' the doctor, are you?"

I nodded. "God, yes, Mabel. I don't know what to do for
him."

She patted my hand and spun me around. "Get back to that
baby, honey. I sent Billy over to the hospital for a doc some
time back. Don't know what's keeping them."

Murmuring my thanks, I walked quickly back to my own
house, hearing Joshua's plaintive cries before I got to the door.

I scooped him up, trying to soothe him. Silas hadn't moved
an inch since I'd left, and his face was slack. I took the cloth
from his forehead and wet it again in the pail of water, wrung it
out, and replaced it. He groaned but didn't raise his head.
Joshua was so warm. I took off his little nightshirt and diaper
and lay him on his blanket, smoothing a cold cloth over his
body and forehead. I lay down on the floor between Silas on the

couch and Joshua on the patterned rug, alternating cold cloths between them. I didn't know what else to do. It was so warm, in spite of the open door and the window I'd propped open, I must have dozed off.

A sharp knock on the screen door roused me, and I scrambled to my feet as a short, little man with a mustache, carrying a black bag, bustled into the room, Billy Samuels on his heels.

"Miz Melvin? I'm Dr. Rush. What do we have here?"

I brushed my hair from my face and held out my hand, which he ignored, seating himself beside Silas on the sofa. Despite my hurried scrubbing, the unmistakable stench of vomit drifted in the breeze, which did little to dispel it.

"My husband is very ill, as you can see," I stammered, "and my son as well, Doctor. Thank you for coming."

Ignoring me, he opened Silas's shirt, probing his throat and belly and then lifting up one of his eyelids. He felt for a pulse on Silas's neck and, after a moment, sighed, turning to me.

"Let me see the child."

I held out Joshua in his fresh diaper, and Dr. Rush took him onto his lap, holding him gently as he did the same examination he'd done to Silas.

"Cholera, the both of them. I'm sorry." He lifted Joshua up to me and shook his head, and my heart plummeted in my chest. "Seems like half the city is infected. The hospital is full, and there's little I can do. Just try to keep them comfortable and cool. Get some water or broth into them; that's about all I can suggest, my dear."

He picked up his bag and adjusted his waistcoat, his face grim. "Your husband a drinker, Miz Melvin?"

I nodded, surprised at the question.

"It goes worse with them, I've found. The baby, well . . . the young ones don't fare so well, either."

Sudden anger surged in my chest. "We'll just see about that,

Doctor. I'm not about to lose my family just because you say so." I couldn't wait to get this overstuffed little man out of my house. What good was he anyway? A longing for my father gripped me, and I nearly swayed on my feet. Outrage suffused Rush's face, but one look at mine convinced him I was about to push him out the door.

"Thank you for coming," I managed as he scuttled down the steps and out of sight. As I stepped back into the parlor, Billy grabbed my hand.

"My Mam, she'll help. She knows teas and such," he said. Then he ran for the door. "Don't worry, Miz Melvin."

When Emily Fisher arrived I was at my wit's end, making chicken broth while holding Joshua and trying to keep Silas comfortable. It was nearly dark outside, the oil lamp in the kitchen holding back the night. Emily took one look at the situation and, with her usual aplomb, took my arm and sat me down at the kitchen table, graced now with a large covered basket. Mabel and Billy Samuels hovered behind her, clearly in thrall, carrying two glass jars of dark-colored liquid and a brown jug.

"Feed the child, Kate, then yourself. There's a roast chicken in the basket, with new peas. No point in you getting sick as well. We'll take care of Silas."

And so they did. Somehow, between the three of them, they got Silas upstairs into bed, cleaned up and between soft sheets, with some spoonfuls of broth and tea in him. Joshua took a little milk from my aching breasts and lapsed into sleep while I picked at the chicken and vegetables Emily had brought. I fell asleep on the sofa, Joshua in my arms, and left them to their ministrations.

Sunlight woke me, and I was surprised to find no baby beside me. Emily lay asleep on the rug beside the sofa, her head cradled on her arms, and I started with guilt to see her so. I dashed up the stairs and found Joshua sleeping, but still hot to the touch of my hand. For a moment I smoothed the damp curls from his forehead and, with my ear to his mouth, listened to the sound of his soft breathing. Assured, I whirled around and ran to the bedroom I shared with Silas.

My husband lay upon his back, his head on the down pillow, hair brushed back from his face. His hands were at his sides, palms up in supplication. His face was once again handsome and peaceful in repose, his blue eyes open. I lifted my hand gently to his mouth, but no breath warmed my palm. I moved to cup his cheek and found it cool, the flesh unyielding. While we had slept, he had breathed his last.

I crumpled to the floor, my hand grasped in his. No matter our troubles, death was no road for a vibrant young man to travel down. Tears gushed hot and salty amid anguished cries that sounded as though there were an animal in pain nearby, though the sounds came from my own mouth. I had loved him once, not so long ago, and his were the arms that had held me in passion and comfort, now to never move again.

I don't know how long I sat there against the bed, but it was Joshua's piteous whimpers that finally penetrated the fog in my mind. My legs trembled as I walked blindly to his room and picked him up from his crib. I cradled him to my chest and, sobbing, changed his diaper and washed him with cool water from the ewer on the dresser, despairing all the while at how warm he felt and how feeble his movements had become. Was I to lose the son as well as the father this horrid day?

"Kate, give him to me." Emily stood in the doorway, her voice a beacon of serenity amid the thoughts swirling like poisonous snakes through me.

"Silas, he's . . ."

"I know, my love." Brooking no delay, she plucked Joshua from my arms and herded me down the stairs. "I've sent for

Captain Fisher. He will be here soon, and all will be put to rights. It is you and Joshua I must be concerned with now."

In the kitchen she sat me down at the table and watched closely as I forced myself to drink the cup of tea she set in front of me. The last things I remember that morning were the plate of scrambled eggs, yellow bright and steaming, that Emily put on the table, and the song she sang to Joshua. "Hush little baby, don't say a word. Daddy's going to buy you a mockingbird . . ."

No, he never will . . . never, never, I thought, and I didn't have another coherent thought for a long time to come.

I watched the brown water of the Mississippi roll by, higher on the grassy banks from the heavy late summer rains. The breeze was cool, and I was glad I'd brought a shawl, hugging it tighter around my thin shoulders. Caught in the grip of the cholera myself, I had not witnessed the dual burials of my husband and son in St. Louis Cemetery, some six weeks ago. It was only ten days since I'd been able to walk steadily on my own, and it still seemed as though the last two months had been a nightmare from which I'd just awakened. I kept thinking, as soon as I got my bearings, I'd go home and everything would be as it was, making dinner for Silas and getting Joshua ready for bed, bundled in his soft, blue flannel blanket. Then I'd remember.

The sun dipped below the horizon before I made my way back to the house. Emily was sitting on the porch, and her shoes were dusty. I knew she had been keeping an eye on me, but she never admitted to that. The captain came out the door, a tray with three glasses of whiskey in his hand, and I joined them, settling into the rocker.

"I'm going down to New Orleans next week, ladies," he said. "Any requests from the Frenchies?"

Emily smiled. "Lace. You know how I love the lace from that little shop on Chartres Street. Kate?"

I shook my head. I couldn't think of a single thing I wanted, except to have my child back in my arms, or to have my memory wiped clean of the pain of missing him. I woke up to anguish, and I wrestled with it at night. When I thought about Silas, I only felt regret—for what we once had together, and that there would never be a chance for him to redeem himself now. I saw the Fishers exchange a glance, and Emily put her hand on my arm. We sat in silence for a long while, sipping our whiskey, as we did for many nights to come.

CHAPTER 6

1872

Taffeta had such a crispness to it, and I ran my hands down the ruffles that spread out from the smooth, corseted bodice of the dress. Not far enough, though. On the right side, the ruffles were hiked up above my knee, and my leg was clearly visible, encased in the black net stockings that Joseph Henry insisted upon for all the girls at Theatre Comique. Even for me, the evening's debuting featured songstress.

"Five minutes, Kate."

"Thank you," I answered, appraising myself again in the mirror. Tessie, the costume girl, had piled my hair atop my head, two curls hanging free, topped with purple feathers and a glittery bow. The bodice of the dress, such as it was, was low cut, and the purple taffeta and lace curved off my shoulders, my bosom held up only by the boning of the corset and certainly not the dress itself. Black, high-buttoned boots added to the effect, my stockinged legs shown off by the raised bustle. Tessie's artfully applied makeup completed the picture, and I scarcely recognized the woman who gazed back at me in the mirror, her red lips glistening and kohl-lined green eyes smoldering.

Just as well, I thought. Someone from St. Louis society could be in the audience tonight, perhaps even Richard Melvin himself. I'd taken the stage name Katie Elder, but even so, you couldn't be too careful. Not that I really cared much, except for the Fishers' reputation. My own had been the object of scrutiny for years . . . and long deemed unfit.

I'd spent over a year existing in what seemed to me now a fog, never seeing clearly through the grief I bore. Less than human, I wandered like a ghost through the grounds of the Fishers' property. I'd come to life enough to help with the boys when they were home, or assist Emily with her charity work, but, truthfully, I don't remember much, and there was probably not much I did that was worth remembering.

One morning last summer I found myself standing on the porch of our old house in St. Louis, and when the door was opened by a startled housewife, I fled. For the first time I realized that I had no life to go back to, and, if I wanted to live, I would have to make one.

I began in small ways, paying attention to my hair and bathing regularly, taking care with my clothes. I started reading again, once my favorite pastime—Shakespeare at first, and then branching out to the new novels Emily always had lying about. I went for long walks along the river, waving back at passengers on the boats, enjoying the sting of the wind on my face. When the boys were home, I played the piano while we all sang some of the songs of the day, and I remembered how much I loved music. I began to do some of the marketing, taking the carriage into town, and it was on Front Street one afternoon that I ran into my old acquaintance from Davenport, Jack Rafferty. He'd come to St. Louis and opened a theater and saloon, the Gilded Lily. According to the Fishers and their friends, it had become quite the talk of the town.

"Miss Kate? I swear, I could never forget *you*," he said, bowing low, his elegant waistcoat practically touching the road. "I have often wondered what became of you."

I smiled and took his hand. "Mr. Rafferty, I am flattered. However, I am sure you have had many more important matters to occupy your time than that."

He cocked his head and stared intently at me. "Indeed I have, to be honest, my dear, but there are some people I never forget. I would be most interested to know what you are doing and how you came to be in St. Louis. Perhaps you could take some time and enlighten me, if I may be so bold?"

So began our twice weekly chats at Miss Dunwiddie's Tearoom, a most respectable establishment. I wasn't certain the Fishers would approve of my friendship with Jack, so I kept these trysts to myself, although they were always most respectable. What a pair we must have made—the flamboyantly attractive gambler and the grieving, black-clad widow—but the employees of the tearoom never so much as blinked, bringing tea and sandwiches to our table, efficient service without a backward glance.

For some reason, I instinctively trusted Jack Rafferty. Perhaps it was memories of how kind he had been to me back in Davenport, or because he was so open with me, but somehow I felt I could be so in turn. Sometimes it's easier to talk to someone who hasn't witnessed your personal tragedies and has had no opportunity to judge or comment. I poured my heart out, and he listened without reproach, comforting me only with a glance and a touch to my hand, over many weeks. Here was a man, clearly one who knew all the sins of life and had bent them to his profit, but so kind and warm to someone who offered him nothing. I never gave a thought to why. When he suggested that I could sing and make a living doing that, I was astonished. Who would pay to hear me, a girl with no training or experience?

"Everyone, my dear. On our walks, you have sung short songs, and I know a good voice when I hear one. With your natural charm, you would be a sensation, if you lent yourself to it. I have a friend, Joseph Henry, who runs the Theatre Comique and who could try you out. Trust me, Kate."

That is how I found myself at this very moment ready to go onstage at the Theatre Comique. Jack had introduced me to Mr. Henry the week before, and I had sung for him. I'd been nervous, but after the first few bars, I was as comfortable as though I'd been sitting at the piano in the Fishers' house. He had been delighted, shaking Jack's hand, and arranging for me to come this evening. I hadn't told the Fishers about this, only that I was spending the evening with a friend downtown. I know they thought it was Rose Melvin, since I had so few friends, and I let them think that so they wouldn't worry. What I truly hadn't expected was the costume and all that went with it. I felt like a completely different person—but somehow still the same person I had always been.

I left my dressing room and waited in the wings for the act before me to finish up, as the stage manager directed. Joseph Henry, a well-fed gentleman who favored yellow brocade waistcoats, joined me, placing his arm around my waist before I could think to protest.

"Darlin', you're going to be fabulous," he said, kissing me on the cheek. I stiffened and then thought, I was starting a new life and perhaps it was high time I relinquished my European snobbery and sense of propriety. I'd continued my education in America, but still I had a lot to learn. This was a country that embraced openness and freedom, and maybe it was time to be open and free myself.

"Thank you, sir," I said pertly and kissed him back, much to his delight. At my cue, I strode on stage behind the closed curtains. I glanced over at the piano player and the guitarist who would accompany me and took a deep breath. The curtains parted as the announcer said my name, and I saw the house was full, all two hundred seats. The gaslights went up, and the piano player began his introduction, barely audible over the conversation of the audience.

I only had two songs this night. I started with a civil war ballad, "Pretty Peggy," but after a few bars that no one heard, I motioned to the piano player to launch into "Mulligan's Guards," the most popular song in St. Louis, my second choice. It was a rollicking song, and just so, it captured their attention, and the noise quieted. They were actually listening, and I began to march around the stage, stopping now and then to strike a pose, which they seemed to like, given the applause. I think it was my right leg that captured their attention, more so than my voice. At the end of the song I received thunderous applause, and then I decided to give them a song I'd learned from the Confederate prisoners back at Rock Island, "Aura Lee."

At first there was some conversation, but by the time I came to the last bars of the song, there was no sound in the theater but my voice and the plaintive guitar chords that accompanied me. I held the last note and looked out at my audience. Some of the men had tears on their cheeks, and when I bowed, the audience not only applauded, but cheered.

Mr. Henry hugged me as the curtains closed, amid protests.

"Kid, you were great! The audience loved you, and the house was packed. I think we need to talk about a contract."

"Thank you, sir," I said. "I'm happy it went well, but I'm not sure this is for me. Let me get back to my dressing room."

I wasn't sure what to think. I only knew this was something I had never expected, while at the same time I was planning what to do next to excite an audience and have another chance to listen to their applause and cheers. I opened the door to my dressing room to find Jack Rafferty lounging on the sofa inside, a cheroot in hand and eyes amused.

"What did I tell you, Kate?"

I shut the door. "I don't know, Jack. What did you tell me?" I stopped and, for some reason, struck the same pose I had on stage, my very revealed right leg curved in front.

He smiled and came over to me, his hand stealing around my shoulder.

"That you could do this, and do it very well indeed," he said and kissed my neck. "I think you're ready for the Gilded Lily, my dear. Do you think you can do that?"

It was as though a flame had been lit inside me, and it flared to life, burning through me. I put my arm around his neck, and it seemed so natural I wondered why I'd never done this before.

"Jack, I know I can do that," I said, and I kissed him for the first time, his lips opening eagerly beneath mine. It didn't feel like a betrayal to Silas at all, but the beginning of a new life.

Jack Rafferty was a very good kisser.

Kisses weren't all Jack was good at. Six weeks after my performance at the Theatre Comique, I was the star performer at the Gilded Lily. My repertoire had expanded to not only the popular songs of the day, but also old songs I had learned in the court of the empire, sung in Hungarian, which became the standouts. I started the audience off with songs they knew, like "Buffalo Gals" and "Silver Dagger," but once I had them, I launched into the folk songs of my childhood. They somehow struck a chord in these audiences, whether they were St. Louis society folk, adventurers, pioneers, ex-military, or rough men looking to head west. Those songs, interspersed with "Aura Lee," "The Lily of the West," and other melancholy ballads that I had learned in Rock Island, spoke to their hearts. The crowds gave me their adoration every night before the curtains closed. I was the sensation of St. Louis, and, before long, even the Fishers learned of my notoriety, despite the different name.

To my surprise, I somehow had fallen in love with Jack Rafferty. Not only was he devilishly handsome, he was exciting, introducing me to a lifestyle I'd never known existed in America. He enjoyed sumptuous surroundings—the best of what could be obtained in St. Louis—and for the first time in years I was reminded of the life I'd left behind in Hungary. I moved in with Jack, at his request, and reveled in the luxury of our third-floor suite at the River Palace Hotel. He bought me clothes, jewelry, and anything else I desired.

What I desired most was Jack himself, and my passion was reciprocated. Silas and I had been caught up in the throes of instant attraction and lust, two innocents learning together, but I discovered there was much more to the arts of love. Jack was an expert teacher, and I was an eager and willing pupil. In his arms, I discovered how to please a man, far beyond sweet kisses and soft touches, and in return, how a woman can be brought to the edge of madness by the knowing caresses of a man who had taken the time to school himself in what a woman desired. Together, we made a couple Eros himself would congratulate.

Every now and then, sometimes when I woke in the mornings or in the evening, when the sun was setting and the shadows first appearing, if I was alone, I would think about my darling Joshua, or even the person I was not so long ago—a simple wife and mother who wanted nothing more. Although, when I was honest with myself, I knew that wasn't true. I knew there was so much more in the world that had reopened to me. Life goes on, and mine had much farther to go. I would not let myself falter and become a ghost to the past. Perhaps even then I had known there was more to discover, but now I was sure of it. I embraced it, and I looked forward to each day with a sense of wonder and excitement. The world was waiting for me, and I stepped into it wholeheartedly.

Far from excluding me from their lives, Joshua and Emily Fisher loved me no matter what course I set myself upon. I had feared their condemnation, but to my surprise and delight, they didn't care what the St. Louis gossips had to say. I made weekly trips to their house on Sunday afternoons, and it was as though

I'd never been away.

If the boys were home, we would go down to the river as always, and helping Emily with her gardens and needlework had become second nature to me, never changing. Sunday dinners were the same as they'd always been.

"You've become quite the sensation, Kate," Joshua said, taking a bite of roast beef. "I always knew you were destined for more than making chicken fricassee, but my imagination didn't go far enough."

I laughed, remembering the first time we'd met. "I guess so, Captain. I wouldn't have predicted this, though."

He smiled across the table and shook his head. "Never think what you do is something you need be ashamed of, my dear. The world is a trying place, but one so full of wonders that no one can say what will be thought of next. In the future, I predict those who make the stage their profession will be most revered."

I shook my head, laughing, and Emily smiled as well. "I cannot imagine that. I will be happy enough to have a modicum of respect from society in spite of doing what makes me happy."

Captain Fisher took a sip of Bordeaux. "Laugh if you will, my dears. The talent performers have will be recognized, I am sure of it. The ability to entertain one's fellow man is a skill not possessed by many of the common herd, which will become increasingly obvious as time marches on. There are few who have it, but you, my darling Kate, are one of them."

I demurred again, and we passed on to other topics, but my heart was happy that they accepted my choice of employment, if not the man I had chosen to live with. Jack Rafferty had yet to be invited to Sunday dinner, but my hope was that one day he would be.

In the summer of 1873, Jack and I boarded the *Delta Queen* to New Orleans, Captain Fisher at the helm. Jack said it was high time we did some traveling and had a change of scenery. I was excited at the prospect of going down the river but especially at visiting New Orleans, a city I'd heard so much about and had never seen.

We were invited to the captain's table each evening, and my hopes were at last achieved. The two men I loved most took to each other from their first handshake, as I'd known they would. Both men of the world, they recognized they had much in common in intellect as well as a fondness for me, and the week we spent on the waters of the Mississippi was a special time. During the evenings I sometimes sang with the musicians aboard the *Queen*, and the passengers were most appreciative. Jack gambled away the nights but still arose each morning, sometimes close to noon, charming and rested as always.

We traveled to New Orleans not just for relaxation, but so Jack could inquire about business opportunities there, I discovered. He had his eye on an establishment on Bourbon Street whose owner had recently passed away. The building was three stories, the upper floors balconied and trimmed with lacy iron filigree in the style of so many buildings in the French Quarter, and I loved it on sight, as I did most everything I saw from the moment the boat docked. This was a city like no other I'd seen in America—so European, and yet so different from anything there. I loved the entire French Quarter, but St. Louis Cathedral and Jackson Square in particular enchanted me, and every afternoon I strolled through the pathways of the park, stopping to chat with the vendors and artists who made their living there.

I hardly saw Jack at all. He was up and away first thing in the morning and didn't return until night, when we'd have dinner together. He seemed completely enmeshed in his business dealings and had little to say. I was happy discovering the city on my own, but I did miss his presence. Still, it was the first time since I'd known him that we hadn't been completely engaged with each other, whether it was at the new Gilded Lily, or just spending time together. Finally, one night after we'd been there two weeks, we sat together and had dinner in our suite at the hotel, the hour early.

"I bought the place, Kate." Jack lit a cigar and leaned back against the sofa, pushing away the room service table.

I took a sip of my claret. "What about the Lily?"

"Bennington will do fine with it. He'll bank my share of the profits every month." He looked at me. "What do you say to living in New Orleans? I rather like it here."

I wasn't so sure. I poured more claret and sat back. "You never stay in one place long, do you, Jack?"

He frowned. "What does that have to do with anything?"

"Just an observation. You know, in all the time I've known you, you've never talked much about your past—where you grew up, your family, those kind of things. Why New Orleans?"

He stood up and began to pace around the sitting room. I watched him, sipped claret, and waited. Finally he stopped, and his face was somber.

"You have an uncanny ability to ask me just the right things at just the right time, you know that?"

"If you say so."

"I do. You want some past history? Here it is. I grew up in this town, Kate."

He gestured towards the windows that fronted on Lafayette. "Oh, not like this, no. I grew up in the Channel, dirt fucking poor. Shanty Irish as they come. My daddy used to come home so drunk he hardly made it up the front steps, but not blind drunk enough that he couldn't wallop me, my brother, and my mother into pulp damn near every night since I was big enough to remember. I ran away from here the night he beat my mother to death, the same night I drowned the bastard in the river, and I've never been back since. I don't know where my mother is buried. I haven't seen my brother in nineteen years, and I don't even know if he's alive or dead. I swore one day I'd come back here and own this town, and this place on Bourbon Street is just the beginning." He threw the wineglass in his hand into the wall, the crystal shattering in bright shards on the carpet.

"Is that enough history for you?"

I didn't know what to do, or what to say. I felt his anguish and his rage like a physical blow, and I once again saw a man I thought I knew turn into someone I didn't know at all. I wanted to comfort him at the same time I wanted to run away. Rage terrified me, and I never thought to see Jack like this. People said he was a dangerous man, but I had never had occasion to see this side of him.

He walked over and put his hands on my shoulders. I was shaking, and his fingers pressed almost painfully into my skin, his breath warm on the back of my neck.

"I'm sorry if I frightened you, sweetheart," he whispered, leaning down. "I've been . . . well, I guess you could say, obsessed ever since we got here." He turned me around and looked into my eyes. "This is the beginning of a new life for us, Kate. It's what I've wanted for a long time. Join me."

There was love in his eyes, and an earnest hopefulness I'd never seen in him before. This man could never be like Silas; they were as different as the sun and the moon. Jack might be angry at the world, or at least a part of it, but this was a man who would never direct his anger at me. He was a man who would only cherish me. I threw my arms around him.

We would make our mark on New Orleans.

CHAPTER 7

1874

New Orleans was a magical place for me, and I fell in love with every brick of it. Each morning I would start my day on the balcony of our suite at the Hotel Royale, watching the sun illuminate the towers of St. Louis Cathedral and light up the city, the air fragrant with the sweet scents of night-blooming jasmine and magnolia. Lush gardens hid beyond the high walls of the houses in the French Quarter, but the streets and balconies of all the commercial buildings were overflowing with baskets of flowers and fragrant vines that proliferated even over the rooftops, engulfing the fragile-looking balconies.

We had developed a routine, Jack and I. Every morning he would kiss me good-bye and go to the club on Bourbon Street, where the work crew was transforming the old warehouse into Jack's dream. Three stories high, with balconies above the street and wide floor-to-ceiling shutters that opened onto the sidewalk, the building was fast becoming the talk of the Vieux Carré, and everyone was anticipating its grand opening.

The first floor would house an elegant restaurant, with a showroom stage at the back, Jack's idea. After the evening's dinner service, the curtains would be drawn back, and the show would begin. Some evenings would feature a play put on by the house troupe, anything from Shakespeare to a French farce, a favorite among New Orleanians. Other nights, Jack planned a variety show with acrobats, dancers, jugglers—almost any entertainment imaginable. On opening night, however, he had decided I would be the star attraction, and I was only too happy to oblige. I loved performing, and my audiences loved me. I was a little apprehensive that sophisticated New Orleanians might not take to me as the more rustic crowds in St. Louis had, but Jack had no such qualms.

One lazy Sunday morning we lounged on pillows, Jack's arms around my waist as I leaned into him. A tray of beignets and coffee sat at the foot of the bed. "The first time I saw you, walking down the street in Davenport, Iowa, there was something about the way you carried yourself, tilted your head, and looked people in the eye. Even then, in that calico dress with a basket on your arm, you looked like a duchess deigning to pick cabbages and pluck chickens, and I wondered where a girl like you had come from, because it couldn't have been Iowa." He kissed my neck. "You're special, Kate. I don't think you realize just how special."

"I looked for you, you know," I said. "From the first time I saw you, standing outside your saloon, you were the only person in Davenport that made me feel that I was of value, and I fell in love a little with a man I was told to never talk to." I kissed him, a quick peck. "I always hoped someday I'd see you again, so I could do this."

The next kiss lasted a long time, and our coffee got cold. Being with a man like Jack was like a balm to my soul, a soul that had been ravaged by guilt and loss. I felt reborn: desirable, beautiful, confident, and everything a woman could be.

The streets of the Vieux Carré became very familiar to me. Every day after Jack left I would stroll the Quarter, and my French served me well. Madeleine's on Royal Street, the most delectable hat shop I'd ever seen, the dressmaker Mme. DuLac, next door, and Mr. Dupree's Perfumerie all became my favorites. I would cut through Jackson Square, watching the artists and performers, and sometimes step into the cool shade of the cathedral itself, its incense-filled serenity calming in comparison to the frenetic pace of life in New Orleans.

I came to know Father Frontenac well and fell into conversations in French with him. He had been educated in Paris and for a short time posted to Vienna. While we knew no one in common, it was gratifying to talk with someone who had been raised in Europe as I had and who knew how difficult the transition to America could be. Most Americans, wherever they had originated, were a breed apart from all we had known. Strangely enough, this French-born priest and I were part of this country now and were Americans ourselves, braving the frontiers of civilization arisen from the hopes and dreams of us all. We would make our mark as thousands of others were doing around us.

By March, the new Gilded Lily was finished. Opening night loomed, and Jack was like I'd never seen him, as easily spooked as a cat in a tangle of terriers. He even snapped at the waiter who brought our room service trays, something I'd never seen him do. I'd been to the club earlier in the day and marveled at the final touches. What a beautiful place Jack had built. Although I'd seen the plans and stopped in every few days, I was impressed with the finished product.

Midnight-blue velvet curtains were closed on the stage, whose lights above and below would show off performers at their best. The restaurant on the first floor and gaming rooms on the second were wonders of elegance. The tables and chairs in the restaurant and even in the saloon areas above were of French design, gilt-edged white with black-velvet seats, softly lit by crystal chandeliers above, as well as more gaslit sconces on walls draped in black velvet and white silk.

The bar areas on all three floors were hand-carved mahogany, their polished curves gleaming beside the welcoming high stools, while the mirrored back shelves hosted the most varied selection of liquors I'd witnessed in any saloon before. The Gilded Lily was truly the grandest establishment of entertainment and gaming I'd ever seen and one that would impress even jaded New Orleans inhabitants. The Irish boy from the Channel had done himself proud.

By four o'clock, Jack was pacing around our rooms like a man possessed. His hair was mussed, and he was still in his shirt, having thrown off his vest and tie twice, declaring them unsuitable.

"Stop!"

I grabbed his arms and pulled him into me. He protested at first, but my grip held firm, and he stood still, looking down at me. "It's perfect, and so are you. Everyone will see that."

"You don't understand, Kate," he began, and I put my fingers to his lips.

"Yes, I do, Jack."

He stared at me for a few seconds, and then I felt the tension ebbing from him. He brought his face to mine, kissing me as though it was the last thing he'd ever do in this world. I dropped my hands from his arms and held him close.

"It's going to be a sensation, and it's all due to you," I whispered in his ear. "Jack Rafferty has returned to New Orleans and given this city something it's never seen before. It'll be the talk of the town in its reality, just like it's been in whispered expectation for months."

How I loved him, this beautiful, driven man who made his dreams become substance.

"The Gilded Lily, on its opening night, is proud to present the toast of the continent, Katherine Haroney, the Hungarian Songbird, now the Lily of the West."

Jack, resplendent in his tuxedo and tails, bowed low, walking into the wings as the murmurs of the crowd quieted in anticipation. The blue-velvet curtains parted slowly, and the stage lights came up as I walked to the center of the stage, my spangled golden gown glittering. I held my neck straight so the elaborate plumes in my hair wouldn't tilt. This was completely different from my debut at the Theatre Comique or the Gilded Lily in St. Louis. No more fishnet stockings. The crème de la crème of New Orleans society was seated before me. I was apprehensive about using my real name, instead of Katie Elder, but Jack assured me it was time I gloried in who I was, and he was right. Never had I felt so exactly Katherine to the marrow of my bones. The orchestra launched into the opening notes of my signature Hungarian ballad, "Heart of Sorrow," and by the time I had sung sixteen bars I knew Jack was right. I had them in the palm of my hand.

For the next hour I sang my heart out, from pretty French love songs that brought tears to the eyes of the most reserved Creole matrons to bawdy frontier ditties that had elegant toes tapping. They loved every note. When the curtains closed, the applause necessitated an encore, and I acquiesced with "Aura Lee," my personal favorite. From that night on, it became theirs as well. New Orleans not only accepted me, they loved me. The Gilded Lily, Jack, and I became a sensation in the city that care forgot.

"Call."

Dunsany peered at me through his half glasses, his face flushed. He shuffled his cards about in his hand.

"Sure about that, are you, Kate?" A bead of sweat fell from his chin and dropped onto the green felt. The other three men at the table pretended not to see it, and I could do no less.

"Call."

He sneered and pushed $1500 in chips to the center of the

table. "You've made a mistake."

Wordlessly, I fanned my cards face up onto the table. Full house, kings over nines.

Dunsany's face paled. He threw his cards down and pushed his chair back, muttering under his breath. Mr. Highsmith stood up and looked down at him.

"If you can't afford to lose to a better hand, Dunsany, maybe poker's not your game. At any rate, there will be no name-calling at this table."

I smiled at Highsmith as I scooped the pot into my reticule. "Thank you, sir. And thank you, Mr. Dunsany."

He stood up. "You cheated."

I took three steps and stood inches from his face. "Listen to me very carefully, Dunsany. I did not cheat. You are a lousy poker player, and you are a fool. You are not welcome in this establishment and will never enter these doors again. Get out."

"Whore."

Jack's fist connected with Dunsany's face before I had a chance to slap him myself, and with considerably more force. The idiot hit the floor, and our bodyguards, Nate and Tom, dragged his limp body through the doors and onto the rain-damp cobbles of Bourbon Street.

"Thank you, darling. You have excellent timing," I said, gathering my skirts and leaving the saloon.

"Dinner at eight, then?" Jack called. I nodded and swept through the door Nate held open for me. My hands hardly shook at all.

Success came with its headaches. The Gilded Lily was famous not only for our food, ambience, and entertainment, but for our gambling saloon. Honest dealers, beautiful hostesses, generous liquor, and no-limit tables made us the most successful place in New Orleans, an establishment where the rich felt safe and secure, even when they lost a great deal of money, which they often did. Dunsany was a Creole from one of New Orleans's oldest families, but he no longer felt secure, having gambled away a good-sized chunk of his fortune. Today's loss to me was a pittance in comparison to his usual losses but the sting of losing to a woman made it worse, I was sure.

I'd taken up poker on the riverboat down, and during our months in New Orleans I'd become quite proficient at the game, much to Jack's amusement. A woman who played cards wasn't usual, but our patrons seemed to enjoy having me in the game, and one or two other women had become regulars at the Lily as well. Gentlemen felt confident that a woman could not best them, and when they found one could, they strived to win again and again. Occasionally they did, but not against me, as a rule. I enjoyed poker immensely, and until today's incident with Emile Dunsany, I'd never left a table with anyone unhappy. I hoped he took my warning to heart.

True to his word, Jack joined me at our usual table in the dining room at eight o'clock. We had a special alcove, one of a dozen in the room hung with heavy brocade curtains, but ours was closest to the stage. It was a cozy spot, a curved upholstered banquette with a half-round table set with silver and crystal, the eight candles in the crystal chandelier creating a shadowed world inside the half-drawn curtains. He sat down, placing a gilt-wrapped box on my empty dinner plate as the sommelier poured our wine.

"What's this?"

"Just open it, Kate."

So I did, pulling off the golden ribbon and paper. It was a wooden box and I lifted the lid to find a pearl-handled, silver derringer pistol, snug in its velvet tray. I cradled it in my hand, and it fit like I'd been holding a pistol all my life, although this was the first time. I loved it.

"Darlin', if you're going to be a gambling woman, sooner or

later you might need this, just in case I'm not around at the time," Jack said. "Keep in mind this only has two shots, but you'll find it fits nicely inside your reticule."

I picked up my beaded jet evening bag and found he was correct. I laughed and placed the pistol back in its box, though. "You'll need to give me a lesson or two," I said.

"First thing tomorrow morning we're going out to Shady Dells up the river," Jack said. "Picnic and pistols—what a pleasant afternoon it will be. I have no doubt you'll be an excellent shot, Kate." He picked up his wineglass and sipped just as our waiter appeared. "Excellent Bordeaux, David. We'll start with the scallops, please."

Summer passed into autumn, and even during those steaming months, the Lily did an excellent business. Jack was talking about buying one of the abandoned plantations up the river. I wasn't sure why that would be better for us, and it was nearly an hour to get down to the French Quarter by boat, but he was entranced by the idea.

I understood it in a way, since coming back to New Orleans was a measure of success for Jack, and living in a grand house was the icing on the fancy cake he'd made for himself, wanting to be sure everyone was aware of it. I never voiced an opinion on the matter, as it had never come to fruition.

Tuesdays were the slowest night at the Gilded Lily, so it was before midnight as we walked hand in hand back to the hotel. Just past the streetlight on Chartres, he stopped and pulled me around to face him.

"Kate, marry me." His eyes glistened in the glow from the gaslight, and his voice had a tremor I'd never heard before.

I'd never thought of this, truly. Even back in Mexico I'd vowed I'd never care what society thought of me, and my dismal life with Silas had affirmed that I was a fish out of water when it came to being a proper wife and mother. The death of both my erstwhile husband and beloved child had confirmed that for me, and I'd never had another thought of a life with husband and babies again. If I'd had any doubts when I took up with Jack Rafferty, I knew that any residual expectation of a conventional, respectable life was thrown to the winds, but this man was a constant surprise. I knew one thing for certain, however. I loved Jack Rafferty and if it was marriage that made him happy, marriage it would be. I didn't have to think about it very long.

"Yes," I said and threw my arms around him as he laughed.

"She said yes!" He shouted and whirled me into the street, but there was no reply from anyone still awake in the French Quarter that warm night, except two cats that yowled in response.

By mid-October the house at Belle Lafayette was finished, its columns once again gleaming white in the moonlight like a ghost ship that had been resurrected from the depths of despair and made whole again. Jack had spent a fortune, not only on the estate, but on furnishings from Paris, from sofas to drapes. The house sat upriver two miles from New Orleans, and on sunny mornings it became our habit to go there and watch the construction and refurbishment. We planned the wedding for the week the house was done, and it seemed as though half of New Orleans was coming—patrons and colleagues, Creoles and Americans alike; no boundaries would be set for this occasion. I was beside myself with gown fittings, musicians, flowers, and caterers, while Jack blithely left everything to me, breezing in and out on his way to the club. I was no longer on the bill (too occupied with our upcoming nuptials), and I didn't spend much time there, only going over to meet Jack for dinner a few nights a week.

It was a Friday with a busy night expected when we sat down

for our usual dinner. Jack had just ordered our steaks, and the waiter had left when the curtain was flung back on our privacy.

Emile Dunsany stood there, a sneer on his face. That he was inebriated was obvious when he began to sway slightly. We hadn't seen him since his family had sent him to Paris months ago, most likely to avoid paying any more gambling debts for a time. I hadn't realized he'd returned.

"You thought I'd forgotten, you cheating whore," he slurred as he pointed at me with his left hand. With his right, he drew a revolver from his pocket and aimed it straight at me. It wavered a bit for a second but then steadied in his hand, only four feet from my face. I was frozen in place, my fork of lettuce halfway to my mouth.

"I didn't." With that, he fired at the same time Jack flung himself in front of me, crashing into the table, sending crystal and china exploding onto the floor. Jack's weight was heavy on my feet, pinning me to the banquette. Screams and commotion erupted out in the dining room, but Emile Dunsany smiled and lifted his pistol again. I scrabbled frantically into my reticule and brought out my pearl-handled derringer, always loaded. I jerked to the right and fired my gun into Dunsany's face just as he fired at me again. His shot went wild, but mine did not, and I saw Dunsany fall. I threw the pistol down onto the table and fell to my knees, grasping for Jack.

"No, no, no," I moaned and turned him towards me, grasping the lapels of his coat. His eyes found mine as I tried to use the tablecloth to staunch the blood surging from the hole in his chest. He batted my hands away and grabbed feebly at my arm.

"No good, Kate, no good," he murmured. I screamed then, hardly audible amid the shouts of the diners and staff converging upon us.

Jack pulled me closer to him, and I cradled his head in my lap.

"Knew that thing would come in handy," he said, the blood bubbling from the corner of his mouth. I wiped it away, my own breath coming in short gasps. He closed his eyes, and I leaned closer. "Live, my darling, on your own terms."

Those were the last words Jack Rafferty ever said, but the ones I will remember forever.

The last time my old companion Death paid me a visit I scarce remembered the feel of his teeth and claws, in part because my mind simply shut him out, and whenever the door to reality cracked open, laudanum shut it softly. Not this time.

My shot hit Emile Dunsany right between the eyes, and he was dead before he hit the floor. The New Orleans police arrested me for murder on the spot, the Dunsany family urging them to a newfound ardor for law and order. Our lawyer, Sam Benedict, had the charges dropped by the next afternoon, but I found a jail cell to be an inhospitable place to display one's grief, and it was only my anger that kept me sane. On returning to our hotel, I shed my clothing, stiff with Jack's blood, and took care of all the details for canceling a wedding and instead organizing a funeral before I fell into our bed. The tears came then, far into the night. I became reacquainted with the wrenching grip of inconsolable loss, a torture like no other. I woke to the steady fall of rain, the first of the autumn, and the rhythm of the water as it dripped past the eaves bored into my brain: no more Jack, no more Jack. Forever, forever.

I buried him at Belle Lafayette, in the crypt that housed the bones of its former owners, with a stone angel standing guard beneath the dripping oaks while Father Frontenac officiated.

The funeral was well attended, according to Sam Benedict, never far from my side, and I recognized many of the attendees—customers and business associates from the city, most with their wives, all dressed appropriately in black with their dripping ebony umbrellas, like a flock of ravens flying unusually close to the ground.

The house stood empty. I refused to hold a funeral dinner in the place where on this day I should have been celebrating my wedding, the tall windows now reflecting only the black trunks of the whispering oaks instead of welcoming light. I couldn't stand to look at the place. When the carriage pulled up outside my hotel, Sam touched my arm.

"I'll be by in the morning, Kate. We need to talk."

I nodded and couldn't wait to escape down the carriage steps.

By ten the next morning he was back, as promised, and my world took another descent into despair.

"There's no money."

I looked at him, incredulous. I knew what kind of income we'd been getting from the Gilded Lily.

"That's ridiculous, Sam."

He shook his head, white hair bobbing with his intensity. "No, it's not. Jack took every penny in income for the purchase and renovation of Belle Lafayette, Kate. And there's still ten thousand dollars outstanding on the mortgage." He peered at me through his spectacles, his finger on the account book. "The Lily has always made good money, but nothing like the money Jack spent on Belle Lafayette. This is a working plantation of five thousand acres. It didn't come cheap, even considering the circumstances. The repairs to the main house and outbuildings alone were horrendous. It's taken every cent the Lily makes to keep it going and pay the mortgage."

"But the Lily makes a good income, Sam, and I'll keep it going."

He didn't meet my eyes. "That was mortgaged, too, Kate. And he had partners. Partners that now own it."

I was stunned. Jack had never mentioned any of this to me. I had thought there was plenty of money. There always had been.

I had a bank account of my own, but there was only a few hundred dollars in it. Jack had always taken care of everything.

"So that means . . ."

Sam patted my hand and looked up at me with sympathy. "That means there's no money, my dear. Unless you can make the payments to the bank for Belle Lafayette, it's as gone as the Lily to you."

My throat was dry, and I found it difficult to speak. Everything was lost—Jack, the house, the Lily, and, most of all, me. I felt like I'd been cast adrift to float to nothingness along with them all.

"I hope the hotel bill is taken care of," I said, wincing at how venal it sounded.

"It is, Kate. Until the end of the week, anyway." He gathered his papers and account books. "I'm sorry, about everything. I wish I could give you better news. Will you be all right?"

I nodded, not trusting myself to say another word. He patted me on the shoulder and took his leave. I couldn't wait to see him go. The gaslight flickered on the brocade wallpaper and the lace bed curtains. The rooms seemed so ugly to me without Jack's laughing presence within them. I hated everything about New Orleans now, especially this hotel. My stomach felt as though something was ripping at me from the inside, and I reached out my arm and swept the coffee service onto the floor, inordinately satisfied at the sound of the cups shattering. I poured a double bourbon from the sidebar and downed it without a thought, then poured another. I lifted the heavy crystal glass to my lips. I needed to not think about anything for a day, but I knew after that, I needed to think about everything, especially my future.

CHAPTER 8

St. Louis, 1875

From the Fishers' front porch, the fireworks lit up the sky and were reflected in the black waters of the Mississippi, accompanied by gunshots clearly audible from the city downriver. I sipped my whiskey and pulled the woolly afghan closer against the winter chill.

"Happy New Year, darling." Emily kissed me lightly. "Don't see in the dawn, my pensive one. It's a cold night." The door shut softly behind her. How well she knew me.

After Jack's death I had fled New Orleans to the only comfort I knew, people who never judged but accepted me with no conditions. When the *Delta Queen* had docked, I had been the first passenger on board and with every mile she steamed upriver, I felt some of the dark burden of grief lift. I wanted to remember Jack as he had been in life—so handsome, so vivacious, so loving—and never as I'd last seen him. Nor did I want to think of Belle Lafayette and its dripping black oaks and what could have been. I had finally learned how cruel life could be, as though I'd needed any more lessons in the vagaries of fate.

Once again, I learned that you can only depend on yourself, no matter how much someone else may love you, or what assumptions most people can make. Things can change in the flick of an eyelash—an importunate word or a bullet from a gun and lives will wink out, or go on without you.

I had to trust myself and not fall prey to the comfort and

love of others, no matter how tempting. While I may accept their offerings and care for them, my first priority must remain making my way in this world despite the loss of those I love. In the midnight hour of the new year, I made this vow: I will make my own road and mourn no more.

"Kate, you're making me rich!" Joseph Henry laughed and kissed me on the cheek, the smoke from his cigar making both our eyes water. "Get out there and wow them again tonight."

"The Hungarian Songbird, Miss Katie Elder!" The slight man who announced all the acts was nearly drowned out by the catcalls and hooting of the audience that awaited me, but I wasn't worried. They were anxious for me, and I'd have them well tamed before the first chorus. The curtains parted, and I launched into my opening song of the night. For the last two months, the Theatre Comique had become my new home. I was back to using the Elder name because to be Kate Haroney again as I was in New Orleans was just too painful when I thought of my days there with Jack.

It was true I spent many hours at the Comique, rehearsing and performing, but I rented a room in a nearby boardinghouse. It was clean and respectable, but hardly what I'd call home. The Fishers had been unhappy to see me leave, but they knew as well as I that I could never make a life for myself unless I did. They weren't best pleased to see me back on the road I'd chosen, rich with pitfalls and lean on respectability.

I was in what I called my dressing room, a makeshift area backstage that Joseph had allotted me, when the door opened and a tall, blonde woman entered. In the mirror I watched her pull up a chair and settle herself beside me, patting her feathered hat to make sure it was in place.

"Good evening, Miss Elder."

I turned to her, wiping the stage makeup from my face. "Do

I know you?"

She laughed, a big booming laugh, and I smiled with her in spite of myself. "No, you do not, but I'm thinking you'll get to know me well. I'm Bessie Earp, and I have a proposition for you, sweetheart."

She was pretty in a brassy kind of way and very self-assured. Normally, Joseph never let anyone backstage, so she must've exerted her charms on him, too.

"Do tell," I murmured, raising an eyebrow. I took off my jeweled headdress.

She laughed again. "You're quite the countess, aren't you? Just what Dodge City needs, a touch of class."

"Dodge City? Where's that?"

"Darlin', it's the liveliest town west of the Mississip', and only getting better every day. You want to make some real money? That's the place to do it, and you can leave it to the Earps to make sure of that."

I'd heard of Dodge City, but it wasn't somewhere I'd thought to be a place for me. It was the end of the cattle drive trails, and from all reports, the rowdiest place on earth, full of cowboys and saloons and dust.

The door opened again, and a tall, well-dressed man entered. He walked with a slight limp, using a cane, but his arresting eyes and attractive smile were the most noticeable things about him. Bessie jumped up and kissed him.

"James! I was just telling Kate here how welcome she'd be in Dodge City."

He bowed and extended his hand, dark eyes appraising. "James Earp, Miss Elder. My wife is correct. Dodge is the place to be these days. I saw your act, and you would be a sensation there. We'd be very happy to sponsor you."

I wasn't sure how to respond to these two. They were as aggressive as anyone I'd ever met, and I was somewhat taken aback. I knew I was good, but I was also aware of a much bigger picture than either of my guests, and I wasn't *that* good. They were recruiting for sure, but for what?

"What exactly do you do in Dodge City?"

They exchanged glances and smiled. "We run a saloon and gambling house, Miss Elder."

"And?" I stood up.

James smiled. "And we're always on the lookout for talent of all kinds. Many young women have found a haven with us, Miss Elder. Talented young women with allure, like yourself. I think you'd be a welcome addition."

Now it was my turn to laugh. "You run a whorehouse, Mr. Earp." I shook my head. "I sing for my supper; I don't fuck for it."

They didn't seem in the least offended, or deterred. Bessie grinned and put her hand on my arm. "Kate, you'd be special. We could ask a lot for you, with the singing and all, and it'd be a grand show as well, right, James?"

"Absolutely right, as always, my dear," he replied, smiling again, but his eyes belied his mouth. "Think it over, Miss Elder."

There was no point in making enemies I couldn't afford, and something about these two made me wary of saying something I could come to regret. I put out my hand.

"Thank you for your offer, Mr. and Mrs. Earp, but for now I must decline. I'm happy here in St. Louis. If I ever find myself in Dodge City, though, I'll be sure to look you up." They both shook my hand, and James opened the door for his wife. He turned and gave me a wide smile.

"We'll be easy to find—just ask for the Earps. People know us. Good evening, Miss Elder."

St. Louis was changing, gentrifying itself to be more like the great cities of the eastern United States. It was no longer a rough and ready port and the sole strike-off point for wagon trains to the West; those attributes had moved westward with the railroad. The Theatre Comique had felt the change in its revenue, and not even the Hungarian Songbird was novel anymore. I was making a decent living, but I knew from listening to the talk in the saloon at night and in the streets during the day that perhaps going westward, where everyone else seemed to be headed, would hold more promise for me than St. Louis.

I thought back to the Earps and their offer. I certainly wasn't interested in prostitution as a livelihood, but the talk of Dodge City and the money to be made there was on everyone's lips.

"Joe, what've you heard about Dodge City?" I asked. It was late, the saloon was all but closed, and we two sat at the bar, having an after-hours drink as we usually did at night.

He threw back his whiskey and nodded at the bartender for another. "You're not thinking of going there, are you, Kate? I know things haven't been as good lately, but that place is rough, no matter what they tell you."

"No, I'm just curious."

"Well, it used to be Wichita where things were hoppin', but with the quarantine and the buffalo hunters, the cattle drovers have moved on to Dodge. There's money to be made there, so they say, but at what cost, my dear? I doubt there's anything like this." He gestured back at the stage and the large gambling area, deserted now. "When they say *cow town*, you had best believe it. 'Course things are changing every day, but still. It's rougher the farther west you get from this river; everybody knows that."

He shrugged, smiled under his white mustache, and signaled the bartender for another drink.

I sipped my whiskey. He was right, but I had never seen anything like the growth in this country of America. People here just seemed to want to keep on going and fill any empty spaces, and there certainly were plenty of those. Towns and railroads were springing up everywhere between here and California, the fabled land of gold, despite hardships and Indian raids, and remarkable progress was being made every day, if the talk and the newspapers were any indication. The ones to go were the ones who made their fortunes, I thought. Perhaps I should be one of them.

Singing wasn't my only talent. Gambling suited me, and I had put away quite a nest egg for myself, playing cards after my shows were done every evening. Women and card games were still considered a novelty but were tolerated, and I found men tended to make foolish bets when imbibing whiskey and attempting to peer down a corseted bosom. Besides, my own card skills were not inconsiderable. I had learned a hard lesson from Emile Dunsany—never leave them with shame—and it had served me well since.

Less than a month later, I played to a hall only two-thirds full, a first for me. It wasn't that they didn't like me anymore, just that there weren't many people filling the St. Louis saloons right now. Although Joe Henry kept up a good front, I could sense the uneasiness in him when the big crowds didn't gather as they used to at the Theatre. Maybe it was time to move on.

At a Sunday dinner at the Fishers', a ritual I never missed, I announced my decision.

"I'm heading west."

Both Joshua and Emily put down their forks and stared at me. I couldn't help but think they'd been expecting me to do something entirely unexpected, and they were right.

Joshua smiled. "You are ever a surprise, Kate, but this one isn't a complete shock. I've been anticipating you'd make a move, although I have to say, I didn't expect this." He took a sip of wine. "Got a destination in mind?"

"Dodge City," I said. I watched Emily wince, although she tried to hide it. "It's booming, so they say."

"So they say," he said. "For how long, and what kind of boom, only history will say. But I understand, Kate. I will caution you—it's a rough place."

He was right, and I knew it, but somehow it seemed my future lay in that direction, and I would deal with the hardships as they came. I was no stranger to adversities, after all.

Emily put down her napkin and came to stand behind me, clasping my arms with both hands, her soft cheek resting on mine.

"Remember this, my chick. No matter where you go, how high or low you fly, there is always a safe haven here." My eyes met Joshua's across the table, and he nodded. I put my hands over Emily's and squeezed them gently, my throat aching with unshed tears and unsaid words. Ironically, it was my love for them that propelled me, in part. They couldn't shelter me forever. There was a world waiting for me, and I meant to conquer it and make them proud.

My arrival in Dodge City was punctuated with gunshots. I stepped down from the stagecoach amid a flurry of activity, and before my trunks were delivered to the hotel lobby, the desk clerk informed me that two men had just been killed in the street. However, he continued, there was nothing to fear, since the marshals were already on the scene.

It wasn't very comforting. My room was on the second floor with a view of the street, and for the next few hours I watched the panorama of violence that played out over and over on the street below. Dodge City was a town that thrived on fury.

It was an ugly place, as towns go. Built on the money and needs of cowboys that arrived there driving cattle herds up the Chisholm trail, it had the look of a hastily thrown together town. Its clapboard buildings and dirt streets rose from the flat prairie floor of its birth. Wooden storefronts, some two stories high, housed hotels, mercantiles, feed stores, stables, and saloons. Some of the boards were so fresh cut, the sap glistened and the wood warped before the signs of what they offered could even be hung. Wooden sidewalks lined the streets, but those thoroughfares were broad and dusty despite the best efforts of the occasional rain. Grit was a constant companion, clouding the windows and coating the clothes of the inhabitants.

There was what the city officials referred to as the "respectable" side of town, housing their families and those of the businessmen of Dodge, replete with a school, houses, and a couple of churches, the lumber on those just as raw as the rest.

Then there was the side where the real business of Dodge City flourished—the saloons and hotels where the men who killed the buffalo and those who drove the cattle to Dodge ended up. When the cattle drovers and their charges arrived, it was chaos—morning and night. In between, the buffalo hunters came to town with their stinking hides, mountains of the things stacked beside the railyard, the men themselves reeking of gore and too many nights on the road hunting for financial salvation. For all of them, women and whiskey were their goals, even before a bath and shave made them rudimentarily presentable, but no one voiced a protest. After a day or two, some were ready for slightly more gentrified pursuits.

Despite its outward appearance, Tom Sherman's dance hall and saloon was one of the better entertainment offerings in Dodge City. Elegance was a quality not readily found in Dodge, but Tom had done his best, and the interior of his establishment was stumbling toward grandiose pretension. Red brocade wallpaper and curtains on the stage gave it an aspect that the men coming in from the trail could appreciate.

Joseph had given me a reference, and I found myself happily employed there, singing five nights a week and, when the cattle drives arrived, every night. I kept my room at the hotel, and after a while, I rather enjoyed the constant show that played itself out night and day, secure in my second-floor box seat. Soon, I knew many of the actors, good and bad, by their faces if not by their names.

Tom didn't mind if I gambled, and I found most of the cowboys and buffalo hunters were blissfully happy to be off the trail, even when parting with their hard-earned cash. Occasionally, there were those who were upset when they lost, but Dodge City's saloon-keepers had learned that law enforcement was their best friend. While the marshals and their deputies could do little to save a victim of the unpredictable fatal disagreements that sprang up like brushfires, they were fairly adept at locking up or killing the perpetrators of these crimes. Word spread quickly that no one wanted to be in the lawmen's sights when hunting down those who had committed a heinous act. While not a perfect system, it did bring some modicum of order to Dodge's streets, and the proprietors of all businesses in Dodge were fast to call on the lawmen as a resource.

It was an epic game of poker, lasting for over sixteen hours, and one in which I found a seat at two in the morning when a rancher from east of Dodge passed out and was dragged to the side of the bar to sleep. I had won some—and was carefully planning on much more—when Texas Jack Vermilion pulled a straight flush. He was a wild one, Texas Jack, come to town with his buffalo hides, but a savvy poker player nonetheless who knew the cowboys fresh off the trail were easy pickings, just as I did. With his hat festooned with feathers and long hair braided with leather and bone, Jack was a colorful addition to the scene in Dodge City. We had become companions, if not fast friends.

Jack's pungent, buffalo-skinner body odor was a little off-putting for me to spend much time in his company aside from the poker table, but I trusted him more than most.

Texas Jack bided his time, and when his winning hand came up, he was jubilant. Even I was happy for him, though twenty dollars of my own hard-earned money was in the pot. He slapped his hand down on the table with a shout and had begun to rake in his winnings when a cowboy across the table saw his money about to disappear forever.

"Cheatin' son of a bitch," he said and stood up, fumbling at the holster at his side. Quicker than anyone could react, he'd pulled a six-gun and stood, weaving slightly, pointing the gun at Jack. Since I was sitting next to Jack, I was fairly concerned about the cowboy's ability to aim straight, to say nothing of Jack's ability to duck. A lot of whiskey had been imbibed.

"You're under arrest," said a tall blond man standing behind the cowboy, and he clubbed him on the side of the head. The cowboy and his gun hit the floor, and the tall man looked around the table.

"Y'all fine here?" he said, and his bright blue eyes met mine. I nodded mutely, as did Jack and everyone else at the table, staring at the gold star on the man's chest, still in shock from the suddenness of our rescue. The tall man's mouth twitched a little in what might have been a smile, and he prodded the cowboy with his foot.

"Let's go, pal. Drawing a gun in Tom Sherman's because you don't like the way the cards fall just won you a night in jail." Another man materialized over his shoulder and dragged the prone cowboy towards the door. The man with the badge tipped his hat. "Evening, friends. Please continue with your game."

Tom Sherman scurried up and shook the man's hand while he was heading for the door. "Thanks, Wyatt. I had a feeling we'd be needing you before the night was out."

I took a seat at the window in the hotel's restaurant and looked out at the afternoon's activities. For Dodge City, everything looked fairly placid. Two wagons stood in front of the mercantile, the wives and children waiting for their men to complete their purchases and load up. The draft horses waited patiently, ears twitching the flies away. People went about their business, women carrying baskets of groceries and notions and passersby, from cowboys to suited gentlemen, treading the sidewalks in pursuit of their interests of the day. I ordered breakfast from the waitress, my normal time somewhat later than most, since I worked evenings. She'd already brought my coffee, and I sipped absently from the cup, not fully awake yet.

"Good afternoon."

I started and looked up at the man standing beside my table. It was the tall lawman who had been in Tom Sherman's a week before.

"Good afternoon to you, sir."

"My name's Wyatt Earp. May I sit with you?"

Many had asked, and my usual response was negative, but I found myself curious.

"If you like." I held out my hand. "Kate Elder."

He shook my hand. "I know. I've heard you sing."

He took off his hat, revealing a head of wavy, blondish hair, and pulled out the chair opposite me. He was handsome in a rugged sort of way, his jawline taut and unsmiling, but the blue eyes were appealing. He folded himself into the wooden chair and pulled it up to the table.

"How did your game go the other night?"

I couldn't help but smile. "I won a little, and I was breathing to spend it, after your kind intervention. Texas Jack did better."

I was rewarded with a slight smile. "He always does."

The waitress arrived, simpering a bit and, unasked, put a cup of coffee down for Mr. Earp. Obviously, she'd done this before. He touched her hand, and she giggled, flapping her apron.

"Thanks, Susie."

I rolled my eyes at her departing back and took a sip of my own coffee. When I looked back up at him, he actually laughed.

"I hardly know her."

"Apparently through no fault of her own," I said. "You seem to be quite the object of her affection."

He shrugged. "As I said." He took a sip of coffee, put the cup down, and stared at me.

I didn't quite know what to do. He was an imposing man, this Wyatt Earp. I thought back to the woman and her husband, Bessie and James, who'd been to see me in St. Louis and wondered if there was any relation. I had a feeling there was. As she'd said, people in Dodge City knew the Earps. A madam and a lawman—an interesting connection, and a rather disturbing one.

"Would you care to have dinner some evening, Miss Elder?"

"Yes, Mr. Earp, I believe I would."

My breakfast arrived, brought by the simpering Susie, and he stood up. "I'll leave you to enjoy your food, Miss Elder. Thursday evening, then, say around six? I will call for you here at the hotel."

So it began. Wyatt and I shared dinners and conversation and discovered each other. He was a very attractive man, made more so by his position and reputation in Dodge City, but my experiences with men, though only two, had taught me that prudence should be my guide. And for me, Wyatt was no Jack Rafferty.

Wyatt was a stolid man who had become so through tragic life experiences, and he was not given to trusting easily either.

For my part, I was finding my way, trying to discern who I was, and where I wanted to be. In Dodge City, this was no easy task.

I sang, flirted, gambled, and saved every penny I could in preparation for I knew not what, only that I should be ready for it when it came. Our relationship was on the most proper of footings, odd in this place, but one we both were comfortable with, perhaps me more so than Wyatt. Many an evening had ended in impassioned embraces with him urging me to no avail to let him spend the night in my room. I had become slow to trust any man's promises after hearing so many light ones, and even Wyatt, as honest as he seemed, was no exception.

Then there was the rest of the Earp clan. James was indeed his brother, and he and Bessie's thriving business ventures were ignored by local law enforcement, as were any complaints about them. There were other brothers as well, and from the little Wyatt had imparted to me, it seemed the whole family was hellbent on profitability, with little regard to legality. That Wyatt seemed to be the exception was curious.

Then came the night when everything changed.

It began like so many others. The show went on at Tom Sherman's, and I was the highlight as usual. During the intermission I wound my way through the gaming tables, looking to see where the best play could be found, or at least where I could make a profit on this rainy evening when my show was done. A new herd had been delivered the day before, and cowboys with money in their pockets were everywhere, eager to make their mark at the tables. Texas Jack and Cowboy John St. Anthony jumped up and gave me a hug as I passed their table, and I promised to come back and be their luck, at least until another seat was available. I had just stepped onto the stage when a man in a duster wearing two guns at his sides entered the saloon and began shooting.

"You're a lowlife, lying bastard, Mike Gleason," he shouted

and fired his guns at the table nearest the stage. Two men went down, one quietly dead and the other clutching his stomach and screaming, while everyone else scattered, some hiding under tables, others running behind the bar and for the back exit. Not content with this, the man kept shooting as he advanced farther into the saloon.

I saw Tom Sherman drop to the floor and scrabble his way towards the back door. No law enforcement had been alerted to the evening's festivities, as it was assumed this was just a normal evening in Dodge, so they would only be coming after the shots were heard and reported.

I knew everyone in range was in mortal peril, but before I could drop to the floor myself, a searing pain like I'd never known enveloped me, and I fell, feeling the warm blood gush down the side of my blue spangled gown, the feathers in my boa spattered with red.

The next thing I remember was being carried in Wyatt's arms. Oddly, his cheeks glistened with tears, and his mouth formed a grim line. "You're going to be all right, Kate. I swear to God you're going to be all right."

I woke in the doctor's surgery area, blinking in the pre-dawn light. I tried to sit up, but the searing pain on the side of my chest made me lie down flat again, a cry of agony escaping my lips.

"Kate, I'm here." Wyatt's face, pale and unshaven, loomed over me, but I could hardly focus, the pain incredible. I stared at him, unable to speak.

"You've been shot, but you're going to be all right," he said, and it felt as though he were speaking to me from very far away. "You'll be fine, I swear." He smoothed my hair, and even this gentle gesture made me wince. "I'm taking you someplace safe."

Yes, please, I thought. Wyatt would keep me safe. God, it hurt. I closed my eyes.

CHAPTER 9

The canopy and bed curtains were purple. Astonishingly so. They made my eyes hurt, even in the gaslight. Feeling smothered, I tried to push the covers away, but my arms couldn't manage the task. Sinking back onto the pillows, the only thing I could think of was that the sheets were purple, too.

When I woke again, thin winter sunlight illuminated the purple curtains in all their stupefying glory, pulled back now to reveal a room that held not only the large bed I lay in, but two chairs, a table, and a sofa, upon which lay Wyatt Earp, snoring softly, his head cushioned by the padded arm. I watched him from within my warm purple cocoon. Eventually, the sunlight reached him, and he blinked, rubbing his hand over his face. Those amazing blue eyes focused on me, and I spoke, although it was a wispy croak.

"Guess I'm not dead, then, unless heaven's purple and you're an angel."

He sat down on the edge of the bed, grasping my shoulders. "Jesus Christ, you scared me some, girl." He closed his eyes and kissed my temple. *Oh, Wyatt.*

For more than a month I lingered in the purple room, the wound in my side healing slowly. At first it hurt to draw more than a shallow breath, but as the days passed, the pain subsided, and I soon was able to hobble about—which felt good for about five minutes before I found myself collapsing back into the soft pillows of my bed, a welcome refuge. A pert maid, Annie by name, tended to me between visits from the doctor and Wyatt. He managed to drop in every day as his duties permitted, sometimes twice or three times a day, depending on the level of lawlessness afoot in Dodge.

My haven was Bessie and James Earp's whorehouse, I discovered in the second week, when I became a little more *compos mentis*. My trunks were stacked across the room, moved here on Wyatt's authority, apparently, and although the activity in the house was raucous on some evenings, no one ever bothered me in my convalescence. I was grateful for the compassionate care I was receiving but I couldn't help but wonder about the state of mind of my hosts.

"Morning, Glory," Bessie Earp said, setting down a tray with coffee and biscuits. "You're looking much better." She poured a cup of coffee, added cream, and handed it to me, waiting as I struggled to sit up, propping pillows behind me.

I accepted the cup and took a sip. It was strong and good, immediately clearing the webs of sleep from my mind. Over the rim of my cup, I glanced up at my hostess. The same woman I'd met in St. Louis sat on the edge of my purple bed, and her eyes were no less sharp now than they'd been then.

"Thank you. For everything. You've been incredibly kind."

Bessie chuckled and patted my hand. "It seems our Wyatt's got a yen for you, duchess, and we keep Wyatt happy." She appraised me thoughtfully. "We look out for our own in this family."

I'll bet you do, I thought, *especially in your business,* but I smiled wanly. "Still, I am indebted, Bessie. If I can repay you—"

"Hush now. No repayment necessary. I told you, we look out for our own." She stood up, brushing her skirts. "You look a mess, but that's to be expected, given what you've gone through, Kate. I've got business to tend to, but Doc says you can be up and about, if slowly. I'll send Annie to help you, and you can take a short stroll around the house, maybe join us for lunch. How would that be?"

I smiled. "Quite wonderful, thanks."

It would be, too. It felt as though I'd been cooped up in this room for weeks, and in actuality, I had been. Forays to the chamber pot and the basin for sponge baths had been the extent of my activities. Bessie's assessment of my appearance was disconcerting, but probably accurate.

After Bessie left, I swung my feet over the edge of the bed and took care of the necessities, this time grabbing a hairbrush from the washstand. My long hair was tangled, and within two minutes I was breathless with fatigue. I set down the brush. Clearly, this was a job for Annie, along with a bath. I smelled musty even to myself, so it was long past time for a good scrub. Going down to lunch was going to be a monumental chore, I realized.

I pulled up my nightgown and gingerly peeled away the heavy, white bandage over my left side. The angry wound was healing, but it was far from pretty and would leave a scar I'd carry for the rest of my life—that was obvious. I pushed in on the two lower ribs and winced. They were healing as well, but the bullet had smashed through them along with a good portion of my side. Anger surged through me like a flash fire. I wanted to kill the bastard that had done this to me, the ignorant cowboy who didn't care who he hurt. I was owed.

I pushed off the bed and stood up, not bothering to put the bandage back on. I wanted a bath and a shampoo and to start feeling like me again. I was on my way to the door when it opened and Annie came in. She was a sweet girl, maybe all of fifteen, and had been aware enough to have kept her innocence, even here. Her brown curls bouncing, she opened her mouth in a perfect "O," and I smiled to soften my words.

"Annie, I need a bathtub, soap, and some very soft towels. How are you at hair styling?"

Three painful hours later I stood on the landing outside my door, listening to the conversation and laughter that floated up the stairway like sounds from another world, my elbow firmly gripped by the faithful Annie, who grinned up at me.

"You can do this, ma'am."

I smiled back and gritted my teeth. Yes, I could. I was Mary Katherine Haroney, schooled at the court of the Hapsburg emperor, companion of princes, scion of a family of distinction, and the Hungarian songbird. The fires of hell couldn't stop me from doing this.

I touched my hair, the clean and shining golden curls piled atop my head by inventive Annie, smoothed the skirts of my sky-blue morning gown, and put my slippered foot on the first step.

All conversation stopped as we entered the dining room. Women in various stages of deshabille were seated on both sides of the long table, with one or two, like the indomitable Bessie, dressed a little more appropriately to greet the afternoon. She was a vision in yellow silk.

"Kate!" Bessie jumped to her feet and came to the doorway, clutching my other arm. "You are truly amazing, my dear. Come, sit beside me."

She led me to a chair, and I sank down gratefully while its former occupant took her leave without protest. Clean china and silver appeared quickly, and my plate was filled with a beef stew and potatoes that, while simple, smelled like manna from heaven to me after weeks of chicken soup, oatmeal, and soft bread. Bessie stood beside me and addressed the open-mouthed women gathered around the table.

"This is Kate Elder, our guest, who has suffered greatly at the hands of a ruffian who shot her some time ago. I know you will welcome her as a friend, as I do." She turned to me and reeled off a dozen names or more of the women around the table, not many of which registered with me. She sat down, picked up her fork, and the meal resumed with scarcely a ruffle or a raised eyebrow, like a river that flows serenely around a rock that has suddenly dropped into its midst. Fresh warm bread and apple dumplings covered with cream arrived without a break in the consumption or conversation until everyone was sated. Then we all sat back in our chairs and surveyed one another more closely.

Several of these women, closer to girls really, were quite beautiful, while others bore the sometimes subtle and other times quite obvious marks of their trade, hardened by alcohol, years, and rough handling. One, Rachel by name, I recall, sat across from me, her dark eyes and striking olive-skinned complexion remarkable. She smiled at me.

"I hear you sing right pretty, Kate."

I smiled back. "Thank you, Rachel. I hope so."

A pretty young blonde beside me spoke up. "That was terrible, what happened to you, ma'am. Terrible."

Bessie put her arm around me. "That's true, Emily," she said. "Dodge City can be a terrible place. Never forget you all have James and me to protect you from that sort of thing."

The blonde smiled. "Yes, ma'am, we do."

A few others nodded their heads, while a couple of women looked down, and one smirked.

"At a price, Bessie, darlin'," said a redheaded woman who stood up. She was dressed only in a white lace camisole and petticoat and was strikingly beautiful. "I'm starting to feel the pinch of this protection, you know? It's costing me more than I thought."

Bessie glared at her. "Mary, we will discuss this later, not now in front of everyone."

Mary grinned and sat down, her point made, while a couple of others nodded, and two women got up and left, pushing in their chairs. I glanced at Bessie, and she was clearly angry.

Laughter from the kitchen was a welcome respite as the swinging door was pushed wide and Wyatt Earp strode into the dining room.

"Bessie, my darlin', I'm a hungry man. Wong says there's beef stew on the table."

He pulled out a chair, glanced around, and froze.

"Kate!" He shoved the chair back in and came around to me, his arms on my shoulders. "You shouldn't be down here. You're not well enough yet." He turned to Bessie. "What were you thinking, Bessie?" His usual stolid composure had slipped, his mouth an angry line.

I put my hand on his arm and rose from my chair, wincing just a little. "Wyatt, I'm fine, really. Bessie was kind enough to invite me to lunch, and it's been quite wonderful. First real food I've had in ages, and the company has been very pleasant. Please sit down and join us."

Bessie threw me a grateful look, while the rest of the women's expressions ranged from horrified to amused. Before I could even sit down again, Wyatt swept me up in his arms and carried me out of the dining room, over Bessie's protests.

I didn't say a word, not that it would have done me any good. He clomped up the stairs I had so carefully gone down and deposited me in the purple bed.

"Kate, you're not ready for that, and especially not in that company." He fussed about, taking off my slippers and pulling the comforter over me, and then pouring a glass of water, which he held to my lips.

I took a sip to satisfy him and leaned back on my pillows. "Wyatt, I'm fine. You're being a little hypocritical, aren't you? This is your family. Surely you wouldn't have brought me to

111

any place you deemed unsuitable?"

He frowned. "Those women downstairs, they're not the sort of people you should be consorting with. Bessie's a good person, Kate, although there's no denying what she and James do here. But, they're my family, and we take care of our own."

I'd heard that before, just this morning. It seemed to be an Earp mantra, canceling out the rest of the world. What a curious family this was. I touched his hand and smiled.

"I took care to not overdo things, Wyatt. For instance, I'm not wearing a corset, nor a bustle."

He looked at me sharply, the frown disappearing.

"And," I continued, "I feel quite well, all things considered."

He laughed low in his throat and leaned down, carefully unbuttoning the top buttons of my dress. "How well is that, Kate?" He kissed my throat and down my breast, his lips lingering and his mustache tickling, and desire surged in me, the first frisson of passion I'd felt since Jack. I didn't think he'd mind, since he couldn't be here, and Wyatt most certainly was.

"Very well indeed, Mr. Earp," I said, and no more words passed between us for quite some time.

In the next two weeks, my time was divided between regaining my strength, seeing Wyatt whenever he could get away, and getting to know the women of the house, activities very divided. The women were a diverse group, and I grew to like most of them very much. Bessie and James were kind overseers as flesh purveyors went, and my initial disdain disintegrated as I got to know them and the girls they not only gained a profit from, but took care of as well. *There but for the grace of God go I* was a refrain that kept running through my head, not that I believed in any religious teachings anymore.

The American West was not a gentle and compassionate place for women, and most of them were here because they had no other choice if they wanted to keep a roof over their heads and their bellies full. There were few occupations for women on the frontier—teachers, shopkeepers of one kind or another, waitresses or entertainers if they were lucky, and whores if they were not. None of these afforded a great living or a long future unless they found husbands or opportunities they created for themselves. It wasn't easy, and for some, even as young girls, there was no option but selling themselves to keep alive. Bessie and James offered a safe option, at least for a time, and I came to see that they were not only good at what they did, but relatively caring in how they did it. There was many a saloon-keeper or brothel owner that wasn't. The girls told stories of beatings, rapes, and other horrors that weren't necessarily inflicted by customers but by their employers.

Sara Brown was seventeen, a beautiful and gentle soul who had been cast out of her Lutheran family for a night's transgression with a neighboring farm boy who had bragged about his prowess the next morning. She found herself on the road with only a small bag of clothes and food enough to get to town—and a heaping dose of shame. Or Mary Hepplewhite, whose stepfather had raped her and whose sobbing mother had named her a liar and thrown her out without so much as a backward glance, having three other mouths to feed and not wanting to join her on the road. Others had similar stories, and I counted myself fortunate for not being among them. The Smiths had been tolerable in comparison, and I knew Wilhelmina and Alexander were in hands, if not the best, at least good enough.

There were others who were different. Harder, more inured to the life or, in some cases, just rotten, I thought. That they were called whores for what they did was of no moment to them; it was somehow even a badge of pride. It was hard to fathom, but there it was. I began to see that many kinds of people made up the world, many of whom I might never understand, but my life had been a learning experience so far, and I had no doubt there was much more to come.

The day Mattie Blaylock showed up was a case in point. Wyatt and I had just sat down to a lunch of Wong's delicious fried chicken and biscuits when a whirlwind in pink taffeta flew through the kitchen door, throwing her arms around Wyatt.

"Darlin'," she cried, kissing him repeatedly while he was busy throwing down his napkin and quite obviously trying to gain his composure. "I've missed you so much these last few months, and I'm so glad to be back with you again."

He stood up, clearly discomfited, and I took a closer look at the lady in pink. That she was no lady was evident, her brassy hair and cheap makeup aside. Her manner was coarse, and in the next few minutes my thoughts were confirmed. She was greeted by a few of the women around the table, and not a few eyes were rolled and glances cast at me. Wyatt wouldn't look me in the eye, so I quietly continued to eat my chicken as she pulled Wyatt away from the table and into the next room.

Bessie patted my hand. "Don't worry about her, Kate. She's nothing to him—a cheating whore he used to take up with before he knew better. Now that he has you, things are different."

I wasn't so sure. Their conversation drifted into the dining room—how she'd been so long with her parents, who'd been ill, and how anxious she was to get back to him—and I knew Wyatt hadn't been exactly truthful with me. My stomach lurched, and despite Bessie's kindness, I excused myself and made my slow way up the stairs to my room, under watchful eyes and whispers. Why could things never be what they seemed? Just when I'd thought I'd found someone I could trust . . .

I stayed in my room the rest of the day and evening. Annie brought me a tray for dinner, as usual. I had never ventured downstairs at night, not wanting to be a part of what went on then. Annie kept her distance, too, I knew, working in the kitchen as much as she could. She perched on the edge of the bed as I ate, and I could see she was debating what to say.

"Miss Kate?"

I glanced up at her and nodded, my mouth full, and with this meager encouragement she launched into her tale.

"See, Mattie's been with Wyatt ever since I been here, off and on. She's crazy about him, always followed him around since she first saw him, no matter that he don't seem to feel the same, making sure no other girl gets near him." She tucked her legs under her skirt. "She's not a nice person, Miss, even for a whore. You need to watch out for her."

I swallowed some tea and managed to smile. "Why is that, Annie?"

"Because everyone knows Wyatt's crazy about you, and now she does, too! Everyone's talking, and Mattie's saying she'll take care of you . . . and . . . Miss Kate, this is bad. Bessie won't do nothing about Mattie—she's some kind of kin to her—and Wyatt just took off."

I sat back on my pillows, exhausted not just with my wounds, but with the emotional turmoil throughout the house and very definitely within me. Goddamn Wyatt.

Annie jumped as the door opened, and as though my thought had conjured him, there he was. Without a word, he strode to the bed, picked up the tray, placing it in Annie's hands and shooing her out of the room. He locked the door behind her and stood there, staring at me. There was no trace of guilt or contrition in his face, and this annoyed me beyond all measure.

"I find myself in a very awkward position. It seems, Mr. Earp, that you forgot to mention you were spoken for. Do you have a faulty memory, or are you just a two-timing liar?"

He took a step toward me, anger flushing his cheeks, and I

saw in that second that Wyatt Earp was never going to be the man I wanted. That man would have seen the justifiable hurt and anger in my words and told me he cared. This one was too proud to do so, expecting too much and giving too little.

"Godammit, Kate, give me a chance to explain about Mattie. She's this girl I been with for a time. Her family and mine, they been close before, and she's a lost thing, sometimes. She's not like you. She works for James and Bessie, but she's got a good soul, and I sort of take care of her. With you, it's not like that at all. You're like nobody I've ever met before."

The words poured out of him, and I waited until he stopped talking and stared back at me.

"So it's different with us, Wyatt?" I said softly. "Tell me how it's different. Looks to me like you take care of lost things, and you thought I was one, too. Is that all it is?" I stood up and walked towards him, smoothing my skirts, although my thoughts had no such comfort, and my hands were shaking.

"You have to understand—Mattie needs me; I'm all she has," he said. "But what you and I have is special, and you have to give me time. I'll talk with Mattie and make her see how things are." His words took on a pleading tone I'd heard before. "Kate, I love you."

His words were like the bullet that had cut me down weeks past, and they hurt just as the molten metal had. I'd had one cheating man in my life, and I swore there'd never be room for another, blue eyes or no. I stared into them and never blinked.

"Get out, Wyatt. Get out of my room and my life. We are done, now and forever." I turned my back, and my heart broke when I heard the door shut behind him.

Two days later I returned to my room and discovered that all my money, which I thought I'd hidden so cleverly in the lining of my trunk, was gone. Annie had warned me, but I hadn't listened. Mattie Blaylock made sure I was in a position no better than she was, just in case Wyatt or I had a change of heart. The stupid whore needn't have worried. Dodge City had hardened my heart to steel, and there was no room in it for Wyatt Earp or any other man.

CHAPTER 10

1876

The bathwater smelled of lavender and roses, and it was bone-achingly hot. My hair was piled atop my head and held with a ribbon, and I could see my skin turning pink the farther I sank into the copper tub. I scrubbed the sponge hard against my skin, but no matter how aromatic the water was or how hard I tried, to me I still smelled like the whore I now was.

"Miss Kate, you want some more hot water?" Annie hovered over the foot of the tub, holding the kettle carefully with a hot pad.

I looked up at her, blinking in the steam. "No, my dear, I'm fine. You go on, now. I just need some soaking time."

She smiled at me and left, shutting the door behind her. It was the same room I'd come to in months past, and still purple, as befitted me now. I lay my head back against the rim of the tub. In another week or two, if Bessie kept giving me the rich ones, I'd be out of Dodge City forever, and I didn't plan on looking back.

Since Mattie had stolen my money, I'd recovered both physically and emotionally from the scars inflicted by the bullet, Wyatt, and his paramour, but I had also changed in other ways. This time I couldn't run home to the Fishers, but I wanted to get as far away from Dodge as fast as I could, and I'd do whatever I had to. I discovered the only way to make a lot of money fast and leave this cow town was exactly what Bessie had proposed, and singing wasn't enough. The real money was in sex, as Bessie and James knew well, and I'd become an apt pupil, even surpassing the expectations of my hosts. Cowboys fresh from the drives and ranchhands in town for a Saturday night were not for me, but those gentlemen of substance— ranch owners, cattle brokers, the town bankers and builders— those who appreciated a woman of education, finesse, and grace—those were my clients, and the Earps made sure I was the shining star in the firmament of their house and, as such, a costly gem indeed. Thus was the arrangement begun, and thus did it go on.

While my bank account rose (on no account was I about to leave my cash in this easily pilfered establishment, as I'd learned to my downfall), my sense of self plummeted, and I knew that only by leaving Dodge City altogether could I hope to regain not only my pride, but also my knowledge of who I was and what I wanted. For I knew it surely was not this.

This. A night spent with my eyes wide open beside a snoring behemoth of a cattle baron from Texas whose money did little to disguise his foul breath or turn his pudgy, prying fingers into anything resembling a soft caress.

This. Three hours being tied to the bedpost by Dodge City's most distinguished banker, his desire only roused by the trickle of his urine on my naked belly.

This. My most lucrative client, cattle baron Wade Tully, whose fee I shared with Mary after we'd whipped him bloody and he still cried out for more. We obliged because we hated him, and it was so prosperous we could have a day or two reprieve before seeing another customer.

This. Hell with liquor, silken pillows, and perfumed air so heady with disgust, sometimes I could hardly swallow. Oh, but swallow I did, disgust and more, for the right price.

This. A small but horrible piece of my life soon to be put

behind me and forgotten forever.

The water was cooling, and I stepped from the tub, surrounding myself with the fluffy, clean towels Annie had laid out. This was a night for me alone. I pulled my nightgown over my head and sank into my clean sheets. Soon this would be only a dim memory. I was becoming quite adept at lying, especially to myself.

"Strawberry jam, Kate?" Bessie handed me the crystal jar, its luscious contents spilling into the silver spoon resting on the lip. I took it and spread two spoonfuls onto one of Wong's flaky biscuits. One bite confirmed it was as good as it looked and smelled, like summer on the tongue, and I greedily took another. I had denied myself most pleasures, but good food wasn't one of them.

We sat, Bessie and I, alone in the dining room, the morning early and the summer sun glittering on our crystal and plates.

"He's on his way back from Deadwood, you know. Bat's hired him back on as a deputy."

"His choice, just as leaving instead of being honest with me was," I said. "By the time he gets here, I'll be in Texas." I took a sip of coffee and looked at her. "Tell him hello and good-bye, will you?" Wyatt and I had not spoken a word to each other since the night I kicked him out of my room. There were times, though, when it felt like a bomb could go off if we were together in the same room for too long. If he was coming back, I couldn't be here.

Bessie sighed. "So you're leaving. Just like that? You been thinking on this some time? As for Wyatt, I'm not telling him nothing. I'm not his mother."

I ignored the last part. "I was going to tell you this morning, Bessie. Mr. Truewell has asked me to be his wife, but before I take that step I'm bound to see this magnificent ranch he says he has. It's some fifty miles north of the Brazos, and, according to him, he's the biggest cattleman in that part of Texas."

Bessie snorted. "Truewell is a blowhard."

I smiled. "Agreed, but a rich blowhard, and sleeping with one man instead of a crowd has some appeal, as I'm sure you'd agree. I can't do this anymore. Although we've made some money, you and I, we both knew it was only for a time."

Bessie put her hand over mine. While she had a good heart, she was married to an Earp. That was an ace that trumped all the cards in the deck, and I knew it. I liked her, but I never fully trusted her, as much as I wanted to.

"I wish you all the best, Kate," she said, her eyes boring into mine. "I'll miss you, girl. You're a queen, especially compared to these little sluts around here. Hell, I'll miss the money you bring in, goddammit, but you're a woman who knows her own mind, and I respect that."

She meant it, and I hugged her, biscuit crumbs spilling from our laps as we stood. The Earps. They'd saved me, damned me, and let me go. Dodge City, all in all, had been a true education, as edifying as the sisters of St. Joseph's. Captain Fisher would have agreed, I thought, if not in everything I learned, at least in the practicality of its usefulness. The thought of the Fishers gave me a guilty pang, and, while I'd thought of going back to St. Louis, my pride wouldn't let me. I was on my own, and I wanted it that way.

It wasn't the heat as much as the dust—interminable and stultifying, miles and miles of it. The stagecoach dragged its way and its passengers through country that consisted of nothing but that and the sun, baking it into our clothes and skin. I looked at my fellow travelers and saw only the weariness I felt myself. Mr. Levitt snored softly across from me, his portmanteau held on his lap like a pirate's treasure he'd foraged, while young

Miss Whittle, a Boston school teacher on the way to her first job teaching in Fort Griffin, stared out the open window, despair etched on her features. Beside me, Mrs. Bidley blew her nose once again and turned to me, sniffling.

"God's truth, Miss Elder, Mr. Truewell will be mighty pleased to see you arrive. That ranch could use a woman's touch, I tell you. The last time we stopped by, that main house was in a sorry state."

I nodded, brushing the dust from my black serge traveling skirt. I'd been listening to Mrs. Bidley for many days now, and, truth to tell, I had learned a lot from her careless comments. That Truewell's ranch was a rundown place was the tip of the iceberg. Being fairly close neighbors, she'd been only too happy to fill me in on the man's history, including his first wife, who had wasted away, occasionally bruised and extremely unhappy in this godforsaken place, pining for Philadelphia and a taste of culture, stymied by Truewell's Baptist leanings and penuriousness. My stomach had curdled along with any desire to be married to the man she described. Perhaps he only desired to save my soul and bind my body to Christ, lust, and dust.

A safe and supposedly prosperous marriage to a man I had had sex with a few times but hardly knew and didn't really like was losing its appeal as fast as the horses' hooves brought us closer to what I began to think was my doom. I patted Mrs. Bidley's hand and dozed off, my handkerchief pressed loosely to my face to ward off the worst of the dust kicked up by the horses.

"Midville Station, passengers."

Dusk had fallen as I slept, and when the coach stopped, Mrs. Bidley bustled about, gathering her knitting, wool so dusty it was colorless now. She jostled my arm.

"Miss Elder, we're here. I'm sure Mr. Truewell has sent a wagon to meet you. Stir yourself."

I followed her and stepped out of the coach, my legs wobbly from disuse. The driver was hauling the mail sacks and luggage from the back and top, assisted by the station agent. I looked around. Midville, the closest town to Truewell's ranch, made Dodge City look like Vienna in comparison. There was a saloon across the street, flanked by a feed store on one side and what looked like a jail on the other. Beside the depot and the water tower were a couple of buildings, closed for the night, and that was all there was to this town.

"Are you going on tonight?" I said to the driver. He turned to me, his hat low over his eyes, and blinked in surprise.

"Yes, ma'am. To Fort Griffin, but that's where we stop."

"Does it have a hotel?"

He looked at me. "Yes, ma'am. Fort Griffin has a lot of things."

"Well, then," I said. "I'm staying on for Fort Griffin."

I think he smiled, but I wasn't sure. "Yes, ma'am. We'll be going soon's as the horses are watered. I'll bring you something to drink."

I climbed back into the coach, settled into my seat, and was content to wait. Truewell be damned, along with Midville and this dust. This wasn't the place for me. I'd take my chances. I'd gotten good at that.

Dawn wasn't kind to Fort Griffin, Texas. It probably wasn't much kinder to me. As I alighted from the stagecoach, bleary-eyed and disheveled by traveling, the only thing I desired more than even a drink of cool water was the nearest privy. The stagecoach driver, looking as tired as I was, and in the morning light, quite a handsome gentleman, took my arm and led me to the wooden sidewalk of the hotel beside the station.

"I'll bring your trunk over, ma'am. I think they're up and about."

"Thank you," I said and staggered up to the desk. I felt as though I'd escaped from something, but I wasn't quite sure yet just what that was. I looked up at the young desk clerk, even early as it was dressed in a starched shirtfront and bowtie, hair water-slicked back, but blinking the sleep out of his eyes. I was clearly the first customer of the day.

"Welcome to the Occidental."

"I would like your best room, please. And a bath, later this afternoon, if that's possible."

He shoved the register towards me. "Yes, ma'am, we can do that. How long will you be staying?"

I looked at him. "I really don't know. How big is this town, and when does the westbound stage come through again?"

He blinked. "Well, as to the first, big enough, I guess, unless you're from St. Louis, and as to the second, in two days."

"I am from St. Louis, and two days will be just fine," I said and signed my name.

'Twas the heat woke me. I shifted position and found I was still in my traveling clothes from the day before, having been so exhausted it was all I could do to throw myself down on the bed. Thirst was all-consuming, and there was nothing but the pitcher and basin on the bureau beside me. Niceties be damned, I picked up the pitcher and held my mouth close as a stream of tepid water poured out. Most of it poured down my parched throat, while some fell into the basin. I tore off my boots, jacket, and skirts and lay back down, my thin cotton shift sticking to my body. Then I stared at the tin ceiling tiles above me.

Jesus God, Kate, I said to myself. *What the hell are you doing?* I stared at the faint patterns on the tiles as though they were a roadmap to self-discovery . . . but they led nowhere. The only route I was likely to find was in my own head, and I realized at that moment that I hadn't been following any path of sense for

quite some time. Since Jack's death—nay, even before that if I
was honest with myself—I had been hell-bent on a road to my
own destruction, and not one that remotely resembled my salvation, much less common sense. From St. Louis to Dodge and
now this place, whatever it was, lying, whoring, getting ready to
marry some randy oaf for money, and turning myself into
someone I hardly knew. I never wanted to marry any man and
put myself in his power ever again. I closed my eyes. I was
nearly twenty-eight years old. After everything that had happened to me, had I learned nothing in that time?

Emily Fisher's face swam into view in the dark, empty places
in my mind, her eyes full of a depthless compassion, and Joshua
appeared close beside her, that lopsided smile of his full of love.
At the same time, both of them shook their heads, very slightly.
I squeezed my eyes shut on the tears that began, and the next
face I saw was my father's, laughing at some quip of mine as he
used to do—not the exhausted gray face of the man I had last
seen in his coffin. The tears ran down my cheeks now, perhaps
the first tears I'd allowed myself since the baby died. Jack's face
was the last and maybe the hardest.

"Where you goin', love?" he said, his dark eyes questioning.
"All I ever wanted was to keep you safe and make you smile
again."

Ah, God! I cried then like I'd never done before, on and on
until my chest was spasming and my head so clogged I couldn't
breathe, until finally I wore myself out. I remember blowing my
nose on the sheet but nothing else until a knock on the door
roused me. It was twilight, or nearly so, the sun coming through
the curtains in long, lazy slants.

"Ma'am?" Another knock, less discreet this time.

"Yes?" I croaked, sitting up and looking around at the
unfamiliar room.

"You asked for a bath, and we got it here, along with your

trunks from the stage. Could you please open the door, 'cause this water ain't getting any hotter."

Unpacked, bathed, and fed, thanks to the well-tipped young desk clerk's tray of soup and biscuits, I sat at the open window and took in the nightlife of Fort Griffin. The stage driver had been correct. This part of Fort Griffin, called "the Flats," had a lot of things but none I hadn't seen before. It was a town sprung up from the arrival and needs of the buffalo hunters and the cattle drovers, much like Dodge City—full of men looking to spend their money. But, from what I could see from my second-story window in the darkening evening, it was a town that was trying to make more of itself—church steeples, a schoolhouse, large new buildings, and a good number of respectable houses, lamplight and candles burning in their windows.

Could I make a life here, or should I move on, perhaps south or east, where the United States had cities of culture and people who led everyday lives of genteel optimism? I sighed and took a sip of whiskey. Somehow, even in my newly enlightened state of self-awareness, that felt like going backwards. This was a country that prided itself on progress, and I wanted to find out not only who I was, but what lay ahead . . . and that direction lay west, for me. It was certainly not the way I'd been doing it up until now, and the time for bad decisions was over. As I well knew, career opportunities for single women were severely limited, and Texas was most likely no different from anywhere else this side of the Mississippi. I did have two skills that I hadn't put to use lately, although neither was likely to qualify as respectable: singing and gambling. Both were preferable to doing laundry or raising children, especially someone else's, and both were a step up from my last few months. I finished my whiskey and turned off the lamp. Tomorrow Kate Haroney would discover what

Fort Griffin had to offer. I would put Kate Elder and all she'd done behind me.

It was already uncomfortably warm at 10 o'clock in the morning as I made my way along the wooden sidewalks of the Flats. I perused the general store, along with a few other women and their children, who waited respectfully while the storekeeper counted out lemon drops and peppermints into their eager palms. The women eyed me shyly, clad in their ginghams and checks, and even though I'd taken pains not to overdo it, I knew my simple brocade suit was not something they'd seen in a while. At least I'd left off the high-crowned suede hat.

"Staying in town a while, ma'am?" the storekeeper asked, his eyes curious.

"Perhaps," I said, paying for the lilac soap he'd wrapped in brown paper and handed to me. "I haven't decided yet." That was true, as far as it went. I stuffed the parcel in my reticule.

Outside the store I shaded my eyes and peered up and down the main street. Saloons, boardinghouses, hotels, and cafes met my gaze. Men were walking and riding up and down the street, waking up from their nights before. I set off for Shaughnessey's, the largest of the saloons and one Tom Sherman had mentioned. It looked prosperous, and Tom swore John Shaughnessey was an honest man, as far as that virtue went in the saloon business.

Even before noon, piano music tinkled from behind the wooden door of the saloon. I pushed the door open and stepped inside. The place was quite large; a long wooden bar arched across the back, and maybe three dozen tables were set around the floor, a few filled with patrons, and one with a poker game going. Shaughnessey's was redundant of pine wood, soap, and the ever-present aroma of leather—boots, guns, and saddles— that was the hallmark of cowtowns and maybe the West itself. It almost covered up the stink of spilled beer and liquor, so at least someone was making an effort, not always the case with saloons and gambling dens. While there was no stage, the piano I'd heard was set in an alcove near the bar. A well-dressed, slender man sat on a stool before it, bent over the keys, Chopin's Etude in E minor his surprising choice—and not badly executed. His sandy hair fell across his face in his concentration as I made my way back to the bar. Chopin wasn't something you heard often in a place like this. *A good omen,* I thought.

The bartender looked up as I approached. His short, black hair stuck up at odd angles above a pleasant face with rosy cheeks, and his burly arms were busy polishing a beer mug.

"Mornin', ma'am."

I nodded. "Good morning to you. Is Mr. Shaughnessey about?"

"You're looking at him."

"Nice to meet you, Mr. Shaughnessey. I'm Kate Haroney. Tom Sherman in Dodge told me to look you up if I ever got down this way. He thought we might do some mutually profitable business."

Shaughnessey grinned, put down the mug, and rested his hands on the bar. "Darlin', mutually profitable is my middle name."

I couldn't help but grin back. "Then I think we must be related."

He laughed and slapped his hand on the bar. "What you sellin', cousin?"

"Myself, of course, but only in the trade I'll bring in with my singing," I said, "and naturally, I'll give the house a cut on any game I deal." I gazed at him point-blank, all levity aside. "Can we do business?"

Shaughnessey stepped back and assessed me from head to toe. "We just might, girl, we just might. We'll see how your cards fall tonight. As for the singing, go ask if Doc over there will accompany you, and then I'll tell you yea or nay."

Fair enough, I thought. The man was no fool. I wouldn't buy on a say-so either. I put my hand on the piano player's slim back and asked him to play "Aura Lee."

He looked up at me, his angular, heart-shaped face startlingly attractive and out of place in this rough town. "A true Southrun ballad, my dear. I'd be delighted," he said, and his bright blue eyes met mine. His face was intriguing, but it was the way his words flowed from that sardonically tilted mouth that captured me. I found it difficult to look away.

Somewhat flustered, I found my voice by the sixteenth measure of the song and plunged in. I needn't have worried. As the song ended and the last plaintive notes of the piano echoed throughout the now silent saloon, all faces were turned to me, including Shaughnessey's. His grin was wide.

"You start tonight, girl, if you want. What was your name again?"

CHAPTER 11

Shaughnessey's had been slow tonight. I'd sung a few songs, but not many customers had paid any real attention, and nobody much was gambling with intention, so I left early. I stared at the ceiling in Room 210, the same room I'd taken a month ago on the night I'd come to Fort Griffin. The moonlight made strange shadows above my head tonight, blending with the water stains and the uneven plaster into shapes that resembled everything from running horses to the waves on the Mississippi.

I closed my eyes, but sleep wouldn't come, although one face kept surfacing and blending into the ceiling's warped and curving images. Doc Holliday. He was a handsome devil with those high cheekbones, square jaw, piercing eyes, and hair drifting onto his forehead. An educated man, he was often quoting Milton one minute and swearing in French the next. I pictured him laughing as he pulled in a pot he'd won, somber as he dealt the cards, pale with anger when anyone had the temerity to challenge his honor, and flushed when he coughed from the disease that was stealing his breath.

From that first day when he'd played "Aura Lee" for me, I'd been fascinated with him, and so far I'd kept that fascination to myself. Doc was an anomaly—a stranger in a land that didn't suit him—just as I was, and I knew he'd sensed it, too. But I'd kept my distance, watching and waiting. My experiences of the last year had made me wary, and I didn't need any more men

130

making trouble in my life. I'd vowed to keep to myself. Besides, he was a busy gentleman, Doc was, with the gambling, the liquor, and the ladies, among them the formidable Lottie Deno.

Lottie was a lady gambler and a damn good one, maybe better than me. She'd made a name for herself, as had Doc, and their tables were not ones I wanted to sit down at and lose my money. I held my own games on the other side of Shaughnessey's and was beginning to make a semi-respectable living between cards and singing because John Shaughnessey was a fair and kind man. After another night of watching Lottie, and especially watching Doc as he trailed his hand across her bared shoulders, I was restive.

All right, *jealous* was the word. The man was the favorite of every girl in Shaughnessey's and maybe half the Flats. For a skinny dentist, he got around. But he'd never so much as put a finger on me, only noting I knew the difference between Chopin and Mozart and who they were. We may have been the only two people in Fort Griffin who did. Still, it wasn't as though I needed the complication of Doc Holliday—or any man in my life—anyway, so what did I care whose shoulders he touched with those elegant hands?

I punched my pillow and turned on my side, tossing my hair back so it wouldn't get crimped up. *Maybe I should cut it, at least a little*, I mused. This heat flattened it quickly, and there weren't any decent hairdressers in Fort Griffin. Braids seemed to be the style here, or piling it up on top of your head and hoping for the best. I thought about the elaborate hairstyles I'd had in New Orleans—and the hats that complemented them, from Madeleine's by Jackson Park. I bet Doc Holliday would have noticed me then . . .

The sun woke me, beaming directly into my eyelids, which couldn't resist opening to see what all the fuss was about. No fuss. Just another day in Fort Griffin, Texas. I sighed and rolled over, blinking at the same stained ceiling of Room 210—no waves, no horses.

Maybe it was time to make it *not* just another day in Fort Griffin. A big herd of cattle had come in the night before, and tonight the Flats would be booming, a perfect opportunity to make a name for myself. I threw back the covers and stretched my arms over my head, my hair hanging to my waist. *I don't think I'll cut you after all*, I thought.

By the time I got to Shaughnessey's, it was only ten, and John was still ordering about the boys who scrubbed the floors and cleaned the tables every morning. There were only a few customers, quietly sipping their beers.

"Morning, John," I said briskly, and he looked up in surprise.

"Well, top of the morning to you, Kate. What brings you out so early this fine day?"

By the time I'd finished outlining my plans, and John had reluctantly agreed, it was noon. John put the boys to work, and by four, we had it done. The tables had been shifted to allow room on the east side of the saloon for a makeshift stage, elevated a foot off the floor, with the piano still in its alcove behind it, and lights illuminating the roughly eight-foot semicircle of raised planks. We'd rigged gauzy muslin curtains, held back with tasseled ropes from an old costume I had, and it looked pretty good, even in the afternoon light. Tonight it would look even better, and I was delighted. There wasn't a place in Fort Griffin that had anything remotely like it.

I hugged Shaughnessey, and he gave me a wary smile. "This better be worth it, Kate."

"Oh, it will be—I promise. You'll see."

I sat down with the piano player, Ben Rutherford, a sweet young man from Boston, who'd been accompanying me. He had come west for adventure, and not finding it quite what he thought it would be, as did so many, he had fallen back on his old profession, music teacher. Fort Griffin offered only a few students, so Ben also played in saloons, and we had immediately hit it off my first night at Shaughnessey's. Ben had been learning my old Hungarian folk songs along with new current favorites. Tonight, we would do an actual show on a stage, rather than just an occasional couple of songs here and there with me standing in front of the piano. It would be a first for Fort Griffin.

"You better go and get ready, Miss Kate," he said. "I'll stay here and get set up. So we start at nine o'clock sharp, then?"

I smiled and squeezed his hand. "Nine o'clock it is, Ben. I'll see you then."

Back at the hotel, I rummaged through my trunks. I had my old costumes from New Orleans, most of which I hadn't worn since then, Tom Sherman's not being quite the venue for them. Nor was Fort Griffin, truth to tell, but tonight was no time for half measures. I decided on a cream-colored silk gown, trimmed with brown satin, the sleeves off the shoulder and the neckline plunging, and dressed my hair in a chignon with amber beads and brown feathers. Bronze leather slippers rather than boots completed my ensemble, and I was pleased with the woman who stared back at me from the mirror. If the ladies at the general store had been impressed with my traveling suit, they would be open-mouthed at this ensemble.

Although it was only three blocks from my hotel to Shaughnessey's, I threw on a black cloak that covered me completely from its full hood to my toes and walked to the saloon, careful to not get my slippers dirty in the dust of the road. Unnoticed, I silently crept in the back door, as Ben and I had arranged, so as to make a somewhat dramatic entrance onto our little stage.

Just as I'd taken off my cloak and hung it over the stack of boxes filled with whiskey, John entered the storage room and stopped, his mouth open.

"Jaysus Mary and Joseph! It's a goddess come to earth."

I laughed and curtseyed. "Exactly the reaction I was hoping for, sir. Will this suit?"

"Darlin', if those boys out there have ever seen anythin' like yourself, I'll eat my boots."

He shouldered a case of whiskey and left, shaking his head, still grinning.

'Course he was, I thought. He was going to make some serious money this night, if all went well. I felt really good for the first time in a long time, and I peered through the storeroom door, catching Ben's eye where he was seated playing the piano, as we had agreed. I gave him a thumbs up. While he finished his song, I checked my hair, smoothed my dress, and took some deep breaths. When the last note died away, Ben walked to the edge of the tiny stage and cleared his throat.

"Good evening, ladies and gentlemen. This evening, Shaughnessey's has a special treat for you. You've seen her some before, but tonight you'll see her as never before. May I present Miss Kate Haroney, our Hungarian songbird, the Lily of the West!"

I gathered my skirts and stepped onto the stage. Ben sat back down at the piano, playing the opening bars of my favorite old Hungarian ballad, one that had never failed to impress the New Orleans crowds. There was a hush in the saloon, cards still in hands, drinks left on the table, and I nodded at Ben as he played the first sixteen bars again, giving everyone time to get a good look. Then I opened my mouth and gave them the very first Hungarian love song they'd ever heard. Time seemed to stop for me, except for the words of that song, and I couldn't focus on anything but the antlered chandelier that hung over the center of the saloon. Frankly, I was afraid to look at anyone in the place.

Too soon, I came to the end of the song, and Ben played the last plaintive chords on the piano. The silence was thunderous in the small wooden building, and my heart stuttered for a moment. I raised my eyes to the crowd and caught Doc staring at me. He stood up, clapping, and as he did, everyone in the place followed suit, clapping and cheering. Cowboys were throwing their hats in the air, and I jumped as a couple of guns were shot off into the roof. Even the formidable Lottie Deno was smiling as she stood at her table, clapping as well.

"More, more, songbird!" came the cries from crowded tables.

"Honey, I love you, sing me another!" yelled a cowboy from the back, and others joined in. I smiled and bowed, then nodded at Ben as he launched into "Buffalo Girls," and we were off amid the enthusiastic shouts.

I only stopped that night for sips of water, but after ten songs I ended with "Aura Lee," and amid the tears from the eyes of the most grizzled cowboys, the show was over, much to the regret of the patrons of Shaughnessey's. John himself was red faced and grinning like I'd never seen him, pouring whiskeys until he was almost out of glasses. He handed me one, and I downed it gratefully, surrounded by admiring fans until I could slip behind the bar and enter the sanctuary of the storeroom, where I was guarded by John's formidable bulk.

"Back off, now," he said, holding up his hands. "This angel of song, Miss Kate, has to rest if you want her back here again tomorrow. Have another drink and sit down. That's what you want, isn't it?"

Shouts of assent greeted this proclamation, and I heard Ben start up a popular song on the piano. People settled back down to gambling and drinking, while I sat down on a wooden box and patted the sweat from my face. I allowed myself a small smile. We'd see what tomorrow night was like, but for now, I knew it had been a success.

"Forgive me, my dear, for not realizin' what a prize was in our midst. One becomes jaded and thinks to never truly see a pearl in the oyster of a place like this."

Doc Holliday stood in front of me, holding out another glass of whiskey, a cigarillo dangling from his other hand. "Miss Kate, you have honored us. Please?"

I took the glass and raised it. "My thanks, kind sir." I took a small sip and smiled. This was a different sort of liquor than John usually poured.

"Private stock, Dr. Holliday?"

"John accommodates me. I had a suspicion you would know the difference, and I'm not disappointed." He stared at me, a small smile playing on his lips.

I took another sip, then stood up and downed the entire glass, staring at him as I did.

"With me, disappointed is one thing you'll never be," I said, returning the glass to his outstretched hand, my eyes never leaving his. "I think I would like to return to my hotel. The evening has been exhilarating but wearying. Would you be interested in accompanying me?"

He bowed quite elegantly, his pearl-grey frock coat nearly sweeping the dusty floor. "My dear, it is my fondest wish." His eyes burned into mine as he raised his head. I retrieved my cloak from the boxes of stacked whiskey and held it out. He draped it across my shoulders, his touch light but firm. Then he opened the back door and stood aside for me.

"Shall we?"

I turned, the cloak enveloping me, our bodies so close I could feel his warmth. I looked up at him in the dim light from the street.

"Oh, indeed, I think we shall."

I ran my fingers gently across his rib cage and then his concave stomach. The man was thin, but muscled, in spite of the disease some said was going to take him soon. I didn't think so. Doc Holliday was a vibrant man, I could attest to that.

I smiled, thinking of the night we'd just spent together. We had a lot in common, in many ways. For some strange reason, this overeducated gambling dentist attracted me like no other man ever had, not even Jack. Maybe it was a desire to protect him, but I had to admit to myself I'd been oddly obsessed from the first moment I laid eyes on him at Shaughnessey's, playing Chopin so well, his long fingers seeming at home at the piano. That they'd been equally so on my body was no surprise. I trailed my index finger down his thigh and was amused when his eyes opened, regarding me appraisingly.

"Good morning."

"And to you." I smiled. "Penny for your thoughts?"

"My thoughts aren't so well-formed as they should be at dawn, darlin', and not worth so much." He turned and pulled me on top of him. "Perhaps you might elucidate and elevate my worth, at least intellectually?"

I fluttered my eyelashes. "Well, I might be convinced, in the interests of economics, say?"

He chuckled and coughed softly. My hair covered both of us as the gentle rhythm began again, and I'm quite certain our worth grew much more than a penny as the sun grew higher.

The day passed, I'm not sure how, in a melange of sensual pleasure that I don't remember ever experiencing before. Somehow food appeared, and then a bath, which we both splashed about happily in, thanks to money and a kind and invested hotel clerk whom we ignored but paid well. As dusk fell, we both dressed in our costumes for the evening ahead and presented ourselves as we knew we should, but we passed the night in a haze of desire and longing that colored our evenings until closing. Our obligations met, we fell into each other's arms at midnight and didn't wake until noon the next day.

As the days passed in this fashion, the Flats came to realize we were indeed an anomaly, an odd couple who'd come together, and together were an entity not to be trifled with. This understanding extended from the cowboys that surrounded me each evening to Lottie Deno and the girls who had grown used to Doc's easy affection. When I'd finished my show for the evening, I took my place at Doc's side, and the games went on with no interference from caressing hands on his shoulders or mine. We began to do well financially, and I made sure all was secured away each morning. Fort Griffin was not a place either of us planned to spend our lives, and neither of us was a stranger to thieves in the night.

We didn't spend all our time in bed or in saloons. Taking a picnic and riding out to a pleasant spot on the river in the early afternoon became a habit we enjoyed. Occasionally we'd take off our shoes and stockings and wade in the water like two children. I think it was something neither one of us had done for a long time, but it was a pastime we both sorely needed. On these sunny afternoons, we shared our histories with each other. Doc grew up in Atlanta, a privileged young man from an established family who had sent him north to study dentistry and been confounded when he'd gone west and stayed—better for his health but offering an uncertain future. My own life intrigued him, and he never tired of hearing stories about Hungary and Austria, holding me close when I cried. I told him of my father—his honor in the face of adversity and how he'd struggled and died, desperate to find new opportunities for his family in America.

"How do you say 'I love you' in Hungarian?" Doc's shirt-sleeves were rolled up, and his waistcoat, hat, and gun were bundled beside us on the blanket we'd thrown down on the grass.

I laughed. *"Szeretlek."*

He leaned over me and smoothed my hair back from my face. *"Szeretlek,* Kate. For now and ever." Before I could even say it back to him, he kissed me, and there was no more talking for a time on our deserted piece of the Brazos River.

Summer passed into fall, and Doc and I talked a lot about moving on and getting out of Fort Griffin, but somehow the days passed without us putting our plans into action, maybe because we weren't certain which avenue was the ideal choice. We were both the sort of people who tended to let fate decide our moves, and that was the one thing we should have remedied before the night Wyatt Earp walked into Shaughnessey's.

Doc was dealing poker at his usual table. I, dressed in red silk with peacock feathers in my hair, was on my last song of the evening's performance. Shaughnessey's was crowded, but not as much as some nights, the drovers having just left town. The door opened, people entered, and even against the stage lights I recognized him immediately. The man was hard to miss.

Wyatt stopped cold, staring at me. Behind him I glimpsed Mattie Blaylock, his brother Morgan, and another woman I didn't know. I didn't falter for a second, finishing my song with a resounding coda from Ben. The appreciative applause drowned out all the conversation in Shaughnessey's for a few seconds, and I quickly left the stage, grabbing a whiskey from John's outstretched hand, our usual routine before I joined Doc or dealt my own game after the show.

Tonight I was in no hurry to leave the back room, with the comforts of a chair and a mirrored table installed in the wake of my success some months ago. After ten minutes or so, John came in.

"Are you feeling O.K., Kate? Usually you're out there in no time."

I looked up and smiled at him. His solicitousness always warmed me. "I'm fine, John. Just not feeling like socializing much tonight, for some reason."

He patted my head, like he always did. "I can tell Doc you

went home, if you want. You need to take care of yourself, sweet-ling."

I shook my head. "I'll be fine, John. Don't worry."

I waited a few more minutes. Facing down Wyatt Earp was something I'd already done, but I didn't relish an encore. I wanted nothing more than to strangle Mattie, the thieving bitch, and my fingers curled just thinking about the pleasure of it. Still, there was nothing for it. I couldn't hide forever. I took a deep breath and went through the storeroom door, feathers held high.

Doc was at his table, his head thrown back, laughing at something the man beside him had said. Wyatt sat at Doc's right hand as if he'd always been there, Mattie standing behind him, and I quickly crossed the floor and put my hand on Doc's shoulder.

"Darlin'." Doc turned and smiled at me. "You must meet this gentleman, my new friend. Wyatt Earp, this is Kate Ha-roney."

Wyatt stood, doffing his hat so gentlemanly. "Miss . . . Ha-roney." His blue eyes betrayed nothing, but I wasn't playing.

I leaned down close to Doc's ear. "Mr. Earp and I are old acquaintances from my Dodge City days." I held out my hand.

"How nice to see you again, Wyatt," I said, "and your little friend." I nodded at Mattie, who had the grace to blush and keep her mouth shut, a novel thing for that odious whore. Wyatt took my hand somewhat awkwardly, smiled politely, and cast his eyes down. I sat down on Doc's other side.

"What brings you to Fort Griffin, Mr. Earp? Chasing after some miscreant?"

"Well, yes, now that you mention it, Miss Haroney. When did you stop using the name *Elder*?"

I laughed breezily, and it cost me a lot. "When I decided to reignite the Hungarian Songbird. After all, it's my real name.

Texans like the real thing, and it's not that difficult to pronounce. It may be difficult for you to understand, the name Earp being, well . . . what it is."

There was a brief moment, and then, being the innocent he sometimes was, Doc laughed. "Kate's rather an expert on language, knowing four of them, so I'd trust her on that, Wyatt."

Wyatt nodded, and then the bastard said, "Oh, I know. She's quite an expert on many things."

He looked at me, and I wanted to kill him in that moment. Mattie wisely turned on her heel and made for the bar, and Doc glanced questioningly at me. The game was on, and it seemed I'd lost already, but I wasn't ready to quit.

"Wyatt's an expert himself," I said. "He's the best I've ever seen at hitting people in the head and making up lies. This is what law in the West has come to. The Borgias could learn from him."

I kissed Doc on the cheek. "Watch yourself, my man. I'll see you later." I gathered my skirts and left before either of them could say a word.

I spent the rest of the evening alternately crying and throwing pillows, finally falling into a fitful sleep until dawn, when I felt the mattress shift with the weight of Doc's body. I turned and found his eyes on me. He lay very still, inches away.

"It's a long story," I said, not moving.

"Well," he said, "it's been a long night, and I heard some of his version of it. Seems the man was crazy in love with you, my dear, although mostly that's the part he left out. I like the bastard for some reason, but I know at least one supremely foolish thing he did."

I waited, my heart not wanting to turn to stone . . . again.

He propped himself on one elbow, clearly drunk but, as was often the case with Doc, in ultimate possession of his faculties. Clarity was one of them.

He stared down at me. "I love you, Kate. I don't give a damn about you and Wyatt, or anything else in your past. We started here, and we'll go on from here. What we have transcends anything before that. I only hope you agree with me and that Wyatt doesn't change anything for you. I got the feelin' that man still wanted to sweep you up and ride away in an instant, like some damned half-assed frontier Lancelot."

I felt as though an anvil had been lifted off my chest. I rolled over on top of him and kissed him, tasting the whiskey, smoky on my tongue. "I love you, Doc. You are the only thing that matters to me in this whole damn world. I want to be with you forever, and every morning I wake up and look at you and think I'm the luckiest woman in the world, you know that?"

He smiled and closed his eyes. "And you are, darlin'. Because I think the same thing every mornin' when I look at you."

CHAPTER 12

Fort Griffin, Texas, 1877

Autumn turned into winter, the blizzards sweeping down from the plains into Texas early that year, but Doc and I kept each other warm and happy under our feather quilts at night and working in the saloons the rest of the time. Lottie Deno moved on to a table at the Den, and while Doc played faro and poker around town, his favorite table at Shaughnessey's remained his and his only, while I continued to sing my heart out and make up for Lottie's absence at my own poker table. I carefully put our collective gains into the Merchants Bank every other day, before one of us could get a wild idea on how to spend it—like on a beautiful Tennessee walking horse that caught Doc's eye one frosty afternoon, or a sumptuous bolt of red velvet that would make a lovely holiday costume for me.

As Christmas neared, I knew I never wanted to spend another one in a place like the Flats. Doc and I were destined for finer things and a better life than this. We stifled our memories of and lust for those finer things, to enjoy at another place and time, and fulfilled our current life with each other instead, a most satisfying method of saving money, and one that provided enjoyable dividends.

"No! Higher, Miss Kate, higher!" cried Jimmy Weston, one of the clean-up boys at Shaughnessey's. He was jumping up and down with excitement as I stretched my fingertips to place the gold Christmas star on the very top of the pine tree, my toes perched on the top step of the wooden ladder.

Task accomplished, I wobbled for a scary moment, then grabbed the top of the ladder and descended, relieved when my boots touched the wooden floor. I smoothed my hands on my green plaid skirt, glad I'd worn it and happy I'd left my hair down, tied back with a red satin ribbon. Now it felt like Christmas.

Doc grabbed my waist and swung me around, my skirts flying as he laughed and kissed my cheek. "An amazin' feat, my dear. Only you were worthy of placin' the star on our august tree. Am I right, John?"

"Never was a man righter, Doc. The queen of Shaughnessey's is our beautiful Christmas angel, so she is." Shaughnessey's face was rosy from the drink but also from happiness. He clapped and so did the boys surrounding us, Jimmy and the other orphan boys who worked at the saloon. Shaughnessey took in any of them who needed a place, and we were now up to five. This was our family. And a good one it was, in this place where so many stayed a day or two and moved on. Those who found solace with John Shaughnessey, the ex-boxer from Boston who had followed his dreams west, were a motley but fortunate crew indeed.

Earlier that morning, Doc and John had ventured out of town with a wagon, cut the most perfect pine tree they could find, and returned to set it up in the middle of the saloon. After the snow melted and the tree warmed, the boys had decorated it with popcorn and the red and green paper rings I'd shown them how to make, along with a tin star we'd fashioned out of scrap metal and then painted. John had kept the saloon closed so we could work our magic. Now, we stood back and gazed at the tree, the boys' faces rapt as we all breathed in the magical and pungent evergreen scent. I thought for a few moments about my own siblings and the Fishers, hoping they were having the holiday they wished for. I missed them all, but I was long at peace with making my own way and the occasional twinges of regret I suffered.

Doc, Shaughnessey, and I exchanged glances and smiled. It was Christmas Eve tonight, a night for anticipation and wonder, and we had created our own little piece of magic hidden here in this frontier bar. If the gamblers and drinkers had to make their way carefully around our tree, we would make damn certain they did. If nothing else was holy in this place, that tree sure as hell was.

Another hour passed as we shared the Hungarian Christmas bread, full of currants and cinnamon, that I'd baked that morning in the hotel kitchen, and the delicious roast beef and potatoes John had made that afternoon. The boys were delighted with their warm new sweaters and their collection of books and gazettes Doc and I had chosen, from lurid penny dreadfuls to Shakespeare, and when John shooed them off to their lean-to in the back, they were tired but happy. For some it was the first Christmas they'd ever had, even Jimmy. I couldn't help but think again of past Christmases—from Hungary to the Fishers— and how different each had been, but I wouldn't have traded this night for any of them. I glanced at Doc and knew similar thoughts were in his mind as he squeezed my hand.

"Merry Christmas Eve, Kate." His blue eyes were misty, and I kissed him gently.

"And to you, my dear Dr. Holliday. May it be the first of many for us."

The banging on the door as the dark fell in earnest shook us all from memories of the past and into the raw present of the Flats. Doc shrugged his waistcoat on over his red-brocade Christmas vest, I pinned up my hair with some sprigs of pine, and Shaughnessey tied on his apron and unbolted the door. The usual crowd flooded in, moving around the tree and into their seats at the tables and the bar. But even among the customers there was a glance at the tree and downcast eyes for a moment as many remembered past Christmas Eves, these men and women from different parts of the world, here now on this night that some used to feel was holy, while to others it was a day for family or just another twenty-four hours on the calendar. Even for the latter, though, there was a feeling that perhaps for this one night, something special was in the air, and the evening passed into Christmas morning with an unusual camaraderie among the denizens of Shaughnessey's, an outpost among the bleakness that was Fort Griffin, Texas. My last song was "Silent Night," and everyone in the saloon joined in, tears on the faces of even the most hardened men. It was a good Christmas.

Fort Griffin was dreary in the winter. Doc and I went to our favorite cafe for breakfast, our boots crunching the frozen mud puddles as we crossed the street. We'd been up late the night before, our usual routine amplified by the latest invasion of cowboys with a late winter herd. Shaughnessey's and every other saloon in town had done a brisk business, as had we at the tables. It was already two o'clock, but every restaurant in town knew that breakfast came late in the Flats.

"I think we should start early today, Kate."

I mopped up the rest of my eggs with the thick toast, cowboy style, and chewed slowly before answering.

"Oh, you do? I don't know. I'm not in the right frame of mind for muddy fingers on my cards quite so soon." I glanced out the window at the sleet coming down and shivered. "I thought a little nap and some reading or . . . whatnot could fill the day." I smiled provocatively, but he wasn't buying it.

"This is a good day to make some money; I just feel it," Doc said. He took a sip of coffee.

I shrugged. There was no arguing with him when he was like

this. I should have noticed he was geared up, coughing half the night and now with that flush on his pale cheeks and his eyes bright. He was even wearing his lucky gold-silk vest.

Over to Shaughnessey's we went, Doc setting up at his usual table, while I sat down at the bar and worked out a schedule with John. Ben came in, and we went over our song choices and performance list for the next week, me humming along as he played a few bars of each tune. The saloon was full; most of the tables had a card game going on. Doc was dealing poker, with the sound of cards and glasses and conversation rising and falling as usual.

"Godammit, Holliday. You skinny, cheating bastard!"

Ed Bailey was standing, his chair knocked over, and his voice carried throughout the bar as silence descended. I saw John set down the glass he was wiping and put his hands under the bar near the shotgun he always kept there in case of trouble.

Bailey was a small, hairy bear of a man, his stomach protruding over his belt, his manner and voice always annoying and arrogant. I'd warned Doc about letting him sit in on his games. The man was a poor loser and a loudmouth, even if he was a regular customer. But Doc was feeling lucky today.

"Ed, sit down," Doc said, his voice low and calm. "Let's talk this over."

Bailey snorted. "Not with you, Holliday. I want my money." He reached over to take the pot, and Doc grabbed his hand and looked up at him.

"Not today, Ed. You lost fair and square. Be a man about it. It near breaks my heart that you would think so badly of me, just because of the fall of the cards." Doc let go of Ed's hand and pushed his own chair back. "Go on home and sober up, and you'll see I'm right."

"You bastard," snarled Bailey. He pulled out his gun and aimed it shakily at Doc.

For a few seconds, the world came to a halt. No one breathed nor uttered a word, and my heart was thumping in my chest. The silence was shattered by the gunshot. Doc weaved to one side, and the bullet buried itself in the back wall, missing Shaughnessey by inches. Before anyone else could move, Doc whipped around the table and put himself chest to chest with Ed Bailey. The gun was still in Bailey's hand, but Doc was so close now Bailey couldn't draw his arm back to aim it. The knife in Doc's hand moved so fast it was a silvery blur, arcing across Bailey's stomach and then coming back to do so again. Bailey fell groaning onto the wooden floor, a crimson ribbon growing wider across his stomach. Blood began to pool underneath him.

Doc stood over him, breathing heavily. "I don't think I'm going to let you shoot me today, Ed." He wiped the knife on Bailey's coat and looked around the room, his eyes unfocused.

I moved then, as fast as I ever had, scraping the money off the table and into my reticule and dragging Doc by the elbow, as he seemed in a daze. We left the saloon, but before we took two steps outside the door, the sheriff was there, gun drawn. It seemed somebody had moved even faster.

I sat in our hotel room, staring out at the street. At least the sleet had stopped, and the air was clear. Doc had been put in a room three doors down the hall, where they were keeping him prisoner until the circuit judge could come by next Wednesday. It seemed even an idiot rancher like Ed Bailey had some powerful friends. Nobody was listening to my side of the story, nor Shaughnessey's. There was a crowd of men outside in the street, drinking whiskey and talking big about hanging "cheating, murdering gamblers," and I was having serious doubts Doc would live until Wednesday.

A knock on the door startled me, and I opened it to John

Shaughnessey. He quickly came inside and shut the door behind him, peering over his shoulder.

"Kate, this is getting out of hand. We got to get him out of here, or he won't last the night, I'm thinkin'." His face was flushed, and he was clearly worried beyond all measure. My heart sank, because I had the same feeling. He grabbed both my arms and turned me to face him.

"Darlin', if you care about your man, you got to think fast."

Well shit, I thought. I cared about Doc more than I had anybody ever, but I didn't know how I was going to save him in this situation. The law had him, and they weren't letting go. I'd been trying to think of something for three hours. I'd stopped at the bank and taken all our money out before they closed, but that was as far as I'd gotten.

John shook me lightly, his face impatient.

"Think, girl. You're not some green farm wife, but a resourceful woman. Start acting like it." I glared at him. "Doc needs you more now than he ever has, and you got to get him the hell out of here before they stretch his neck."

He was right; it really was up to me. Nobody else could do it, not even John. It was as though the cobwebs cleared out of my brain. It wasn't much of a plan, but it would have to do. John must've sensed something in my face, because he dropped his arms and stood back a little.

I picked up my portmanteau full of money and shoved it into his arms. I trusted John Shaughnessey, and I prayed I was right to ask this of him.

"Go back to the bar," I said, my mind racing. "Take this with you, but stop at the livery stable and arrange for two horses to be saddled and carrying some blankets and food. Jimmy and the boys can manage it, 'cause we'll need it, along with everything in there." I nodded at the bag. "Tell Jimmy to wait and keep the horses ready. This might take me some time. Let's say two hours from now, all right?"

He nodded, grinning slightly, and kissed me on the forehead. "Darlin', whatever you say, you know it'll get done. Don't tell me nothing else; I don't want to know. But them horses and everything you need," he said, holding up the portmanteau, "will be waiting for you."

I hugged him. "I love you, John, and always will. If I'm ever back this way, I'll buy you a drink. You're a good man."

He laughed. "That I am, my sweet girl, that I am. I don't think I'll be seeing you for a while. You take care of Doc, now."

I dressed in the warmest clothes I could find, a triple layer, but left our cloaks for later, stuffing extra socks and anything remotely warm into a large raffia bag I had from the general store. I listened for a while as men went up and down the hall, and after a bit, when all seemed quiet, I opened the door and went quickly down the hall to the back stairs.

Slipping outside, I made for the street behind the hotel. There was a storeroom for lamp oil and supplies on the back street, and that was where I headed. The street was deserted, all the activity concentrated on the main thoroughfare, and I crept to the storeroom door. My hand was shaking as I turned the knob, but the door was unlocked, as I hoped it would be.

Straw littered the floor, and I scraped it into a goodly pile beside the barrels and wooden crates. I spied a crowbar leaning against the wall, and I smashed it into one of the barrels, standing back as lamp oil gushed out of the side onto the straw. It seemed I wouldn't need the glass jar of kerosene I carried, after all. I set it down and backed out of the shed, my hands cold and fumbling at the matches. After the third try, one flared, and I leaned down and touched it to the dry straw. It caught quickly, and as the glowing straw burned its way to the oil, it grew into flames. I smiled and shut the door. I waited only a couple of minutes until I saw flames licking under the door and a good amount of smoke rise up before I turned back to the hotel. I came up the front stairs to our room as two of the deputies rushed past me, shoving me aside in their haste to get downstairs.

"What's the problem?" I asked, and the youngest one turned to me as he dashed past. "Fire, ma'am, fire. This here's a town all built of wood, and things go up quick. You best get outside."

"Oh, I'll do that, thank you," I said and walked farther down the hall to the room where they were holding Doc. The door was open, and my man sat on a plain wooden chair, his hands tied to the back of it. A deputy stood there, watching him and casting glances out the window at the flames on the street behind the hotel. Distracted, he looked at me and frowned.

"Ma'am, this is no place for you; go outside or back to your room. We got us a situation out there."

I looked up at him. "Looks to me like you got a situation in here, too."

He never saw the butt end of Doc's Colt coming at him. I guess I learned something from Wyatt after all. Doc laughed softly as I cut the ropes that bound him, coughing only once, his eyes bright in his lean face.

"Kate, you are a caution, I swear." He kissed me as we raced down the hallway. "I knew I took up with the right woman."

I kissed him back. "Holliday, you have no idea." I handed him the Colt. "Now get moving."

Morning found us thirty miles north of Fort Griffin, snow falling fast. John had been true to his word, and we had our money, a carpetbag with water and some food, and two tired horses, for all the good it was doing us, stuck in a bleak landscape with no shelter anywhere. We finally made camp in a grove of stunted cedars and built a small fire that kept us warm intermittently as the falling snow put it out. We kept building it back up with

151

green boughs, coughing in the smoke and taking comfort from the little warmth it provided.

I nestled against Doc and pulled the blankets around us, some cedar branches we'd cut underneath. He hugged me close.

"I love you, Kate. I don't think anyone else in the world would have done what you did for me back there." He kissed my temple, and I nestled closer, breathing in the smell of tobacco and that sweet, intangible, and fascinating scent of Doc.

"Probably not," I managed, half asleep in spite of the cold and smoke. It had been a long night, and the day looked to be a longer one.

I felt him sigh and then take a deep breath where I lay against his chest. "Woman, it's us against the world." He gave a chuckle and coughed just a little.

"It's not the world, my sweet. It's just the Ed Baileys of the world. The rest is up to us," I murmured. I wiggled my toes in their cold leather boots. My stomach was protesting our beef jerky and cornbread breakfast but grateful for it all the same.

"So it is," Doc said, his voice slurring with fatigue. "Given that, after a brief respite, I think we should make for Dodge City. Your friend Wyatt was most persuasive in that regard. It sounds a capital place. We are through with Texas."

CHAPTER 13

Dodge City, Kansas, April 1878

"Kate, how does that look?"

I glanced up from the battered copy of Shakespeare's plays I had found buried in a stack of pamphlets at Kirkland's General Store. God knows how it came to be there, but it must've had a fascinating journey. I was still wearing a black lace peignoir and little else, since mornings started late for us, and afternoon was prime reading and nap time for me at the Dodge House—and usually for Doc as well. Lately, however, he'd become obsessed with setting up his dental practice. From the looks of the teeth of many of Dodge City's citizens, and considering Doc's excitement at once again practicing dentistry, it sounded like a passable idea. He'd already wired his friend John Seegar in Texas to ship his dentistry chair to Dodge, and Doc always carried his instruments with him. I'd packed them into that portmanteau nearly as carefully as I had our money when we left the Flats.

He'd been at the desk for an hour now, with his shirtsleeves rolled up, vest unbuttoned, and pencil clenched alternately between his teeth and his hand. When he handed me the paper he'd been writing on, his sandy hair fell across his forehead.

"John H. Holliday, Dentist, respectfully offers his professional services to the citizens of Dodge City. Office at Room 24, Dodge House. Where satisfaction is not given, money will be refunded," I read out loud.

"Most excellent." I handed it back. "You sending it to the

153

newspaper?"

He grinned, as happy as I'd seen him in days. "And postin' it outside the hotel. It sounds good, then?"

"Yes, I think business will be brisk, Doctor." He really did love practicing his skills. I put the book down and stood up, leaning over him, my unbound hair falling around us both. "I think you deserve a reward for all this work, sir. Perhaps I could offer my services to the dentist?"

He carefully put down the pencil and ran his hands languidly through my hair. "Why, madam, how kind and what an enticin' offer—one no proper Southern gentleman could refuse." There was no further discussion of mandibles or advertisements that rainy spring afternoon.

Our trek through Texas and northward had taken some time, but we'd been in no hurry once we left the law in Fort Griffin behind. After that first cold night spent in the open, we'd been fortunate to find the occasional ranch house and small town, and we managed to purchase a pack mule and supplies. Somewhere north of Sweetwater, Oklahoma, well-stocked with provisions, we found an abandoned cabin and settled in, content to wait out the worst of the winter and just to be with each other. We were weary of other people and their vagaries. We had begun to find the world a hungry place, one that could swallow your morals and self respect in a few chosen bites. It was crowded with people who lie and cheat, with few exceptions, but the worst thing was, we had become just like them in self defense. We needed time to learn to like ourselves again, a respite that was essential if we were to make a life on our own terms.

We'd shot mostly pheasants and prairie hens and once a hapless deer. We cooked, ate, slept, made love, and in that time alone, crept into each other's hearts and minds. From childhood fears to first loves and all that came after, Doc and I came to know each other like few men and women ever do. With no distractions, there were no barriers, no judgments, and no shame between us.

When the buildings of Dodge City loomed on the horizon, I'd been eager to taste the fruits of civilization again, but I was filled with regret for the roles we would once again assume. One look at Doc's face told me he felt the same. The moment had passed, as they do, and we'd pushed our horses forward towards perdition.

Dodge City was much as I remembered it, a dirty cow town, full of hastily put together clapboard buildings thrusting up from the prairie floor like a raw-boned forest, full of muddy streets and rowdy inhabitants. But in the short time I'd been gone, it had grown: another two-story hotel, several saloons and gambling halls, more stores, and even another church or two, their steeples poking towards the gray, low-hanging clouds. There was some pretension to elegance now in a few of the storefronts, and the town had more sidewalks to better traverse the spring mud, but all in all, it felt pretty much the same.

To Doc, however, it was a haven that could provide future revenue, and he'd turned to me, his eyes bright with fever. "Darlin', we'll make a killin' in this hellhole, and we'll be the most elegant couple in town while we do." He'd laughed, kissing me on the cheek. "What's the best hotel in Dodge?"

"Things have changed a bit. We'll have to look. Tour of Dodge City coming up, my man. But the minute we decide on a room, you're going to bed for a few days."

He'd waved his hand, ignoring my concerns as he always did. Tuberculosis had been Doc's companion for years now, and he worked hard at dismissing it. To give him credit, he managed quite well, but I knew he was nearing a bad spell. He'd done well when we were snug and warm in our snowbound little cabin, out of cigarettes and whiskey, and he even put on a couple of pounds, limited as our diet had been. Traveling on horseback in the cold wasn't a good prescription for him, but we'd had no choice.

Once settled, into bed he'd gone, while I fed him broth and whiskey, which did ease his cough. Within a few days he was eager to explore. Our room at the Dodge House was large, with big windows fronting on the street and a separate sitting room. While it was perhaps a little noisier than a room at the back, both Doc and I preferred to observe what was going on in town through our "windows on the world," as we called them.

"It's important to see what and whom to avoid, as well as what we should participate in, my dear. Surprises aren't always a birthday party and can sometimes be unpleasant," he said, tucking his revolver in his waistcoat.

I couldn't disagree with that, and with that credo and from that vantage point, we made our plans. Gambling and dentistry proved a heady mix.

"Call."

"Why, Mr. Masterson, you are a lucky man," Doc said, as Bat's full house was exposed. The gentleman in question chuckled and scraped the pot towards him, eyes twinkling, his derby hat pushed back on his handsome head.

"I'd no idea dedicated lawmen such as yourself were fortunate gamblers as well. Nicely done, sir." Doc gathered the cards and shuffled, his fingers dancing over the pasteboard figures.

"Holliday, it's up to me as sheriff of Ford County to be sure you're running an honest game here at the Long Branch. Dodge has a reputation to maintain."

Doc nodded his head, and although I felt his shoulders tense under my hands, his manners didn't allow him to show that in his face or voice. He wasn't especially fond of Bat.

"Of course, sir, I quite understand." Doc smiled at Bat Masterson, and his blue eyes were guileless. "My granddaddy always said the best way to know a man's mettle is to watch him with horses or sit with him at cards, and it's a rule I follow to this day. Another hand, then?"

Masterson laughed. "Deal, Dr. Holliday. The night is early, the game honest, the whiskey excellent, and the county quiet."

We spent a profitable evening in the Long Branch, as we had most of the nights we'd been in Dodge, either there or at the Alamo. Although Masterson and lots of men like him thought they were gamblers, there wasn't a one to match Doc, or even me, although I'd yet to start a table of my own. For now, I stood behind my man, content to get the feel of the place again, establish my presence, and learn who now had power in this town.

Masterson did, for sure, but since Bat's brother Ed had been gunned down, Charlie Bassett was the city marshal now. Wyatt wasn't around, rumored to be in Deadwood again, but I'd seen James Earp briefly with his brother Morgan. All was cordial, but I didn't stop in at Bessie's for a chat. I wasn't feeling all that friendly. Even though our past troubles weren't her fault, I knew the Earps and their friends stuck together no matter what, and I had no desire to revisit my former life in Dodge. I was done with that for good. If it hadn't been for Doc, I'd never have come back to this place.

"More wine, sir?"

Doc nodded, and the white-aproned young waitress refilled his glass. Dinner at the Dodge House dining room was a fairly refined affair, or so they thought, and one in which we regularly participated, since we lived just up the stairs. I'd rather enjoyed my decidedly ill-equipped but tasty culinary adventures during the winter, working with the wild game we'd shot, although cooking was something I hadn't done since Davenport. The Dodge House put on a varied and respectable menu, not something that could be said of most of the establishments in Dodge. It wasn't New Orleans, but they were learning.

I took the last bite of my steak Delmonico and put down my fork. Doc was enjoying his, and it always made me happy to see him eat, as there were some evenings he didn't touch a thing.

I picked up my full wineglass and smiled at him.

"Tonight, I'm going to start dealing at the Long Branch," I said. "I've talked with Henry, and it's all set. I'll split with the house."

He frowned. "But, darlin', I need you. Haven't we talked about this?"

"I know, Doc. But we have to make a real stake if we're going to head west, remember?"

He drained his glass and nodded at the waitress. I sighed, knowing this wasn't going to go well.

"We talked about this, Doc. Your dentistry practice will open tomorrow, and you'll be busy there. So, I'm going to make some extra money gambling until you're well established. You knew I was going to start sometime, and tonight's the night, my love. I've been feeling like I'm not contributing, and I know I can. Make me happy and wish me well."

He stared at me. "Kate. You're my woman, and a gentleman provides for his woman; that's all there is to it. Do you want me to feel like you don't trust me to do that?"

I sighed—and instantly regretted it as his eyes flared. "Doc, of course I trust you, my love." We'd already had this conversation, and I thought it was finished. Unfortunately, I would come to learn it never would be. "Let me be who I am, and trust me to make things easier for both of us." I took his hand in mine across the table. "Please."

He took a moment, sighed, and nodded. "You're right, my

love. This isn't Georgia. I'm sorry, I'll have to learn to adjust, won't I?"

"Yes, Doc, we both will. This isn't an easy world anymore, and we've created a road in front of us that needs to be paved with all the gold we can give it. I'm your woman, and you wouldn't want to be with me if I didn't understand that, would you?"

He smiled, and it was as if the sun came out, brightening the crystal and silver and lighting the entire dining room. How I loved this strange man, but how difficult he could be. I held my breath.

"Take 'em down, darlin'." He leaned across the table and kissed me. "Luck be with you, although you scarcely need it."

"I hate to interrupt this warm and tender moment."

Sweet Christ. My stomach plummeted. Wyatt Earp, dressed in his usual black clothing, wide-brimmed hat on his head, and mustache jaunty, slapped Doc on the back. "Holliday, Bat told me you were in town. I see you took my advice." He nodded at me, eyes deliberately disinterested. "Kate, nice to see you again, too."

Doc, clearly delighted to see his new friend, shoved back his chair and shook Wyatt's hand. He pulled an empty chair from a nearby table and motioned for the waitress to bring another glass.

"Heard you were in Deadwood, but I'm damn glad to see you. How is that place?"

Wyatt smiled a little, his mustache barely moving, and shook his head. "Deadwood's a sewer since Wild Bill got himself killed. Did a little law work up there, but that place'd take twenty of me to make a dent, so I came back here where they got some respect for the law. Charlie Bassett just made me his assistant marshal." Wyatt pulled back his topcoat to display the silver star on his vest.

"Indeed," Doc murmured. "Congratulations to you, sir." Doc filled Wyatt's glass and held his own wine glass up.

"Here's to furthering your illustrious career, Marshal Earp. I am certain of your success."

We all clinked glasses and drank, and I don't believe Wyatt for one second caught a single whiff of sarcasm from Doc. Wyatt was never a subtle man.

High summer in Dodge City arrived, bringing more dust, heat, cattle, and the cowboys who drove them. It also brought us a very good income, which I dutifully banked every afternoon. We were becoming very well established between the gambling and Doc's dentistry practice, which didn't make as much money as cards did for us. Nevertheless, dentistry marked him as a professional man who cared for others, something his reputation sorely needed. Tales of Doc's short temper and ability with a weapon had circulated far and wide on the frontier. Not all of them were justified, but there was enough truth among the chaff that he couldn't profess innocence. He was gossiped about, and some took a wide berth when he stepped their way. My own reputation wasn't much better, especially now that I was gambling again myself, but at least whoring wasn't in the equation, and so far no one had brought it up. I was grateful for that small measure of mercy.

Tom Sherman had approached me the first week we were back in town, but my days of singing in Dodge were done. Memories of the last time I'd sung in Tom's saloon were the stuff of nightmares for me, and I preferred to keep a lower profile on the evenings I gambled. I dressed conservatively—no plunging necklines, feathers, or high-legged bustles for me, although I couldn't resist expensive fabrics and well-made gowns. There was a seamstress here who was a wonder, with the latest patterns from New York and even Paris, so she said. Her creations fit me perfectly, accentuating my small waist as well as my ample curves above and below it. I always felt wonderful when I wore her designs, from evening dresses to the dark-green riding habit she'd fashioned. I even had her make me two pairs of breeches, which I wore riding with Doc. They were much more comfortable than skirts, and I hadn't worried about genteel convention in a long time.

We would often venture out of Dodge and onto the prairie in the late afternoons. These frontier towns had grown up so quickly from nothing that in a few moments you could look around and see only endless waves of grass and sky—with no buildings or people to spoil it. I felt like I could breathe again out there, and in spite of the continuous wind that swept across the plains, Doc could, too.

In early July, after a stint at the Long Branch, I decided to set up a table at the Alamo, which tended to be a little less boisterous than some of the saloons in Dodge. I dressed carefully, choosing a black and gray striped skirt with a black-velvet jacket and lace cuffs. Doc had changed and left after our ride, and I hadn't seen him for dinner, not an unusual occurrence lately, but not my preference, either. He loved spending time with Wyatt and his other cronies and gambling well into the night. I wasn't thrilled with that, but I kept my worries to myself.

The Alamo had some pretensions to grandeur, with crystal chandeliers, brocade wallpaper, Turkish carpets, and mostly matching furniture. When I arrived, it was early, and only a few tables were occupied, but that would change rapidly as the evening wore on. I said hello to the bartender, told him where my table would be, and made arrangements for one of the girls to be aware and bring drinks when I signaled. Keeping customers well supplied with alcohol was a priority.

Texas Jack Vermilion and Turkey Creek Jack Johnson were two of the first to sit down with me tonight, and I was glad to see both of them. They were flamboyant characters to be sure, but good-hearted ones. I hadn't seen either of them since we'd arrived.

"Kate, sweetheart, it's good to see you back in town," said Texas Jack. "How'd that side heal up?" His long mustache and large hat gave him a clownish look, and the man favored striped pants on top of that, but many a fellow had made the mistake of underestimating how quickly Jack could draw a pistol if threatened. He'd been a good friend to me when I first came to Dodge, and still was.

"Good enough to take your money and run, Jack." I pointed to the chair beside me and shuffled the cards.

He kissed me on the cheek and sat down. "I've missed your singing, girl, and I've missed your sass." He took off the ridiculous hat and placed it on the table, where it was promptly shoved aside by Turkey Creek, who gave me another kiss and plopped down on my other side, his long hair brushing my shoulder. He entwined turkey feathers and leather strings into his braids and was as inordinately proud of his chestnut locks as were many ladies of their own.

"You gonna sing for us tonight, Kate?"

"No, boys. I'm not singing for a while; I'm a serious business-woman now," I said. "Ante up your money, and I'll give you a song of a different stripe."

Before long, the table had filled with a couple of drovers, then Charlie Wright and Bat ambled by and sat in, and I dealt some poker. I guess it was a quiet night in Ford County. I took the drovers' money early on, and they went in search of other dealers. The original four players were no mean hands at the game, and only my skill and a little luck provided me some income for a while.

Players came and went. Around midnight, in came Doc and Wyatt, arm in arm, convivially drunk. The two had become fast friends, unlikely though it was. On top of that, Doc had fixed up Wyatt's teeth, and you'd think he'd given the man the holy grail. Wyatt smiled a lot these days, especially with his pal, Doc. Occasionally I wanted to slap them both, but I'd learned to keep my thoughts to myself. My sometimes uneasy truce with the Earps, especially this one, had been in effect for months.

"Katie, my sweet Hungarian dove," Doc said, planting a kiss on the top of my head as he placed his arms around my shoulders. Wyatt nodded, smiling at me. "What do you say, Earp, should we sit in on my love's game tonight?"

Goddamn you, Holliday, I thought. Just what I needed. You sit in here, and I'll take you down. Turkey Creek and Texas Jack exchanged smiles and looked pointedly at me. There was no mystery about who I was keeping company with these days, and they also knew just who I used to spend my time with, but I knew not a word would ever pass their lips.

"Take a seat and ante up, boys. I could use a new pair of French shoes, and you're just the gentlemen to provide them." I grabbed the whiskey bottle, filled my glass, and while they chuckled, I dealt out the first hand.

"Damn, woman." Doc opened one bleary eye and looked at the table, where I was counting up the profits from last night's game. "Don't you know you're not supposed to fleece your own true love?"

I didn't dignify that remark with a reply . . . I just kept counting the money. I'd had a good night, especially after Doc and Wyatt had come in, and was several hundred dollars richer than I'd been when I sat down at the Alamo last evening. A goodly portion of it came from their drunken pockets.

He propped himself up on an elbow and stared at me. "My dear, have you gone deaf and mute? Or are you simply being rude?"

I stood up, hands on my hips. "Me, rude?"

"Well, if the shoe fits, madam." He was the picture of affronted dignity and even sighed softly as he lay back down.

"Damn your eyes, Holliday! How dare you talk to me that way after crashing my game with your dear friend Wyatt last night? You're goddamn right I took your money, and his, too, and I'll beat you both any time you want to play. Don't you dare do that to me again and then have the audacity to complain to me the morning after. Next time I'll take your hide with it."

He shot up out of bed faster than I could've imagined, his hand at my throat, shoving me back into the curtains at the window. His eyes were bloodshot, burning in his pale face, and for the first time, he frightened me.

"Bitch. We'll see whose hide you think you can take." His fingers tightened, and it was difficult for me to draw a deep breath. Suddenly, my knee seemed to rise of its own volition, jamming itself into his crotch. He fell back against the bed with a strangled cry.

My knees were shaking, and I clenched my hands into fists to stop their trembling. I couldn't remember being this angry in a long time, but perhaps my anger reflected an accumulation of everything I had compromised since I'd returned to Dodge. I'd sacrificed a lot for this man who, in his selfish stupor, had betrayed me.

I leaned over him. "Don't ever do that to me again. Not last night, and sure as hell not right now," I hissed. His eyes flew open. "I taught you a lesson. Be a man and take it, like the Southern gentleman you so profess to be."

I slammed the door so hard I was worried for a second about the hinges, but the door stayed up, and I made my way to the bank. Men could be idiots—even Doc.

The weeks passed by, Dodge City looking and smelling the

worse for it, and Doc's cough got worse as the summer wore
on. I didn't know what to do for him. He was drinking a lot to
compensate for the pain and anxiety it gave him, which led to
our first spat and quite a few more. He could be an ornery
bastard when he was drunk, as more than a few people had
found out to their demise or at least their detriment. I'd taken
to bolting the door of our room some nights just to avoid the
confrontations that erupted, and the next day I'd find him
passed out in his dentistry office down the hall, snoring peacefully in his leather chair. He was usually contrite and apologetic,
and I never asked where he'd been or with whom. It didn't
matter to me. If it wasn't one of our fraternity—Wyatt, Morgan,
Bat, Charlie, Texas Jack, and a few others—it may have been
some whore, but I knew it was a passing whim even so. Doc
was particular, and whores didn't generally come into the equation. Whether Doc was drunk or sober, I was his woman, and
everybody knew it, none more so than him.

While I made an honest living, more or less, Doc was treading in some deep water with a few of his cronies, and the ones
who were designated lawmen turned a blind eye to his
shenanigans. He charmed most of them—with the exception of
Bat Masterson, a pretty straight arrow who knew Doc was a
slippery one. Still, there was nothing he could hang his hat on,
and Bat preferred to be his friend instead of his prosecutor.
Still, he kept a close eye on him.

I don't know why Doc loved to deceive people, but it was
something he thoroughly enjoyed. Maybe it was his way of getting back at society, which he scorned, or perhaps he just got
bored. I'd never met a man as smart as Doc Holliday, and it
wasn't just his classical education, something we shared. He
was brilliant—always the first to pick up on any nuance, to
pronounce judgment and be correct, and to see what others
failed to notice. Even when he was full of whiskey, his senses

were seldom fogged, a phenomenon I'd never seen in anyone else before or since.

His inner demons drove him into dark places that cost him, physically and emotionally, but the man had an iron will. I sensed it from the first night we met, and as our lives together progressed, I knew it for a fact. I also knew I loved him so much I would defend him, protect him, and do anything I could to keep him safe, even though his worst enemy was himself, and that was the devil I battled from time to time. The sure knowledge he would do the same for me was the glue that kept us together. Cynical, intolerant, and duly singed by our brushes with fate, the two of us persevered.

Tensions flared throughout the summer as Wyatt gained a reputation as a lawman not to trifle with. His habit of striking a man on the head with his gun, rather than shooting him, was becoming legendary.

Near the end of July, Doc and I got dressed up and went to see Eddie Foy, headlining at the Theatre Comique. It was a warm night, and the gray-silk dress I'd chosen was quickly dampening as we sat in our seats at the show.

I carried a pretty, enameled Spanish fan Doc had given me, and I needed it in this crush, fluttering it constantly. Foy always drew a big crowd—he loved Dodge, and Dodge in turn loved him. It was very close, not just hot, and the variety showroom seethed with cigar smoke, liquor fumes, perfume, leather, and the close-packed odors of bodies unwashed for too long. I thought about going outside for some fresher air, but I remembered that Wyatt had been out there, obviously on sentry duty for trouble, and I had no desire to run into him.

Doc ordered more drinks and began to deal a game of three-card monte after Bat joined us, even though the show was still going on.

"Holliday, nothing stops you, does it, not even our famous

showman," Bat chuckled, picking up his cards.

Doc raised an eyebrow and smiled. "You don't seem to be troubled by any scruples in that regard, either. Besides, I'm sure the man wouldn't begrudge any of us a hand of cards." He glanced up at the stage, where Foy was dancing and singing his heart out. I was enjoying the show myself, in spite of the heat. "Look at that man, he's just makin' a livin'—like the rest of us."

Making a living Eddie Foy certainly was, and he was also making full use of the small stage. He gave it his all, and I was impressed with his energy and his talent. The man was inspiring. Maybe I should get back into show business myself. I did miss it, no question. I began to relax and took another sip of the very good bourbon.

As I reached for my cards, shots rang out, and I froze, flashing back to the night I was shot at Tom Sherman's, only now I wasn't on the stage. Doc dragged me out of the chair and pushed me down onto the floor, where already Bat and half the patrons in the room were lying on their stomachs. Doc grabbed my hand, and we had begun to crawl our way to the door when the shooting started outside. I stopped, paralyzed. Doc stood up, dropping my hand and peering over heads to the street outside. He reached down and pulled me to my feet.

"Come on, Kate. Wyatt's out there, going after the shooter."

We shoved our way to the door. Doc drew his pistol and joined Wyatt, who was standing in the middle of the street with some other men, all shooting wildly into the darkness at the dim outline of a man on a horse, now on the bridge headed out of town. The rider toppled and the horse careened wildly across the bridge and galloped away.

"You got him, Wyatt!" Charlie Wright yelled, and they all ran towards the bridge, Doc included. My knees were wobbling, and I sat down on one of the chairs that lined the wooden sidewalk outside the Comique. The men were acting like a pack of wild dogs, all of them.

"Here." I looked up. Bat held out a tumbler of whiskey. Well, perhaps not *all* men were dogs in the pack.

"Thanks. Just the man with a glass I wanted to see."

He sat down beside me. "You're just the girl with a glass I'd like to see more often."

He took a sip of his own whiskey and looked at me over the rim. "Just wanted to be sure you knew that, in case you ever grow weary of our charming dentist. After all, I am a reliable man with a steady job, Miss Haroney"—he glanced down the street—"with expanding opportunities on a constant basis."

Bat always made me laugh. "I believe I heard you had prospects, sir. I'll keep that in mind." I lifted my glass to his, and the crystal gave a soft chime as our glasses met.

A week later, poor George Hoy, the erstwhile shooter, died of his wounds, and everyone said Wyatt Earp had killed his first man. I always wondered exactly whose bullet had found its mark that night.

CHAPTER 14

Fall was in the air, along with a lot of dust and the ever-present stink of cow. I rolled out of bed, shut the window we'd opened during the night, and lay back down. Doc had left early, coughing, to greet dental patients already lined up in the hallway outside. I leaned over and breathed in the scent of him on his pillow, pulling it close. That pillow was a sight more comforting than Doc himself these days.

I turned over on my back and stretched out, my arms over my head, staring at the patterned tin ceiling as though it held the secrets of the universe. I sure as hell wished it did, because I could use them. I wasn't sure where my life was going, but I was fairly sure getting out of Dodge City was in my future. Of course, I'd said this to myself once before, and it hadn't exactly worked out, but this time I was determined. Doc's disease was progressing, and it wouldn't get any better unless we went to a place kinder to those with tuberculosis—cleaner air, perhaps drier and higher altitude. I'd been talking with Doc Watson, and he assured me that New Mexico and Arizona were better climates for Doc. From the sound of it, any intelligent human being would consider them better climates than Dodge City, Kansas, which wasn't fit for much except cows, cowboys, and making money from them.

I sat up and stared out the window, seeing the same panorama as usual, the one we fed off like parasites: cowboys, cattle, and dust—coming, milling, and going—just grist in the grinder. I tossed my hair back, poured a glass of whiskey, and lit a cigarillo. "Time for a change, Kate," I said out loud, "way past time for a change." I caught my reflection in the mirror, the smoke curling in lazy patterns around my head, and for the first time in months I really looked at myself.

Long golden hair, messy and falling onto bared shoulders; green eyes pretty but undeniably bloodshot; an angular face with a prominent nose and chin, skin now too puffy and not getting any younger. My appearance was arresting, yes, and with cosmetics very much so, but there was a cost to our lifestyle, and it was a heavy one. But that wasn't what bothered me as I looked at my reflection. It wasn't the obvious; it was what the glass didn't show that worried me. Behind that face and those eyes resided guilt, fear, and the glimmer of hope—hope for a life of promise, a life of intent realized, a life cleansed.

Or at least, I wanted to believe it did. Something beyond this, beyond some of the things both Doc and I had done, even though our intentions had been for the good, mostly. We were people who made the situation work, no matter what we had to do and even if it cost other people their lives; to us, our lives mattered more. That was a hard but true fact we had both accepted. Hell, I'd lived with that for a long time, and so had Doc. It didn't mean we never thought about things like Silas, the Fishers, Doc's family in Atlanta, Emile Dunsany, Ed Bailey, the countless cowboys whose money we easily took, or many others whose names were beginning to pale.

I stared at the reflection and smiled at her. Who was this woman? The eager pupil in the Hapsburgs' schoolroom? The nubile debutante in the emperor's court? Perhaps the eager-to-please daughter or student; or the young wife and mother, cowed by grief? Closer yet, the showgirl, the whore, a poker player, all anxious to show the world defiance fueled by anger and disdain? Hurt me, and I'll hurt you worse. Or, the cynical mistress, elegant companion, and a true gambler, jaded and skeptical enough to show no compassion at all? All of them were me: Kate Fisher, Kate Melvin, Katie Elder, all Mary Katherine Haroney.

I dropped the cigarillo in what was left of the whiskey. I had things to do, and the day wasn't getting any longer. Twenty minutes later, dressed in boots and breeches, I set out for the livery stable, and twenty minutes after that, Dodge City was a smudge on the horizon. I'd discovered a passion, thanks to Doc and his obsessive love of horses. He'd infected me with it, and for the last month I had been working with Bat Masterson and the foreman at his ranch outside Dodge, learning to break and train horses. Every minute I could spare during the day I spent out there. It had been a hard road, working both nights and days, and I was bruised but determined. I'd taken more than one nasty spill, but that only made me more eager to learn.

I wanted to surprise Doc, who had taken a dim view of my horsemanship when we first met, but it was more than that. Although I'd grown up with horses at the court, I'd had little opportunity to ride for pleasure in the years since. This was different, because in working with wild and green-broke horses, I found an affinity with these animals that I'd never really had with most people. Talking to them, soothing their fears, and gentling them firmly to my will woke a feeling deep inside me, one I'd kept buried for a long time. I could help them and make their lives better, and they believed in me with a simplicity and lack of judgment that human beings never had. I was working now with an Arabian mare named Rula and was in the last stages of negotiation with Bat to buy her for myself.

I rode through the wooden gates and down the dusty track to the corrals north of the ranch house, tying up my livery horse on the rails. George Adams, Bat's foreman, joined me, and we watched Rula and two other horses as they ran around the large corral George used to break horses. Originally from England, George had worked with horses since he was a boy. His hair was graying now, but his lean, tanned face and blue eyes were as sharp as a 30-year-old's. I'd learned more about horses from him in a month than most people ever knew in a lifetime.

He grinned at me. "She's a beauty, Kate."

"You think Bat's ready to sell her to me?"

He shrugged. "It's hard to tell with him—you know that. You got a natural touch, girl. Let's see how you do with her today and not worry ourselves about buying and selling, OK?"

I patted his arm. "Deal."

He handed me the hackamore bit and reins. "Put it on her."

Hackamores utilized a nose bit, unlike the harsh metal bits that fit into a horse's mouth, and a lot of horses couldn't be broken with one. For Rula, though, I'd insisted. Arabians were sensitive and high-strung, and I wanted nothing to break this horse's spirit. I hoped the pressure of the bit across her nose would be enough. I knew that even with hackamores, the horse could feel a lot of pain across her nose and face, but I knew some force would be needed. I'd been working with Rula for some time and had even slid onto her back once, before she let me know firmly she wasn't ready for that. I'd slid off before she could take matters further, and we'd made friends again. Now she was cautiously walking nearer to the fence, not taking her eyes off me.

I climbed over the fence slowly and approached her, the bit held behind my back, as she shied away. I stopped and waited, and she edged back, huffing gently. I placed my hand on her neck and softly stroked the coarse, cream-colored hair. From my pocket I fished out a small apple and held it in the palm of my hand. She took it gently, crunching and watching me as she ate.

"Pretty, pretty girl. You know I love you," I whispered in her ear. "Gentle, gentle now, stay with me." I kept repeating the words as we moved here and there, and finally I dropped the hackamore over her head and onto her nose, the reins dangling as she danced away, fixing me with a betrayed stare. I waited for her to show her displeasure and ignored George's quiet chuckling as he leaned against the corral fence. The fine dust from the corral, stirred by our movements, covered my clothing and invaded my nose, but I knew I couldn't sneeze or rub my nose or eyes, though I was blinking somewhat frantically. Any noise from me except gentle words would spook Rula, perhaps beyond recovery for today.

She tiptoed back to me, hooves puffing in the dust, and our eyes met. I reached out my hand so she could sniff it. Then I smoothed it over her nose and the hackamore. She stilled, and I took the reins in my other hand. Before I could think more about it, I vaulted onto her back, clutching her long mane in one hand and the reins in the other.

I tucked my legs around her belly, and she shot across the corral, both of us ignoring George's shouts. She bucked, she shied, and she ran—while I held on. After what seemed hours but wasn't, Rula stilled. I leaned over her neck and whispered in her ear.

"You and me, girl. That's all we got, just you and me." She was trembling, and so was I. I waited a minute or so and began to pull gently on the right rein. For a second, nothing happened. Then she turned, her eye rolling, but her stance giving me permission. I pulled on the left, and she turned—reluctant, but she turned. We walked over to the fence.

"Hello, George."

He took off his hat and bowed his head, no grin this time. "Ladies, good afternoon."

I nodded, turned Rula, and walked away. This joy was entirely mine and Rula's, although she might not see it quite the way I did. She stopped when I gave a gentle tug, and I slid off her back. I took off the hackamore, and she turned to look at me before bounding away to the other side of the corral. Next time it would go even easier; I had no doubt.

Bat was sitting on the porch, a glass in his hand. He was casual today: no derby hat, hair mussed by the breeze, shirtsleeves rolled up, wearing old boots. A second frosty glass of iced tea was on the tray beside him. I plopped down on a chair beside his and grabbed the tea, drinking half of it straight down. He laughed.

"Hard day?"

I smiled. "Good day, too."

"I know. I saw you." He sipped his tea. "You do have a way about you, Kate. Cards, horses, men. For a little thing, you make your mark."

"I'll take that as a compliment, Mr. Masterson. You going to give me a fair price on that mare?"

"You get right to the point, don't you?"

I stared at him over the rim of my glass. Bat was a very handsome man, in the prime of his life. From his brocade waistcoats to his polished boots, he was apparently unmarked by the violence of his livelihood. The exception was his eyes, and those he kept hooded a great deal of the time. Today, they weren't.

"I do, and I want that horse. I've gentled her, worked with her, and today I rode her with a hackamore bit." I smiled in spite of myself, thinking back on the experience. "She's my horse; I'm her rider. So we might as well make it legal."

He laughed again, heartily, and shook his head. "Girl, what am I going to do with you? I guess I don't have a choice, do I? You'd probably take that beauty right out of my corral some night, and who could ride her back?"

His hand covered mine, lightly. "I guess the only thing we need to figure out is what she's going to cost you." He turned my hand over, and his fingers traced the lines on my palm.

I resisted the urge to snatch my hand away. I knew very well what Bat wanted for that horse, but what he wanted and what I was prepared to give him were two very different things, even though he didn't think so. Men were tiresome, always thinking with something besides their brains when it came to women—at least I had found that to be consistently true. For now, Doc was my man, and while I was no blushing debutante, neither was I unfaithful once declared. At least Bat was acting like a gentleman so far, and I wanted it to stay that way. I stood up, gently disengaging my hand from his, smiling all the while.

"I guess we will," I said. "Right now, I need to get back to Dodge and clean up. Are you coming into town tonight? Perhaps we could discuss it further then?"

He walked beside me down the steps and out toward the corral. "I think that's a capital idea, Kate. I'll see you at the Alamo. If our streets are calm tonight, most likely around ten."

He waved as I rode off. I waved back, but my eyes were on Rula, trotting around the corral as though she wanted to come with me. *Soon you will, my beauty,* I thought. *Soon you will.*

"Fifty-dollar buy-in, five-card stud, no limits."

I was tired of dithering tonight. The drover looked at me incredulously and drifted off, the three men around the table watching a little wistfully as he left.

"Jesus, Kate, you'll scare all of them off," Turkey Creek said, downing his whiskey.

I pulled my bodice down a little further and grinned. "No worries, boys, there's fresh meat coming in the door, and it looks ready for a roast."

There was, too. Right off the trail and just out of the bathhouse, a crowd of cowboys came into the Alamo, their hair still wet and slicked back, smelling a lot better than they had an hour before. They stared wide-eyed at the red velvet wallpaper and the chandeliers and drifted through the room, uneasy but wanting to feel accustomed. Two months on the trail, eating dirt and beans, was a long time.

Morgan Earp, always a jolly one, poured Turkey Creek another shot. "Here they come, just like Kate said, Turkey, so shut up and laugh like it's Christmas mornin'. They picked up their pay this afternoon." He grinned at me, and I dealt a hand while the new arrivals stood and watched, not sure what game they wanted to try. I'd give them a show, and maybe even Morgan would go home with his pockets full. I liked Morgan. He wasn't near as hardbacked as his brothers, and he made me laugh.

Doc was dealing faro at a table across the room and doing well if the occasional shouts of consternation were to be believed. None of them, of course, came from him. We had a bit of a competition, my man and I, and tonight I wanted to win it just out of orneriness if nothing else.

By midnight, Morgan, Turkey Creek, and Josh Barriman were doing well, and I was doing even better. Doc had stopped by for a quick look and a kiss, coughing up a fit.

His face was paler than usual, and his eyes bright with fever. Telling him to go home and get in bed was tantamount to pouring whiskey down his throat; I'd learned that the hard way. I caught Morg's eye as Doc weaved his way back across the room. Morg shook his head and shrugged. He knew Doc pretty well, too.

"Evening, my dear."

Bat Masterson pulled out a chair and sat down beside me. He sported a dark-green waistcoat, derby hat, cigar, and a grin, as usual, looking as though he'd just stepped out of some fancy Chicago hotel instead of locking up drunk cowboys.

I smiled as Turkey Creek said, "Fifty-buck buy-in, Bat. She's not messing around tonight."

His eyes on mine, Bat nodded. "Hell, boys, I knew that. Kate never does."

He knew more than that. There was a horse on the table—along with my questionable morality—and Bat and I were the only two people who knew it.

"Ante up, boys," I said, and so they did.

By two in the morning, with three passed-out cowboys in their chairs, there were only four players left—Morg, Turkey Creek, Bat, and me. As the pot grew, Morg and Turkey Creek folded until there were only two. Doc had closed his table and was standing behind me, coughing but alert as only he could be.

"I raise." Bat threw Rula's papers on the table and didn't even look at me.

"Call," I said, without throwing in a nickel. We both knew what my bet was.

He had a full house, kings over eights. He smiled in anticipation. I laid down my straight flush, queen high, and stared at him as my fingers spread the cards.

"I'll pick her up tomorrow afternoon," I said and kissed Bat on the lips, lingering until I heard Doc growl behind me. "Around four good for you?"

"It's such a comfort for me to know your chastity is not in danger, my dear," Doc drawled, pulling off his tie. He placed it carefully on the table and set about unbuttoning his waistcoat, one gold disc at a time. I took off my shoes and stockings and waited, sitting on the edge of the bed.

"Not, of course, that you have been chaste since . . . well . . . somewhere in your very dim past, but it's a figure of speech," he said. "Perhaps we should say your reputation?"

I took off my earrings and pulled the pins from my hair, not responding. Perhaps it would stop here. Likely not.

He stood up, pulling his shirt out of his pants. "I beg your pardon again, darlin'. Your reputation is beyond redemption. How remiss of me."

Oh, he was picking up a head of steam now, and I knew better than to say a word. My head was pounding, and all I wanted was to lie down on the pillow behind me, but self-preservation kept me upright. I began to unlace my stays, but when my head bounced off the headboard from his blow, I knew it was going to be one of those nights.

"You gutless little cracker," I said. Dizzy, I rolled across the bed anyway and punched him in the stomach with everything I had. It was enough to knock him over, and Doc landed on the floor, clutching his midsection.

It didn't take him long to get up, unfortunately, and he was mad with the desire to retaliate, grabbing my hair as I lunged for the door of our room. I flailed at him to no avail, but enough so that both of us landed on the floor he'd so recently vacated.

His face was inches from mine, his hands tangled in my hair as he banged my head against the floorboards. His eyes were bloodshot, his breath was redolent of whiskey, and he spat the words at me.

"Whore! Take your horse and ride back to Masterson where you belong."

Spangles of light clouded my vision, and my arms felt like lead. Somehow I managed to lift my hand to his throat.

"Let me go, or I'll kill you this time, Doc." His eyes widened in surprise as my fingers dug in, and he choked. "I swear to God I will."

He relaxed his hold, and as he did, I let go and rolled away. A mistake. The tubercular bastard was quick as a snake and not as drunk as I'd thought. Before I could get to my feet he kicked me hard in the back, and I screamed with the pain of it.

"Kill me, will you? I think not, madam," he snarled, giving me another kick. Somehow I scrambled to my knees and took shelter behind the marble-topped table in the sitting area. He strode towards me and knocked the table over while I scuttled behind a wing chair. He was laughing now and fumbling at his waistcoat, where he kept his knife. He'd never done that before, and for the first time I was truly frightened. When the pounding on the door began I was thankful that someone might intervene, because it had never been this bad.

Doc ignored the banging and grabbed me, pulling me to my feet. "Time to pay for your many sins, my dear." The same knife he'd stabbed Ed Bailey with glittered in the gaslight, and Doc's eyes were mad. Terrified, I screamed again, and the door crashed open. Wyatt Earp barreled through and grabbed Doc's shoulder.

"Not tonight, Doc."

Wyatt spun Doc around and instead of clubbing him on the head in his usual style, he punched him in the jaw and dropped an unconscious Doc onto the bed in one graceful move.

He picked up the knife where it had fallen to the floor and put it in his pocket, then turned around and held out his hand to me.

"Kate."

I took his hand, and he pulled me to him, holding me close. I could smell him, that indefinable Wyatt smell—leather, smoke, and bay rum—and for a long moment neither of us moved. I gently pulled back, and Wyatt put his hands on my shoulders, as though reluctant to let me go, and we truly looked at each other for the first time in a long while.

"This isn't the first time, is it?"

I leaned my head on his shoulder. "Hell, no. This is Doc Holliday we're talking about, Wyatt. Your friend and my love. Drawing his knife on me is a first, though."

"It's going to be the last, too." He kissed the top of my head, and we stood there for what seemed like hours until I gently pulled away.

"I don't need a white knight."

Wyatt blinked like a man waking from a dream. He glanced over at Doc, unconscious on the bed, and then back at me. I must've looked like a harridan from hell, but that wasn't what I saw reflected in his eyes. What I saw there was regret, and maybe I felt just a tinge of that as well.

"Well, Kate, maybe you don't," he said. "But you got one, anyway."

I watched the plains roll by as the train carried us towards Las Vegas, New Mexico, a new start and a place where Doc might heal. They said it was a good place for lungers, but I knew Doc needed to be away from the dust of a cow town, not only for the good of his lungs, but to escape the damnable life we'd been leading before one or both of us got killed. At the rate we'd been going, it could even be one of us who was responsible. God help me, I loved this man, and he loved me, but between the two of us, our tempers were a contention. I knew Wyatt had talked to Doc, not just about that, but about Wyatt's concerns that Dodge City was not a good place to live and where better opportunities might exist. I chose Las Vegas, hoping it might be a haven to heal us both. I didn't care where the Earp faction might be headed in the months to come, but I'd be just as happy if they stayed far from us.

Doc was asleep, head cradled by the red plush seat behind his neck. I leaned my head back, too. The seats were comfortable, just like the Atcheson, Topeka, and Santa Fe Railroad said they were. I closed my eyes, but I knew the bad dreams of gunshots and quick death wouldn't be held at bay for long.

CHAPTER 15

Las Vegas, New Mexico, February 1879

I opened my eyes, but it was just as dark as when they'd been closed, which was a little disconcerting. I lifted my hand and wiggled my fingers, but I saw nothing in the inky blackness. I felt like a blind thing struggling towards the light of redemption. Doc's breath, labored, stirred my hair against the pillow. I smoothed his hair from his forehead and let my hand fall gently back to my side. Morning came late in Las Vegas in winter.

The constant drip of the icicles outside our window woke me again, and I opened my eyes in the gray light that signaled morning. Doc was sitting at the table across the room, pouring coffee from a silver pot. As he saw me lift my head, he poured a second cup into the sturdy mug on the tray. The air was warming from the fire crackling in the stone fireplace.

"Morning, darlin'."

I pushed back the quilt. "And to you, my dear. You're up early today. Feeling better?"

"Measurably." He coughed, but it ended fairly quickly, and he took a sip of coffee and smiled. " 'Course, that's a relative thing lately. Meanin' they should put down the shovels, because I've outfoxed the reaper for another day. To be completely honest, though, I do feel some better today."

I sat down beside him, cradling the coffee mug in one hand and clasping his in the other. I took a sip and felt the warmth glide down inside my chest.

"I'm glad, Doc," I said. "It's been a rough few days, and this time I was really worried."

"Hadn't been for your lovin' ministrations, Kate, I might not be havin' coffee right now."

He put down his cup, reached over and gently put down mine, and gathered me into his arms.

"You are my balm of Gilead, my dear, she who keeps me whole through the thorny trials of life." He kissed my temple and looked down on me. "I swear I don't know how you put up with me, but I'm damned glad you do."

My arms crept around him, loving the familiar warmth of his thin frame. Sometimes I didn't know why I stayed with him either, but all I knew was that this half-crazy, dangerous man was my destiny, and he was my other half that made me complete. He didn't have the boyish wonder of Silas, the handsome glamour of Jack, nor the compelling fierceness of Wyatt, but Doc had infected me with real magic—his crooked grin, quick wit, and Southern charm, and besides, who else of my acquaintance could converse with me in French, discuss Aristotle, debate the merits of Shakespeare, or make love to me as though it were an apocalyptic event? Nothing in this life or the next was likely to match that.

Las Vegas hadn't been especially kind to us. We had come overland on the stage from Trinidad, which was as far as the railroad had been laid. After that, the bone-jarring stagecoach ride on stony mountain roads fair rattled my teeth out of my head. The town was quaint, as frontier towns went, trying hard to make a life for itself. Many Spanish families had settled here, with extensive ranches around the area, and the charming adobe and brick buildings were laid out in a pleasing landscape. There was a hotel, a boardinghouse or two, quite a few stores, a livery, a few saloons, a church, and even a bank, along with a populace determined to make it a destination. That wasn't what we'd come for, though. We'd come for the climate, or so we'd been advised. Las Vegas was high and dry, with clean, crisp air—the ideal spot for anyone with tuberculosis. It was a place of healing, promise, and benediction. So they said, and so it was for the first month or two.

We'd found a cozy cabin near town and had settled in, fixing it up with furniture and supplies. The late autumn was beautiful, the aspens golden in the sunlight. We loved sitting out on the porch, watching the sunset and breathing the air that tasted of pine and hopefulness. Doc was better after we'd been there just two weeks. His eyes were clear, and and he was taking a full breath for the first time in many weeks, the taint of Dodge City working its way out of his system. We'd brought Rula and Doc's horse, Hercules, on our journey, and every afternoon we rode out, coming home to our cabin and settling the horses in their stable beside it.

Then, just before Thanksgiving, winter hit, and it was the winter of nightmares. I'd never lived at high altitude before, nor known the kind of snow that could come with it. At first the locals said it was just a storm or two and would pass, like it always did. But the blizzards just kept coming, and Christmas became a frozen concept that nobody could get out to celebrate. We were lucky to just have enough food and firewood to keep going. It was the worst winter anyone in Las Vegas could remember, even the old Navajo women who shook their heads and spit their tobacco juice into the snowbanks.

Although doing better at first, Doc grew worse as the weather fell upon us with all its fury. For the last month, caring for him had been up to me. The doctor in Las Vegas was little better than a novice at his trade and certainly not up to the task of dealing with Doc and his illness. I'd brewed tea, made tisanes, applied chest poultices, but finally resorted to Indian herbs and remedies offered by the squaws in town—most of which turned out to be the best medicine we'd found yet for lung ailments. I had no prejudices about the native people, knowing full well that the people who lived in a geographic area, whether it was the Walesians, the Viennese, or the Navajo, knew what they were about when it came to treating the illnesses of their own areas, including the city people who came to them for a cure. The Indians of the American Southwest were no different, and they became the practitioners of healing I could rely on, rather than some ill-trained idiot from Massachusetts who didn't know the difference between tuberculosis and a chest cold.

Two weeks ago I thought Doc had breathed his last, but after taking the local herbs and tea I'd brewed, he pulled through. This morning, for the first time since, he was out of bed and looking as though he'd live.

After finishing my first cup of coffee, I was awake enough to really register the drips outside our window. I pulled back the curtains and hauled up the window frame. The air was still cold, but not freezing, and the ice that had covered everything for weeks was gone, while the sun warmed the frozen landscape. A couple of kids wandered down the road in front of our cabin, a dog following them, the snow slushy in their footsteps.

"Doc."

He joined me at the window, his arm snaking around my waist and his mustache tickling my neck as he kissed me.

"Darlin', it looks like we're in for a thaw. A life-savin' one at that."

"Since you're feeling so well," I said, sliding my hands under his bathrobe and onto his bare chest, "maybe some mild exercise couldn't hurt. You need to make sure your muscles don't atrophy with all this snow and altitude. Keep the blood pumping, so to speak."

He kissed me, the taste of coffee and desire on his tongue,

and so it was we missed the brief February thaw.

Real spring was a long time coming to Las Vegas. Blizzards came back, and once they stopped, the entire town was awash with floods and mud instead of daffodils and new hope. I'd never seen anything like this and apparently neither had the long-term residents of the town. I trudged, slipped, and fell on my way into town and the general store, arriving home muddied and angry, clutching the sacks full of groceries I'd managed to glean from Mr. Toravason.

Doc's cough returned in full glory—without the fevers and sweats, but still he wasn't doing as well as I hoped. From what I had learned from the Indian women, dry and clean air was a good thing, but the altitude itself was not, especially for someone who was gasping for oxygen. Every time the women came by and heard Doc cough, they kept pointing downward and shaking their heads. It made sense from not only a native perspective, but from scientific and common knowledge. There was simply less oxygen at altitude. Why did doctors think this was a good thing for tubercular patients? I was starting to think doctors didn't know shit from snake oil.

On top of that, our stake was getting low. We hadn't been able to ply our trades in Las Vegas since we'd arrived, between Doc's illness and the godforsaken weather. True, spring was in the air, but it was bringing the need for serious change along with warmer temperatures. If we didn't do something fast, we'd be stuck penniless in this town on top of the world with no way to get out of it.

Bat's telegram was the incentive we both needed. It seemed there was a railroad war going on, and Bat needed all the best gun hands he could find, with the promise of hefty remuneration if the right side won—the right side being Bat's, of course. I didn't pay much attention at first, but Doc was all afire. Within two days, I was kissing him good-bye as he boarded the stage for Trinidad. He was still frail, but the color in his cheeks was the good kind, and I hoped that his longing for action would heal him more than sipping tea and gambling ever could. There was no stopping him anyway, once he had the bit in his teeth, and if I hadn't learned that fact in loving Doc, I never would have lasted this long with him.

"I'll be back in no time, sugar. With Bat in charge of this thing, we'll take them down fast."

He didn't care who was fighting whom, and, frankly, neither did I at that point. He was right; Bat would most likely figure the right side of it all, and, as little as the two of them liked each other, they were and always would be comrades in arms who had a history and trust that transcended all other issues. That was the way of things on the frontier, I'd come to learn. There were a lot of people out here, but few who had honor, were trustworthy, and knew how to stand up for themselves amid a sometimes wavering sense of justice. They all knew each other and called on each other when needed. I had no doubt Wyatt and his brothers were involved as well, and I had no worries about that either. Those were men I could trust to make sure Doc came back to me, and there were none better to have his back, as he'd done for them before.

I kissed him soundly and clung to him for only a brief moment, sensing his urgency to board the stage and leave this winter of pain and weakness behind him.

"I love you, Doc. Don't do anything too rash."

He gazed down at me, sandy hair falling on his forehead, blue eyes bright, and mouth in the sardonic twist I knew well.

"Kate darlin', I'll be back with you before you know it. Set Las Vegas on its ear while I'm gone, and we'll take it over when I get back. Guaranteed."

Charlie Ross pulled out a chair at my table and sat down with a satisfied sigh, coffee in hand. He watched as I licked powdered sugar from my fingertips, and we both laughed.

"I can't resist," I said. "Those are the best beignets I've had since New Orleans."

Charlie's eyebrows rose, and I laughed again. "Well, all right, maybe the *only* beignets I've had since New Orleans, but they're damn good."

"I know it," he said, but this time his sigh wasn't satisfied. "Trouble is, that's pretty much all Andre will cook—pastries and bread. Not that they aren't good, but on top of that, he doesn't understand much English. Since Anna left, I've been spending nearly all my time in the kitchen, and I can't keep doing that and run this whole place, too."

Charlie's Plaza House, a restaurant and small hotel in the heart of Las Vegas, was a gem. I had rented one of those six rooms, moving into town when Doc left. The food was wonderful, the rooms tasteful and clean, and the hotel was close to Downey's saloon, where I was dealing in the evenings. Life in Las Vegas was calm and, for the moment, secure, and I found myself actually enjoying being on my own. Much as I loved Doc, last winter wasn't one I wanted to repeat.

I put down my napkin and had started to rise when a hand on my shoulder pushed me back down into my chair. Startled, I bit back my angry question when I saw the badge of Sheriff Johnson six inches from my nose.

"Kate Haroney?"

"Yes."

He threw some papers on the table. Charlie was frozen where he sat, hand on his coffee cup. I raised my eyes to the sheriff's glare. "Technically, you're under arrest for violating the gambling laws of Las Vegas. There's a twenty-five-dollar fine, and if you can't pay it, I'm going to have to take you across the street."

I opened my mouth to protest, and he slammed his meaty palm down on the papers. "No sense in lying. We've got witnesses, and we don't want any trouble around here with your kind."

Anger sizzled in my veins, and I wanted nothing more than to slap his face. Doc had warned me that Las Vegas, like many towns in the West, had an ordinance against gambling, but no one took it seriously, as card games went on all the time in the back rooms of all the saloons in town. I guess somebody had lost too much money or didn't like the way I dealt and took it upon themselves to make sure I wasn't able to do it anymore. I took a deep breath.

"Sheriff. I assure you I was unaware I was in violation of any law and am most deeply regretful that I have broken one in my ignorance. When and where can I pay this fine? Would right now do?"

Sheriff Johnson stepped back and, thankfully, took his hand off my shoulder, as I don't think I could have stood it a moment more. Charlie was clearly enjoying this by now and took a sip of coffee, his smile mostly covered by the rim of the cup. I shot him a glance, and he winked.

The sheriff conceded that now would be fine.

I dug into my reticule and laid the money down on top of the papers on the table. He snatched it up like it was gold dust, stuffing the money and the papers into his pocket, and turned to go.

"Sheriff."

He glanced back at me, clearly surprised I had anything to say.

"Do I get a receipt?"

He frowned and looked at Charlie. "He'll do. He's a witness, right, Ross?"

Charlie nodded solemnly, and Johnson turned on his heel, slamming the door behind him.

I picked up the last beignet. I took a bite, and the powdered sugar exploded on my tongue. At least one thing was still good about the morning. We sat in silence for a time.

"Apparently I've lost my job," I said, chewing reflectively on my beignet.

Charlie took another sip of his coffee, eyeing me over the rim of his large cup. "Can you cook, Kate?"

"Well, you know, Charlie, yes, I can. I've never done it for more than ten people or so, but I think I could manage more."

Charlie laughed and stood up, untied his white apron, and handed it to me. "Well, girl, I think you just got a new job, if you're game. You don't, by any chance, speak French, do you?"

"As a matter of fact, I do." I smiled, and I knew Charlie wasn't at all surprised. This was a fortunate turn of events for him, all things considered.

"Well, then. Lunch time'll be here soon. Let's see what you can do."

I took off my apron and headed outside for some air. Breakfast at the Plaza, light on eggs, pancakes, and bacon, and heavy on Andre's heavenly beignets and croissants, was over for another day. I'd been head cook, or "chef" according to Andre, for some months now, and I found, much to my surprise, that I loved it and was damned good at it, too. Andre was much more than a baker, and once he had someone to communicate with, we had made the Plaza's restaurant into the best in town, replete with more than pastries. Our coq au vin, beef bourguignon, and Andre's Languedoc stews were legendary, as was my humble chicken fricassee and other recipes from my Iowa days. We spent hours poring over Andre's spattered, old French cookbook and coming up with new dishes nightly for the uninitiated citizens of Las Vegas. There was something wonderful about creating culinary delights that fascinated me, and it made my imagination soar like it hadn't since my time in New Orleans with Jack. Quite a few of the railroad people had sampled our food and had been impressed—even the hard cases from back East.

I woke early this morning in Room Six of the Plaza Hotel and found I was happy, oddly enough. It made me smile, and I was content to rise with the sun and begin my day. I felt good, my head and eyes clear, and I was eager to see what the day would bring; today promised to be quite a day for Las Vegas. The railroad was scheduled to arrive for the first time at two o'clock this afternoon, the fourth of July, 1879.

Las Vegas had discovered late, however, that the Atcheson, Topeka, and the Santa Fe wasn't exactly pulling into the middle of town. It turns out the tracks and depot itself were on the other side of the river, nearly a half mile from the town center.

Last night our staff had set up two huge tents across the river, right beside the depot itself, one for diners and one as a makeshift kitchen. We were roasting a hundred chickens, just as many steaks, and fifty racks of ribs in preparation for this auspicious day. Las Vegas and most of its citizens had been in a frenzy ever since the announcement of the July fourth railroad arrival. I had to admit this was a historic moment, and, even though I knew more than most about the problems railroads could bring, I was excited about it. I knew it wouldn't take long for the other side of the river to become a hotbed of saloons, restaurants, and God knows what else. They built things fast out here.

I had just lit a cigarillo and plopped down on an empty crate when Andre pulled up with the wagon. We had brought wagonload after wagonload of tablecloths, furniture, cutlery, and china—not to mention food—over to the depot this morning.

"Katee, more sauce, *s'il vous plaît*," he said, his long blond hair flying out of the rawhide tie at the base of his neck. Andre was a slender man, so French that I sometimes wondered how he'd managed to survive and get this far west from New Orleans, his first stop after Paris. "We cannot make the sauce over there. Too *primitif.*"

"Andre, sweetheart, we've got plenty of time. Don't fret," I said. He stopped only when I firmly put my hand on his arm.

"*Ma chère,* it's only eleven o'clock. I have two huge buckets of barbecue sauce ready for you. Those chickens and my sauce will be stone cold by two o'clock if you don't slow down. Here, have a smoke."

He sighed and took the cigarillo I held out.

"*Oui, oui,*" he said. He sat down beside me, blowing out smoke, shooting me his sweet smile, and relaxing for the first time today. He was just a kid, maybe twenty-two, and I knew he wouldn't be around for long, especially after the railroad came. Someone with his talent in the kitchen was destined for San Francisco, or even New York, even though he didn't know it. Andre's passion was food, and that passion would lead him to much bigger venues than Las Vegas, New Mexico, and my rudimentary assistance with American-style dishes. In a way I envied him, because Andre had a path, and I knew that as surely as I knew I had none.

Cooking had given me back a dimension of myself I wasn't entirely comfortable with, bringing back memories of the Smiths, but in spite of the satisfaction, I knew it wasn't something I'd want to do forever. I smiled at Andre and patted his shoulder. We were good for each other, and both of us had learned a great deal.

"I'll get the sauce. You stay here," I said, my voice firm, and he nodded. "I'll handle whatever else you need, as well as the desserts, just like we planned. Send Manuel and Jimmy for them around one. We need you to stay focused and calm."

He nodded again, only understanding half my words, but fully grasping my intent. Most of the time we didn't speak French because he was working diligently on his English, and, except for recipes, I did my utmost to ensure he'd learn it. Trial by fire was the surest teacher, I'd found.

I headed back into the kitchen, where things were under control. The girls were making salads, biscuits, and beans. This was no day for French specialties, but western fare and only the most expected and delectable. Cat-head biscuits and barbecued beans went with everything, and that was what our esteemed guests wanted with barbecue—along with strawberry shortcake made with berries I'd gotten from Mexico. I headed towards the dining room, empty now of diners and half the furniture gone.

"Wipe those glasses. I see spots!" Charlie yelled at the hapless young waiter who was closest. "We can't have spots, for God's sake. Not today!"

I put my hand on his shoulder, as I had with Andre. "Charlie, nobody's going to see them until tomorrow, anyway."

His head whipped around, and he stopped short. "Kate, it's a nightmare. They're going to think we're a bunch of hicks."

I laughed. "Charlie, we *are* a bunch of hicks, if you compare us to New York and Chicago. Darling, that's just what they're expecting. Our food, on the other hand, will be fabulous, as will the presentation. Everything's going well over at the depot. Maybe it's time you headed over there, just to ease your mind. Take Andre with you, and I'll be along."

He visibly relaxed, his shoulder easing under my hand, and turned to me, his face expectant. "You think so, really?"

"Really." I nodded at the waiters and drew Charlie with me to the bar. "It'll be fine. You hired me to run the kitchen, as well as the dining room. Trust me. Have I ever let you down?"

I poured him a stiff whiskey and watched as he swallowed it, relaxing even more.

"No, Kate, you haven't." He looked at me, and he seemed to believe it. I poured myself one, too, and felt the better for it.

"All right, then. Go on over there."

Charlie slid off the barstool and walked towards the door, his portly frame outlined in the bright sunlight pouring through the windows. He turned back to me as he reached the doorframe, grinning, and I smiled back. It was going to be a red-letter day for Las Vegas, and I was going to make sure it was one for the Plaza Hotel as well.

I rode Rula over the bridge after I'd sent the last wagon of food away. It looked like the Second Coming here, with people lined up six deep around the depot. I couldn't imagine where they'd all come from. Cowboys, ranchers and their wives, gamblers, bar girls, railroad men, townfolk, Indians, and some I couldn't categorize—all were waiting for the train to arrive, with children running around them like small dogs herding cattle. Red, white, and blue bunting decorated the depot itself; a brass band of uncertain origin had materialized in the last half hour, playing alongside the mayor of Las Vegas and prominent citizens seated on a makeshift dais that had been erected seemingly overnight. People with parasols, hats, frilly dresses, and dust-free suits dug out of closets vied for a position as close as they could get to the tracks.

I tied up Rula behind the tents and tugged the strings of my apron-front tighter. I knew my worth was behind the scenes, at least until the festivities were over and everyone turned to the food and drink they were anticipating nearly as much as the train.

The magic hour approached, and, right on time, the rumble of the train itself was felt on the tracks, guided by those intrepid spirits who galloped in on horseback shouting its imminent arrival. Heads bobbed up and down with excitement, ladies' parasols dipping and gentlemen's hats in eager hands, ready to be thrown in celebration.

When the train pulled into the depot, the crowd exploded, trumpets blaring, hats flung to the wind, cheers heard and echoed from the mountaintops all around. Las Vegas was on the road to progress. Passengers and railroad executives stepped off and joined the crowd.

The mayor's speech flowed over the dignitaries from the railroad as they paid obeisance to his words, and within moments of the last toot from the brass band, hordes of people made their way into the large tents of the Plaza Hotel. We were more than ready for the onslaught.

Our alfresco setup was quite charming: carpets laid over the ground, tablecloths fresh and white, and the crystal and silver gleaming. Before even the first fork was lifted, I looked at Charlie, and we both grinned. Our Great (impromptu) Railroad Picnic was a success. The champagne corks popped, and the toasts began. From railroad honchos to town fathers, everybody had what they wanted on this day.

The waiters were charming and helpful, and the diners enjoying themselves immensely. We sent some of the boys back to the hotel for more champagne and whiskey and the occasional request, but half an hour in, I knew all was well.

I wandered outside to get Rula and ride back to the hotel. Only a few children played in the dust beside the train, with a few curious adults checking out the engine and the massive wheels of this amazing machine. I inspected it as well, empty now of its crowd of people, its engine still puffing and cooling from the long ride of the day. There were at least ten passenger cars idling on the track, and, as I watched, a man, black suit elegant on his slender frame, stepped carefully down from the third car. This man was never in an ungentlemanly hurry. His

long fingers pushed his hat back from his brow, and he stopped
on the last step down from the train, his angular face curved
into a smile.

"Darlin'. You didn't think I'd miss this for the world, did
you?"

Apron flapping, I ran to Doc like he was the best thing I'd
seen in months, because he was. He laughed as I collided with
him, and his arms hugged me so tight I thought I'd stop breathing. I kissed him all over his face until his lips found mine, and
that lasted some time. He finally pulled back and looked at me,
his eyes dancing.

"Like I said, you ready to take on Las Vegas, Kate?"

CHAPTER 16

My room at the Plaza Hotel was now next door to Dr. Holliday's Dental Clinic, and the dental business was brisk, even with the hours the good doctor spent supervising the construction of his new saloon on Center Street, across the river. My bed was now occupied by the same doctor, and we got reacquainted on those pink flowered sheets that had once been the province of my lone feminine repose. Perhaps it was time to speak to the chambermaid about a change of style in the linens.

I still worked at the Plaza, although once Holliday's Saloon officially opened, I'd be leaving to take over there. We weren't going to serve food, of course, with Julius Graaf's Restaurant and City Bakery next door, but a firm hand on the decor and liquor were right up my alley, and Doc had ceded this to me.

New Town, as the area near the railroad depot had been christened, was chaos. Buildings were springing up practically overnight, and the most profitable job in Las Vegas for now and some time to come was construction. The sounds of hammering and sawing filled the air day and night.

Many of our old associates from Dodge and points east had arrived with the railroad's six trains daily, some welcome and some not so much. Among them was Hoodoo Brown, who was all right and had managed to get himself appointed temporary marshal of New Town—frankly, a job that was sorely needed. Gunfights, robbery, and assaults were occurring almost nightly, with so many people flooding into the new territory, and Hoodoo was just the man for the job . . . if you didn't look too closely at his resume. Folks in the West rarely did, for the most part, although Doc's reputation had followed him. The dentistry practice was helping, though. People in pain didn't care who helped them out, we found. Doc's skills, paired with his natural charm and elegance, meant things had gone smoothly, indeed. As for me, I'd kept a low profile since I started working with Charlie, and I knew a thing or two about charm and elegance myself.

"Seventeen feet. Seventeen fuckin' feet!" Doc spread his hands in front of him, looking at the men swarming over the frame construction in front of us. "I hope the sign will fit."

He looked at me and grinned, and for a minute he looked like a mischievous ten year old. "My name isn't the longest, but it surely is one people will remember."

"Oh, they will," I said, slipping my arm around his scarlet waistcoat. "Holliday's Saloon will be the most illustrious establishment in New Town."

I didn't add, "Well, for New Town, Las Vegas." We both knew that went without mentioning. Still, it was the first time Doc had something to call his own, apart from a dentistry shingle, and it was something he wanted more than anything. This crude saloon in the middle of nowhere, really, was our future and helped make up for mislaid plans of our pasts. Doc had invested everything he'd made from riding with Bat in the railroad war, and I'd put in my savings from dealing in the spring. It was a fresh start for both of us.

"You think thirty feet will be enough space for you to sing, Kate? I would surely like to hear you sing again, in our own place." He looked down and kissed me softly. "Could you do that for me, for us?"

"I might could," I said, gently mocking his Southern accent, and he smiled. I wasn't sure, but I thought maybe it was time to unlock some of the fear and memories and again do what I liked. This was our time and our place. What could be safer, if not that?

August 12th, 1879, was opening night for Holliday's Saloon, and a highly anticipated event for us and many of our old friends from Dodge City, St. Louis, and new ones from Las Vegas, including Miguel Otrero, whom Doc had met on the train, a son of the most prominent family in town. Only twenty-three, Miguel had taken a strong liking to Doc and was eagerly awaiting our big night. I liked Miguel. He was a nice kid, and we'd spent many an afternoon watching the saloon come into being.

The new space looked very good, with the wooden tables and chairs arranged around the thirty-foot-long room. It had a bar along the back, with a mirror that had arrived from St. Louis on the train just three days ago, and a piano that was carefully positioned along the west wall with, indeed, a small stage for me. The smell of sawdust and fresh pine mingled with the scent of bourbon and the perfumes of the four bar girls, strategically positioned to deliver drinks from the bar.

"Darlin', you look glorious."

Doc's arm slid around my waist and held me close, his lips tracking up and down my neck in a way that nearly led me to entice him into the back room of the saloon, just as I had the night we'd first gotten together so long ago. The man was incorrigible, and we'd found it difficult to get up in the mornings during the saloon construction, not from gambling and drink, but from sheer lust. There must have been something special in the water back there in Georgia, because no one had ever affected me the way Doc did, and he mumbled much the same about Austria to me many a night. Whatever it was, I wanted it to never end. And whatever we'd found with each other in the godforsaken climate of the American West, it was magical and worth holding onto forever. I wasn't much of a believer in the mystical side of things, but every time I kissed Doc Holliday, I knew there was a God.

"Thank you, sir, but magnificent is what you are, Dr. Holliday," I said in return, and it was true. His waistcoat was forest green, embroidered with subtle gold thread in circular designs. His shirt and neckcloth contrasted snowy white against his black silk trousers and high boots, and a gold silk vest with well designed pockets (holding both a pocket watch and a derringer) was the shining touch.

He knew it, too, and he grinned and twirled me around, causing the white and gold taffeta skirts of my dress to flare. The white ostrich feathers and gold braid wound around my upswept hair remained in place, and I laughed and did an extra spin, curtseying before him.

"Oh, sir, may I have this dance?"

He swept me up, and across the floor we went, sans music and privy to bemused looks from our staff as we waltzed around and around.

"Kate, you may have this dance and all the dances we may ever have," he whispered in my ear as we whirled. "You are my love and my muse, darlin'."

An hour later, we were in the thick of it. From town leaders to the lowest scum off the trains, people packed Holliday's Saloon. There was standing room only, with every seat at a gaming table jealously guarded and prospective gamblers standing in line behind the chairs, eager to claim a seat when anyone vacated one. The bar was doing amazing business. Sam Hicks and his helpers poured as fast as they could, with customers lined up three deep.

"Ladies and gentlemen, I give you the Lily of the West," said Doc, his sonorous tones rising above the general din. I stood up beside the piano, Jim McDonald smiling up at me from the keys, fingering the intro to the song we'd practiced the day before. "Aura Lee" was usually the song I'd end a set with, but somehow I thought it should be the song I begin with, and so I did just that.

As the last notes of the song died away, it was quiet in Holliday's Saloon. I looked out at the people gathered there, and once again I saw hard-bitten men blinking back tears and others with introspective looks. As the applause swelled, Jim launched into "Buffalo Gals," and the mood turned back into the boisterous, devil-may-care feeling that had started the evening. I got what I wanted, however. Sometimes people need to be reminded that life is more than just a moment's pleasure, and it cannot be cherished unless you value what was lost. No one knew that better than me. Sometimes those memories need to be awakened so you know how sweet life can be. I saw Doc deal a hand of poker, and those at his table were eagerly watching the cards, nothing more. Moments pass quickly.

"Goddamn, Doc!"

I jerked up in bed at the man's painful yell and the sound of boots hitting the floor, blinked, and just as quickly fell back down in the soft pillows. Dr. Holliday was dealing with patients this Monday morning. Dentistry was not a painless business, even though this dentist had a gentle touch. Most of Doc's practice consisted of pulling teeth that were making life miserable for his patients, and an occasional yell most likely meant that the offending tooth had just been dispatched. Silence followed, usually along with loud sighs of relief, and the gratified patient left with a wad of bloody gauze pressed to his mouth.

I had always been scrupulous about cleaning my teeth, using a little boar-ristle brush when I was very small. And even in the wilds of America, I always found a replacement when I needed it, sometimes making one myself. Since meeting Doc and listening to him talk about dental hygiene and what could happen to your teeth, I'd been even more religious about it—never missing a night or morning brushing. Well, almost never. Fear was a great motivator, as were the moans of his patients.

"Sleepyhead."

Doc sat down on the bed and nudged my hip, making room. He held a cup of coffee in his hand and grinned down at me. "I've already pulled three teeth and given a lecture on the virtues of tooth brushin' to five people."

I wrinkled my nose at the scent of carbolic acid and chlorine that clung to his skin, but I made a swift pass at the cup. He laughed and held it out of reach. "Nope, you have to sit up, at least. I swear, Kate, you sleep more than any woman I've ever known."

I growled and rolled to the other side of the bed. "How many women have you lived with, Holliday? I didn't know you had such extensive experience. My heart is crushed at the thought I'm not the only one."

He stared at the ceiling, lips moving as though counting, and I pounced delicately, placing both hands under the cup, which he relinquished with equal care. That first sip was always a delight, and I sighed with pleasure at the dark, acrid taste I'd come to love as much as the aroma.

"You're the only woman I've ever lived with, besides my mama, Kate," he said. He took the cup from my hands, setting it on the bedside table. Then he untied the ribbons on my night-shift carefully, his hands pushing it off my shoulders and caressing my breasts. "Now that you're awake . . ."

I pulled him down closer, and my fingers fumbled at the buttons on his trousers. "Must be lunch break for the dentist, eh? Allow me to make it worthwhile. You've had a hard morning . . . ah . . . indeed."

This had become our routine, sort of, for the weekdays at

least. No matter how late we stayed at Holliday's Saloon, Doc opened his dental office at nine o'clock sharp and closed at three in the afternoon, after a break around noon for lunch or . . . well, me. It suited us, although I worried the man didn't get enough sleep—only a nap in the afternoon before we headed to the saloon for the night. He assured me he was fine, and his cough and physical condition were much improved from the last winter. I was still dosing him with the remedies I'd learned from my Navajo friends, and he tolerated my ministrations for the most part, only grousing now and then. I knew tuberculosis wasn't considered curable, but had its ups and downs, and for now, it was an up for Doc. He would never stop drinking and smoking, and, unfortunately, I joined him in both those pursuits. But then, I didn't have the disease. If I thought for one minute my not doing either of those things would stop him from doing them, I would have quit, but I knew my man. Doc Holliday did what he wanted to do, everything else be damned, including his own body and soul. I loved him not because we were so different but because we were so much the same—hellbent.

"Goddamnit, Hoodoo, this won't stand." Doc threw the latest papers down on the poker table and stalked off to the bar to pour himself a whiskey, his heels clicking on the wooden floor.

"Kate, talk to him," Hoodoo said, shaking his grizzled head. He pushed his hat back and wiped his forehead with a bandanna. "This is serious. He ignored the first one that stupid sheriff served on him on opening night, and now there's another. There's no telling what that sheriff will get up to next, and I ain't got no legal power to stop him."

I picked up the papers. "The Territory of New Mexico vs. John Holliday, Case Number 990, Keeping a Gaming Table, Second Offense." The same moron who had stopped me from gambling in the spring was now after Doc. Hoodoo Brown was the acting magistrate, but the sheriff outranked him, and even though gambling was going on openly everywhere in Las Vegas, the sheriff could pick and choose whom to prosecute. He didn't like outsiders much, and I knew that only too well. We'd been open two months, and business was booming, but if the proprietor ended up in jail, our fortunes could take a steep downfall. Our fate depended on how hard the sheriff wanted to push. Maybe just paying the fines over and over was the best option, but that might not last forever.

Miguel Otrero was sitting at the bar, talking to Doc. I walked over and sat beside him. He was dressed for a night on the town, like a Spanish hidalgo, as usual, black boots gleaming, with skintight pants and a brocaded short jacket. The ladies loved him.

"Miguel, we have a little problem. The sheriff is going after Doc for gambling. Do you think your father could help?"

The Otrero family was one of the oldest in town, and Miguel's father owned the local bank and half of old Las Vegas. I didn't know how he felt about his son hanging around with us, but it was time to find out. We needed influence.

"Miss Kate, you look lovely this afternoon," Miguel said, his soft, brown eyes warm but stalling nonetheless. "Tell me this trouble."

"I just did, Miguel."

He had the grace to look down and then back up at me, apologetically. "I will see what I can do, but my father is an old-fashioned man, *comprende*?"

Doc set his glass down on the bar with a thump. His hand slid inside the pocket of his vest and rested upon what I knew was the pearl-handled derringer he always kept there. His eyes were unfocused, gazing across the room towards the door. "Forget it, both of you. I fight my own battles. I've found no one else ever does." He twisted around and glared at me.

"Besides, it is the height of bad manners to air one's troubles in public, *comprende*, Katerina?"

"Don't take this out on me," I said, gathering my skirts. "I warned you that the gambling ordinances around here were a shifting mess, and it's public knowledge you've been cited, anyway." I slipped off the barstool. "I'm going to dinner. Join me if you like."

I walked out the door, and he didn't follow, although Miguel did, slipping his arm through mine as we stepped onto the sidewalk.

"I'm sorry, Kate, I shouldn't have hesitated, or at least not voiced my doubts."

I sighed. "It's all right, Miguel. I shouldn't have brought it up, even though you already knew. There's no talking to Doc about it tonight."

We entered the restaurant down the street and ordered steaks and whiskey, both of which made me feel better. We sat at a window table and watched the town ramp up for the night.

"It's not just the gambling citations," I said, taking a bite of apple pie. The pie at Julius Graaf's was wonderful, as was everything else. I did miss having a kitchen to bake my own, which was even better. If we could keep the saloon open without legal interference, hopefully we'd be able to build a house of our own before winter set in.

"Oh?" Miguel raised an eyebrow and took a sip of his whiskey. "You mean the weapons issue?"

"You knew about that, too? Damn, this town is small," I said. "Not that Doc isn't still carrying a gun, and his knife as well. There's little chance he'll give up either one."

Miguel smiled. "Nor should he. A man should have his weapons. That was a stupid charge, and I can't believe they have not dropped it by now. Likely that rancher who tried to shoot him last week got nervous and went to the sheriff again.

Of course, I heard he's not been seen lately, so there shouldn't be any more problems."

I put my fork down, appetite gone. "What? When did someone pull on Doc, and where was I?"

Miguel's glance slid away from mine, and a flush bloomed on his smooth cheeks. He took a gulp of whiskey. "It was the night you weren't feeling well and left early." He took my hand. "I'm *estupido* when I drink. Doc told me to say nothing. I'm sorry, Kate."

I wasn't listening. Las Vegas was especially prickly because of the railroad and the people, rumors, and gossip that traveled with it. Neither of us was a stranger to violence and death—the American West was rife with it, and to not realize it and take defensive measures was tantamount to writing your own epitaph. Doc had a nasty temper, but every time he'd ever hurt another human being there had been a damn good reason for it, once even to protect Wyatt from getting shot in the back in Dodge City. Still, a legend had grown that Doc was a fast gun killer and I was nearly as bad—a whorish harpy standing behind her man. I'd been dubbed Big Nose Kate, and that sure wasn't a moniker anyone could relish. Hell, my nose wasn't that damn big. I think they were more likely referring to my propensity to poke it into Doc's card games. This wasn't gossip we wanted to flourish, especially here in the town we wanted to settle in. We were already in negotiations to buy the lot next door to the saloon.

"Kate?"

I blinked and grasped Miguel's hand tight. "Sweetheart, don't worry. I'm not angry with you or Doc. It's just that we need to be very careful. You understand, don't you?"

Miguel nodded. I wasn't concerned about him at all. The young man had a huge case of hero worship for Doc, and for me by extension. No matter what Doc had done, or what might come next, he was our ally.

I pulled the reins up, and Rula stopped beautifully, as always. My darling had lost none of her feistiness but had trained well. I gazed out at the valley before me, the golden rays of the noonday sun illuminating a paradise: the cottonwoods rustling in the breeze, the green and gold of the verdant meadow, and the gloriously blue sky above it all. The perfect place for a house, small farm, and a horse ranch, just like we'd talked about.

"Pretty damn perfect, wouldn't you say?" said Doc, drawing up beside me, Hercules snorting from his gallop. Doc grinned and reached out to grasp my hand. "It's not Georgia, mind, but 'a heaven of hell,' I think?"

I laughed. "Or 'a hell of heaven.' You could be onto something."

He drew my hand up and kissed it. "And only you, my divine Kate, would know Milton."

I raised an eyebrow. "Well, ain't we a pair! So how much does Otrero want for this?"

He frowned. "Too damn much, but I think he'll come down. We could start buildin' and get something up, maybe the barns and the start for the house, before the snows."

I took a deep breath of the mesquite-scented air and felt better than I had for weeks. It was so clean, so pure out here, and I never wanted to go back to the saloon and the stench of beer, smoke, and unwashed cowboys. Already, at Holliday's, if you closed your eyes, you could be in Dodge City, minus the cows. Still, it's where we made our living, for now anyway.

"Let's make him an offer. Miguel will help." I turned Rula around reluctantly.

Doc dismounted and tied Hercules's reins to a pine tree. "Where you goin', darlin'? I've got a surprise."

He unfolded a blanket that I hadn't noticed behind his saddle, spreading it out on the ground, and from his saddlebags he produced two heavily laden sacks. He smiled up at me. "Best tie up that horse, lady. We're going to be here a while."

I swung my leg over the saddle and threw Rula's reins over a mesquite bush. There was plenty of grass up here—she'd be busy. We did need to talk about this . . . and other things.

I sat down heavily on the blanket and watched as Doc busied himself laying out food, along with a bottle of wine he expertly uncorked and held out to me first. I couldn't help but laugh. "We're so cosmopolitan and then, *voila!* No damn crystal. Savages after the grape we are."

Doc watched me as I drank. "Desire is one thing, my sweet, small saddlebags are another." He shrugged in that way I knew and loved so well. Insouciance was in his very bones. He lay down beside me in his languid way, and I held the wine bottle to his lips.

"Damn good Bordeaux. Graaf knows his stuff."

"Indeed," I murmured and took another drink. "Doc, we need to talk about Jim Whitney."

He closed his eyes. "The fuck we do, Kate. That's my business, not yours."

I kept my temper, biting my lip. "You're mistaken. What you do always affects me, too, Doc, especially if we want to stay in this town. If you killed that stupid rancher, I want to know so I can figure out the best way to handle this situation. Tell me the truth."

He opened his eyes and propped himself up on his elbow, his muscles taut. "All right then. I didn't kill him, least I didn't mean to. I shot him, but it wasn't a kill shot. He took off into the night, and that's all I know. If the dumb bastard bled to death it wasn't my doin'." He took the wine bottle from me and took a long pull, watching my reaction.

"Anybody see you shoot him?"

Doc sighed and took another drink. "Hell no. I'm an impetuous sort, but I'm fairly cognizant, Kate." He held the bottle out to me.

I sighed. Goddammit, his arrogance was going to ruin us. "Since nobody's found his body, there's been a lot of talk. How do you suppose he disappeared into thin air?"

Doc shrugged, and that little smile of his played around his lips. "Only the good Lord knows, darlin'. Strange things happen out here in the wild West. No accountin' for it."

I took the bottle from his hand and set it up beside the saddlebags. "Spirited up to heaven, most likely."

I stared at him for a minute and began to unbutton my shirtwaist. I knew how to pick my battles, and this wasn't one I was going to win. Besides, it was warm out here. "Hungry, Doc?"

He smiled at me, his face angelic. "Ravenous, Kate."

Doc's fingers played idly with the laces of my stays, loose now, as I lay on my back watching the fluffy clouds flitting overhead. The drone of bees and the occasional call of a hawk circling lazily in the sky were the only sounds but for us.

Graaf's honey biscuits, strawberries, and coffee had been delicious, but not as delicious as Doc's honey-laden tongue sliding down my stomach and his hands spreading my legs, pushing my petticoats aside. To have my man inside me here in this paradise, clasping my arms around him as though we were the first people to ever make love on this hillside, the scent of sweetgrass crushed beneath us, was all I wanted forever and more.

We would build something here, made with love, memories, and pride, knowing that all we'd been through could never take it from us. We would make a life, John Holliday and I, the woman and the man who were meant for finer things than the fires of hell we'd been forced through. We would make an Eden for ourselves and find the peace and serenity we longed for. What had happened in the past was just that, the past, and we'd done what we had to do.

I reached over and kissed him, the taste of honey still on our lips and the promise of paradise in our minds.

"What the hell are you talkin' about, Miguel? What do you mean he won't sell?" Pink patches of anger suffused Doc's pale cheeks, and I instinctively put my hand on his sleeve. He was worked up good and threw me off, grabbing Miguel's ruffled shirt front. Miguel tried to pull away, and Doc jerked him closer.

"Doc, believe me, I tried everything I could think of. He's adamant and he won't listen to me. Or maybe he won't listen because it is me," he stammered. "He thinks you're a bad influence."

Doc froze, his hands still covered with ruffles. He took a look at my face and abruptly pulled Miguel into an embrace instead.

"*Lo siento, mi amigo,*" he whispered, looking hard at me over Miguel's dark head. "Your father loves you, but he doesn't see clearly, as we do."

I poured them both a whiskey and watched as they drank it while I sipped my own. Our dream of a ranch in the valley was in dire jeopardy; Miguel's family owned the entire valley north of here. There had to be a way to make his father relent, although I couldn't think of one offhand.

"Maybe if we talk to him tomorrow, over at the bank," I suggested, but Doc shook his head, and Miguel was silent. "Surely there must be some way."

Doc poured another whiskey and gave a mirthless laugh. "I don't think Señor Otrero likes Anglos much, darlin', and especially not the likes of us."

I was getting mad now, too. "Goddamnit, that's not fair. He

doesn't even know us, just rumors he's heard. We are more than some people that own a saloon."

Doc laughed now, for real. "Oh, that's the truth, my love. Our reputations have preceded us. More, indeed."

Even Miguel smiled at this. "There has been talk, Kate. My father knows everybody."

I slammed my glass down on the bar. "I'm tired of this. Doc and I are not the people everyone thinks we are, Miguel, and you know it, even if a lot of folks don't. People do what they have to, sometimes, but that doesn't change where they came from or who they really are."

Doc looked at me, and I saw something in his eyes I'd never seen before. He put his arm around my waist and pulled me close. "Maybe not to us, sweetheart, but nobody cares who we used to be, only what they see now." His lips were soft on my cheek, and what I saw in his eyes I now heard in his voice: regret. "We're both a long way from home."

I kissed Doc fiercely on the mouth, and then I pulled away, stamping my foot. "No. No, I won't have it!" I nearly shouted, startling both of them. "There's other land in this place, and people who will sell it to us. We'll find something even better, and to hell with those who don't want us here. We're here, and we're staying, and not just in a saloon, goddamnit!"

There was a lot of land, most of it empty. In the next two weeks, I think I rode over all of it, sometimes alone, sometimes with Doc or Miguel. I was sore from the saddle, and even Rula got tired, but every time we found a nice piece of acreage, the story was the same. Either the Otreros or someone they knew—or influenced—owned it, and nobody would sell. Anger gave way to discouragement, and time was not on our side. Winter was coming to the mountains, and the thought of another winter without our own place a little farther down the valley wasn't something I was looking forward to. Doc was unhappy, too, and he began drinking more and becoming argumentative—never a good thing with the man.

The saloon was making good money, but the sheriff was riding us, and Hoodoo could only do so much. Doc stopped his dentistry practice, which was likely a good thing because his temper was too high. He was supposed to be fixing people's teeth, not thinking about putting his fist into their mouths. Then came the mayor's cease-and-desist order for Holliday's Saloon. Don Francisco was a friend of Miguel's father, and apparently Señor Otrero was putting on the pressure to get rid of us once and for all, sensing that his refusal to sell us the land we wanted wasn't enough.

Doc paid the fines, but that was only temporary, and the despair in his face chilled me through. This was a man with pride, trying to do the right thing, even if it was running a legitimate saloon with his name on the sign board out front. Maybe it wasn't what his family would have wished for, but it was a start. For the first time since he'd left Georgia, he had a venture that was successful and his, and that was what mattered. Being successful in the eyes of his family was important to Doc. I know he wrote to his cousin fairly often, and that the rest of his family was aware of how he was creating what I'm certain he described as a professional career in the West.

For me, it was much the same. My family had scattered. Wilhelmina married a farmer in Iowa, and Alexander, too, had married and was now in some mining camp in Colorado. We kept in infrequent touch, but I wanted them to be proud of me, or at least know that I was making my way. As for my younger brothers and sisters still in Austria, I'd never heard from them since my father died, and melancholy overtook me whenever I thought too long about them. I didn't know how to contact them, and I could only hope their lives were happy and

worthwhile and they hadn't suffered any adverse effects from
their separation from my mother and father. The world was a
large and terrible place sometimes.

What Doc and I both wanted was a place to call our own. To
raise horses, to be independent, and to leave our past lives
behind. Every morning we woke to that desire, our arms around
each other, and every morning when I held Doc and felt his
cough, I knew that time was running out.

"Doc Holliday, you lucky bastard! You're a sight for these eyes."

Wyatt Earp shoved his way past tables and patrons and pulled
Doc out of his seat at the poker table, his exuberance stopping
all conversation in Holliday's Saloon.

"Man, I missed you."

Doc's arms wrapped around Wyatt's sturdy frame, and I knew
that, from this moment on, we were destined to whatever that
damned man wanted us to do. These two were more than brothers, no matter how I tried to fight it.

The Earps had come to Las Vegas, and I had a feeling our
lives were never going to be the same.

CHAPTER 17

"Maybe Wyatt's right."

I buried my face in my pillow. Maybe he'd fall asleep before I had to respond to that asinine comment.

"Arizona's just heatin' up, Kate. There's a lot of opportunity there. Gold, silver—it's growin' like crazy. Wyatt says this Tombstone's the place where the real money is, and Virgil's the marshal in Prescott, and he says the place is boomin'. Morg and Lou are in Tombstone already."

I felt him prop himself up on an elbow and lean over. "Kate."

I sighed. "What?"

He put his hand on my shoulder and pulled me over. I could smell the whiskey on his breath. His eyes searched my face, looking for a reaction. Well, he was going to get one. That goddamn Wyatt.

Shrugging off his hand, I sat up in bed. "Doc, what the hell do you care what the Earps do? What about our plans here? What about the ranch? Two days with Wyatt and you're ready to run after him like a damn puppy. Be your own man."

I stood up and pulled on a wrapper before he could grab me. You never knew how Doc was going to react sometimes, but truth was truth.

He turned over on his back, folding his arms under his head and gazing at me contemplatively.

"I got another citation. We may get shut down for a while. Plus the sheriff's askin' around about that stupid rancher.

Maybe leavin' for a while isn't a bad idea."

My heart lurched. Stupid rancher indeed. This wasn't good. I sat back down on the bed.

"Well."

"Yes."

It looked as though a sojourn in Arizona with some friends in law enforcement could be in our future after all.

If there was a hell on earth, I was pretty sure it was sitting in a stagecoach for days on end with Bessie and James Earp across from me and Wyatt Earp and Mattie Blaylock beside me. So far, amid the heat, dust, and aching bones, it had been a journey punctuated by protracted silences and idle musings about the weather or about life in Arizona. My prior history with the Earps wasn't something any of us were eager to touch on, and navigating around those shoals—as well as their own family skeletons—was an awkward business. Our supply of polite chat had run out about 200 miles ago.

Gazing out the low stagecoach window, I realized the terrain wasn't any more exciting than the conversation—mile upon mile of stunted trees, sagebrush, sand, and sunlight. My nose wrinkled, and I sneezed as dust churned from the wheels and drifted inside. Every time we stopped, however, I wandered away from the little way stations and there was something about the emptiness, the purity of nothingness, that spoke to me.

I was surprised at my reaction, but pleasantly so. I had resentfully embarked on this journey only through circumstance and was prepared to be petulant and unhappy, especially with our traveling companions. But this was a place I'd never imagined—the clear air and vistas of the untouched country opened a space within me that I'd never known. In country like this, people could be reborn, could be whoever they wished to be, and could start over in a land swept clean of taint. I kept this feeling to myself, hugging it close. Even Doc wouldn't understand, and I needed no mockery or disillusionment. It was my secret place, full of hope and untouched by any plan, manipulation, or so-called opportunity.

On our third day, as we went through northern Arizona, Doc caught my eye from his seat beside James and rolled his eyes, his fingers turning his watch chain over and over. Mattie had just finished telling us a turgid tale about her first dance and there was nothing in this world I wanted to do more than strangle her. It was normally my first impulse anyway, but today's homicidal urge was a combination of irritation and excruciating boredom at every word that came out of her mouth. I couldn't resist a glance at Wyatt, who looked away after briefly meeting my eye. How could any man find life tolerable with this stupid woman? His misplaced gallantry was tinged with sheer laziness. Better the slut you knew, I supposed.

Bessie smirked, but I knew she was close to the breaking point, too. "Say, Mattie, how's your headache? Maybe a touch more medicine?" Bessie held out a brown bottle that I knew was laudanum, and Mattie took a long, grateful swig before handing it back. Maybe she'd sleep for a while and we could have some peace.

When we stopped to change horses and get water, I climbed out to breathe some fresh air and brush the dust from my clothes, as did everyone except Mattie, who snored in her seat, drooling a bit onto her lace collar. We all ignored her, grateful for the respite. The men walked away into the desert, laughing at some sally of Doc's—like as not about Wyatt's lady love. Chivalry had its limits.

Bessie handed me a cup full of water and stretched her arms behind her. "We should get to Prescott tomorrow, with any luck."

The water tasted of dust, but I drained the cup and handed it back to her. "Christ, I hope so. I've been wondering if anyone would stop me if I shoved Mattie's ass out the door on the next mountain pass."

Bessie laughed, and James, coming up behind me, clapped me on the shoulder. "I'm your ally there, my dear." His dark eyes gleamed with mischief, and I couldn't help but smile. Family or not, the Earps were a pack of rogues, and I doubted even Wyatt would miss Mattie for more than ten minutes. Imagining her demise was a pleasing fantasy, at any rate.

We spent the night at a ranch west of Williams. Doc and I managed to get a bedroom to ourselves, while the Earps shared. The bed wasn't particularly comfortable, but anything was preferable to sitting in the stagecoach, and at least we were alone for the first time in days. We took full advantage of that, aching bones or no. I woke up to pale light, filtering through the window across the room, while Doc snored softly beside me. I gently disengaged his arms, dressed, and went in search of coffee.

The driver was sitting on the porch, sipping coffee, and I sat down beside him with my own steaming cup. He looked to be about thirty-five and had skin bronzed from the merciless sun and wind, unlike Doc and the Earps, who spent a good deal of time indoors.

"Morning."

He nodded in acknowledgement, and we sat in silence, watching the sun rise on Arizona, like statues waiting for light to animate us. When he stood up, I did, too, knowing it was time to wake Doc and ready ourselves for another day on the road.

"Interesting company you keep, ma'am." The driver rolled up his sleeves and glanced at me. "I knew them in Dodge." His face betrayed nothing, and neither did mine.

"Really? Remember me, too?"

He shook his head. "No, but I remember your husband pretty

well. He's a twitchy one sometimes, though you most likely know that by now."

"Yes," I said and pulled open the door. "But he suits me, sir, right down to the ground."

"Sorry, ma'am," he stammered, his face flushed. "I didn't mean to offend or nothing."

"No offense taken, mister." I smiled. "But if I were you, I'd keep my opinions to myself. Healthier, you understand."

He set down his cup and didn't waste much time getting off the porch. It always amazed me how fast and far gossip could travel, but stage drivers could cover a lot of ground.

For a territorial capital, Prescott was pretty small. It was kind of a pretty town, and someone had taken the time to lay out the streets on a grid of sorts, which was unusual in the West. But then, this wasn't a town disrupted by cattle drives and cowboys. It was aiming to be a real city, and, even with the bustling saloons that catered to ranch hands and cattlemen, it had the possibility to become one.

Virgil and Allie Earp were waiting when we pulled in late that afternoon, and you would have thought those Earps hadn't seen each other since they were boys. Doc and I hung back on the sidelines while the hugging and kissing went on, but soon Wyatt dragged us into the familial circle, and we all went to dinner together, celebrating their reunion.

"Virg here is the U.S. deputy marshal," Wyatt said, saluting his stern older brother with a glass of whiskey, "so y'all be on your best behavior now."

Everyone laughed at that, even Doc, and I managed a tight smile. Sometimes the hypocrisy of these people was unbelievable to me. I was certainly in no place to sit in judgment with my history, but I knew too much about all of them to consider them law-upholding citizens. They were opportunists, every last one of them, including Morg, who had shown up with Louisa as we sat down to dinner.

What a group we were, and little wonder we drew everyone's eye. All of us women had come to maturity in saloons and whorehouses and wore cosmetics, colorful (if now somewhat understated) clothing, and hairstyles that weren't the braided products of a broken-down frontier rancher's wife. We looked normal to ourselves—citified women but without the accoutrements of stage costumes and saloon girls' feather stoles. Doc and the Earp brothers, in their black suits and hats, looked like undertaker crows escorting fancy women, and not a one of us seemed approachable to the earnest citizens we encountered. Clearly, the sober denizens of Prescott hadn't been exposed to many people like us before. They weren't sure exactly what to think, but I had a feeling they'd figure it out soon enough. We were a little bigger than life, and somehow that appealed to me.

Doc and I took a room at a Victorian boardinghouse on the west side of the Plaza square. It was quieter, but still close to the action on what the locals called Whiskey Row, where saloons and card rooms dominated the street on the east side of the newly constructed courthouse. The Earps were scattered here and there; that was fine with me as long as they weren't next to us. Wyatt was eager to head on to Tombstone, but Virgil still had business to wind up. It was pleasant to have a few days of breathing room from both of them and their enthusiasm.

Doc took an instant liking to Prescott, but I wasn't sure why. Perhaps it reminded him of Atlanta, with its Victorian houses, town square, and people determined to make it a proper place to live. Even I had to admit it had its charm, and it was the territorial capital, so interesting folks were always coming and going. But for some reason, it didn't appeal to me the way it did to him. Perhaps it was the looks I received from the women I encountered. Of the ranch women, shopkeepers' wives, and even the ladies married to the political types that frequented our boardinghouse, not a one seemed happy to see me or was more than just civil to my face. I could just imagine what they said behind my back! Propriety seemed to be the most desired virtue in Prescott, and it was never one I yearned for. Doc seemed oblivious to this, and, rather than complain, I found myself seeking out Bessie Earp for companionship. There was no judgment there, for certain. Today, however, there was a sharp edge to Bessie's usual careless demeanor, an edge she usually kept concealed but one I knew only too well.

"We're leaving for Tombstone next week, Kate. It seems to me lately that Doc's pretty comfortable with Prescott." Bessie put down her coffee cup and gazed at me with some speculation. I wasn't surprised she'd noticed that.

"I'd say he is, Bessie."

"Wyatt won't be happy about that. You know he dotes on Doc."

We were having breakfast at their hotel, something we'd made a habit of the last few days. I glanced around the restaurant, took a bite of my cinnamon roll, and chewed thoroughly before I answered that one.

"Jesus, Bessie. What is it with you Earps? You just gather people up and think they'll follow you anywhere."

She chuckled. "And usually they do, missy. You know that better than anyone. Besides, the plan was to go to Tombstone. That's where the real money is, and everybody knows that."

I looked at her. Still pretty if a bit overblown, her blonde hair was just a touch too brassy and her dress a shade too blue. To my eyes she was clearly a madam, but she passed for respectable most of the time.

"Bessie, I'm thinking I'll follow Doc's lead, not Wyatt's, and if he wants to stay the winter in Prescott, we just might do that, no discourtesy meant."

Her face darkened, and she pushed back her chair, shaking her head. "Your decision, Kate." She stood up and took my chin in her hand. "And I know it's yours as much as Doc's, sweetie. Maybe more so."

I brushed her hand away and picked up my own cup, careful not to let my temper show. "I guess we'll see you in the spring, then." I smiled, and she smiled back, but it wasn't a smile you'd ever want to see from a friend. She sailed out the door, and I was glad to see her go.

I was just as glad to see all the Earps pull out a week later. Doc and I stood arm in arm and waved as they drove away, wagons packed and horses tethered to the back, on their way south. Wyatt, as predicted, had been fairly unhappy when Doc announced we were staying in Prescott for a while, but in the bustle of packing up Virgil and Allie and getting supplies for the trip, he'd been busy enough not to complain too much. I tugged on Doc's arm and reached over to kiss him on the cheek.

"I'm looking forward to a Christmas in Prescott. How about you, Dr. Holliday?"

He laughed and spun me around, right there in the street. "Absolutely, my dear. I can't think of a finer season nor a finer place to spend it than right here with you in Prescott. My luck's been runnin' high, and there's no interfering sheriff. I think this town has a lot to offer us."

Snowflakes dusted Doc's shoulders and my fur muff as we stood in the courthouse square, our voices rising with a hundred others as we sang "Silent Night" together. For this night, we had sworn off gambling and spent Christmas Eve joining the festivities with our fellow citizens of Prescott. Plank tables had been set up in the square, and two bonfires lit up the night, warming us as we ate barbecue and sipped mulled cider that had been generously spiked with whiskey. Doc was in a happy mood, and because he'd made so much money in the last few weeks, he was full of Christmas spirit. I was only too happy to bask in his bonhomie, my fur muff warming my fingers—one of which now wore a lovely new sapphire and diamond ring.

The moon rose high above us, seeming to shine especially for this night and our acknowledgement of its difference. Some things never change, no matter where in the world you are, and Christmas Eve was one of those rare events that men paid tribute to, no matter how they'd spent their lives. Buried memories surfaced, and emotion and kindness came into play in the most hardened of people. I had seen it before and marveled at the magic evoked for a brief moment in time, even in myself. I was not religious, though raised Catholic, having abandoned religion when I realized God had most assuredly abandoned me and my family to our fates long ago, in spite of my naive prayers.

What I witnessed on this night was a drawing together of the human spirit, a realization of oneness and forgiveness, that was unique and forged solely through human desire to connect and love each other, if only for a brief time. This was one of the many philosophies Doc and I agreed upon—just one more reason why I loved him.

"Feelin' the chill, darlin'?" He kissed my ear as he whispered into it, his breath warm and welcome.

I turned my head and met his lips. "Not so much as I could be, but not so warm as I will be in our bed." The chorus of the carol swelled around us.

He laughed softly. "Not so silent a night will *we* have, then."

"We must be mindful of our neighbors on so holy a night, my dear," I said. "Let's have another cider and take our leave after one more carol."

We headed over to the tables, amidst the greetings of our

acquaintances, drank our cider, sang our noels, and bathed in the moonlight before saying our good-nights.

The rain was spitting inside the stagecoach again. I pulled the oiled canvas down, cutting off the rain but most of the light as well, showing only the dim outlines of my silent companions, a couple from Prescott and a portly banker headed south to Tucson. *Just as well,* I thought sourly. *They weren't exactly glittering conversationalists, anyway.*

This wasn't my first lone foray into the wilds of Arizona; in fact, it was the third. I nearly giggled, imagining Doc's face when he read my note, as he'd surely done by now, even though I'd left at dawn, and he still wasn't home. He'd likely wake up between the sticky thighs of some saloon girl he'd taken a fancy to the night before, as was his predilection lately. Whoever she was, she was welcome to him, not that it was likely she'd see him again.

Sometimes Doc's success at cards turned him into a man possessed, thinking only of winning, the cards, a pretty woman, or whatever struck his fancy before and after he'd taken the pot. He was rarely sober, and even when he was, his eyes were never still, always looking for the next excitement. It was damn lucky he hadn't killed anybody, because that happened sometimes, too, almost without him thinking about it, before or after. I nearly hated him when he'd get like that, and those times had become very frequent during our stay in Prescott.

So, I left now and again. It seemed to clarify things for him, at least for a time. When I returned, he'd be loving and contrite, and, frankly, I'd be refreshed. Not that I always told him about the places I'd been or what I thought about them. I wasn't sure he'd care, but it would be worse if he did, because then maybe that would be our next destination and I was slowly becoming not at all sure I wanted to share that with him, not like he was at the moment. I was looking for something and I didn't even know what it was, but I knew that it would be mine, and when I found it, I'd know. Then I'd decide when to share it with Dr. Holliday.

I loved him so much it hurt. I decided a long time ago that loving someone that much could kill you, and I'd been there before. Doc was dangerous, not only to the world, but to me. I had to protect myself from him or he could destroy us both. I traveled and looked around because I knew Prescott wouldn't last, and Tombstone was the last place I wanted to go, into the arms of the Earps, but I knew it was always in the back of Doc's mind as the next step. I was determined to find another option.

"Rest stop!"

The stagecoach slowed down and lurched to a halt. We all stumbled out, eager to walk about and get some blood flowing into our legs before we hit the trail again. There wasn't much to the place—a couple of adobe buildings, one clearly a barn with a corral for changing horses, the other doubling as office and living quarters for the hostler and his wife, who had set up some coffee and sandwiches on the porch. I took some coffee and wandered off a ways. We were coming down in elevation as we headed south and east, the pines of the high country giving way to mesquite and cactus, but the air was still cool and crisp. I was headed to Globe, one of the copper mining towns. A few people had spoken well of the place. They said it had a future beyond a boomtown and not just in mining, but from the farms and ranches that surrounded it, as well, and I wanted to see it for myself.

"Miss Haroney? Kate?" Tim McCann, the stage driver, came up beside me. "We're ready to move just as soon as they finish harnessing." He put his hands on his hips and gazed out at the landscape, much as I was doing. "Pretty country. Empty, though." He chuckled as much to himself as to me. "Maybe that's what makes it pretty. No damn people to mess it up."

I smiled and finished off my coffee. "You may be on to something, Tim. For now, though, I need more than prairie dogs to commune with, so I guess I'll get back on the stage."

"We'll be in Globe by dark," he said. "You'll get more than prairie dogs there."

We walked slowly back to the adobe buildings. I'd gotten to know Tim, as this was the second time he'd been the driver on one of my sojourns. He was also the driver who'd been so observant on our trip from Las Vegas. He'd been solicitous of my welfare then, if wary. Now, minus my companions, the wariness had gone, and he was free with advice—not that I always took it.

Globe surprised me, and Tim was right. There was more than prairie dogs here. The town was thriving, with restaurants, shops, saloons, churches, and even a bank. Many of the structures were built of solid brick or quarried local stone. The silver mining business was booming, all right. In fact, they said the place was called Globe because some miner found a piece of silver the size of a globe, and that started things off a few years back. I took a room at the Globe Hotel and set out the next morning to look around. It was a hilly town, as mining towns tend to be. After leaving the businesses of Broad Street, I headed up the hill on Oak Street, past nice houses and businesses, for a couple of blocks.

I wasn't used to walking long distances, particularly uphill, and my feet hurt, so I turned in at what looked like a boarding-house, hoping to find somewhere to take a brief rest. The place looked nice—a two-story building, half brick—and as I stepped up onto the planked porch, a woman came out, wiping her hands on her apron. She was a sturdy-looking woman, maybe in her forties. Her face was stern, but when she smiled and held out her hand to shake, I responded immediately and held out my own, smiling in return.

"Morning. New here, aren't you?" Her hand was calloused but firm and warm in mine.

"Pretty obvious, I guess," I said, looking down at the high heels on my shoes. "I'm not used to these hills. I'm from Prescott."

"Come on in and sit a spell. I've got some coffee on." She opened the screen door, and I followed her inside, down a black and white tiled hallway, to the kitchen at the rear of the house.

"I'm Mary Newhouse, and I own this place," she said, pulling out one of the wooden chairs around a scrubbed oak table.

"Kate Haroney." I sank gratefully into the chair. Within seconds she set down a steaming mug of coffee and took a chair herself.

"What brings you to Globe, Kate Haroney?" Mary asked, eyes shrewd and assessing.

I smiled. "Just looking around, Mary. I'm new to Arizona, and I want to get a feel for the place."

She laughed, a short barking sound. "Ha. Not much to see around here, Kate. Just a mining town in the middle of nowhere. I came out here ten years ago, and I'm thinking about moving on. I hear San Francisco's the place these days."

I sipped my coffee. It was good. "Oh? Business not so good?"

Mary glanced at me over her coffee cup. "Business is fine; I'm not. Tired of Globe, truth be told. Still, it's a good business, miners and all." She waved her hand, as though taking in the place. "Six rooms, and six more out in the addition I'm planning on. Good men. I don't put up with the ones that aren't, if you know what I mean."

"Oh, I know exactly what you mean," I said. I did, too, and Mary knew it. I didn't meet many women that I got on with, but this was a rare exception, perhaps for both of us. There was something in her eyes that said she'd been in many of the same places I had, and not just geographically. I'd sensed it the minute I took her hand.

I finished my coffee and stood up. "Thank you, Mary. I'm very glad I met you this morning. Perhaps we could get together again, for dinner or . . ."

"I'm pretty busy around suppertime, Kate," Mary said, gathering up our cups and putting them into the sink. "I've got hungry men to feed. Maybe if you're around during the day tomorrow, you could stop by. You'd be welcome."

"I'd like that," I said and shook her hand. "Thank you again for the coffee."

In the next few days I got to know Mary Newhouse very well—and Globe, too. Mary had come here with her husband, a rancher, and when he died a few years back, she'd sold off the stock and bought the boardinghouse. She'd been through her own hard times and was a restless and not very happy woman. I avoided sharing any specifics about myself and especially Doc or the Earps. All of us had developed reputations, and, even if Globe was a bit off the track, news traveled faster than one would think out here. I liked Globe, and I sensed an opportunity I didn't want to jeopardize.

"Bastards." Doc threw his boot across the room. "What is wrong with these penny-ante bureaucrats, Kate?"

I took off my corset and sighed. "I don't know, Doc. They are very eager to ape their Eastern counterparts but don't seem to realize where they are. Stupid men do stupid things."

"Idiots." He threw his other boot, narrowly missing the window.

The Prescott city council had decided to enact anti-gambling ordinances, and the latest was charging every gambling establishment $500 if they allowed gaming, along with the earlier rules the council had thought up in the new year, which included serious penalties for carrying a weapon—as Doc always did. After various misadventures, he was never without a pistol, wisely so.

"Kate, I'm going back to Las Vegas to see how things are goin' with Holliday's saloon. We'll leave tomorrow on the stage. Pack your things."

There was no future in Las Vegas, especially since Doc had left things in a hurry, with a couple of gambling charges against him. Hoodoo Brown was looking after the saloon, but I didn't have high hopes of a profitable future there, and certainly not a ranch.

"I think I'll stay here, Doc," I said. "There's things to look after."

He rounded on me angrily, as I knew he would. "Nonsense. This place is finished for now, unless they come to their senses. What possible reason would you stay for?"

"I'm doing well at the Palace, Doc. If they pay the fine, I'll stay on." My face was guileless, but he stared at me suspiciously, as though I was the one who'd been fooling around. That was always the way with him.

"Kate, they'll be closed down in a week. Don't be silly, darlin'. Come with me." He put his arm around my neck. "I need you." He kissed me, his hand sliding softly on my thigh, and I lay back down in the bed. There would be time to talk about this in the morning.

Doc's face was a stoic mask as I waved good-bye. We'd had a breakfast battle, but there was no way in hell I was getting on that stage. He finally conceded, or as Doc put it, "Madam, I see that I will be doin' business on my own, without your counsel and attention. I am disappointed that apparently our affairs don't matter to you as much as I thought."

Whenever Doc played the martyr card, I knew I had won the

game. When it came to emotions, the man was as transparent as glass. Luckily, emotion was the furthest thing from his mind when he was playing cards. He really did need to wrap up his business in New Mexico, but I had no desire to ever again see the place where my hopes for a normal life for Doc and myself had been crushed. I had new hopes now. I was determined to find a place for us, despite the Earps and everything else that had been thrown in our way. Arizona had a lot to offer, and I was searching and ready to grab the opportunities that lay ahead when I found them.

CHAPTER 18

Globe, Arizona, June 1880

Mary clinked her glass on mine. "Congratulations, Kate. You're in for it now."

"I know it," I said. The whiskey hit the back of my throat like a lava flow, and I couldn't wait to pour another one.

Mary laughed, held out her own glass for another, and turned around and faced the crowded saloon, raising the glass.

"Hey, you slags, hold up your glass and drink to the newest business owner in Globe, Kate Haroney. She's the new owner of the Miner's Rest, and she's going to take good care of you boys." Her voice rang out over the noise of cards, glasses, and conversation, and all heads turned to us. "And the next one's on us. Cheers!"

An echo of "cheers" rang out amid the clatter of boots rushing to the bar. Hands slapped me on the back repeatedly, and I received a few hugs and kisses from men I'd never seen before. Meanwhile, Mary laughed a lot and kept pouring. Whiskey was nothing new to me but this was the first time I'd seen Mary drink anything but coffee since I'd known her.

"You are sure damn happy to be getting out of here," I said. I was starting to think I'd paid too much or the place was falling down from termites, maybe both. "You know something I don't?"

Mary peered at me and sighed, putting her arm around my shoulders. "Kate, I'm sorry if I've been a little too, well . . .

relieved. There's nothing amiss with our dealings—don't fret about that. It's just that I've developed such a hankering for California, I can't wait to light out. You showing up has been a godsend."

Relief flooded through me, although I wasn't entirely certain she was telling me the truth. I had learned to trust no one, not even Doc. Still, I had come to think of Mary as a friend—maybe not the best person to do business with, but there it was. "What's so damn wonderful about California, anyway?"

She pulled me over to a table, and we sat down, the bottle of whiskey between us.

"You ever been somewhere you just can't wait to see again? Somewhere that made you never want to leave it?"

"No," I lied, thinking of the green forests of Hungary and knowing I'd never see them again. There were some things you couldn't do anything about.

Mary patted my hand comfortingly. "Damn, that's too bad, Kate. That's really sad." She kept patting my hand distractedly. "You've never seen California, but I think you'd find something different there, maybe change your mind. 'Course, I don't want you thinking about that, since you just bought my boarding-house." She laughed and poured herself another whiskey. "They got these trees there, they call 'em redwoods, and they're like no trees you've ever seen in your life." She went quiet, her eyes seeing something that wasn't in this room. Lost in it, she was.

I poured another whiskey and looked around. This was another saloon, much like others I'd seen in the last ten years, this one maybe a little rougher than some. The sophisticated crowd, what there was of that in the West, didn't often find its way to Globe. Still, money did, and these miners and cowboys had plenty of that, digging it out of the ground or herding it around. I could do all right here. I could have something steady and a comfort, instead of dealing cards or worse, to make my living. Miner's Rest would be just what I needed. I was used to taking care of men, that was one thing for sure, and cooking was something I'd always loved. That was peculiar, since I'd learned how to cook as practically a slave for Mrs. Smith, so long ago now back in Iowa. But I had also learned from Andre and the Plaza Hotel. Maybe I'd show Globe a little something new in the culinary area. I couldn't resist a smile at that thought.

Mary cocked her head. "Happy about this, Kate?"

"You know, Mary, I really am." Maybe she was right about California, but, for now, Globe had the look of a haven for me.

Much later, under a full moon, Mary and I wound our way up the hill to Oak Street. It was quiet, and the adobe and wooden buildings appeared silvery in the moonlight. We made our way upstairs to Mary's room and, giggling like little girls, shed our boots, corsets, and skirts in a muddle and lay down on the featherbed. Mary clasped my hand in hers.

"I'm going to miss you, Kate," she said, "even though I hardly know you." She turned her head on the pillow, and I could see her eyes shining in the dimness.

I squeezed her hand. "I know it's strange, but I feel the same way. You're a friend, and I haven't had many."

Mary sighed. "Nor have I. It's hard to be a woman alone out here. You have to do things you never thought you'd do, and then you just go on, because you have to. Pretty soon, you put the bad things in a box somewhere in your mind and never open it."

"How well I know."

Mary laughed softly. "Oh, I know you do, Big Nose Kate."

I stiffened. "What?"

She leaned over and kissed my cheek. "Not to worry, but you've got quite the reputation, as does your friend Dr. Holliday. Even in Globe we hear things, although as far as I know, no one else has put this together. Is he coming here, too?"

I was so shocked I couldn't think. I sat up, pushing my hair off my face, feeling sick. I thought I'd been so careful. This was supposed to be a new start, and though Doc might eventually decide to come as well, this was my venture all the way. I felt betrayed, the anger surging up. I wanted to put my hands around Mary's throat and squeeze her lifeless.

I swung my legs off the bed and put my head between my knees, the nausea welling. Perhaps it was a good thing I'd had so much whiskey, as my stomach was outweighing my ability to follow my murderous impulses.

Minutes passed. Then I felt Mary's hand on my shoulder.

"Jesus, Kate, I'm sorry," her voice was ragged. "I would never tell anyone. You don't have to worry. You're my friend, I mean . . . this is just between us. I was stupid to tell you, especially like this."

I swung around, knocking her hand off me, and put my hands on her shoulders, shaking her. She hung her head, and her long, dark hair fell over her face.

"I trusted you, Mary. Now I don't know what to think." My hands fell into my lap, fingers twitching.

"You can still trust me, Kate," she whispered. "Please believe me."

I took a deep breath. "All right." I lay back down on the bed, spent. It was what it was. I knew, somehow, that I could trust Mary even though she'd not been honest with me. Maybe I wouldn't have been either, in her place. In any event, I had little choice.

It seemed like forever before sleep overtook me.

"You bitch! I thought I could trust you." Doc's face was contorted with rage, and his fist hit my cheek with a sick, crunching sound. "Can't ever trust a whore, can I?"

I fell on the carpet, its pattern of cabbage roses wildly pink and green, then red where my blood trickled onto the petals. The room was spinning, and I couldn't breathe.

Doc's boot landed in my stomach, and I screamed with the pain of it. He jerked my head off the floor, his fist wrapped around my hair.

"What made you think I'd ever live in some shithole like Globe, wherever that is? How Wyatt and Bessie would laugh at that!"

"Stop . . ." I managed. "Just stop . . . Doc, I love you."

He laughed, and when I saw the glitter of a blade I knew I was going to die. How could I have been so blind? I closed my eyes, and all I could hear was his mocking laughter.

I sat up fast, looking wildly around me. The bedroom was bright with sunlight, and I blinked owlishly, the pain in my head blinding. I heard the laughter again, drifting up from downstairs. I flinched, reality chasing away the horrifying remains of the nightmare.

"You're a crazy man, Alf, God love you." I heard Mary's voice. "Now get out of here and find me that nugget you keep talking about. I'll be waiting. Chicken stew for dinner."

I heard the front door slam, and I put my head in my hands. One more day and that would be me. The dream receded, but the dread did not. What the hell had I been thinking? If my nightmare was any sort of premonition, Doc Holliday wasn't going to be too happy about my investment in Globe.

"Twelve pounds of sugar, thirty pounds of flour, one pound of salt, yeast, twelve dozen eggs, eight pounds of butter." I ticked off the list on my fingers as Mr. Bailey nodded. "Plus the bill for the beef and the chickens from Goodall's ranch."

"Don't forget Simpson for the hams," Bailey said, tallying up all of it with his pencil, the point of which was going dull by this time. "You owe him for last month, too."

"Christ, don't I know it," I said. "These goddamn miners eat like every night was the last supper."

Bailey laughed and leaned back against the counter. "They sure do. As good as I hear your cooking is, what'd you expect, Kate? Maybe you should up your rates."

I grinned ruefully. "Maybe I will."

I loved Bailey, likely because I never had to worry about being proper around him. I arranged for the groceries to be delivered by Bailey's hired boy, George Hunt. Then I set off for Maggie Sweet's shop down the block. The silver bell over the door tinkled as I came in, and scents of cinnamon and wool—a unique but welcome mix—met my nostrils. Maggie looked up from the colorful balls of yarn she was putting in display baskets and smiled broadly.

"Well, hello, Kate! I was hoping you might be in today. Wait until you see the new fabrics I just got in."

"I think you may be the anti-Christ, Maggie," I said, putting down my basket of produce. "I want damn near everything in here, as usual." She smiled knowingly, poured me a cup of tea, and then produced shortbread cookies on a pretty plate painted with pink flowers.

Maggie's shop was unusual, and so was Maggie. An elegant, red-haired woman, she ran her shop with grace and style. Most stores in the West were the general dry-goods variety, pretty rough and tumble, but Maggie had taken things up a step. She stocked fabrics, sewing supplies, yarn, embroidery materials, and upholstery fabrics, along with a selection of ready-made clothing and furniture she'd re-covered herself. The shelves were stocked with a colorful variety of decorative wonders, from drapery tassels to the finest bolts of silk, and there was nothing you could imagine, from a fancy dress to new curtains, that you couldn't find right here. She filled orders as far away as Tucson and Las Vegas but did a steady business in Globe, a town that was growing fast. Ranchers and miners had wives, and wives liked adornment.

Before she left, Mary had introduced us, and in the six weeks I'd owned Miner's Rest, I'd spent a good deal of time and money with Maggie Sweet, and we'd become good friends.

"How's the new addition coming along?"

"Very well," I said, taking a sip of tea. It was refreshing, even though the temperature was nearing ninety degrees out there already. Tea had a way of making me feel calmer. "It'll be done in another two days, according to Jim. So I'll be needing extra quilts and curtains for those six rooms, which is why I'm here." I smiled. "And to say good morning to you."

"You picked out the fabric for the quilts last week, and I've had Juanita and her girls busy with them. I think the white muslin for the curtains would be just the thing, and we can start on those tomorrow."

"Perfect, and I'll need two more pair, for a total of eight." I knew there were hotels and boardinghouses that didn't care about windows, much less the curtains that covered them, but I knew the patrons and customers did. Myself, I couldn't imagine sleeping in a room without a window and fresh air, and none of my boarders would ever be resigned to that fate. Even though many of my customers were a rougher sort, they appreciated the small touches that Mary had offered, and I had not only continued, but built on in the short time I'd been the proprietress. I'd gained a reputation in Globe since I'd been here, and it was a good one—that I was not only honest and fair, but my boardinghouse was one you were lucky to live in, with nice decor and delicious food. I was proud of my new reputation and determined to keep it up. The addition would have another six rooms, and I'd had the downstairs back parlor space remodeled to provide a bedroom and sitting room for me as well, freeing up two additional rooms upstairs. I'd quickly learned the only way to make money in this business was to have more space to rent, and that was my first priority.

"How'd the new curtains and bed linen work out for your private retreat, Kate? I can't believe you wanted to do those yourself, when Juanita could have done them for you."

"They're beautiful, Maggie." I thought of the pale-blue silk curtains that hung at my windows and my bed, and the way the sunlight filtered through them each morning.

"I loved making them, and, frankly, I filled up quite a few evenings that I didn't have to prep food, or paint railings, or think too much." Maggie smiled thinly back, and I knew my friend had her own past that she'd put behind her, as I had mine. "I think working on the house has been good for me, and it's not something I'll ever stop doing, one way or another."

Maggie laughed. "That's good to hear, customer dear. Now all I need is to teach you to knit and do embroidery, and I'll make even more money off you."

I thought of the long hours the Hungarian governesses had spent with me and embroidery needles and shook my head. "Sorry, but embroidery never seemed to take with me, not for lack of trying. As for knitting, it never gets cold enough in Arizona to work on something you can only wear two days a year, so the hell with that. Besides, wool socks make me itch."

"Maybe you could make some for your sweetheart, then," Maggie said, eyeing me slyly. I didn't take the bait. I wondered if she'd heard anything, but I didn't think so. Mary had said she'd kept quiet, but I couldn't help wondering where she had heard about me and Doc.

"Maggie dear, I don't have a sweetheart, and neither do you," I said pointedly. "Unless you've been keeping something from me? Some rancher catch your eye?"

She laughed and cleared our teacups, returning from the

back room with a ball of lace, which she spread out on the table.

"Take a look at this, Kate. I think you'll appreciate this more than anyone I can think of. It's Austrian lace, very intricate."

It was beautiful, three inches wide, handwoven in an intricate pattern, one I recognized from my childhood. It was the work of the nuns of the Abbey of Forschweigen, who spent their lives doing this delicate and wonderful work to support their small holding near the river Trier. My mother had been very fond of it, and I blinked to hold back the sudden tears the memory brought.

"Wherever did you get this?" I whispered, my hands gliding lightly over the lace as though I could feel the years in between then and now.

Maggie smiled and put her hand over mine. "From a supplier that sends me precious things sometimes, from New York. I had a feeling someone from your part of the world might recognize it."

I looked up at her and saw only kindness and an awareness that I hadn't seen in some time. In spite of my well-earned guardedness, my early history poured out as Maggie held my hands in hers, and then she returned the confidence. She was an Irish girl, orphaned and sent to America, landing not in New York but in New Orleans where, at the age of twelve, she'd been a high-priced addition to a French Quarter whorehouse, one I'd heard of with misgivings when we lived there. One night she'd knifed a tormenter of some means and insensibilities. She had fled, embarking upon a journey that eventually led her to this outpost, determined to never look back and to have a life of her own choosing. This child of famine and exploitation wanted to make a life of beauty for herself and others to escape the horrors of unhappy childhood and adolescence, and nothing would stop her.

To my surprise, no one interrupted us for that hour, and it was one of the most gratifying of my life. To be able to be honest about my past, and she of hers, to someone trusted, was a great gift for us both. I thought that fate had brought me to Globe and to a friend like this.

"Jesus, Kate." Maggie looked at me, her eyes somewhat red but her face composed, as I stood up and gathered my basket. "This has been an unexpected morning. I had a feeling about you—and not just that you would appreciate Austrian lace."

I hugged her. "I can't say I didn't suspect something of the sort about you, Maggie. We need to look after each other, if you don't mind my saying so."

Maggie hooked her arm around my waist as we walked to the door. "Oh yes, I quite agree, my Lily of the West."

I looked up, but I wasn't surprised. "You know pretty much all of it, don't you, Maggie?"

"None it of matters to me, Kate, and you know it. I'm your friend, just as Mary was, and I know you're mine. That's what does matter."

She opened the door and ushered me out onto the boardwalk. "I'll have Juanita bring the curtains up by Thursday." She kissed me on the cheek, and I began the walk up to Oak Street, feeling bemused but also buoyed by the warmth of trust, something that had been alien to me for a long time. Independent women in the West were a rare breed, and I was happy to have found one I could call a friend. I was also quite delighted with the length of lace that rested on top of my basket.

I opened the door to Miner's Rest and headed towards the kitchen at the back of the house, unloading my basket into the pantry and cold chests. I glanced out the back door, watching Jim and his crew as they worked on the addition. It seemed to be going well. I went outside, the screen door creaking as it shut behind me, and watered my vegetable gardens, all raised three feet off the ground in wooden boxes. Jim had built these, too, according to my specifications. Gardens on the ground in Globe were beset by rabbits, raccoons, and any pest interested in seedlings, and they were many. Now I had tomatoes, peppers, lettuce, squash, and beans—all doing well even in this heat, protected by muslin sheets stretched overhead. The Apache women of Las Vegas had taught me about many things, including growing food, all part of survival in the West. I'd added the muslin and tomatoes, with a dollop of common sense, knowing the sun overhead for the enemy it could be.

"Miss Kate."

Jim Stewart, his straw hat pushed back on his head, stood just behind me, grinning.

"Hey Jim. How's the work going?"

"Well, very well. We'll be done day after tomorrow, like I promised. This is going to be the best boardinghouse in town, and believe me, everyone's talking about it. Those six new rooms are going to go fast."

I smiled in satisfaction. "Good. I hope so, Jim. Your work is excellent. I love my new rooms." I gestured towards the main house, and his face lit up.

"Yeah, they're pretty nice, eh? Listen, we're going to take a break and be back when it's a little cooler, if that's all right with you."

"Fine."

I turned back to the kitchen and thought about tonight's dinner, which needed to be on the table for my boarders around four-thirty in the afternoon. The menu included sourdough biscuits, beef stew, blackberry pie, and maybe some fresh tomatoes, if there were enough. I tied on a red-checked apron and began peeling potatoes.

"Hello, Miss Kate. Got some groceries here."

Young George Hunt lowered a large, heavy box down from his shoulder. "I've got two more outside in the wagon." He grinned. "Those miners sure can eat."

I smiled. "They certainly can, George. You can put the rest beside that one; I'll get to them later."

He nodded and was back quickly with the rest. He picked up a paring knife, sat down at the table, and began peeling potatoes with me. George was a nice kid, maybe nineteen or twenty, from back East somewhere. He'd been a big help since I bought the place, and I enjoyed his company.

"You don't have to peel potatoes, you know," I said. "The lemonade's in the icebox."

"I don't mind." He did get up and pour himself a glass, and he brought me one, too. We worked in companionable silence, and soon two large pots of vegetables and meat were simmering on the stove. We wandered to the front porch to cool off in the afternoon breeze.

"You sure you can't hire me on?" George said. "Mr. Bailey wouldn't mind. Besides, I could do both jobs, sometimes."

I sighed. "You know I can't afford it right now. Soon as I get those new rooms rented out, we can talk about it." Having George around to help with maintenance, repairs, and cleaning would be wonderful, and it wouldn't be long now. "You know I need you, so be patient."

"I could work for room and board," he said, looking at me imploringly, and I smiled. George fancied himself in love with me, I knew, but I couldn't take advantage of that. In fact, I'd have to make sure to dash his hopes soon. Boys had never been my style, and, cute as he was, I couldn't risk any gossip along those lines.

I shook my head. "Soon, George, and you need to stay at Mr. Bailey's. I can't give up a boarder's room. Besides, people might get the wrong idea."

He bristled at that. "The hell with what people think, Kate."

"I used to say that, too, George, but sometimes it matters, and I can't afford to have my reputation, or yours, tarnished." I stood up and ruffled his hair.

"My sainted mother used to say those very words, darlin'," said a soft, drawling voice, "but you are the last person in the world I expected to hear them from. I think there have been a few things I missed lately. You'll have to catch me up."

The screen door hissed shut as the porch floor creaked behind me. The scents of bay rum, bourbon, and cheroots drifted over the porch. An icy finger seemed to run down my spine, and I was afraid to turn around. When George's eyes widened, I knew I had no choice.

Doc's hands grabbed my waist and held me fast. His smile grew wider as he took in my workboots, cotton dress, apron, and disheveled hair. "Why, Kate, how fetchin' you look, with the sweat of honest labor on your brow." He pulled me close, kissed said brow, and slowly licked his lips. "I surely have missed the taste of you."

At this, a red-faced George Hunt wasted no time in removing himself from the porch, and, with a furtive backward glance at Doc, he hurried down the hill with his wagon.

I raised my eyes to the level of his mouth, which was slightly smiling, and then to the unfathomable blue eyes, which were not. A second or two passed, and he kissed me again, savagely, and it was all I could do to remain standing.

"Holliday. I missed you."

He stared at me, and his hands squeezed my waist, hurting now. "Really, Kate? You have such a mysterious way of showin' it. The minute my back's turned, flyin' off to . . ." he looked around with disdain, "paradise? Makes my trust in you turn to Missouri dust, I swear." His gaze shifted back to mine, and I looked down. That was a mistake, and not the first I'd made.

He threw me back into one of the porch's wicker chairs and turned his back. That's when I knew he was really angry.

"I've spent a good portion of the day lookin' over your hotel or whatever it is. Then I took a nap in your parlor while you and that young lout who just wisely skedaddled made soup. Got quite a feel for the place." He turned back to me, and I saw for the first time the pearl-handled Colt .44 peeking up beside his embroidered burgundy vest—another reason George had taken off like a scalded rabbit.

"Does the proprietor include herself along with the price of a room? How many times a week do the boarders get to bed the cook? I can vouch she's worth more than the dinner," he drawled. "When she's got a head of steam on, anyway."

I'd had enough. I pushed myself out of the chair. "That's all I'm taking from you, Doc. Come inside and let's talk." I pushed past him and opened the screen door. I wasn't sure if he'd follow me or shoot me right there. Only when I was three feet down the hallway and I heard his footsteps behind me did I draw a breath.

We talked. While I made three blackberry pies and he drank whiskey, we talked. When the miners came home, ate dinner, and drifted off contented to the porch and their beds, we talked. And later still, when Doc lay waiting on my bed hung with silken curtains, we talked even more. Truly, there was a lot to talk about, stored up over months of leave-takings and goings, dissatisfaction, and hopes. A constant thread ran underneath all of it, as it always had with us, as though it had been bred in the bone and when we met, sewn together. We loved and needed each other like a drug neither of us could break free of, nor wanted to. When the talking was done, we sated ourselves on each others' bodies, tearing off clothes and baring our skin and souls. It was a night long in its coming, and one that we both knew signaled a new phase for us. Together or apart, Doc and I were complete again.

"Darlin'. Tell me where a man could find some amusement in this charmin' town in which you've chosen to purchase an establishment." Doc put his boots on the railing of the porch and sipped his coffee while lifting an eyebrow at me.

It was early. The boarders had left for work, and I had Juanita's two girls in the kitchen, cleaning up breakfast and sweeping. For four days Doc had kept to himself, Shakespeare, and me, but I could tell, despite the Bard and my best attentions, boredom was setting in for him. Boredom and Doc weren't a good mix, so I was a little worried. Across the street, Mrs. Gleason, sweeping her porch a lot more than was necessary lately, waved good morning, and when Annie Milsap went by with a chirpy hello, her basket on her arm and her eyes on Doc, I knew his presence was noted and being discussed around town. He was rather difficult to miss, with his black frock coat, tapestry waistcoat, and gleaming black hat—not to mention the pistol in his holster. The pale face of a Botticelli angel with a mocking smile beneath a perfect mustache wasn't the norm for the working man of Globe, and certainly not one likely to be renting a room at the Miner's Rest. I feared my reputation as a respectable boardinghouse proprietor was in great jeopardy, but perhaps it always had been, really. Still, it was a small price to pay for Doc in my bed.

George Hunt, laden with the groceries I'd ordered, came up to the porch. Doc didn't move a muscle, but George was clearly nervous.

"Morning, Miss Kate." His eyes skittered towards Doc as he bravely mounted the porch steps, and I held the door open for him.

"Morning, George," I said. "Good to see you. Let's bring

those things on back to the kitchen."

George was uncharacteristically silent as we put away the supplies, and I didn't venture any conversation myself. By the time he returned to the porch, Doc was gone. Relief mingled with apprehension flooded through me. Doc could certainly find myriad ways to entertain himself down on Broad Street, and I knew without a doubt he'd find the most dangerous ones. I wasn't sure Globe was ready for Doc Holliday but he surely was more than ready for Globe.

I slid the last of the sunny-side-up eggs onto the platter and carried it into the dining room, pushing the swinging door open with my hip just as a raucous burst of laughter erupted from the men sitting around the long table.

"Doc, you sure are one devil of a fellow," Joe Smits, said, a wide grin on his face. "I never heard of nobody ever calling Myron Bodeen a card cheat before, though we all knowed he was."

Doc was sitting at the head of the table, cheroot in hand. "I can't abide a dishonest man. Civic duty, if you will, gentlemen." He looked up at me and nodded. "Good mornin', Miss Kate. You are lookin' especially lovely today."

Murmurs of agreement rose around the table, and Joe took the platter of eggs from me, passing it down into eager hands. Christ, I was doomed now. I could only wonder how Doc had passed himself off as a boarder here. Breakfast resumed with scarcely a ripple, and soon all that was left in the room were empty platters, a few crumbs, and Doc and me, as the rest of the men departed for the mines. Spears of morning sunlight slanted through the shuttered front windows, creating stripes of shadow in the room, and I sat down beside him.

"Have an entertaining night, Holliday?" I hadn't seen him since the morning before, and the signs of extreme fatigue were evident in his face, the man's charming manner aside.

"Indeed." He coughed, and his eyes gazed at me through half-lowered lids, all he could manage. I took the cheroot from his hand, putting it out on the remains of an egg. "Miss Kate, Globe is an undiscovered treasure."

As I guided him towards our bed, I knew what that meant. He'd won quite a bit yesterday, and rather than quit when he was ahead, he was more than ready to venture out again. For some, gambling was a pastime, but for Doc it was a calling.

As the summer heat waned, the miners and I were happy, but Doc grew restless. Miner's Rest was doing well. Even the new rooms were occupied, and I had hired a new girl to help in the kitchen, as preparing meals for that many men and keeping Doc happy was a double job for me.

One evening, before Doc headed down for the saloons and the men had gone to their much needed rest, Doc and I sat on the quiet porch. He took my hand in his, turning it over and over, his fingers tracing lines on my palm. It was warm, but not unbearably so; the pleasant evenings were a welcome respite from the heat of the day. The night birds were beginning to gather in the mesquite trees, their songs a plaintive but sweet reminder that life thrived even in the heat of a desert summer.

"Darlin'."

"Mmm," I murmured. Whenever Doc started a conversation this way, I knew more was coming, and it wasn't necessarily going to be something I wanted to hear.

"While Globe seems to be a nice enough place, Kate . . ."—he drew on his cheroot and blew out a cloud of smoke against the red streaks of the setting sun—"I'm thinkin' about going down to Tombstone. Wyatt says the place is thrivin'."

I'd been wondering how long he'd be content here, my porch, body, and easy pickings aside. That goddamn Wyatt.

Doc's hand gripped mine tighter. "You think you might come

along? For a time, see what you think?"

"Yes," I gripped his hand back, even tighter. "Worth checking out Tombstone, I suppose. But I have responsibilities here, Doc; you know that. It'll take some doing."

He pulled my hand to his mouth and kissed it. "I know that, Kate. I'm not askin' you to give this up. I can see you have a good business here, and I know how much ownin' your own place means to you." He pulled me closer. "But there's more out there, Kate; we both know it. Globe is an all-right town, but this country is on fire, and opportunity is everywhere. From what Wyatt says, Tombstone is the place where fortunes are made, in a lot of different ways. This could provide us with the ranch and the future we almost had in Las Vegas, only ten times better. We can't afford to ignore it."

I shifted uncomfortably in my chair, because what he was saying I knew to be true. Globe was a step for me, but after listening to Doc, I had to admit that maybe it was only that, and perhaps nothing more than a safe dead end. I wasn't sure what I aspired to, but I knew as well as he did, there was more. I thought back to New Orleans, a part of my past that I always closed down. Death and desolation had torn my soul there, but I could never bury it, as much as I tried. Meeting Doc had brought me back to real life again, even if our constant battles took their toll. Tombstone, even with the Earps involved, could be exactly what we needed to move towards our goals of a better life, one we both had been brought up to expect and revel in. We could worry about the Earps later. I stood up and took his face in my hands.

"I love you, Holliday," I said and kissed him. "Do what your heart tells you to do. You know I'm with you all the way."

CHAPTER 19

Tombstone, Arizona, October 1880

"Strike!"

Louisa Earp and I laughed and clapped our hands in delight, although we weren't really sure why.

"What the hell is a strike?" I said, fluffing the black feather boa around my shoulders.

She shook her head. "I don't know, but Morg seems delighted about it."

The noise level in Vogan's Bowling Alley was deafening. A hand fell on my shoulder, and I looked up at Doc, who deposited another whiskey on the table. James Earp was the bartender here, so I knew it'd be good. Morgan Earp, always happy, was in ecstasy at the moment over his bowling prowess. I watched as two Chinese boys reset the wooden pins in an arrow pattern at the end of the wooden pathway where he'd thrown a large ball only seconds before. Morg had managed to knock down all the pins, quite an accomplishment from the looks on the faces around us. I guess we had a lot to learn about bowling.

This was my third visit to Tombstone, and each time there was something new to experience. Though practically in its infancy, the town still crackled with energy—new buildings and new businesses exploding overnight. From one silver strike, the mines had honeycombed the earth beneath, and the wealth of all the silver brought forth had transformed the empty, high desert barrenlands into a bustling and wealthy populace demanding luxuries and entertainment. Restaurants, hotels, saloons, and bars mushroomed into being, along with rapidly built houses for the new inhabitants, who continued to arrive in throngs on an almost daily basis. Sophisticated merchants, way beyond general stores, offered goods (sometimes right from the bed of a wagon minutes after pulling into town) seldom seen this far into the West—French corsets, Campbell's tinned soups, German wines, Swiss chocolate, Belgian lace, Schweppes tonic water, tins of deviled ham, 30-year-old Scotch (much to Doc's delight), and even silk panties from New Orleans (much to mine).

Restaurants, like Nellie Cashman's Rush House and the Grand Hotel's, offered wonderful food every evening without fail, including lobster and fresh oysters. After overindulging, we often went to Schieffelin Hall for the best in entertainment, from operas to Shakespeare. Doc had taken rooms at the Grand Hotel, and the amenities were nearly as good as the best New Orleans or even Vienna could offer, opulent and supremely comfortable. I relished waking up in our nest of silken sheets and brocade tapestries, beguiled by the rich and intoxicating aromas of fresh coffee, chocolate, and croissants that rivaled those I'd had in New Orleans.

Each time I came here, though, I had the feeling I was living a fantasy that couldn't last. One night I had a dream that the veins of silver below us shrank into thin black snakes that shriveled and grew skyward, their bony fingers pointing up through the earth like dead winter tree branches and whispering "you have taken all we have to give," then encircling the town and pulling it back into the hard desert ground. I didn't bother to mention this to Doc. He appreciated poetry but gave the fantastical short shrift.

Of course, we spent a great deal of time with the Earps, which

I didn't really mind except for Wyatt, who was always glowering about something, and that idiot Mattie, who was likely the cause of most of Wyatt's moodiness. Everyone seemed to ignore her when she surfaced from her laudanum dreams and actually came out of the house, which wasn't often, but even once was too often for me. Doc irritated me because he felt sorry for her for some reason and was invariably kind. I'd never told him the whole truth about what happened back in Dodge, and after all this time I likely never would, but he knew I detested her, and we'd had more than one argument about his gallantry to the likes of Mattie Blaylock.

After a few more games, even Morg tired of bowling, and we made our way over to the Alhambra for sport of a different stripe. The Earps had invested in silver mines, but along with Wyatt being appointed deputy sheriff for Pima County and Virgil the U.S. deputy marshal—and their stints as Wells Fargo guards—they'd also taken to dealing in various saloons around town. Law enforcement didn't pay terribly well, and the mines weren't as lucrative as they'd thought they would be.

Tonight it was Wyatt's turn at dealing faro. The place was nicely done, like a lot of Tombstone, with Turkish carpets on the floor, velvet upholstered chairs, and a long, gleaming bar. We sat in for a few hands before a group of men came in and loudly demanded drinks at the bar, glancing around to be sure they were noticed. They were a motley crew—dusty and hard-bitten, some wearing red sashes and all with an attitude for trouble. Wyatt shot Doc and Morgan a look, and they both nodded, eyes on the newcomers.

"Who are those men?" I whispered to Doc. His eyes flicked to me, and he took a drink from his flask, the polished silver twinkling in the light from the chandeliers.

"They call themselves the Cowboys," he said, with such contempt they might well have been the lowest form of life on earth. "Vermin who think the law doesn't apply to them, wearin' those raggedy red sashes so they can recognize each other, I suppose. They terrorize the countryside around here, stealin' and murderin', and that so-called lawman, John Behan, doesn't do a damn thing to stop it, mainly because he's in league with them. Every time one of them actually gets arrested, the others in the gang step in to alibi him, and it just goes on. For now."

Wyatt nodded. "Behan's as big a crook as the rest of those scum and an even bigger coward. Whenever they come into town, there's trouble. Poor Fred White can't do much about them."

I'd met town marshal Fred White the last time I was here. He was a nice man, but not one to pick a fight, especially if he was on his own. Behan was the sheriff of Cochise County, and a bigger dandified phony I'd never seen, useless as a lawman. "Surely somebody could do something. Can't Virgil as a federal make a difference?"

Wyatt, Morg, and Doc all looked at me with amusement. "Kate, that's not how it works," Morg said. "These things tend to work themselves out if you just walk around them. Eventually the local law will handle things. No point in getting into a fuss if you don't have to."

The Cowboys scattered throughout the saloon, drinking, pawing women, and gambling, and eventually a few of them drifted over to Wyatt's faro table. The most unkempt of them all sidled close to Doc, staring at him and smirking. He sported a long, straggly beard that looked as though pieces of his dinner could be lurking in it somewhere.

"Hey, lunger, you like it here? I heard you was some bigshot gambler where you come from," he said, and his companions sniggered. "You ain't no big shot here, are you? Just some gin-soaked lunger."

Doc ignored him, but the man threw a glance at his friends

250

and, taking their smirks for encouragement, kept it up.

"I'm talking to you, fancy boy. Are you deaf or just stupid?"

Wyatt put his cards down and looked at him. "He can hear you, Ike. The entire place can hear you, but I don't think my friend feels like talking to you."

The man called Ike staggered back a bit, and another man steadied him.

Doc turned his back on both of them and took a few steps over to the bar. I followed him.

The man who had righted Ike grinned wolfishly, teeth white against his black mustache. He seemed to be the man in charge. "I'm Curly Bill Brocius . . . you may have heard of me. I know you're Wyatt Earp, and you used to be some kind of lawman in Dodge City."

Wyatt stared at him. "Oh, I've heard of you, and your friends here as well, haven't we, Morg, Doc?"

"Indeed," Doc murmured, glancing at three men who still stood beside the faro table. "Your reputations quite precede you, gentlemen." He coughed gently and leaned into me almost imperceptibly. He was fairly drunk himself.

"As does yours, lunger," said the third man. He was better dressed than the others. His hat was banded with silver, and his face and frame had a lean and hungry look, handsome and compelling. He stared at me, and I blushed as his eyes raked my body and interest flared in his dark pupils. His gaze shifted to Doc. "You're Doc Holliday, right?"

Doc stared back at him, a smile playing at the edges of his mouth, a smile I'd learned to be wary of. "In the flesh. I don't believe we've been formally introduced."

Curly Bill laughed, clapping the younger man on the shoulder. "This here's Johnny Ringo, fastest gunhand in the West, right, Ringo?"

Ringo's eyes never left Doc's face.

"Care to find out, Holliday?"

Unfazed, Doc took another sip from his flask and turned to me. "Darlin', don't we have other business to attend to this evening, besides satisfyin' Mr. Ringo's jejune curiosity?"

I smiled at him. "Yes, Doc, we do."

It was very quiet in the Alhambra for a few moments, and the stillness was broken by Curly Bill's raucous laugh. "Come on, boys, we've got other joints to visit. Nice getting to know you all."

Ike and Curly Bill ambled away, but Ringo took a second before turning on his heel and looking back over his shoulder. "I'll be seeing you, lunger."

"I have little doubt of that," Doc said, saluting him with his flask. Ringo's eyes passed over me, and I shivered. That was a dangerous man, for both of us.

"Christ, Doc," Morgan said. "I don't know why those idiots went after you tonight. Usually they go after Wyatt here."

Wyatt's face was grim. "I don't like it, either, Morg. Doc, you need to stay out of their way. I'm serious."

Doc shrugged. "I generally do, but I will not run nor hide from animals like them. They best stay away from any path I take, Wyatt. Y'all need to follow your own advice."

Another hour passed as we desultorily played a little faro, drank some excellent bourbon, and listened to Doc play Chopin on the out-of-tune piano. No matter how much he drank, Doc's fingers never seemed to fumble on the keys. I always thought he should've been a concert pianist, but anything that demanded daily discipline was not Doc's forte—except for whiskey.

As I gathered up my reticule and shawl to leave for the hotel, shots were fired in the street outside. Within seconds, everyone in the saloon ran for the door, abandoning Wyatt's faro table.

Curly Bill Brocius stood in the middle of the street, careening wildly in circles and shooting his gun at the moon. That he was very drunk was clear, but that made the situation even more dangerous. Fred White approached him cautiously.

"Now, Curly Bill, you know this has to stop," he said. But Curly Bill laughed wildly, and another shot exploded into the sky. Who knew where the next one would go?

Fred shook his head. "Just hand me the gun, and we'll sort this out in the morning."

Brocius focused blearily on Fred and stopped shooting. "Well, sure, Fred, anything you say. You know I always follow the rules," he laughed. As Fred reached out for the gun Curly Bill seemed to be handing him, it went off, and Fred White fell down in the dusty street.

Wyatt moved so fast it was like a blur, grabbing the gun out of Curly Bill's hand and buffaloing him across the head with it. Curly Bill fell to his knees, and Wyatt grabbed his collar.

"Get the doctor, now!" Wyatt yelled and dragged Curly Bill, who was still laughing even with blood running down his face, off to jail. Morgan followed them, gun in hand, watching Wyatt's back. People milled around in clusters, murmuring and shaking their heads. The doctor showed up, and Fred was carried off to be ministered to. From the looks of it, I didn't think he'd last long.

"Jesus God," I said, clutching Doc's arm. "This is a dangerous place you've chosen, my man. We've seen our share of bad actors and gunplay, but Tombstone and these Cowboys are like nothing I've run across before. Somebody needs to stop them."

Doc had said nothing at all since the first shots rang out, even after Fred White was taken away. I looked at him, his angular features softened by the gaslight from the Alhambra, and his eyes glittered as he looked down at me.

"Oh, darlin'. I think somebody just did." He nodded in the direction taken by Wyatt and Morgan. "But this could be act one of a tragedy not even the Bard himself could foresee." He coughed delicately. "Or I could just be very drunk." He laughed and kissed me on the cheek. "Let's to bed, my sweet Hungarian songbird. The morn comes too soon, and there is no good to be done here."

Doc was right. Fred White died of his wound, and, in no time at all, Curly Bill was released because, as Judge Spicer pronounced, "If there is no witness, there is no crime." It had been too dark, and everything happened too fast for anyone to reliably testify that Curly Bill shot Fred in cold blood instead of the accident he claimed it to be, and that was that. The Cowboys rode triumphantly out of town, and Virgil Earp was appointed town marshal to replace Fred, much to Wyatt's dismay.

"That goddamn Virgil. We can't afford to get caught up in this," Wyatt said, slamming his fist on the table. He, Doc, and I were having dinner at Nellie Cashman's. Doc put his hand over Wyatt's, while smiling reassuredly at the diners close to us, who then turned back to their dinners with lowered eyes.

"It'll be fine, Wyatt," Doc said. I didn't offer any placatory remarks because, frankly, I didn't think it would matter. Virgil was a rigid man, and he believed in enforcing the law, no matter the circumstances, and the circumstances in Tombstone were a lot different than anywhere else I'd been. It had too many jurisdictions, too many politics, and too many guns.

I was leaving for Globe on the morning stage and couldn't be happier about it, even though leaving Doc was always hard for me. I didn't like Tombstone much, and in the last few days I'd come to fear it. I wished he would come with me, my reputation be damned, but the twin demons of Doc's own greed and his loyalty to Wyatt had effectively stopped that. For me, I couldn't wait to get back to my placid and uneventful life at the Miner's Rest, even if it lacked the excitement and passion of

Doc. It also lacked being shot by a drunk Cowboy or, if I was honest, the lure of Johnny Ringo. I had no idea why the man had affected me the way he had. Maybe it was his utter lack of respect for anything—or just the heady, dangerous aura he projected. He reminded me of myself long before I'd met Doc, and I knew I needed to stay as far away from him as I could get. Globe was my refuge and, at the moment, my salvation.

We didn't spend the evening gambling after dinner, but said our good-byes to Wyatt and went back to our hotel room, where we did what Doc and I do best. I needed a surfeit of him and he apparently felt the same about me. Around two o'clock, he raised himself up on an elbow and looked down at me.

"Kate, how am I to get by in this place without you?"

I caressed his cheek and kissed his chest, tasting the salt on my tongue, and silently mourned at the thinness of his frame. "The way you always do, my dearest, in your own inimitable way. Holliday, I love you like no one ever, but you are the devil himself when it comes to advice from me or anyone else."

He laughed softly and slid his hand back between my legs. "I am indeed the devil himself when it comes to you, Kate. Let me show you just how depraved I can be."

Much to my delight, he did just that.

Globe at Christmastime was like a small town pretty much anywhere, at least a small town in the American West. When I was a child in Hungary, there had been balls, feasts, tall houses, and palaces of the nobility decorated with garlands and trees with tiny, lit candles, and sleighs piled high with laughing merrymakers, their bells ringing out to mark their passing. I missed it greatly, as I always did this time of year, and I missed my family as well. I wondered once in a while what my life would have been like if my father had chosen to stay in Europe but I tried not to do that often. Globe had some garlands and tinsel decorating the stores and many of the houses—even the banks and offices—and while it hadn't snowed yet (some years it never did), there was always hope on people's faces, especially the children's.

It was cold, though, and I walked briskly down to Broad Street with my empty basket swinging on my arm, my braid-trimmed gray cloak on my shoulders, and leather gloves on my hands to keep me warm. The sky was whitish and rather ominous, so perhaps those snowflake wishes would come true after all, but I wouldn't have bet on it.

I stopped at Bailey's and ordered my turkeys for Christmas dinner, picked up a few extra supplies for cakes, brandy for plum pudding, and peppermint candy, and then I headed for Maggie's.

The wonderful scent of cinnamon tea greeted me as I entered, and I was immediately drawn to the displays Maggie had created for the season. Gold voile, threaded with green and red silk, was draped all around the small shop from ceiling to floor, creating a cozy nest. The scent of bayberry candles, another of her creations that the ladies of Globe bought avidly, filled the room. Arrangements of pine swaths and cones decorated the sales counter and the table where we sat as Maggie poured the fragrant tea.

"This is delightful," I said, sitting down and peeling off my gloves. "Reminds me of home more than anything I've seen in years. Wherever did you get the pine boughs and cones?"

Maggie laughed, sipping her tea. "Juanita's nephew. He was going up to a ranch on the Rim two weeks ago, and I paid him to gather them for me. The pine forests are thick up there. He thought I was crazy, but people love them. You know how it is, Kate. Everyone here is from somewhere else, and not that long ago, and most of us grew up with greenery and decoration at Christmas."

I nodded. "Yes, we did, and it's important. Last year we were in Prescott, but here . . ."

"I have some cones I saved for you, Kate."

I smiled. "That would be wonderful. Thanks . . . you know me well." I leaned over the table and kissed her on the cheek. "I think I need some fabric as well. The Miner's Rest needs some glitzing up. Most of those men haven't had too many festive Christmases, I think. Maybe I can give them one this year."

I made my way back up the hill, happily burdened down with all my purchases, and smiled as the first snowflakes began to fall. I had three days before Christmas—plenty of time to make the cookies and mince pies I had in mind. I thought about Christmases with my family and at the Fishers', as I always did this time of year, remembering when Emily taught me how to cook those very treats. I'd had a letter just last week from her, with news about Alexander. He had four children now and was in Colorado, some place called Penny Hot Springs. Wilhelmina still lived in Iowa, and, from what Emily wrote, I was an aunt there at least once over, too. It was unlikely I'd ever see my sister again, and, while I wished her well, I didn't much care. As for Alexander, he wasn't all that far away, and it sounded as though we had a sense of adventure in common.

I sent my girl Betsey home to be with her family after we'd put the two stuffed turkeys into the ovens. I surveyed the dining room at the Miner's Rest and was very pleased at the result. Pine boughs and cones decorated the table, along with platters of Maggie's red bayberry candles, and I had draped the gold, red, and green fabrics in swags over the doorways as Maggie had done in the shop. I wasn't very creative at decorating and was glad I had a friend who was. My energy went into the food for this repast—with Betsey's help, there were mince pies, lemon cakes, and iced gingerbread cookies that were already set out on the table. The enticing aroma of roasting turkey spread throughout the house, and some of the boarders had poked their heads in to sample a cookie or sweet, drawn by the savory smells.

"Miss Kate, this smells like home," Joe Smits said, his mouth full of gingerbread. "Thank you for bringing that back to me." His blue eyes were watery, and I knew he was as full of memories as I was. I patted his hand.

"I'm happy to do it, Joe. It is special, isn't it?"

He hugged me, and, startled, I hugged him back. "Merry Christmas."

"Merry Christmas to you, Miss Kate."

The sound of boots filled the room, and I looked over Joe's shoulder to see all the boarders at Miner's Rest coming into the dining room. Tom Murphy held out a package wrapped in silver foil to me, pressing it into my hands, and all the others had grins on their faces.

"We did this for you, Miss Kate, to thank you for all you done for us. You are something special, and we wanted to let you know how much we appreciate it."

I was taken aback, and mouth open to protest, I clamped my lips shut instead. *You will always be gracious, Katherine,* said my mother's voice somewhere in the back of my mind. It had been a long time since I'd had occasion to be gracious. Willing my hands to be steady, I carefully peeled back the foil paper. A delicately wrought silver and copper bird lay in my hand, its wings etched in careful patterns, the graceful curve of its head and body already warm to my touch. I couldn't speak, my throat closing with emotion.

"Our Timothy here, he's the one who molded it," Joe said, motioning to a young blond man, who blushed with the attention, while the rest patted him on the back. Joe smiled at me.

"We saved some bits here and there, and he turned it into what you see."

I swallowed. "Thank you," I managed, blinking back tears. "It's beautiful. I will cherish this always." I cradled the glowing bird in my hands. "All I have for you is dinner. Merry Christmas!"

"Oh no, Miss Kate," Joe said. "What you've given all of us is a home, and we wanted to let you know how much we appreciate it. Merry Christmas to you."

By five o'clock, it was near dark, and the bayberry candles had been replaced twice. It had been snowing since mid-morning and showed no signs of letting up; even the weather was festive for the holidays. Replete with food and drink, everyone was leaning back in their chairs. Maggie had joined us for dinner, along with George Hunt—both Christmas orphans like the rest of us. Platters still held turkey and stuffing, and we had taken to singing the old carols while indulging in the mince pies, plum pudding, and brandy. The front door banged shut, and a few errant snowflakes floated into the room, accompanied by one Doc Holliday—a sardonic grin on his face, his hat and cloak covered with snow.

"Ladies and gentlemen, greetin's of the season to you all! It's been the very devil of a journey to get to you, but on this holiest of days, the good lord has seen fit to deliver me." He took off his hat with a flourish and a bow, snow scattering on the wooden floor. "Kate, my angel of mercy, for Christ's sake as well as mine, where's the brandy?"

I sat at the kitchen table, the sky still dark outside the windows, and sipped my coffee. God, that was good. I'd disentangled myself from a sleeping Doc and in the last hour had cleaned up the kitchen from the ravages of Christmas dinner, put two large pans of sweet buns in the oven, and finally sat down. It was still snowing, that much was visible. This could be a landmark storm for Globe, from what I'd heard, and Mother Nature couldn't have picked a better time for it.

"Morning, my dear." Maggie crept into the kitchen, poured herself a cup of coffee, sat down beside me, and gave me a quick kiss on my cheek. She had spent the snowy night in the spare room upstairs rather than brave the storm outside, and I was glad.

"Quite the Christmas we had," I said, smiling into my coffee cup.

She laughed. "I'll say." She eyed me as speculatively as she could, given how much whiskey my elegant friend had consumed the previous evening. "Now I understand, Kate. Sorry I was such a doubting Thomas before. An evening with John Holliday has made me a believer."

I laughed. People could be charmed by Doc when he was in the mood, but I had thought Maggie could be immune, given her gloomy predictions on our long-distance relationship.

"Well, it seems he has made himself quite a coterie of admirers in Globe, Maggie, and now you're in the club." I poured myself another cup of coffee. "Should I be jealous?"

She set down her cup, and her eyes were clear as she stared at me. "Oh, my dear, I don't think you ever need to be jealous of anyone. Can you not see how he loves you? He's mad with it."

I smiled in spite of myself. I was doing a lot of that this morning, but having Doc in my bed always made me happy. "He's mad, period, but I'm just as mad, loving him the way I do."

"Then it's perfect," Maggie said, hugging me. Contentment suffused through me; on this day, that was all I felt.

New Year's Eve found us still somewhat snowbound but content in our snug nest. We had spent the evening with the miners, who had slogged to the mines for the last week, snow or no. I had been busy cooking warming soups and stews for all of us, to say nothing of amusing Doc, which didn't involve much cooking but proved to be more enjoyable. Evenings were pure entertainment, as Doc and I led everyone in songs he played on the old piano in the parlor. It was slightly out of tune but still serviceable. I could tell Doc was longing for the piano at the Grand Hotel in Tombstone. Nevertheless he was happy playing his favorite Chopin and even the songs I knew from my dance-hall days, which he had no trouble accompanying, as he had in the past. Globe was serene, and so were we.

"Ah, Holliday." I snuggled into him, and his arms held me gently as he kissed my temple.

"Just stay in Globe. Tombstone is a hellhole, and you know it. We can buy a ranch and make a life here, or if that's not enough, a stake to get us to San Francisco or Denver. We don't need Tombstone."

I refrained from the words "or the Earps," but it went without saying. He was silent for a long time, and I felt my heart sink.

"Kate," he whispered. "While it's true Tombstone is a 'hellhole' as you call it, there's a place for me there, and it's a place to make a lot of money. And Wyatt and Morgan need me, whether they know it or not." He turned me over and looked into my eyes. "They're such babies sometimes, and they don't understand the true nature of evil, which abounds in Tombstone. I can help."

"You're not your brother's keeper, Doc. Wyatt can take care of himself." Even as the words came out of my mouth, I knew it was the wrong thing to say, but there it was.

Doc sat up in bed, still cradling me in his arms. "I know that, Kate. Sometimes, though, you see bad things comin', and you have a choice whether to help or to walk away. I think I need to stay for a while, at least. Besides, I don't want to show up in a

new place like some down-at-the-heels Georgia cracker, so we
need a big stake. By this time next year, we can be on our way
to San Francisco in style. So for now, I'm goin' back."

He coughed lightly, and my arms tightened around him. This
man had so little left to give, and I wanted him near me, so I
could keep him whole and safe for whatever time we had. I
kissed him.

"Doc, that's a date. New Year's Eve, 1881, right here. I'm
looking forward to it." Even as I said those words, a frisson ran
down my spine, and, God help me, I knew the words were a lie.

CHAPTER 20

Tombstone, Arizona, July 1881

My hand brushed across the sheets beneath me, and I was surprised by their rough contour. They didn't smell particularly sweet either. The standards of the Grand Hotel had sunk since my last visit. I guess I'd have to have a talk with them. At the thought of Doc, something chimed in my memory, but I fell asleep again almost instantly.

When next I woke, it was to Virgil Earp's voice. The sheets had improved some, but not my memory.

"Get up and put some clothes on, Kate. I'm putting you on the stage in ten minutes, and I don't ever want to see your face in Tombstone again."

I blinked blearily, and Virgil's face swam into view, his usual stern visage rigidly angry. What in hell had I done to deserve this? Because I hadn't moved anything but my eyelids, he grabbed my arm and jerked me up in the bed.

"I'm not wasting any more time with you, woman. Get dressed, now, before Wyatt gets back here. I don't want to have to lock up my brother, too." He thrust some papers in front of me. "You're recanting those lies you told Behan. Sign these, or I swear to God I'll throw you back in jail or hand you over to Doc. Believe me, that is not something you want to happen right now."

Wyatt? Doc? I struggled to keep sitting up and to remember where I was and why, but my mind was proving false. My eyes skittered around the room. It was my usual room at the Grand. I saw my clothes crumpled on the floor and my traveling trunk, the one I always took with me on my visits to Doc and Tombstone. A flash of laughing faces crossed my mind—Johnny Behan, Milt Joyce, Johnny Ringo . . . then others, angry ones: Wyatt's and, of course, Virgil's. I shook my head, my hair falling back into my face. I pushed it back with trembling fingers. What had I done? I must've said that out loud because Virgil glared at me, shouting, and spittle landed on my cheeks.

"You expect me to believe you don't remember the havoc you've caused in the last three days, Kate? I don't believe you, and I don't think Doc ever will again, either."

He thrust an envelope at me, and banknotes spilled out onto the bed. "This is from him. He said to leave town, and he never wants to see you again. I'm here to make that happen."

With a befuddled but growing sense of dread, I fumbled my clothes on and signed the papers before Virgil rushed me onto the stage. It was early, and the good citizens of Tombstone were mostly still abed, at least the ones I knew. By the time we were halfway to Globe, I began to remember most of what had happened. As it came back to me in bits and pieces, I wanted nothing more than to throw myself out of the stagecoach the next time we rounded a steep cliff.

Globe was my haven, and one I badly needed. I threw myself into cleaning and refurbishing Miner's Rest, which I had neglected and left to Juanita and her daughters in my frequent travels to Tombstone this year. While they did a passable job, there was nothing like a homeowner's spring cleaning, long delayed, that gave a place its real polish. I fell into my bed and slept like the dead for nights on end, until early one morning I woke to the smell of coffee, obviously not brewed by my hands. I dressed hastily and made my way to the kitchen in the dark pre-dawn to find Maggie sitting at my kitchen table, sipping a mug of coffee, and another mug steaming in its place beside an empty chair. Just one candle burned in a pewter holder on the table, the flickering light warming the room.

"Morning, sunshine," she said, but her eyes were worried, and her smile was tight.

"And to you," I said, sitting down and picking up the cup. It was great coffee, nearly as good as mine. "Haven't seen you in a while."

She snorted and put down her cup. "You haven't seen anybody in a while, Kate. You've been holed up in here like a cornered rat. Time for a come-to-Jesus chat, I think. What in hell happened the last time you went to Tombstone?"

I stared out the window into the dark, but there were no answers out there. I turned back to Maggie. "I made a mistake, a bad mistake."

"We all do that sometimes," Maggie began, looking at me carefully, and her breath caught in her throat. "Jesus, woman, how much weight have you lost?"

I shook my head. "I don't know . . . It doesn't matter." I'd stopped looking in the mirror, because I didn't like what I saw. I knew I'd lost some weight, but from the look on Maggie's face it was worse than that. I didn't really care. I looked down at the floor.

Maggie lifted my chin, forcing me to meet her eyes. "All right, start at the beginning, back in July, when you went to Tombstone to see Doc. What was the first thing you did when you got there?"

I shook the dust from my skirts and descended the steps from the stagecoach, grateful for the driver's hand on my elbow. Hours of sitting inside the bumpy coach always took its toll, and my legs felt like rubber, but it was always worth it. As they unloaded my trunk and the boy from the Grand Hotel took off with it, I waited a moment to get my bearings. It was always like this when I visited Doc in Tombstone, and he hardly ever came to Globe anymore. I glimpsed Wyatt crossing the street a block ahead, going into the Oriental, and I made my way in the other direction to the Grand. Doc knew I was coming, but he rarely met me, usually busy with some thing or another, and the stage schedule was hit or miss, depending on many things—Apaches, bandits, broken wheels, lame horses, God knows what. I'd been lucky so far, as all my trips down here had been relatively uneventful. There was the occasional hysterical wife, lecherous salesman, or drunk rancher, but that was to be expected and nothing I couldn't handle.

It was getting dark outside by the time I finished my bath and dressed for the evening. I'd brought my blue silk, trimmed with black braid and jet bugle beads, one of Doc's favorites, and I'd put my hair into a chignon adorned with jet beads as well. There was still no sign of Doc, but I was hungry, so I headed downstairs to the dining room. He'd show up sooner or later; he always did. We'd agreed I would come July second, and we could spend the fourth together, sort of an anniversary for us, since we'd met back up in Las Vegas on the Fourth of July two years before. As I sat down to my table, I smiled at the memory of watching Doc step off the train that day.

Tombstone put Globe to shame in the culinary area, and I thoroughly enjoyed my solitary dinner, beef Wellington with an oyster appetizer. It was delicious, and the waiter had just delivered my ice cream and a chocolate gâteau when the other chair at my table was pulled out and Johnny Ringo bowed, his eyes locked on mine.

"May I join you, pretty lady?"

This is interesting, was my first thought. *Doc would be furious,* was my second. For some perverse reason, I nodded. Since my true love was making himself scarce, this would serve him right.

The waiter was hovering at Ringo's elbow when he gestured towards my half-full wineglass. "I'll have what the lady's having . . . a burgundy?" The waiter nodded, pleased. He produced another glass and poured, topping off mine as well. "And the gâteau, please; it looks marvelous."

I smiled. "It's unusual for a Cowboy to know a gâteau from a gambling chip, Mr. Ringo," I said, sipping my wine. "But then I don't think you've always been a . . . Cowboy, have you?"

He inclined his head. "Of course not, Miss Kate, but you understand that, don't you? Just like you're a touch out of place here yourself, you and Holliday?"

"Perhaps, *étranger dans un pays étranger?*"

He saluted me with his wineglass, and something close to a smile crossed his thin lips. "*Oui, madame. Etranger celui qui a appris, n'est-ce pas?*"

"We have all learned, Mr. Ringo. Strangers must adapt. Mere survival is insufficient, I quite agree."

We finished our dessert and the wine, and we ordered another bottle. It was a delight to talk and parry words with someone who could not only keep up but challenge me, and after he graciously paid the check, we made our way to the street and the evening ahead. I peered owlishly up and down the street, much to Ringo's amusement. The burgundy was having an effect.

"Looking for someone, *cherie?*"

I flushed in spite of myself. There was still no sign of Doc, and I was starting to get angry. I clutched Ringo's arm. "Not really. Let's play some cards."

Midnight came and went, as did we, moving from saloon to saloon—with the exception of the Oriental. I lost some money, then won some more, and I can't remember laughing as much in a long time. There was something about Ringo, and not just his looks. He was darkly handsome and clearly dangerous, which always appealed to me, but he was also a sophisticated, charming man and God only knew how he'd ended up here. I was hardly one to judge, given my own past and Doc's as well. The West harbored refugees from other lives, and once in a while you ran into someone with similar tastes and backgrounds. It didn't happen often. Perhaps we didn't always want to find out, more likely. Even so, I knew I was treading on quicksand with this one.

"Well, Miss Kate, how lovely to see you this evening." Johnny Behan sat down at our table, briefly lifting his derby hat, and his companion, Milt Joyce, echoed his greeting and pulled out a chair. They poured shots from the whiskey they'd brought along, and time spun away again. I knew Doc disliked him, but tonight Behan seemed quite the gentleman. Milt, not so much. But then, just because the Earps hated these people, that didn't mean a lot to me. Tombstone politics were convoluted, and every time Doc had started up that everyone in town was a cheating bastard except him and the Earps, I stopped listening. I hadn't been listening tonight, either, but when Milt Joyce swore and slammed the whiskey bottle down, I couldn't help but pick up on the conversation that had been going on while Ringo and I were absorbed in the merits of Byron versus Keats.

"You know damn well Doc and the Earps had a hand in it, John," Milt said, his face red. "I'm going after those lying bastards if it's the last thing I do."

Behan put his hand on Joyce's shoulder, leaned over, and whispered in his ear, and I saw Joyce flick his eyes in my direction before the two of them got up and headed over to the bar. I looked at Ringo.

"I haven't been paying attention, but there seem to be some political convolutions going on here," I said, "and it doesn't look like it's a real happy family here in Tombstone between the

Democrats and Republicans. What's the story tonight?"

Ringo gazed at me, eyes hooded. "It's your boy Holliday that's got them riled up. They've got reliable information he was behind the stage robbery where Philpott got killed last March, but the Earps are protecting him, like they always do."

Righteous indignation shot through me. "That's bullshit. Doc's no stage robber. He's a gambler, not some common criminal."

Ringo laughed. "Come on, Kate. We all know better than just an honest gambler. Doc's got his fingers in a lot of pies, so to speak. Maybe you don't know him as well as you used to, since you've been in Globe so much."

I stood up, and Ringo gently pulled me back down. "Do you know, for instance, where your man is at this moment? Because I do."

My head was spinning. I'd had way too much to drink, even for me at my finest. Ringo's words were buzzing in my head, and that chocolate gâteau was threatening to make an encore, but the worst of it all was a sick feeling that he knew something I didn't. I put my head down and took a deep breath. Then I sat up and looked Ringo in the eye, at least as much as I could manage.

"Where is he?"

"Oh, I'll show you. First, let's visit the Chinaman. You'll like it, I guarantee."

I'd never tried opium, but somehow, with Ringo's urging, I believed it would be all right. When we left the Chinaman's, the dark alley seemed lit like a kaleidoscope, full of colors and even scents I'd never noticed before. Were we still in Tombstone? It seemed like a different world.

It was very dark. Ringo held my arm and guided me as we passed unfamiliar buildings. He turned into an alley and then into the hallway of a two-story building. We passed inside and through a corridor that smelled faintly of perfume, stopping before a closed door. He opened the door silently, and the occupants inside, bathed in a softly lit world of their own, were oblivious to us. Doc was bent over a pretty, dark-haired woman, cradling her in his arms, and the look on his face was one of such tenderness I caught my breath. It looked as though this was no whore for the evening but clearly someone he cared for. I had always known he amused himself when away from me, but the depth of this betrayal was like an arrow to my heart. I stumbled and clutched Ringo's arm, and he gently shut the door and led me away.

I didn't remember much after that, only drinking as much as I could. I think more opium was involved somewhere along into morning. I do remember the humiliation and blinding rage that led me to sign the papers Behan put in front of me, incriminating Doc. I knew it was a lie, but I only wanted to hurt him as he'd hurt me. I know I woke up in a cell in Behan's jail. I think I was truly mad, then, and when he let me out, admonishing me slyly to "look after myself," I went to the nearest saloon and drank away the hurt until I couldn't remember anything else I did that day at all. When Virgil Earp took custody of me and put me back in my hotel room, and then onto the stage to Globe the next morning, I still hadn't seen Doc. I have never known such hurt and despair—to the point where I didn't care if I lived or died—but I only knew that everything I held dear had ebbed away.

When Virgil handed me the money and said Doc never wanted to see me again after what I'd done, I collapsed into the seat on the stagecoach. On the long trip back to Globe, I never left the stage except to use the facilities twice. I only drank water and slept, wanting to wash away the last four days of my life but knowing that I never could.

Maggie bent over me, enveloping me in her arms as I lay my head onto the familiar, scrubbed wooden table. She held me as I sobbed for the first time in years, and it felt as though all the anguish and shame I'd held in for so long was pouring out of me with those salty tears. After a time, Maggie held a damp cloth to my face and sat me up. I couldn't breathe, and I took the cloth from her, blowing my nose ferociously.

"Come on," she said. She pulled me out of the kitchen and into my bed, tucking the sheets around me. "Don't even think about moving, Kate. The girls will be here any minute, and between the three of us, we'll feed these miners and get them on their way. Sleep now. I'll be here."

I started to protest, and she put her cool hand on my forehead, shushing me softly. In a swirl of skirts she was gone, and my eyes closed, the damp dishcloth still clutched in my hand, the words stilled on my tongue.

Summer lost its grip, and the evenings grew cool as October arrived. Maggie came by every couple of days, or I stopped in at her place. I felt as though I'd come back to life, even though it was one short on enthusiasm, let alone passion, for much of anything. After my confession I felt better, not about where things were or my life, but that somehow I could begin to atone for the havoc I'd wreaked in Tombstone. I knew Doc was in no legal trouble because of my recant, but that wasn't enough. I wrote to Wyatt, knowing the chances were he'd throw away the letter unopened, but I had to try. He was the only person who could get Doc to listen to my explanation and apology. For old times' sake, or maybe some lingering compassion, I hoped he would talk to him. As the weeks passed, though, I knew it was a feeble hope, and the odds were I'd never see Doc again—and I couldn't blame him. That I was stung by his betrayal and insanely drunk was not justification for what I'd done to him in retaliation, and I knew it. It was highly likely the entire thing had been plotted days in advance, and if Behan, Ringo, and Joyce were standing in front of me, I'd take great pleasure in shooting them all dead. In reality, they were in little danger, as they weren't likely to show up in Globe, and I'd have to be so drunk to actually do it, I'd miss anyway.

My garden had long given up the ghost in the heat of summer, but I decided to plant squashes and potatoes that would ripen before the December frosts. Anything I could grow helped feed my ravenous boarders and saved me money. Every morning after the men left, I would don an old apron and tend the plants, taking off my shoes and socks and reveling in the feel of the soft dirt between my toes. I'd never really spent time or actually gotten my hands dirty in a garden before coming to Globe, and I found that I loved it. The sun, not so strong now, dappled my face as I worked, and the air was fresh and cool. Little birds, my nemeses in spring when they got to my tomatoes before I did, swooped around me from their perches in the two cottonwood trees that shaded the yard, and now I smiled at their antics. As I weeded, I thought how affronted my mother would be to see me working like a servant, or what the cowboys would think to see the Hungarian songbird grubbing in the dirt and covered with sweat, and that made me laugh out loud. How things change.

I finished watering and put the tools and watering can in the shed, stretching my back to work out the cricks from bending over so long. I turned back to the kitchen door and stopped when I saw a man crouching on the porch, his face hidden by his hat, hands resting on his knees. When he stood up I drew in my breath, stunned with disbelief.

"Kate," Doc said, and I sank to my knees in the dirt.

The delectable spiced beef in the fried tortillas burned my throat, but I quenched the fire with a concoction of tequila and lime juice the street vendor had handed me with a knowing smile. I took another bite. It was delicious, as was all the food Doc and I had eaten since we'd arrived down here. We'd been in Tucson for two days now as the guests of Señor Leo Carillo, and it had been delightful. Carillo's estate was beautiful, and he told us of his plans to expand his gardens to include boating ponds, orchards, and even a dancehall and a restaurant. Doc certainly knew some interesting people.

Tucson was a mix of American newcomers of every stripe but was built on the Mexican culture of its founders. It was different from all the other hardscrabble villages or towns I'd seen in the West. Most Eastern newcomers tried to emulate the culture they'd left; Tucson was already unique in its own right, from the architecture to the food. The rest of Arizona's cuisine literally paled in comparison with the exotic and abundant fare here, from the tacos to the cheese-covered tortillas and beans, and so much more—I could eat myself into another dress size.

This night the Carillos hosted a grand party, or *fiesta*. Flickering colored lanterns and Spanish guitars accompanied the bright swirl of the women's skirts and shawls, accentuated by the attractive tight black suits of the men, and smiles and flashing eyes promised excitement beyond that of the dance. I reveled in the colors, the music, and the passion.

"Care to dance, señorita?" Doc held my elbow and grinned, and I laughed and followed him into the crowd, twirling my own full red skirt bought just this afternoon.

We'd been together nearly every minute since Doc had shown up in Globe, almost as though we were afraid to let each other out of our sight. We'd agreed to never discuss it again, but not before I'd poured my heart out, most of which he knew from everything I'd written to Wyatt, and I explained why I'd been so crazed. We put it behind us, and, somehow, we managed that. For a few days we'd spoken to no one, holing up in my rooms at the boardinghouse while Maggie and the girls took over. When he suggested the trip to Tucson, I agreed. I met with Maggie and cut her in for twenty percent of the Miner's Rest, which she richly deserved, and we boarded the stage without a backward glance. Sometimes you find out what really matters in life—I'd learned that my feelings about the boardinghouse didn't even come close to what I felt for Doc. Right now, we needed to be together and to put our mistakes behind us.

We fell asleep in each other's arms after the excitement of the fiesta, and when the maid's gentle knock signaled chocolate and pastry on the tray outside the door, I slipped away. I sat on the balcony and watched the town come alive while I sipped chocolate. I wasn't sure what would come next, but for once I didn't care, as long as we were together. Doc's coughing signaled his wakefulness, and I poured another cup for him. He wasn't doing well, much as he tried to hide it. I had refrained from chiding him, and at least he'd gotten some rest since he came back to me. And he had stayed away from saloons, although I knew that wasn't likely to last.

"Darlin', good mornin'," he said, leaning against the balcony door and blinking in the sunlight. His face was paler than usual, and I felt a guilty pang about our exuberant dancing but tamped it down. Doc would do as he pleased, and the last few days had pleased him greatly.

"Good morning to you," I said, handing him a cup. He took it and eased down into a chair beside me. "How you feeling?"

He took a sip of chocolate, coughed, and bent over, the cup clattering back onto the table.

At least he hadn't thrown it. I knew better than to say anything, but I stood up and helped him back inside. When he got this bad, all that helped was rest.

"Remember when we talked about headin' up to Colorado?" Doc said, taking my hand as he leaned back on the pillows. "I think we should do that before the snows come. Arizona's tirin' me out."

I smoothed his hair back off his forehead. "Then that's what we'll do, my love. Tomorrow we'll head back up to Globe, and I'll make arrangements with Maggie. We need a fresh start, someplace with a real future."

He smiled and closed his eyes, and I sat there until his breathing quieted and he fell asleep. *Thank God*, I thought. Away from the Earps, and away from Tombstone and Globe, neither of them places I wanted to stay, and both rife with bad memories.

While Doc slept, I readied myself and went downstairs. I said good morning to Señora Carillo and headed out to find a pharmacy or herb shop to get medicine for Doc. The town was bustling with energy and growth. Stone and adobe buildings housed banks, assay and business offices of all kinds, as well as shopping emporiums, perhaps without the imported glossiness of some of Tombstone's more garish comparisons, but seeming of a more permanent, traditional stripe. I found a Mexican store selling herbs and bought several packets, getting what I needed for Doc's breathing. A block farther, I saw an ice cream parlor with marble counters and pretty chairs and tables, and I had another breakfast of vanilla ice cream and a sweet roll. The menu was strictly American, this town of two worlds coexisting well together. I stepped out into the sunshine, feeling satiated but a little anxious about Doc.

"Kate!" I turned around and saw Morgan Earp running towards me. "Christ, I've been looking everywhere for you—but in saloons, not ice cream parlors!" He laughed, wiped his forehead, and put his arm through mine. "It's good luck I saw you. Where's Doc?"

Oh, no. How did they always manage to find us, and what in hell could he want? "Hello, Morg. Doc's not feeling his best," I said. He was clearly agitated, and his clothes were dusty from the road. "Why are you here?"

"It's them goddamn Cowboys," he muttered darkly. "There's going to be trouble. Wyatt sent me to find Doc 'cause he's likely to need his help."

I didn't like the sound of this at all, and I liked Morgan's frantic demeanor even less. Doc didn't need this sort of problem right now, and the only way I could imagine him being of help to Wyatt sounded ominous. I wished I'd never ventured past the Carillos' front door this morning. Morgan would never have known to come there. There didn't seem to be any choice, so the two of us walked back to the Carillos' while I tried to think of a way to keep Doc safe within those thick adobe walls, serene against the needs of Wyatt Earp and his brothers.

As we entered the cool front hall, Mrs. Carillo met us. I introduced Morgan, who was clearly impressed with the elegance of the place, but we didn't have much opportunity for him to become better acquainted.

"Kate, Doc was feeling better and left to go downtown," she said, frowning in disapproval. "He didn't look very well to me, but he told me to tell you he 'felt like a game,' and that you'd understand."

We found Doc playing faro at Charlie Brown's Congress Hall Saloon. Morgan put his hands on Doc's shoulders and whispered in his ear while I sat at the bar and had a whiskey. *Everything is falling apart,* I thought. *Damn Doc and damn the Earps.* I had no desire to leave Tucson and even less to go to Tombstone on command, but I'd be damned if I'd let Doc go alone. I knew better than anyone how nasty the relationship between the Earps and the Cowboys had become. Tombstone was a powder keg, and I didn't want us to be anywhere around when the fuse was lit.

"Kate, I think you should stay here with the Carillos and then go on to Globe," Doc said. "I'll meet up with you there." We were on our way back to the Carillos' house to pack, Morgan trotting alongside.

"Good plan," Morgan said. "We're taking the freight train to Benson, and then a buckboard to Tombstone. It's a rough ride for a lady."

Presumptuous ass, I thought. I stopped dead in the street and put my hands on my hips, wanting nothing more than to punch Morg in the face, much as I liked him. "If you are taking a freight, I am taking a freight. If you are taking a buckboard, I am taking a buckboard. Where you go, I go, and that's not up for discussion, Holliday."

Doc laughed until he started to cough, his face flushed. "You heard the lady, Morg. She's comin'." Morgan was not pleased, but there was little he could do about it. Two hours later, we were on the train, and by the next day, we were in Tombstone. Morgan was right, it was a rough ride and not just for a lady. By the time we got to Doc's room at Fly's Boardinghouse, we both collapsed on the featherbed like it was a cloud in heaven. Whatever Wyatt needed, he'd have to wait until Doc was up and walking, and if I had anything to say about it, the first place he'd be walking was straight to the stagecoach for Globe.

CHAPTER 21

Tombstone, October 25, 1881

I rolled over onto my side but that didn't stop my lower back from silently screaming. God almighty, that many hours bouncing on the seat of a buckboard had taken a heavy toll. I heard the jingle of a watch chain and opened my eyes. Doc stood beside the bed, fully dressed.

"Kate, you never cease to amaze me," he said. "That was quite a devastatin' journey."

I thought of a lot of other names for it, but then I *had* insisted on coming. "Where are you going, mister? You've been coughing up a storm, and you should get right back in here with me." I held out the sheet invitingly, and he laughed.

"Darlin', I get back in there with you, and I won't get any rest at all. I need to find Wyatt and see why he was in a such a hurry to get us back here. Then I'm going over to the Alhambra to work. If you want to get to Colorado soon, we need a bigger stake. Maybe you could scare up a game or two yourself." He raised an eyebrow. "If your backside's feelin' up to it."

I snorted and pulled the sheet over my head. "Go, then. My backside and I will be just fine without you." He pulled off the sheet, kissed me on the forehead, and shut the door softly on his way out.

I tried to go back to sleep, but I couldn't. My back hurt, and my mind was racing too fast. By the look of the sun coming through the window, it had to be around noon. Doc was right.

If we wanted to get to Colorado, we needed to make as much money as we could, and Tombstone was just the place to do it—much as I didn't want to be here. As for whatever Wyatt wanted, it couldn't be good. Ever since Doc had saved his life in Dodge City, Wyatt always turned to Doc when he needed somebody to watch his back. With the Cowboys rampaging around the county, that could be now. I sighed and threw off the bedcovers.

"Hello, Mollie," I said, coming down the stairs. Mollie Fly was at her desk in the photography studio, as usual. She was a little thing, an inch or two shorter than me, but she carried herself like a queen. She commanded the respect of one, too, from everyone in town, including her husband. Buck Fly was always off here and there with his camera, and Mollie held down the photography business and boardinghouse in perfect order. I liked her, and the feeling was mutual. She was fond of Doc as well. He did have a way about him with the ladies.

Mollie looked up and smiled. "Hi there, Kate. I saw Doc leave a while back, and I figured you'd come back with him. Coffee?" She gestured towards the kitchen, where she always had some brewing, one of the things I liked about staying here. Doc found it comfortable and homier as well as much less expensive than the Grand's elegant sterility, and he'd been here for six months now.

"Thanks, Mollie, that'd be lovely." I got a cup of coffee and wandered back into the gallery. The Flys' photographs were wonderful, and I never tired of looking at them. Mollie specialized in studio portraits, capturing the very essence of a person, while Buck traveled around the West, posing his subjects wherever he found them. They were eclectic: Indians, ranchers, miners, farm women, and children. He was a true genius with a camera. It always surprised and delighted me to find such artistry on the frontier. Finishing my coffee, I headed down to the Alhambra to deal some poker myself.

By seven o'clock, I was tired of sitting, and I'd made around $200. I stood up and fanned the cards.

"Sorry, boys, this lady's taking a break," I said, to a general chorus of groans. "Go have a drink or two, and we'll get back to business in a while." The bodice on my blue silk dress was cut low and I leaned down, smiling enticingly. "You boys behave yourselves now." The six men grinned back, and I gave them a little something to remember as I sashayed out to the lunch counter. Doc had stopped by earlier and said to meet him there, where we usually ate when we were working the games at the Alhambra. The Alhambra was pretty elegant, especially for a frontier saloon, and I particularly liked the crystal barware. Whiskey always tasted better in a good glass. The Oriental was even more spectacular, with its chandeliers and Brussels carpet, but I was giving Milt Joyce a wide berth after last summer. Besides, Wyatt ran a faro table there, so I always avoided the place on principle.

I sat down beside Doc, who was engrossed in his fried chicken dinner, and ordered the same from the smiling waiter who appeared instantly.

"Goin' well?" Doc asked.

"Fairly," I said, settling my reticule on my lap. "Nobody's losing the mine yet, but the night is young. You?"

Doc nodded, taking a bite of mashed potatoes. I was glad to see his appetite had returned after the spell in Tucson. "Quite well, my dove. We will need to go to the bank tomorrow."

I laughed. "That's quite well. I'll have to up my game to match you."

"Indeed."

The waiter brought my dinner, and it smelled so delicious I discovered I was ravenously hungry. I don't think we'd really eaten anything except some biscuits and apples on the way to

Tombstone the previous night. Before I'd taken a bite, a shadow fell across the table.

"Holliday, you goddamn pimp, you got a lot to answer for!" the man said, knocking the fork out of Doc's hand. "Stand up like a man, and stop telling lies."

Doc put down his napkin and eyed the drunken, smelly Cowboy who stood beside our table.

"I have no idea what in hell you are talkin' about," he said mildly. "Who are you, again?"

"Ike Clanton, as you well know." He spat the words in Doc's face. "I'm the one you're selling out, you fucking liar."

Doc was genuinely surprised, and I was so shocked I wasn't sure what to do. Looking frantically around the restaurant, I saw a couple of waiters standing open mouthed, and I knew they weren't going to be much help. Two of the other diners threw down their napkins and made a hasty exit.

Doc stood up, fingering the pistol in his waistcoat. "You, sir, are a lout whose breath smells like he's been dinin' on corpses. Since I have been in this community, I have had to put up with people such as yourself—a sub-species of humanity lower than dogs, who are likely dismayed at the comparison. I'll no longer lower myself to do so. You disgust me. If you want to fight, be a man and get yourself heeled, for I will not countenance another second in your company."

I pushed back my chair and started to stand up, but Doc pressed me back down. Bright spots of color blossomed on his cheeks, and I knew he was lethally angry. Ike Clanton was about to die.

"Apologize to me and my lady," Doc said, his voice tight. Clanton, his eyes wild, didn't seem to hear him.

"You're all in on it, you and those goddamn Earps. You're going to pay," Ike shouted, his hands twitching as he slammed them on the table.

Doc's hand tightened on his pistol, but before he could draw it, Morgan and Wyatt Earp converged on our table and dragged Ike outside—while he cursed and fought them every step of the way.

I drew a deep breath and put my hand on Doc's arm. "Let it go, Doc. We don't need this kind of trouble."

Dazed, he looked down at me, his eyes bright with anger, and started to step away from the table. Virgil Earp loomed up at his side like a frowning fencepost, the marshal badge shining on his brocade vest.

"Sit down and calm down, Doc," he said. "Any more trouble out of you or that Clanton moron, I'll have to jail you both. I won't have a choice."

To my surprise, Doc did so, and Virgil left, apparently to deliver the same message to Ike Clanton, still ranting outside in the street.

We sat in silence for a few minutes, dinner forgotten, so I went to the bar and got us two whiskeys. When I returned, Wyatt was sitting at the table. I handed Doc his drink.

"God, Doc, I'm sorry I didn't see you earlier today. I didn't know Ike was in town," Wyatt said. "He's convinced you're going to sell him out, and this whole damn thing is my fault. He agreed to testify against some of his Cowboy friends, but it's just been between him and me. For some reason, he thinks you know about it, and he's been scared crazy." He looked at Doc pleadingly, and I watched him squirm. This was just the sort of thing Wyatt would try to pull, and I'd be damned if I'd help him wriggle out of it.

Doc gazed at him, face weary. "Wyatt, you are my friend, and I always support you, but these people are like rabid dogs, and there's no end to it. That idiot is threatenin' to kill me, along with you and your brothers, and he's got backup with the rest of his moronic pack. We are going to have to put an end to this, or leave."

For the first time, Wyatt didn't meet Doc's eye. "It'll blow over; it always does. Ike's just drunk. By tomorrow, he'll go back to his ranch."

Doc took my hand and stood up. "I hope so, Wyatt, because my patience is at an end. Kate and I are headin' up to Colorado."

Wyatt shot me a baleful look, and I smiled innocently and downed my whiskey. The hell with him. A favor from him didn't mean I owed him anything; it only made a small dent in his debit account from the past. He didn't want to lose his best friend, even though he knew leaving Tombstone was the best option for Doc.

"Gentlemen," I said, setting the glass on the table and smoothing my skirts, "I have a game to play, and I'm sure I will see you during the course of the evening." I swept out of the restaurant, and, when I looked back, they were silent, staring at my departing skirts. Men.

The evening passed without further incident, even though some Cowboys sat in on my game for a while. I made another couple hundred, and I knew Doc was doing fairly well, too. A few times I heard shouts from the street outside, and I recognized Ike Clanton's voice, along with some of his Cowboy friends. The idiot never seemed to shut his mouth. I wasn't frightened, necessarily, but it was unsettling to know someone who threatened dire harm to those you cared about was running loose through the town. It was around two o'clock when Doc stopped at my table and nodded towards the door on his way to the bar. I dealt my last hand and closed down my table, and we stepped outside together in the cold air. I pulled my shawl closer, and our footsteps made little sound on the packed dirt. We were joined by Wyatt as he left the Oriental. It was mostly dark, although in Tombstone the saloons and bars never really closed, and lights flickered in windows. A surprising number of people walked quietly home or on to other pursuits.

"Pimps and lying whores, that's what they are. Come tomorrow morning, I'll shoot the first Earp I see, I swear to God." Ike Clanton careened into the Occidental saloon, staggering against the door frame. People looked over their shoulders and walked a little faster. The door slammed shut. For the first time, I was genuinely worried. I stopped dead in the middle of the street, and Doc and Wyatt did, too, both turning to look at me in the dim light.

"That was charming," I said acidly. "I would not say this has 'blown over.' Do any of you have a plan on how to deal with this, besides drowning the elegant Mr. Clanton in the nearest horse trough?" I looked at Wyatt first, and then shifted my gaze to Doc. "I suggest you get one because I have no intention of mopping up blood or burying either one of you. He sounds serious to me, drunk or not. What's Virgil doing, besides threatening to jail anyone Ike decides to yell at?"

Doc gripped my arm. "Kate," he said, "stop it." The threat was implicit, and I knew Doc was much more agitated than he'd let on. Wyatt, however, started to laugh and doubled over, in the grip of nervous hysteria. Doc and I stared at him.

"My dear brother Virgil, whose self-righteousness could get us all killed," he gasped, "has been playing cards off and on with the McLowrys and some of the Clantons since midnight, and likely still is." He wiped his eyes, regaining composure. "This town is a madhouse, and damn near all the people in it are insane."

None of us said another word. We resumed walking towards Fly's, and we couldn't get there soon enough to suit me. When we stepped onto the wooden porch, Doc turned back to Wyatt.

"Madhouse or not, as far as I'm concerned, Wyatt, Tombstone, and I are about done. Ike Clanton comes at me one more time and I'm likely to gut him like a rabbit."

He turned, his cape swirling. He escorted me through the door, and Wyatt turned and walked off into the dark, alone.

Upstairs, Doc sank back onto the feather pillows of our bed and watched wordlessly as I undressed. After I unpinned my hair and when I was down to my shift, he sat up and took off his waistcoat, then his vest, and finally his belt. He studiously put his cufflinks on the nightstand, unbuttoned his shirt, and resettled himself on the pillows. Two fresh crystal glasses and a bottle of whiskey stood on the nightstand. He poured the amber liquid into both of them, raising one to me.

I knew he shouldn't drink any more tonight, especially with the looming possibility of trouble tomorrow, but at the moment I didn't care. I took the glass from his hand and sat beside him. I caressed the pale skin on his chest, and he took my hand, turning it over and pressing his lips into my palm. It was a simple gesture but one that ignited a searing wave that reached to my core. He knew it, and he smiled as he pulled me close.

"Ah, Kate. We make each other truly alive, don't we?"

"You know we do," I murmured, my lips soft on his belly. "Do nothing foolish until we're out of here, and we can have this every day for the rest of our lives."

He wrapped his hand around my hair and twisted, pulling me gently up to look into my eyes. "Do not dictate to me, darlin'. You of all people know better than that." His hand tightened, and my neck arched. He gazed into my eyes, and I saw no smile there now. "I will do what honor demands, as I have always done and always will."

This was not an evening for defiance. Doc was edgier than I'd seen him for a long time. I lowered my eyes, and he released his hold on my hair. I poured another whiskey for each of us, straddled him, and held the glass to his lips.

285

"For now, our world is here in this room, and that's all we need," I said. I took the glass and set it on the table, then smoothed his hair back from his forehead. Some silver strands shot through the sandy blond locks, although he was only thirty, less than a year younger than I was. Then I dedicated myself to the one thing I knew would bring him solace, very likely what I did better than any other woman in the world.

Pre-dawn light filtered through the muslin curtains. Doc slept like a baby, his breathing easy. I eased away from him and went to the window, staring into the vacant lot beside Fly's. I could see Fremont Street around the corner of the building, and, as I watched, a tall figure strode down the street. Virgil Earp was done with gambling and on his way home to bed at last.

I dozed off and on for a few hours. Then I threw on a wrapper and tiptoed down to the kitchen. Mollie was already there, a stack of photographic plates before her on the table. I poured a cup of coffee and sat down across from her.

"Up early for you, Kate," she said. "It's not even nine. Can't sleep in?"

"No, but I'll go back up soon and try again." I yawned. "Not much going on for us until later in the day."

Mollie chuckled. "I never did hold with that Puritan 'early to bed, early to rise' silliness myself."

We drank our coffee companionably in silence, and in Mollie's calming presence I began to feel easier. After a while I nodded gratefully at her and went back upstairs, stretching out on my back beside Doc, who slept peacefully on. I didn't want to do anything today, and, clearly, Doc needed rest, too. As I sank wearily into oblivion, I thought maybe today would be a fine day in Tombstone after all.

"Kate!" Mollie Fly was knocking insistently on our door. I

looked over at Doc, who was still asleep, and got up and opened the door.

"That Ike Clanton is downstairs, looking for Doc. He's far from sober, as usual, and he's armed." She clutched my arm. "He scares me, Kate, and Buck's out somewhere. We need to get rid of him."

Christ. If Doc had to put up with Ike Clanton right now, he'd likely kill him. Doc stirred, and I pulled the door shut softly and hurried Mollie down the stairs before he could hear us.

"Where's that chickenshit pimp, Holliday?" Ike stood in the photo gallery, brandishing a rifle, with a pistol shoved into the waistband of his baggy pants. "Hiding behind your skirts?"

The man was crazy, as well as drunk. If Virgil saw him like this, he'd lock him up for carrying guns in town. Then I remembered seeing Virgil at dawn, so maybe he was still home in bed.

"Ike, listen to me," I said, not reacting to his slurs. "Doc's not here, but I'll tell him you're looking for him. He's probably already over at the Alhambra, so maybe you could check there first?"

"That's right," Mollie said, backing me up. "Doc left here some time ago, saying something about breakfast."

Clanton stared suspiciously at both of us. "That goddamn Wyatt already buffaloed Frank McLowry this morning, and we're being treated like dogs. You tell Holliday we're after blood this time." Then, apparently deciding we were being truthful with him, he turned on his heel and left, weaving his way up Fremont Street.

Mollie shook her head. "This is getting nasty, Kate. I saw Wyatt lose his temper this morning on my way to the bank, and he sent Morgan to get Virgil. There's more Cowboys with guns coming in, too. I saw the Claibornes, the McLowrys, and Billy

Clanton on the way back."

I started back up the stairs. "Don't worry, Mollie. I'm going to try my damnedest to keep Doc out of it, at least. I'm sorry you had to be involved in this."

Mollie patted me on the shoulder. "Not your fault, Kate. Life in Tombstone, I guess."

Soon after, Morgan showed up. I had to tell Doc that Ike Clanton had been looking for him, and he and Morg exchanged glances.

"If the bastard will let me get some clothes on, he'll see me all right," Doc said. He looked a little peaked, but he was in no mood to listen to me, and I knew better than to try. He was building a head of steam, so when he and Morg left, I decided to spend the afternoon reading and avoid any further turmoil on this chilly afternoon. I'd made good money yesterday, and I needed a day away from the saloons anyway.

When I heard voices outside and looked out the window, I ran down the stairs and out the front door of Fly's. Wyatt, Morgan, Virgil, and Doc stood in the street, facing the Cowboys in the corral. I saw the McLowry brothers and Billy Clanton.

Wyatt yelled, "This is not what I wanted!" and I knew something terrible was about to happen. Ike Clanton, eyes wide, came running out of nowhere and was practically on his knees grabbing onto Wyatt, drunkenly babbling something.

"Get to fighting or get out of the way," Wyatt snarled. Ike nearly toppled me as he staggered to his feet and ran past me into Fly's, then off again down Fremont Street, just as Buck Fly appeared in the doorway. I grabbed onto a porch post and saw Wyatt shoot Frank McLowry in the stomach while about a dozen guns went off at once. Frank was still shooting, along with Billy Clanton, who fell but got up and staggered towards us as he tried to reload his pistol. Buck Fly stepped out and grabbed the gun from him, and Billy turned back towards the horses, falling as I watched. It was hard to tell who shot Billy, since all the Earps were shooting, and Doc as well. Powder smoke swirled, and I tried desperately to see Doc, but I knew better than to step from the porch—and even there I had an urge to dive for the wooden boardwalk. I saw Mollie poke her head up in the window, then dive back down.

Virgil Earp crumpled to his knees, shot in the leg by Frank McLowry, who was wounded himself, but they both kept shooting. Then, Morgan screamed as Billy Clanton's last shot went into his shoulder.

A scared Tom McLowry had stood behind his horse up until this point, and I saw him reach for the shotgun in his saddle scabbard. As I screamed a warning nobody could possibly hear in the din of gunshots, I saw Doc raise his shotgun and shoot Tom, who fell over in a spray of blood.

Wyatt stood untouched, firing off shot after shot from the revolver in his hand. Frank McLowry, incredibly, was still standing, blood spattered on his shirt and pants. He staggered into Fremont Street towards Doc, who backstepped in anticipation. Frank raised his pistol.

"I've got you now, you son of a bitch."

Doc smiled. "Blaze away. You're a daisy if you do." Doc's shotgun boomed, and Frank toppled into the dust.

As suddenly as it began, the shooting stopped. It couldn't have been more than a minute, but it seemed like an eternity to me. I ran to Doc through the fog of gunsmoke. He'd sunk to his knees, blood trickling down his trousers.

"Ah God, Kate," he muttered, leaning on my shoulder. "That was awful, just awful."

I saw Louisa and Allie Earp arrive, running to their men, but Mattie Blaylock stood out on Fremont Street in her usual laudanum haze, staring at all of them and then walking away.

Johnny Behan arrived, waving his cane. "Wyatt, I have to arrest you."

Wyatt stared at Behan like he was an annoying fly. "Johnny, you deceived me and told me you disarmed them. I don't think I'll let you arrest me today." Behan, flustered, turned away, and Wyatt stood still as a statue, feet planted where he'd started, in the dust of the O.K. Corral.

I wrung out the cloths I had soaked in disinfectant according to Doc's instructions and passed them to Dr. Goodfellow, who accepted them reluctantly.

"Dr. Holliday, I don't think this is necessary," he said.

Doc, impatient, barked in his face. "Infection will undo everythin' else we've done here, George. Just do it, please."

Both Morgan and Virgil had nasty wounds, which we were still caring for many hours after the gunfight. Tom and Frank McLowry and Billy Clanton were in coffins, rouged and suited up, and neither doctors nor God would save them now. We were all on edge, holed up in Morg's house, and worried about retaliation from the Clantons, Curly Bill, or some of the other Cowboys. Rumors were swirling around town that they had vowed revenge, so all of us were armed, except for Dr. Goodfellow. A coroner's inquest had been held this morning, but, so far, no decisions had been made, as far as we knew.

"Go lie down, Lou," I said, gently pushing her towards the bedroom in the small house she shared with Morgan, where we had set up our makeshift surgery. She hadn't slept a wink, holding Morgan's hand, and neither had Allie, who hadn't left Virgil's side, either. Both of them were too upset to be of much use in changing dressings or blood-soaked bandages, so I had stepped into that task and, along with Doc, assisted George Goodfellow. Wyatt, gaunt and grim-faced, had hovered over all of us until I finally wiped my hands on my apron and took him by the arm.

"Get out of here and sleep," I said, gripping more firmly as he tried to pull away. "You are doing no one good, and only yourself harm." His blue eyes blazed at me, but I steered him outside into the porch. "If you don't want to go home with Mattie, go to our room at Fly's, or to Josie's room at the Grand—I don't care which."

I dropped his arm, and he stood still, gazing into the fiery sunset over Tombstone.

"Jesus, Kate. How did we ever get to this?"

How indeed, I thought. *Most likely through the greed and evil that exists in the human condition.* But I kept silent. This confrontation had been a long time coming, and I hadn't seen any way to avoid it. Maybe if we'd all left town weeks before . . . but hindsight is always more effective than foresight. Wyatt was blaming himself enough, even though it wasn't deserved. He was a complicated man, as was Doc, and I loved both of them, knowing just how complicated they could be.

I kissed his cheek and pushed him off the porch. "Go, Wyatt. We'll see you in the morning. Doc and I will be here."

He turned to me, his face bleak. "Thank you, Kate. Take care of my brothers."

"You know I will."

He walked slowly away, not stopping at the small house he shared with Mattie but continuing on down the street. I couldn't blame him for that, and I hoped that Josie Marcus could give him the comfort he needed.

From the *The Tombstone Epitaph*, Thursday Morning, October 27, 1881:

Yesterday's Tragedy
Three Men Hurled Into Eternity
in the Duration of a Moment.

Stormy as were the early days of Tombstone nothing ever occurred equal to the event of yesterday. Since the retirement of Ben Sippy as marshal and the appointment of V. W. Earp to fill the vacancy the town has been noted for its quietness and good order. The fractious and much dreaded cowboys when they came to town were upon their good behaviour and no unseemly brawls were indulged in, and it was hoped by our citizens that no more such deeds would occur as led to the killing of Marshal White one year ago. It seems that this quiet state of affairs was but the calm that precedes the storm that burst in all its fury yesterday, with this difference in results, that the lightning bolt struck in a different quarter from the one that fell a year ago. This time it struck with its full and awful force upon those who, heretofore, have made the good name of this county a byword and a reproach, instead of upon some officer in discharge of his duty or a peaceable and unoffending citizen.

Since the arrest of Stilwell and Spence for the robbery of the Bisbee stage, there have been oft repeated threats conveyed to the Earp brothers—Virgil, Morgan, and Wyatt—that the friends of the accused, or in other words the cowboys, would get even with them for the part they had taken in the pursuit and arrest of Stilwell and Spence. The active part of the Earps in going after stage robbers, beginning with the one last spring where Budd Philpot lost his life, and the more recent one near Contention, has made them exceedingly obnoxious to the bad element of this county and put their lives in jeopardy every month.

Sometime Tuesday Ike Clanton came into town and during the evening had some little talk with Doc Holliday and

Marshal Earp, but nothing to cause either to suspect, further than their general knowledge of the man and the threats that had previously been conveyed to the Marshal, that the gang intended to clean out the Earps, that he was thirsting for blood at this time with one exception and that was that Clanton told the Marshal, in answer to a question, that the McLowrys were in Sonora. Shortly after this occurrence someone came to the Marshal and told him that the McLowrys had been seen a short time before just below town. Marshal Earp, now knowing what might happen and feeling his responsibility for the peace and order of the city, stayed on duty all night and added to the police force his brother Morgan and Holliday. The night passed without any disturbance whatever, and at sunrise he went home to rest and sleep. A short time afterwards one of his brothers came to his house and told him that Clanton was hunting him with threats of shooting him on sight. He discredited the report and did not get out of bed. It was not long before another of his brothers came down and told him the same thing, whereupon he got up, dressed, and went with his brother Morgan uptown. They walked up Allen Street to Fifth, crossed over to Fremont and down to Fourth, where, upon turning up Fourth toward Allen, they came upon Clanton with a Winchester rifle in his hand and a revolver on his hip. The Marshal walked up to him, grabbed the rifle, and hit him a blow on the head at the same time, stunning him so that he was able to disarm him without further trouble. He marched Clanton off to the police court, where he entered a complaint against him for carrying deadly weapons, and the court fined Clanton $25 and costs, making $27.50 altogether. This occurrence must have been about 1 o'clock in the afternoon.

The After-Occurrence

Close upon the heels of this came the finale, which is best told in the words of R.F. Coleman who was an eye-witness from the beginning to the end. Mr. Coleman says: I was in the O.K. Corral at 2:30 p.m., when I saw the two Clantons and the two McLowrys in an earnest conversation across the street in Dunbar's corral. I went up the street and notified Sheriff Behan and told him it was my opinion they meant trouble, and it was his duty, as sheriff, to go and disarm them. I told him they had gone to the West End Corral. I then went and saw Marshal Virgil Earp and notified him to the same effect. I then met Billy Allen and we walked through the O.K. Corral, about fifty yards behind the sheriff. On reaching Fremont street I saw Virgil Earp, Wyatt Earp, Morgan Earp and Doc Holliday, in the center of the street, all armed. I had reached Bauer's meat market. Johnny Behan had just left the cowboys, after having a conversation with them. I went along to Fly's photograph gallery, when I heard Virg Earp say, "Give up your arms or throw up your arms." There was some reply made by Frank McLowry, when firing became general, over thirty shots being fired. Tom McLowry fell first, but raised and fired again before he died. Bill Clanton fell next, and raised to fire again when Mr. Fly took his revolver from him. Frank McLowry ran a few rods and fell. Morgan Earp was shot through and fell. Doc Holliday was hit in the left hip but kept on firing. Virgil Earp was hit in the third or fourth fire, in the leg which staggered him but he

kept up his effective work. Wyatt Earp stood up and fired
in rapid succession, as cool as a cucumber, and was not
hit. Doc Holliday was as calm as though at target practice
and fired rapidly. After the firing was over, Sheriff Behan
went up to Wyatt Earp and said, "I'll have to arrest you."
Wyatt replied: "I won't be arrested today. I am right here
and am not going away. You have deceived me. You told me
these men were disarmed; I went to disarm them."

This ends Mr. Coleman's story, which in the most essential particulars has been confirmed by others. Marshal
Earp says that he and his party met the Clantons and the
McLowrys in the alleyway by the McDonald place; he
called to them to throw up their hands, that he had come
to disarm them. Instantaneously Bill Clanton and one of
the McLowrys fired, and then it became general. Mr. Earp
says it was the first shot from Frank McLowry that hit
him. In other particulars his statement does not materially
differ from the statement above given. Ike Clanton was not
armed and ran across to Allen street and took refuge in the
dance hall there. The two McLowrys and Bill Clanton all
died within a few minutes after being shot. The Marshal
was shot through the calf of the right leg, the ball going
clear through. His brother, Morgan, was shot through the
shoulders, the ball entering the point of the right shoulder
blade, following across the back, shattering off a piece of
one vertebrae and passing out the left shoulder in about
the same position that it entered the right. The wound is
dangerous but not necessarily fatal, and Virgil's is far more
painful than dangerous. Doc Holliday was hit upon the
scabbard of his pistol, the leather breaking the force of the
ball so that no material damage was done other than to

make him limp a little in his walk.

Dr. Matthews impaneled a coroner's jury, who went and viewed the bodies as they lay in the cabin in the rear of Dunbar's stables on Fifth street, and then adjourned until 10 o'clock this morning.

The Alarm Given

The moment the word of the shooting reached the Vizina and Tough Nut mines the whistles blew a shrill signal, and the miners came to the surface, armed themselves, and poured into the town like an invading army. A few moments served to bring out all the better portions of the citizens, thoroughly armed and ready for any emergency. Precautions were immediately taken to preserve law and order, even if they had to fight for it. A guard of ten men were stationed around the county jail, and extra policemen put on for the night.

Earp Brothers Justified

The feeling among the best class of our citizens is that the Marshal was entirely justified in his efforts to disarm these men, and that being fired upon they had to defend themselves, which they did most bravely. So long as our peace officers make an effort to preserve the peace and put down highway robbery—which the Earp brothers have done, having engaged in the pursuit and capture, where captures have been made of every gang of stage robbers in the county—they will have the support of all good citizens. If the present lesson is not sufficient to teach the cow-boy element that they cannot come into the streets of Tombstone, in broad daylight, armed with six-shooters and Henry rifles to hunt down their victims, then the citizens will most assuredly take such steps to preserve the peace as will be forever a bar to such raids.[1]

1 The Tombstone Epitaph, October 27, 1881

CHAPTER 22

Although we were on the lookout for any bullets that could come our way, it turned out the biggest threat came from what passed for law and order. After the coroner's inquest and based upon a statement from Ike Clanton, warrants for Doc and the three Earp brothers were issued. Since Morgan and Virgil were incapacitated, only Doc and Wyatt were taken into custody. The bail of $20,000 was quickly raised from friends and supporters, and the two men were released pending further action by Judge Spicer. I was outraged, but when your enemies are lying thieves and murderers who have the ear of a bent sheriff, this is what happens—and what passed for legality in Tombstone long before the Earps ever set foot there.

"Jesus Christ," Morgan groaned from his makeshift bed in the front parlor. "This is going to be a mess, now. That goddamn Behan." He started to prop himself up, and Doc gently pushed him back down.

"We've got this under control, Morg," he said, checking the bandages across Morg's shoulders. "Tom Fitch has agreed to represent you, and Tom Drum will go for me. You know those boys throw some serious legal weight."

Wyatt paced back and forth in the crowded room. "They sure as hell do. I don't care what sort of lies the Clantons and McLowrys throw out there; with those two on our side, I'm not worried."

That was clearly untrue, but perhaps it wasn't as evident to everyone else as it was to me. I'd sat with Wyatt, Doc, Tom Fitch, and Drum this afternoon, and I knew it was going to be a battle. A preliminary hearing was scheduled to begin in the morning, and Tom Fitch's plan was to effectively try the case at the hearing and avoid a trial altogether. It was unusual, he said, but we trusted him. With his reputation, as well as Drum's, I had no objection to any strategy he suggested. He was a brilliant lawyer and orator and a former senator. Luckily, he had moved to Tombstone just a few months before. Listening to him today, I'd been impressed with not only his legal knowledge, but also his sharp-edged, no-nonsense philosophy.

Since Spicer had ordered the hearing, things had quieted down. The circus of the funeral for Clanton and the McLowry brothers drew a big crowd, and we all stayed far out of range. On the one occasion I went to Fly's to get extra clothes for Doc and myself, some Cowboys had made remarks, but I ignored them and kept walking, much as I wanted to spit in their faces.

Still, we were all uneasy.

The Cowboys were convinced they would win in court. Their arrogance and false statements added to their braggadocio on the streets, and they could easily be planning revenge in many forms. As soon as court convened in the morning, the Earp women and I would be packing and moving us all to the Cosmopolitan Hotel for the duration of the hearing. We couldn't all continue to stay in Morgan and Lou's little house, and this would give us another layer of security as well.

Before we settled in for our last night in the cramped quarters, Doc and I went outside to the porch. We sat in the dark, the glowing end of Doc's cheroot providing the only light. The night was chill, and I pulled my shawl closer as we sat down on the porch steps.

"Doc, talk to me." He said nothing, but the end of his cheroot pulsed a bright cherry red. He took my hand and gripped it, hard.

"I want you to go back to Globe."

"No," I said. "I'm going to be here for you and see this thing through. I'll be fine."

"This is bad, Kate. All that brave talk with the lawyers today, but you know it could go either way. I won't have you goin' through this nonsense, and it's not safe."

"When this is all over, we'll both go to Globe and then head up to Colorado, just like we planned."

He laughed, a harsh bark. "Maybe not, darlin'. All my money, and now yours, has gone to my defense. It's going to be a while before we can get another stake that size. Colorado is a long way away, and we're poor as Georgia church mice."

It was true, but I didn't want to hear it. "I've got the boardinghouse—that's worth something, and we'll make it back, Doc. I know we can. Maybe in Globe, or Tucson . . ."

He leaned over and kissed me, his mouth tasting of tobacco and despair. "Stop it now, Kate. I never wanted anythin' like this, you know that. I always keep out of it unless I have to defend myself. They've made me into this gun-crazy killer because I stood beside my friends, and if history is any judge, my dear, I will remain so, no matter what the law decides."

He pulled me close, and I buried my face in the curve of his neck. "Our future, at this point, can only be seen through the proverbial dark glass, I think. These people are animals, Kate. If you go to Globe, keepin' you safe is one less thing I have to worry about, so do this for me."

Early the next morning I helped Ally and Lou get settled in at the Cosmopolitan, and then I headed over to Tom Fitch's law office before court convened. Luckily, he was just packing his leather case when I stepped into the office.

"Good morning, Tom," I said, smiling at his startled expression, "I stopped in to bid you a good day in court, and to say good-bye as well. We've decided I'll go back and stay in Globe for the duration of the hearing."

Recovering quickly, Fitch came around the desk and took my hand. He was an impressive-looking man, his silvery hair brushed back in waves from his face, and his penetrating eyes missed little. I found him very appealing, and from what I'd heard and witnessed yesterday, if any lawyer on earth could ensure the Earps' and Doc's safety, he was the one.

"Kate." He smiled down at me. "Doc is a lucky man. Although I'll miss seeing you during this deliberation, I think you're doing the right thing. Tombstone is not safe for any of you right now, and I know Doc will rest easier with you out of this maelstrom—and maelstrom it will be, although I tell you, it's one we'll weather." He kissed my cheek. "Take care, my dear."

We walked together to the courthouse and met Wyatt and Doc on the steps. Fitch handed me over to Doc and shook his hand and Wyatt's as well. Quite a crowd had gathered, supporters as well as Cowboys, but we ignored them all.

"Gentlemen, let us begin," Fitch said, and he strode into the building. I hugged Wyatt, and then turned to Doc, holding him close. His thin frame felt terribly frail against my hands, but this was no time for nutritional advice.

"I'll see you soon, my man," I smiled, my false bravado brooking no argument. "Mr. Fitch has assured me that all will be well. My bags are already on the stage. Christmas in Globe, then."

"Of course, darlin'." Doc's mustache tickled me as he whispered in my ear. "There's not a thing I look forward to more than your plum puddin', unless it's your silken . . . sheets."

They turned and disappeared into the crowd entering the building, and I walked across the street to the stagecoach. I hated looking back and watching someone I loved walk away—a superstitious phobia, perhaps, but one that was ingrained in me.

Globe wasn't all that far, and there was a telegraph, I told myself. I stared at the stark landscape as the high desert rolled past, hardly blinking and not wanting to even think about the last few weeks. Leaving Doc to face what could be the end of him was the hardest thing I'd ever done. He had Wyatt, but then he always had, and I didn't know if that made it worse or better. I didn't start to cry until we were at least twenty miles out of town.

On November 30, Judge Wells Spicer ruled there was no cause for a trial, and the longest hearing in Arizona history came to an end, with Wyatt and Doc walking away free men. A grand jury upheld Spicer's decision on December 16th, and, legally, that was the end of it. I knew as soon as I heard it, though, that things were far from over in Tombstone. I had gotten a few letters, some from Lou and Ally and a few from Doc. Things sounded very tense. Doc urged me to stay in Globe, and while I worried about him, I felt a guilty sense of relief in not being there. It wasn't just my own safety, but the swirl of emotions that engulfed everyone in that place. Tempers were short and tensions high—and not just among our friends and allies, but all those on the opposing side. Tombstone was a town divided, and it would be for some time to come. Doc wanted me to stay in Globe until things calmed down.

I threw myself into cleaning and sprucing up Miner's Rest, welcoming the sore muscles as I brought it back to my exacting standards. Maggie had done her best, but it was good to have a purpose, and the project took my mind off what was happening farther south. Christmas neared, and decorations were going up all over town, so I enthusiastically decorated the boardinghouse and joined in the festivities, at least on the surface.

"There," Maggie said, setting the tinsel crown atop my hair. "You're the Queen of Christmas now, no question." She danced away, laughing, and while I felt rather silly and a bit hypocritical, I shrugged off my melancholy over Doc's absence. I couldn't expect him to show up like a Christmas present another year in a row, but as the days passed I somehow couldn't help hoping that he would.

Tonight was Christmas Eve, and all my boarders were home for dinner and holiday the next day. Maggie and I had outdone ourselves—baked ham crusty with honey and spices, sweet potato pie, creamed peas, fresh baked rolls, plum pudding, and all the whiskey punch they could drink—and drink they did. Before we even sat down to dinner, the house resounded with Christmas spirit and mirth. Someone produced a guitar, another a violin. As improvised drums beat out the rhythm, we danced the dark away.

"To Miss Kate, and Miss Maggie," Mike Sullivan said, holding up his glass before we began dinner. "You ladies make this house a home, and this is another Christmas we'll all remember." Cheers resounded around the table, and dinner was served, while Maggie and I exchanged smiles. I was happy to be able to provide this for all of them, and I knew she was, too. So much was wrong in my life, but this, here and now, was right. I hoped that Doc was having a Christmas he would enjoy. At the same time, I wanted it to be empty without me. That may not have been a very charitable feeling, but at least it was an honest one. I piled my plate full and enjoyed every bite.

The telegram was terse. "Virgil shot. Bad but will live. Rest of us fine. Must stay here for now. Doc."

Over the next week, details drifted in from stage drivers, travelers, copies of the *Epitaph*, and a letter from Doc. Feeling was running hot, even in Globe, that it was long past time the

Cowboys were hunted down and put in jail. I made no secret of my feelings, and I no longer hid my associations. Support for the Earps—even Doc, now notorious himself—was high, even as far as Globe. Arizona was still the frontier, and between Apache raids and outlaws, people were tired of being threatened. They wanted to travel, as well as sleep soundly in their beds at night, so law and order was their shield, and the Earps personified that.

Doc's letter provided me more details. Three days after Christmas, Virgil was alone, walking back from the Oriental around midnight, when he was ambushed and shot. No one saw the shooters, but everyone knew they were Cowboys, just not exactly who. Virgil's arm was likely to be crippled the rest of his life, but he was alive. Doc said he, Wyatt, and Morgan, along with some of our old friends, were on constant guard around the Cosmopolitan Hotel.

Maggie and I were sitting at a table at McGarry's and had just finished lunch. I put down the letter. "Sounds like an armed camp down there," I said. "Not a good place to be, but I know Doc won't leave, especially after this."

Maggie sipped her tea. "You didn't really expect he would, did you?" She raised an eyebrow, which for Maggie was tantamount to derisive laughter.

I glared at her. "No, but you could at least commiserate."

She did laugh, then. "Kate, the man has a white knight complex at this point and has had since that gunfight back in October. There's no way he's going to desert his pals." She leaned over and kissed my cheek before finishing. "Even for true love, sadly."

She was right, and I knew it. Doc had found a calling. I'd seen that before I left Tombstone. It was in his eyes, the turn of his jaw, even the way he walked. He was dedicated, perhaps for the first time in his life, to a noble cause—to righting a wrong and protecting his friends. I couldn't deny him this and call myself someone who cared about him. He needed to do this, and I would have to be patient and see it play itself out, no matter where it led. I worried every single night that it would lead to his death, but it was something I could do nothing about. All I could do was be here for him when it ended, or whenever he needed me. That, I had come to learn, was how it worked with loving Doc.

The winter went on, but winters in most of Arizona weren't like winters anywhere else I'd lived. Instead of dark skies, rain, and snow that forced everyone to be housebound, the weather was nearly always pleasant: blue skies, comfortable temperatures during the day, and chilly and sometimes cold at night. Spring came early, and around the first of March I replanted most of the vegetables I'd started in little pots in the kitchen. Enjoying the sunshine outside this time of year made me feel like I had something special the rest of the country would have to wait months to have.

Virgil was doing OK, according to Doc, but would never regain full use of his arm. There were minor altercations, legal hassles, warrants, claims, and counterclaims, and it seemed there would never be a resolution to the feuds until one or the other of the sides was jailed or killed.

I kept busy running the boardinghouse and relaxed with reading and seeing Maggie frequently. I'd never been a person who had a lot of friends, especially women, and my past—some of it true, some highly embroidered—had made the rounds in what passed for polite society in Globe. Most of the so-called respectable ladies kept a wide berth, which suited me just fine. Afternoon teas, the ladies' garden society, and church suppers weren't of any interest to me. They were attended by a bunch of ignorant busybodies who hadn't really lived, as far as I was concerned. These were women who would likely faint at the sight of a gunshot wound or the glimpse of a thigh under ruffled taffeta, and whose husbands took every opportunity to help me with my packages or wish me good afternoon while I smiled and gently removed their hands from places on my person they shouldn't have been. All in all, I was a model citizen when I would have liked to shoot a few of them right in the eye. Being a land-owning businesswoman had taught me self control in ways nothing else would have done, but there were days it was very difficult to control my temper, which had ever been volatile.

When I was ready to explode, Maggie would shake her head and pour me a whiskey. There was next to nothing she didn't know about me now, and she kept me sane when it seemed I couldn't go another day not knowing what was happening down south. One morning I'd had enough. I packed a carpetbag, issued orders to Juanita and the girls, and stopped in at Maggie's shop on the way to the stage.

The bell tinkled as I opened the door, and Maggie looked up from the lace she was rolling onto a paper tube. As usual, she missed nothing.

"So, a week, maybe two, then?"

I nodded and set down the bag. "No more than that, but I have to see him. Whether we're together after this or not, I have to have it set in my mind one way or the other."

Maggie hugged me. "Just go, Kate. I'll handle Miner's Rest."

Louisa Earp came down the stairs as I entered the lobby of the Cosmopolitan Hotel. "Kate!" she cried and enveloped me in her arms, maybe holding on just a little too long. "Damn, I'm glad to see you. Come upstairs, and we'll catch up. Doc will be so surprised."

I'll bet, I thought, but it was too late for second thoughts now. Lou led me up the stairs to Doc's room, and I put my bag beside the washstand while Lou plopped down on the bed. I sat beside her, and her smile faltered, tears filling her eyes.

"It's been awful," she said. "Poor Virgil and Allie. I'm so scared every day that someone will get killed. I just want out of here. But you know how they are. They won't leave. They think it's their sacred duty to make things right."

Within twenty minutes, I was fully up to date with the happenings in Tombstone, and it was even worse than I'd imagined. It wasn't just the Cowboys, but a constant wrangling with different law enforcement agencies—between the counties and towns. Depending upon who was in league with whom, the authorities were harassing the Earps and Doc with arrests one minute and appointing them officers the next. I was beginning to understand the enormity of the problem, the tightrope they were walking, and the distinct possibility of further disaster. Tempers were high and patience in short supply. As Lou was drying her eyes, the door opened, and Doc strode in, stopping short at the sight of us.

"What in hell are you doin' here?"

While not the greeting I was hoping for, I put my arms around his waist. "Wanting to see you for a day or two, if you can spare me some time." Lou took the opportunity to sidle around us and speed off down the hallway, in search of less problematic surroundings.

Doc sighed but pulled me closer. He kicked the door shut, and we fell onto the bed.

"You are one stubborn woman, Kate, but I'm damn glad to see you."

By the second time around, we'd managed to divest ourselves of most of our clothing, boots, and Doc's knives and guns, so we were more comfortable but no less enthusiastic. A while later, he raised himself up on an elbow and poured us some whiskey. He dribbled a bit onto my stomach and licked it off while putting the glass to my lips.

"You better stop that or . . ." I managed, but he growled something, and I left him alone. Apparently his affinity for chivalry or what passed for it had increased his stamina and done wonders for his health. I was past any complaining.

It was dark when I woke and heard Doc snoring softly on my shoulder. I gently disengaged and then put on my chemise. I poured a little whiskey and sipped it while I watched him sleep. His color was good, and his breathing was, too. He seemed to have put on a little weight, even. Adversity was beneficial to the man. Wyatt had done what I could not, I thought ruefully, but I didn't begrudge any of it. Except, of course, that I hadn't been here. There was one thing I knew, though, and it was worth coming back to Tombstone for that. Doc loved me, and that was all I needed to know.

Breakfast the next morning was a crowded repast. Along with Doc and me, there was Morgan, Wyatt, Virgil, James, their wives, as well as Warren, the youngest Earp brother, who'd come to town after Virgil was shot. We all sat at a long table laden with eggs, pancakes, bacon, and coffee. There may as well not have been another person in the place, with our conversation reverberating through the room.

"Ringo makes to draw on Doc again, he's a dead man," Wyatt said, shoveling pancakes into his mouth. "Can't countenance that."

Doc smiled and sipped his coffee. " 'Course he's a dead man, but it'll be me that makes him one. He's my huckleberry, no one else's."

Morgan laughed. "Doc's right about that, Wyatt."

Virgil grimaced as he adjusted his sling. "He may be, but that doesn't stop the rest of them. Bullets from cowards in the dark are out of our control. We need to get out of here."

Allie, Bessie, and Lou nodded, but James shook his head.

"We got a good thing, here, brothers. I'm not letting this scum run me out of Tombstone just when things are getting good."

Bessie rounded on him. "Good? You call walking down the street every day in fear of our lives good? I sure as hell don't. I think San Francisco sounds good, not goddamn Tombstone."

Silence fell around the table. Bessie had a point, and we all knew it. The way things were going, there was little future here for anyone. I sure didn't disagree, but I knew better than to say so.

Wyatt stood up and threw down his napkin. "I got things to do. Going to sell the mines to Casey today, just in case."

James began to protest, but Wyatt fixed him with that blue stare. "Don't even start up with me. They aren't producing anymore, so it's a good move."

We all watched him walk away, and before he reached the door, Doc kissed me on the cheek and stood up as well. "I'll see you later, darlin', at the Oriental." He followed Wyatt out the door before I could say a word.

I looked around the table. "So, what's he, Wyatt's bodyguard? Are things so bad here that he needs one?"

James looked down at his plate, and a few seconds passed before Virgil coughed. "Well, no, but it seems like we all watch out for each other now, Kate."

I pushed my chair back. "I'm going back to the hotel. Lou, Allie, anyone else coming?"

No one met my eyes, and I made my way outside to the street. I really didn't feel like going back to the hotel, but when I glanced up and down Allen Street, I felt like I was being watched. I saw Curly Bill Brocius and another man walk into a nearby saloon. Whether they saw me or cared, I was uncomfortable enough that when I entered the lobby of the Cosmopolitan, I breathed a sigh of relief.

When I walked into the Oriental later that day, I saw Doc

dealing poker, while Wyatt was at the faro table in the back of the room. All seemed normal, and I didn't see any Cowboys among the patrons. I ordered a whiskey and walked over to stand behind Doc, where I'd stood so many times before, my hand resting gently on his shoulder. He glanced up and smiled and dealt smoothly, never missing a beat. A couple of hours passed, and when Doc stood up and joined me at the bar, he raised my fingers to his lips, and I felt his breath soft on my skin.

"I was thinkin' we should have some supper and then seek our amusement elsewhere. How do you feel about that, Kate?"

I smiled and put my arm through his. Wyatt materialized at Doc's side.

"Evening, Kate." He tipped his hat. "I'm going to shoot some pool with Morgan. It's been a long day. I'll see you in the morning."

The pounding on the door woke both of us. Doc grabbed a pistol and opened the door a crack. James Earp burst into the room. "Morg's been shot, Doc. He's at Campbell & Hatch's pool parlor."

Too shocked to say a word, we threw on our clothes and ran down the stairs and into the street. There was a crowd of people in front of Campbell & Hatch's, and Doc shoved them aside while I trailed behind him. Morgan was lying on a lounge in the card room, blood spreading beneath him, while Wyatt bent over him and Louisa sobbed and clutched Morg's hand. I'd seen plenty of gunshot victims, but never one who'd lost this much blood.

"Ah, goddamn them," Doc murmured, and I knew then there was no hope. A knot of despair twisted inside me. Morgan was the best of us all. If it could happen to him, there were no roads out of this mess.

"Do you know who did this?" Morgan whispered to Wyatt.

Wyatt nodded. "I do, and I'll get them." Wyatt's face was pale, streaked with blood and tears.

Morgan gripped Wyatt's bloodstained hand tighter. "Don't let them get you, brother." Those were the last words he spoke. Louisa howled and lay her head down on Morgan's still shoulder until Virgil gently pulled her away. Wyatt looked up at Doc, and some unspoken agreement passed between them. Doc nodded before he turned away.

We walked slowly back to the hotel, neither of us saying a word, but I knew that after tonight, nothing would ever be the same. Morgan's last words rang in my ears, and I kept seeing a horrifying vision of Doc, the next one to lie so very still in a lake of his own blood.

We slept little, and I was alone when I woke to gray light filtering into the room. A bleak morning presaged an equally bleak day, I was sure. I washed and dressed, packing my things into the carpetbag, and noticed Doc had already organized his belongings as well. His trunk sat by the bed, full saddlebags resting on top.

I went downstairs to the restaurant and ordered coffee and toast. The tables were empty so far, but through the window I saw Wyatt and Doc coming down the street. They joined me, and we sat in silence for a time.

"James, Warren, and I are taking Morg to Contention today, and James and Bessie will go on to California with the body," Wyatt said, not looking up from his coffee. "They aren't coming back. Doc will watch over things here, and tomorrow when I get back, we're taking Virgil, Allie, and Lou to Tucson to the train. They aren't coming back either. We're done with Tombstone."

I put a hand on each of their arms, and both Doc and Wyatt looked up at me. "And then? Tell me what happens then, gentlemen?" I asked, although I already knew.

"We do what we have to do," Doc said. "We don't have a choice anymore. If the law doesn't do its job, we have to do it."

I nodded. "I see that. I don't like it, but I understand why you think so."

Doc shook my hand off. "Goddammit, Kate, we talked about this. Don't backslide now."

"I'm not 'backsliding,' Doc," I said, "but I don't have to like it. I'm going to get on that stage to Globe, as ordered once again, but I'll be damned if I'm happy about leaving you to the hell you're about to call up." My fists were clenched, and to my chagrin, tears were running down my cheeks. "I don't want anyone else I care about to die."

Doc stood up and took me in his arms. "Darlin', not one more person will die at the hands of these bastards, that I can guarantee. We're too damn mad and too damn mean. But you know these murderin' scum have to be called out for what they've done, and we're the only ones who'll do it. It's not a vendetta. It's simple justice and long overdue."

Wyatt pushed back his chair, leaned over, and kissed me on the temple. "Take care of yourself, Kate, and we'll do our best to take care of everyone else." He gave me a wan smile, fingertips brushing my cheek. "I got to meet James. I'll see you tomorrow, Doc."

I'd said my tearful good-byes to Allie and Louisa, and Doc and I stood outside in the cold, waiting for the stagecoach to arrive. Texas Jack Vermillion and Turkey Creek stood nearby like guardian sentinels. Doc and I were talked out, and there was little left to say. It was going to be a long while before I saw him again, and all that kept me going was the hope that I would, indeed, see him again. Regret at past decisions colored my thoughts, but I couldn't let it cloud the now, which was all we had.

Before I climbed up the steps to the interior of the stage, I clung to Doc and kissed him.

"Don't forget to come back to me, Holliday. I'm going to think about you every day and keep you alive."

He chuckled. "You are a caution, Kate. I'll think about that every night, and it'll keep me warm." His arms were like steel bands around me as he whispered in my ear, " 'Life every man holds dear; but the dear man holds honor far more precious dear than life.' "

I pulled back and looked in his eyes. "Don't you dare quote Shakespeare to me, and don't you dare die on me, Doc Holliday. I'll haunt you."

He laughed. "God, Kate, I know you would. No one else could ever be like you." He pushed me onto the stage, smacking my bottom through the layers of silk. "Justice, darlin', justice. I'll see you before you know it."

CHAPTER 23

Globe, Arizona, 1887

It was a lovely spring morning. I could hear the birds outside in the garden, and I swung my legs out of bed and padded to the windows, pulling the blue silk draperies open to the predawn light. I'd been thinking maybe I would have Jim Stewart put doors here instead of a window, so I could step outside rather than just wish myself part of that world. For now, I shoved my feet into slippers and went down the hallway to the kitchen, where I opened the back door and breathed in the fresh, cool air. I walked outside onto the porch and sat on the bench. For the thousandth time, I pictured Doc standing there, one leg crossed over the other, head tilted, with the smile I so loved on his face. I hoped he still had that smile. I hadn't seen him in five years, and I was doubtful if time had been so kind.

I hadn't changed much, if the mirror was any judge—a few more lines here and there around my eyes, but not so many around my mouth. People said you get those from smiling too much, and I hadn't smiled nearly as much as I wanted to in the last five years. Avoiding late nights, whiskey-dulled mornings, and sinful shenanigans was a recipe for good health, I suppose, but hell, it was boring sometimes. I laughed softly in spite of myself. Be careful what you wish for, they also said, and it was true.

I got letters from my old friends now and then, and in the first year or two, from Doc. Our future together had been in dire jeopardy since the first gunshots at the O.K. Corral, but those hopes and dreams had finally breathed their last alongside Morgan Earp in a pool hall in Tombstone, and neither they nor he were ever going to be resurrected. That night, Doc's Southern code of honor had fully surfaced, and he took to the role of protector and dispenser of justice in the cause of the Earps' brand of law, order, and—frankly—revenge, as though it had been a mantle he'd waited to don all his life, one that fit him like a bespoke waistcoat.

For a long time after that, I wallowed in grief and self-pity, moving through life like a mechanical doll, waiting for some sort of resolution and hoping it would involve Doc coming back to me. The newspapers and penny dreadfuls were full of the Vendetta Ride, as they called it, chronicling in purple prose the hunt for and deaths of those they rode down. And after it was over, the reputations of Wyatt and Doc were the stuff of legend. Legends do not make good bedfellows. Legends also do not settle down and rest in obscurity.

I'd lost those I loved before—my parents, my child, Jack—but Doc wasn't dead, just gone. That made it more difficult in one way, but easier in another. I was done following him across the West—comforting him one night and being in jeopardy the next, whether from Doc himself or the latest candidate for sainthood or revenge. Maggie said I'd finally grown into myself, and there was something to that. I thought it was a kind of epiphany, a realization of what I truly wanted. It was serenity, or at least as much peace and comfort as I could provide for myself, admittedly at the cost of being alone, but there it was. After all the death and blood, I wanted no part of the excitement or involvement. The world was an uncertain and dangerous place, so I had made myself a nest of safety, and I liked it. An independent woman was unusual in the West, and I was proud of myself.

"Miss Kate?" Juanita stood inside the screen door. "You want

I start the breakfast, *por favor?*"

I stood up. "Yes, *gracias.* I'll just be a moment. Pancakes, bacon, and scrambled eggs today."

Another day begins, I mused, pretty much like the last one, but there are pleasures to be had and much to be done. I began making lists in my head before taking one last look at the garden. A single daffodil had emerged since yesterday, its buttery yellow petals glowing in the early light. *Good morning to you, Doc,* I thought. *Wherever you are, I wish you well.*

"I've got some new fabrics in . . . light summery sort of things," Maggie said. "We're making you up some new dresses, madame. You look like a washerwoman." She laid out a half dozen bolts of cloth and looked at me expectantly. I sighed. Once she got an idea in her head, there was no arguing with her, and besides, she was right. In the back of my closet hung dresses, but not the sort I could wear everyday anymore—beaded silk, lace-trimmed taffetas, and embroidered satins, to say nothing of the hats—elegant confections with ostrich plumes and velvet ribbons—none appropriate for the proprietress of a boardinghouse. The good folks of Globe would be convinced I was running a very different sort of house had they seen me in those. There had been rare occasions in the past few years to enjoy my favorite clothes. Most of the time, I had opted for cotton shirtwaists, dark skirts, and lots of aprons. Style had become a thing of the past, like so much else.

Maggie looked up at me and snorted. "Stop looking so glum. Just because the love of your life is no longer around doesn't mean the rest of your life is over, Kate."

Anger flared briefly, but I knew she was right about that, too. "All right, let's see what you've got. It is time I had some new clothes. Aprons will cover them just as well as these dumpy things, and when they come off, I'll be the belle of the kitchen ball."

Maggie grinned. "I've got plans for that, too, Miss Gloomy." She piled up a sprigged muslin, a pale-green chintz, a sky-blue cotton voile, and a dusty pink with roses. The last one I took off and replaced with a pale gray. Rolls of trimming were on the counter, and I ran my hand longingly over some white cotton lace and tiny silk flowers intertwined with green leaves.

"Don't worry," Maggie said. "You'll get that, too. I've got the new patterns from New York, along with your measurements. Now, let's have some tea."

Smiling a little to myself, I left Maggie's and continued down Broad Street, stopping in at Old Dominion Commercial, where dear George Hunt was now elevated to clerk and secretary. I placed my grocery orders and then moved on to the post office. I hadn't had a letter from Doc in years, but when I saw his handwriting on the envelope, my heart skipped a beat, and I couldn't wait to get back to the house and open it.

"Dear Kate, I hope this missive finds you well. I know it has been some time, but I was hoping that you could perhaps want to visit me in Colorado. I am in Glenwood Springs, near your brother Alexander's place in Penny Hot Springs. I stopped in to see him and his family and gave them your regards. I have been doing some work for the mines here, security and so forth. It is going all right but I have been thinking of your herbal concoctions that were so effective back in Las Vegas. I am always thinking of you. Love, Doc."

I crumpled the paper into my lap and stared at the clouds drifting across the afternoon sky. With Doc, I always had to read between the lines, and in the spaces between these lines, a lot of things were lurking. My hand curled tighter around the flimsy paper, crushing it into a ball. I wouldn't need to read it again; the words were burned into my brain. Going all right, my ass. The bastard was sick. I threw the letter into the trash and got up to start dinner.

Maggie flung her arms around me. "I wish you'd reconsider, Kate. What more can I say to convince you this isn't a good idea?" Tears were pooling in her eyes, and I had to look away or I'd be crying as well.

We stood at the stage stop on Broad Street with my trunk beside me, packed with the lovely new dresses, along with pretty much everything portable I owned. The summer sun beat down on us; it was warm already, even though it was only nine o'clock. I pulled back and clutched Maggie's shoulders.

"This is something I want to do more than I have anything in years," I said, and as the words came out of my mouth, I realized it really was true. I wanted to be with Doc, no matter where, more than anything else I valued, or thought I did. My boardinghouse, my livelihood, perhaps whatever serenity I'd cobbled together for the last five years—all paled beside that, and I didn't care. The veils fell away, and I took a deep breath. "Take care of the boardinghouse like you've done before, and if I don't come back, it's yours, Maggie. You've been the best friend I ever had, and I'll miss you terribly, but this is who I am and what I want." I kissed her and smiled, wiping the tears off her cheeks with my gloved thumb.

She gazed into my eyes and nodded her head. "If that's what you want, Kate." She raised her eyebrow in her Maggie way and smiled back. "I love you, my dear, and I understand. In fact, I envy you. I don't think I've ever loved somebody the way you love Doc, and that's something special that doesn't happen very often in this life." She looked up at the stage that was pulling up beside us. "Go, Kate. Be happy."

I waved to her as we pulled away, and the last thing I saw of

Globe was Maggie Sweet, standing in the dusty street, waving at me while tears glistened on her cheeks.

Colorado was somewhat cooler than Arizona, but both my dress and I were sticking uncomfortably to the seat in the stagecoach, glued there by dust and sweat, crammed in beside five other passengers. The journey had been long and relatively unpleasant, but at least there hadn't been any Indian attacks or holdups to impede our progress, and now we were only five miles out of Glenwood Springs. Apparently it was a holiday destination for the other passengers, who were happily chatting about the hot springs and the delightful accommodations that awaited them. I was as eager to arrive as they were, if not for the same pleasures, but I was a bit more apprehensive. I'd had a lot of time to think about my impulsive decision and wasn't nearly as assured as I'd been when I left Globe.

I hadn't seen Doc since I left Tombstone, and a few letters aside, our great love for each other had been stretched thin along the course of five years. He could have come to me, but he had chosen not to—and I had not set off to find him, either. There were many good reasons, or if I was being honest, excuses, why we hadn't made those decisions, and some of them weren't just geographic or circumstance. Everything we'd planned together for a future had been put aside when Doc chose to support the Earps and rode off with Wyatt. After that, his reputation became that of a hothead shootist, with both law enforcement and every young, ambitious gunhand looking to arrest him or best him. Somehow, he'd managed to survive all of it, but what we had, our hopes for a life together, had dissipated like a desert sandstorm, impossible to reclaim.

What hadn't disappeared, though, were the feelings I had for him. I was trusting, perhaps foolishly and based upon one letter finally asking me to join him, that his feelings had remained the same. As the distance lessened between us, my fears intensified that it might not be so. For the last few days I hadn't been able to eat a thing, afraid I'd not be able to keep it down, and I fervently wished I'd brought my old traveling companion, a flask of whiskey.

The gentleman across from me, who'd gotten on in Denver, smiled at me. In the relatively short time we'd had together, I didn't think he was the predatory sort, though he was clearly a dandy and perhaps a gambler, judging by his somewhat world-weary attitude.

"Sometimes destinations can be more worrisome than the journey," he said, holding out a small silver flask, concealed from the others by his leather gloves. "Please."

I looked up at him from under the brim of my hat, and my hand shot out, seizing the flask.

I smiled. "Thank you, kind sir. I believe you are a mind reader." I turned my head to the window and took a sip, and then a longer one, before I passed it back. "A kind favor I will remember and attempt to return." It was good whiskey, and for the first time in days, I felt a warmth inside just when I needed it.

He inclined his head and tucked the flask back in his pocket. "No need, pretty lady, but you are very welcome."

I never saw him again, but he was a nice man who had given me hope, and for the first time on this journey I began to feel maybe things would be all right.

Glenwood Springs was hacked out of the wilderness like many other frontier towns I'd seen, but it was rapidly approaching sophistication with an eye to the future. Solid stone buildings, proper sidewalks, banks, mercantiles, and the magnificent Hotel Glenwood graced the main street, which was full of respectable looking people going about their business as we pulled in. I hired a boy to bring my trunk to the Hotel Glenwood. Doc had said he was staying there, and I had sent a telegram before I left. After asking the desk clerk to inform him I had arrived, I sat down on a velvet banquette and tried to quell my anxieties. The hotel was elegant, with Turkish carpets, lofty green ferns, brocaded drapes on the lobby windows, and a string quartet playing quietly in the restaurant through the archways on the right of the lobby. It was warm and quiet, and I must have dozed off, blinking awake when I heard my name.

"Kate."

The man who stood in front of me was a faded image of the vibrant Doc Holliday I had known, as though seen through a mirror that had gone shadowy with age. His blond hair and mustache were shot through with gray, his skin ashen, and his eyes dull. His hand below the frayed cuff of his shirt was bony and shook slightly when I took it in mine and stood up. Only the smile was the same, rakish and genuine. I dropped his hand and put my arms around him, burying my face in the lapels of his waistcoat to hide the shock in my eyes.

"Darlin'," he whispered in my ear. "I'm so damn glad to see you."

I said nothing and simply took his hand as we walked across the lobby and up the curving staircase. Upstairs, his room was small but nicely appointed, certainly not the most lavish in this hotel but more than adequate. There was even a private bathroom, with hot and cold running water and, wonderfully, electric lights. The short walk to the second floor left Doc breathless, and he sat down heavily on one of the chairs by the window. I took off my hat and gloves and rearranged my hair, unsure exactly what would come next. It was not a comfortable silence.

"It seems the mineral baths have not been quite as edifyin' as they claim," he said, and his laugh was swallowed by the violent cough that came with it. He gazed bleakly at me. "I must apologize, my dear. I've brought you here on a fool's errand. I'm not quite the man I used to be . . . isn't that a daisy?"

It felt as though a dam broke inside my chest, spilling out the doubt, pain, and longing and washing it all away. I sank down beside his chair, my skirts covering his legs, and I took his face in my hands. "Jesus, Doc. I'm here because I love you, and you're all the man I've ever wanted."

We made our way to the bed and collapsed on the silken pillows. We held each other at long last, talked, and cried and then finally went to sleep in the solace of each other's arms. This, for so long, was all we wanted.

Room service at the Hotel Glenwood was very efficient—and a good thing, because mornings were not kind to Doc. After he drank a few cups of coffee and my herbal teas, his chest loosened up, and he breathed easier, but it was a process better done behind closed doors. Usually he was eager to be out and about by early afternoon, even if it was only a short stroll down Glenwood Springs's main street, or to a restaurant nearby. For the first two days, though, we spent most of our time in the room.

At first, we talked a lot about the old days, both in Tombstone and before. Doc had mellowed a great deal, and it wasn't just that he was sick. He told me the truth, all of it, about riding with Wyatt and killing the Cowboys they found, starting with Frank Stillwell at the depot in Tucson.

"It took on a life of its own, after that," Doc said. "We were so hell-bent on revenge for Morgan and for everything those bastards had done, we just kept going. It was like chasin' sewer rats, and they just kept runnin' . . . we never knew which way they'd go some days. Wyatt wouldn't listen to me or to any of us—Turkey Creek, Texas Jack, McMasters, even Warren. Then they killed McMasters, and Wyatt was like a crazy man, and the rest of us were no better. The law in three states was chasing us just as hard as the Cowboys before we packed it in." He stared at me, and his blue eyes burned with the old fever he'd always had. "You know, Kate, I don't regret a damn thing we did, and I never will. Never did get that idiot Ike Clanton, though."

"He's dead," I said. "Shot down near Globe by a private detective hired by some rancher down there. This spring, in fact. I was glad to hear it myself."

Doc laughed. "You always were a vengeful little thing. I'm glad to hear that, too. At least I've outlived that moron. Wouldn't be fair any other way."

"No," I agreed. "It wouldn't. Doc, I was never angry that you went with Wyatt. In fact, I admired you for it, and if I'd been a man, I would've gone with you. What I hated was that I knew I wouldn't see you for a long time, maybe ever." I poured us both a whiskey and handed one to Doc. "I don't want to dwell on the past or the could-have-beens. I won't be getting on a stage to Globe, and you won't be riding off to New Mexico with Wyatt. We're here, and that's all I want."

Doc clinked his glass on mine. "Now, and us."

And that was that. I knew when I came to Colorado that I had to put all the resentment and anger behind me—the anger towards the loathsome Cowboys, the Earps, and Doc himself. I wasn't sure I could do it, but once I saw Doc again, those years of loneliness and pain fell away, and I knew the present was all that really mattered. It had been five years since we'd seen each other, a long time by any measure, but, oddly, we fell comfortably into the same patterns we'd always had when our lives were relatively placid—talking, reading, and making love. And we had a lot to make up for. What was missing, thankfully so, was the carelessness, the violence, and our impatient plans for the future. Doc was dying. There was little future to be had, but whatever there was, I'd make it the best I knew how for both of us. Just being with Doc again was like having the best time of my life every day, and, God, how I'd missed those times.

"The doctor will be by this mornin'," he announced one day, looking out the window and sipping his coffee. "You'll likely hate him. However, he has been quite kind."

I was still in bed, my own coffee on the nightstand. Happy to hear there was medical care involved, I smiled. "Why would I hate him? Is he a bad doctor?"

He shrugged. "I suppose not, but he'll not like the whiskey, nor you in my bed." He grinned. "He's a bit of an innocent, I'd say."

"Hmm."

"I'm sure you'll have more to say than that."

"Well, 'fuck him' comes to mind," I said, "since I'm not leaving you or your bed, and whiskey is one of the few things that stops your coughing. I don't have patience for some wet-behind-the-ears, so-called professional telling us what to do. We've been at this for a while now."

Doc chuckled. "Indeed we have. At any rate, you may want to get dressed before he gets here. Think of it as armor for an Amazon warrior. I, on the other hand, will remain in my dressin' gown."

True to his word, when Dr. Crook arrived, Doc greeted him in his dressing gown, introduced me in my prim starched shirtwaist, and then lay silently on the bed through the doctor's examination. When he finished, Crook accepted a cup of coffee and turned to me.

"Mrs. Holliday, you must be aware how serious your husband's condition is," he began.

I put out my hand, stopping him. "It's Miss Haroney, Doctor. We never married, but that's not important. What is important is I'm fully aware of Doc's condition."

Crook coughed. "Well, I doubt that. In any event, I must insist that there will be no strenuous exercise, which of course," he coughed again, "includes any uh . . . relations . . . or alcohol." He eyed the whiskey bottle on the table. "He must have rest at all times. He is a very sick man. In fact, I recommend he be placed in a sanatorium where that rest will be certain . . . for the little time he has left."

Doc looked at me and raised an eyebrow. I stood up and strode to the door. "Doctor, thank you for coming. I hope it was not an inconvenience, and I thank you for your advice." I opened the door. "We will be sure to call upon you when we have need of your services."

Crook's mouth fell open, and he snapped it shut, glaring at me. "You're making a mistake," he said. "You don't know what you're doing."

I gestured towards the hallway. "I know exactly what I'm doing, you pompous ass. Good afternoon." He grabbed his bag and scuttled into the hallway. He pointed his finger at me and opened his mouth, but I slammed the door.

Doc laughed and didn't cough. "That was most entertainin', Kate. I never liked him, anyway." He patted the bed beside him. "Now get that damned starched dress off and get over here so I can get on with this business of dyin'. I don't have any time to waste."

The next morning I got up early while Doc was still asleep, and before I left, I checked to be sure his breathing was easy. First, I established a bank account. Then I stopped and bought him four new shirts, since I couldn't abide those frayed cuffs a moment longer. Back at the hotel, I ordered breakfast to be sent up, and I picked up Doc's waistcoats and trousers from the bellboy, Art Kendrick, who'd been vigilant in seeing to our needs, which included sending Doc's clothes out to be cleaned and pressed.

"Thank you, Art," I said, pressing a dollar into his hand. "I appreciate everything you're doing for Doc."

Art caught my arm. "Miss Kate, I'd do anything for Mr. Holliday. He's the nicest gentleman that's ever stayed here." He blushed. "And for you, of course. You just let me know what you need, and I'm your man."

Doc had apparently made a lot of friends in his time in Glenwood Springs. I wasn't surprised. He had that sweet way about him, especially when he wasn't bedeviled with holding off angry gamblers or defending the Earps. His reputation was that of a dangerous man, and I knew better than anyone it was more than just reputation, but looking into Art Kendrick's eyes, I clearly saw that didn't make any difference here.

I hung Doc's clothes in the closet and put the shirts on the bed. He came out of the bathroom, still in his underclothes, his hair still wet. He was painfully thin, but the color was back in his face, and his eyes were clear. I didn't know if was my herbal concoctions, sex, whiskey, or getting rid of the quack doctor, but he looked much better. Of course, that was the tricky nature of tuberculosis—one day good, the next awful—so I hesitated to get hopeful. He eyed the shirts and cocked his head.

"Shoppin'?"

"I certainly was. I'm giving those old shirts to the maids for rags, mister. I can't have my man looking anything less than elegant." I held up a shirt. "Try one on?"

He grinned. "Why, thank you, ma'am, I do believe I will."

Later, we set out for our afternoon stroll, me in my new sprigged muslin and Doc looking quite resplendent. Nearly everyone we passed said hello, and quite a few stopped to have a few words with Doc, who was obviously a popular figure around town. He introduced me to a few people, and eventually we stopped by a saloon. The hanging sign said "Riverfront Club." He held open the door, and in we went. As saloons go, it was nice, and quite subdued in comparison to some of the raucous hellholes Doc and I had known in the past. Electric lights were in sconces on the walls, and the layout was nice, with a beautiful bar across the back wall and even a piano and small stage in one corner. Perhaps a dozen patrons were playing cards at the green felt tables. The bartender waved hello, and Doc and I took a seat at the bar, ordering two whiskeys.

"Nice place," I said. "Come here often?"

Doc smiled. "I work here, darlin'. I deal faro a few nights a week but I've been a little under the weather for the last week or two."

I couldn't help but laugh. "Holliday, you never cease to surprise me, but I guess that's one of the reasons I'm here." I leaned over and kissed him. "Aside from the fact I love you, you sneaky bastard."

For a time at the Riverfront we fell into our old pattern, Doc dealing and me standing behind him. He tired early, and we walked home long before the wee hours. But he was feeling better, so he said, and he did look much better than the day I arrived. One evening at the Riverfront Doc sat down at the piano, playing his beloved Chopin, while I sat on the seat beside him. Everyone seemed to like the music, and after a while, he fingered out the chords to "Aura Lee," the old Civil War ballad I used to sing.

"What about it, Kate? Want to give it a go? I think Glenwood might enjoy some first-class singin'."

I laughed and shook my head. "It's been a long time, Doc." It had been years since I'd sung in a saloon—since Las Vegas, in fact, at the ill-fated Holliday's. "I'd likely sound like a frog croaking."

He just smiled and kept playing "Aura Lee," and the song brought back memories from as long ago as Davenport, where I'd first heard it from a Confederate soldier under my father's care. It had always been my signature song, and, for some reason, tears pricked at the back of my eyes.

"I'd like to hear you sing it, if you want to," Doc said quietly, hardly audible over the sound of the piano. "It's always been my favorite."

I looked sharply at him, but he kept his eyes on the keys. Then I thought, *By God, if he wants it, then I'll sing it.*

"Well then," I said, "let's do it."

He smiled and stood up. "Gentlemen, and ladies," he said, bowing to the crowd sitting around the tables and the bar. "We have an unexpected pleasure this evenin'." He then bowed to me. "The Lily of the West has agreed to favor us with a song."

People murmured in surprise and quieted in anticipation while Doc sat back down and played the opening bars. Where had he dredged up that old memory, I wondered, but I stood up and took a deep breath, launching into the vocal as I'd done a hundred times before. The first verse was a little shaky—while not froggy, it was tentative. It had been a while since I'd sung for anyone but myself and the birds, but my confidence soon came back, my voice soaring into the rafters of the Riverfront Club and lowering to a smoky whisper at the final notes. Tonight "Aura Lee" wasn't just a song, but it somehow symbolized all I had loved, and I sang it in honor of those Southern boys, my father, myself, and, most of all, Doc, who had fought battles just as fierce and was still fighting.

As the last notes of the piano died away, complete silence fell in the saloon. I thought, *Well, at least I loved singing it.* Then the applause built and filled the room like a wave. I turned to look at Doc. He smiled and launched into one of my old Hungarian ballads, his hands sure on the keys as they always were. I sang three more and did an encore of "Aura Lee" before we finally shut the piano and took a table. People came over and introduced themselves, eager to meet me, while most of them already knew Doc or at least who he was.

"My dear," one august gentleman said, taking my hand, "that was the loveliest sound I've heard in a very long time. Glenwood should thank its lucky stars that Mr. Holliday and you have graced our community with your presence."

The president of the bank where I'd opened an account pumped my hand enthusiastically and assured me that anything we needed, he'd be happy to accommodate. It went on like that for a time. Finally, Doc went to deal his faro table for the evening while I thanked everyone for their compliments. *For God's sake*, I thought to myself, *I should have sung myself silly in Globe and Tombstone. Who knew what sort of charm could've been wreaked on those populaces?*

I stood behind Doc for the rest of the evening, filling his whiskey glass when he asked and rubbing his shoulders occasionally. At midnight we walked slowly back to the hotel.

"Thank you for that," he said, taking my hand. "I did want to hear you sing again."

The next morning, Doc surprised me. "What do you think about goin' down to Penny Hot Springs and seein' your brother and his family?"

My coffee cup clattered as I put it down in the saucer. "What?" I said, stalling for time. I was surprised. Alexander and I had written, but we hadn't seen each other since I left Davenport, and I'd always felt guilty for not getting in touch with him. What the hell prompted this?

He was doing his Doc best to appear insouciant. "A couple months back, I was doing some security work at a mine over there and we got to know each other. He's a good man. I thought since you're here, you might want to see him."

"Are you sure you're feeling up to that?" I eyed him suspiciously.

" 'Course I am," Doc said, somewhat impatiently. "It's a short trip. We can be there by supper."

329

I was a little skeptical about that, to say nothing of the entire idea, but curiosity won out. I agreed to rent a buggy, and off we went on a fine Colorado morning. The Rockies towered above us, and I loved the clean, woodsy smell of the forest, so different from the dusty, scorched scent of the more familiar desert.

Doc was in an inordinately good mood through the journey and seemed genuinely eager to spend time with Alexander. I, on the other hand, was feeling quite apprehensive. What would my little brother be like after all these years? I still had mixed emotions about leaving him and Wilhelmina to fend for themselves, but I'd had little choice at the time, and they'd seemed to get along in Davenport much better than I had. My life since then had been so chaotic, I hadn't had an opportunity to hunt them down and see how their lives had evolved. And even though I shouldn't have felt guilty about that, somehow I did. However, from the sound of it, they were both much more settled than I was.

The road into Penny Hot Springs was a little rougher than the more traveled one from Glenwood Springs, but we made it without incident. Doc confidently pulled up to a good-sized log cabin set among tall trees and granite boulders. He had obviously been here before. A man wearing work clothes, red suspenders, and boots came out onto the porch, his hand shading his eyes from the setting sun, and I saw two children hovering by the front door. I don't think I would've recognized my brother in a crowd, but as I stepped onto the wooden planks of the porch, he grabbed my shoulders and smiled, his craggy face suddenly transformed into the twelve-year-old I remembered.

"Kate, my God," he said, pulling me into a hug. "It's so good to see you." I hugged him back and burst into tears. I sure hadn't seen that coming, but he just smiled and kissed my cheek.

"Eva, get on out here and meet my sister!" His voice was

suddenly husky, and a slim, dark-haired woman with a sweet smile came outside, wiping her hands on a white apron. "Looks like we'll have two more for supper."

Doc stepped onto the porch and took off his hat, bowing slightly. "How lovely to see you again, Miss Eva. You are lookin' as lovely as a Georgia peach."

She chuckled and held out her hand to me. "This charming devil promised he'd bring you to us, Kate, and I'm so happy to meet you. Alexander never stops talking about you, and I've been pining to see you in the flesh." Her hand was warm and soft, just like her manner. "Come on in the house, and let's get better acquainted."

Dinner was a savory venison stew, and by the time the peach pie was served, I had my lap full of my three-year-old nephew, Jonathan, nodding off with his yellow curls damp against my shoulder. I looked around the table, and my heart was full. My brother had done well if four beautiful children and Eva were the marks of success, and I felt sincerely that they were. Doc, incongruously enough, was involved in a game of cat's cradle with Lisa, the oldest girl. She solemnly led him through the finger movements, and he assiduously followed her instructions, looking up at me through veiled lashes.

"This was wonderful, Eva," I said, as she rose to clear the table. "Let me help you."

She shook her head, motioning me to keep my seat, and I saw the three oldest children get up from their seats, pick up the dishes, and take them to the kitchen.

"You stay right there," she said. "Jonathan's a devil to get quieted down, but you've done wonders with him. We've a method for the rest of this."

I settled back, Jonathan's soft breathing unchanged, and listened to Alexander and Doc talk about the mines, silver prices, and life in Penny Hot Springs as darkness fell outside and the candles grew brighter in their pewter holders. Alexander had a stake in a silver mine, and it had paid very well in the last few years, but he was concerned it was nearly played out. He'd invested in coal as well, which Doc agreed was a solid idea. Clearly, Doc was well acquainted with the mining business in Colorado, and the two of them had become friends. The man never ceased to amaze me with his capacity for becoming well versed in so many avenues and his ability to strike up relationships with the unlikeliest of people.

Eva put the children to bed, and we sat out on the porch, talking, drinking brandy, and watching the stars—so many here so much closer to the sky. For the first time since I'd arrived in Colorado I felt at peace, content to simply be here in this place with the people I loved. Doc had given me a valuable gift bringing me to see Alexander, and I took his hand in mine as we sat there in the dark. We slept that night in Lisa's room, while she generously bunked in with her little brothers. The featherbed was soft, and the pine-scented night breeze wafted through the open casement.

"Thank you," I whispered. "I didn't know how much I needed this."

His hand caressed my cheek. "I did. Your brother did, too. Good night, my lily."

Breakfast was a raucous affair at the Haroney household: blueberry pancakes, eggs, sausage, hungry children, and plenty of coffee to wake up the adults to engineer it all. Convincing Eva I really could cook, I took charge of the pancakes and turned out three dozen while she handled the rest. I was happy to see Doc eat three pancakes under the watchful eye of Lisa, who had appointed him her personal charge. I made his herbal tea, and she watched while he drank every drop. Then she presented the empty cup back to me.

"Does he need another?" she said solemnly. "He's been quite sick, you know."

"Yes," I said. What an astute child. "He has, but he's some better now." She went out with the two older boys, Doc, and Alexander to harness the buggy, and I turned to Eva.

"Thank you so much for everything," I said, and she hugged me close. She was all I could have hoped for in a sister-in-law.

"Don't be a stranger, Kate, now that we have you again. Come anytime; we'll be here."

I gathered the overnight bag Doc had thoughtfully packed, and we went outside. Doc stepped up into the buggy, and Alexander walked me around to the other side, grasping my hand and pulling me to a stop.

"Kate, we're here for you; I want you to know that." His brown eyes bored into mine, and I felt a little uneasy. "I'm not good at this, but it's made me very happy to see you again, and I love you." He hugged me awkwardly, and his voice dropped to a whisper. "Doc loves you very much. Send word when you need me, and I'll be there."

I kissed his cheek and pulled away, glad to take my seat on the buggy. I tucked in my skirts and waved good-bye as we turned onto the road out of Penny Hot Springs. My brother had accepted what I only hoped to stave off, that Doc's disease was in its end stages, and right now I only wanted to get away from anyone who knew the truth, loving and supportive or no. That was truth way too close to the bone.

One morning not two weeks later, Doc simply didn't have the strength to get dressed and leave the hotel. I bustled about, putting on a brave face, but inside I was coming apart. The capricious nature of tuberculosis had made its unwelcome appearance once again, and after a month with no improvement, it looked like it had come to stay. It was all I could do not to rage and throw Doc's untouched plates across the room. Even when the railroad came to Glenwood on October fifth, Doc was simply too weak to get outside to see it. We watched through the window and reminisced about the July Fourth railroad celebration in Las Vegas. In fact, that came to be how we spent a great deal of our time after that—remembering all the times we'd had together, and some we'd had separately. It proved to be quite interesting.

The days passed, alternating between hope and despair. My latest creation of strawberries and chocolate mousse was tempting for only two bites before Doc smiled apologetically and pushed the plate away, his eyes closing. I added his dish to the others already piled on the tray. Then I carried the tray down to the kitchen, thinking that even my herbal teas seemed of little use anymore and wondering what to try next.

One afternoon Art stopped me on my way through the lobby.

"How is he today?" His face showed genuine concern, and I squeezed his hand gratefully.

"No better, I'm afraid. I'm on my way to the kitchen to see what I can come up with. I was thinking I'd try chicken soup with dumplings."

He smiled. "That sounds good, Miss Kate. He'd like that. Maybe some cherry pie with whipped cream for dessert?"

"Absolutely grand idea, Art. You can have some, too."

I hurried off to the kitchen, and an hour later, with the soup cooking and the pie in the oven, I wandered outside the back door just like I used to in Las Vegas when the cooking was momentarily done. I sat on a packing crate and lit a cheroot, thinking of Andre and where that boy could possibly be now . . . likely San Francisco, creating food that would make those who could afford it weep with joy. I smiled just thinking about it, and a snowflake brushed my cheek. I looked up to see more coming down. Today was my birthday, and the first snow of the season a gift—but really, another day with Doc was all the gift I wanted. I'd never cared much for November, and no matter where in the world I'd lived, November was one dreary month. It seemed like the year was dying along with everything else, and that was not something I wanted to think about at all. I stomped out my cheroot and went back inside.

Doc ate half a bowl of soup and a little cherry pie. I was elated. After dinner he sat beside me in one of the two wing chairs in front of the window, and we watched the falling snow blanket Glenwood Springs. It was like a fanciful marzipan town being frosted with spun sugar, and then, as the streets became deserted, it was enchanted in its isolation. I thought of Glenwood's original name, Defiance, a name that seemed more fitting every day as I dared this hateful disease to take the man I loved.

"Open the window, Kate."

I hesitated. "It's cold out there. I don't want you to get a chill."

"For Christ's sake, woman," Doc said, "I'm dyin' of tuberculosis. At this point, catchin' a cold is the least of my problems."

He made a valid point, but I covered him with a quilt anyway before I pushed up the window. Doc reached over and stuck his arm outside, and within seconds it was covered with big, fluffy flakes of snow. He smiled, and we watched them melt away on the velvet sleeve of his dressing gown.

"Do you think it's true?"

"Is what true?" I said.

"That every snowflake is unique, never the same design as another." He looked at me. "Sort of like people."

"Yes," I said.

He nodded. "There will never be anybody else like us, Kate. We're just like those snowflakes."

I shut the window, and we watched the snow fall until Doc fell asleep.

When I opened my eyes the next morning, it was dim in our room, although I knew it was past eight o'clock. I pulled back the curtain, and the snow was still falling, mounds of the stuff on all the roofs, balconies, and streets. Only a few brave souls were outside. Some were clearing off the sidewalks in front of their businesses, but most were children, staggering about gleefully and hurling snowballs at each other.

Doc was still asleep, his breathing very shallow, but that was normal lately. I turned on the lamp by the window, dressed, and went down through the lobby to order breakfast, wanting to see people's reaction to the storm. It was very quiet—only a few people in the restaurant, or looking outside at the snow, the hotel half empty this time of year. I thought about Alexander and his family, but I wasn't worried about them. They'd been living here a long while now, and this was normal weather for Colorado.

Art came by and dropped the *Glenwood Echo* on the tray, its headline reading, "November 8th, First Snow!" Then he carried the tray upstairs for me, chattering away.

"They must've been up all night over at the newspaper, getting that out," he laughed. "Before their breaking news headline melted away on them, like it usually does this time of year."

I opened the door to our room, and Art put the tray down on the table beside the windows, as usual, while I leaned over the bed to check on Doc.

His arm shot out and grabbed mine, viselike, pulling himself off the pillows.

"Can't breathe, can't . . ." he gasped, and a torrent of blood shot from his mouth, covering the front of his pajamas and me as well.

"Holy shit!" Art said. "I'm getting the doctor." He ran out

through the open door while I sank down on the bed beside Doc, holding him to me while more bloody coughs racked his thin body. There had been blood before, but nothing ever like this. The coughing subsided for a moment, and I lay him down gently and grabbed towels from the bathroom so I could mop at the blood on him and the bedclothes.

"Kate," he gasped. "Oh God, help me." His face was bone white, cheekbones sculpted in his narrow face, eyes blazing in terror. My heart clenched, despair shot through me, and for the first time, I didn't know what to do. He grabbed my hand.

"I'm so cold." His body shuddered. "Whiskey'll help warm me up."

I hesitated. That may have been true, but it didn't seem like a good idea, and I'd kept it away for some time. Still, at this point, maybe that and some hot tea wouldn't hurt. I held a cup of tea laced with whiskey to his lips, and he swallowed it in three gulps, easing back down. He closed his eyes and breathed without coughing.

"Doc, I'm going to clean things up," I said, and he gave me a feeble nod. I took off his soiled nightclothes and washed him gently. Then I tore off the bloody top sheet and pulled the silk comforter around him. I smoothed his hair back, and he smiled faintly.

"You're my huckleberry, darlin'," he said. Then he fell asleep.

I was afraid to go more than four steps away. I poured a cup of coffee and sat on the bed beside him, mesmerized as I watched his chest rise and fall in a gentle rhythm. Soon, Art arrived with Dr. Crook in tow.

He nodded at me, clearly not happy I was still here. "Ms. Haroney. I understand Mr. Holliday was hemorrhaging earlier?"

"Yes."

He took Doc's pulse, listened to his chest, and did a few other medical passes. Then he stood up.

"He's dying," he said.

"I know that," I said. "He's been dying since I got here."

Crook shook his head impatiently. "No, he's dying today, Miss Haroney. There is nothing I can do." He picked up his black bag. Art hovered in the doorway, and his face was ashen, tears glistening in his eyes.

Crook said, "As I am the coroner, please have someone contact me to handle the death certificate." He nodded at me and walked out. This supercilious, arrogant bastard made Johnny Ringo look like a saint. In another time and place, Doc would have shot him. In this one, all I could do was shut the door softly. I lay down beside Doc, my hand in his.

Two hours later, Doc opened his eyes and smiled at me.

"We've had quite a time, haven't we?"

I nodded, my throat too constricted to speak. I'd seen death come calling before, but this time was the worst. I squeezed his hand in mine and sat up, but he shook his head and smiled faintly.

"My Lily," he said, and that was his last breath.

My feet were frozen as I stood beside my brother in the slushy mud of the Linwood Pioneer Cemetery. The Reverend Rudolph finished his eulogy, and I threw the first handful of dirt onto Doc's casket, followed by many more. Nearly a hundred people had turned out for Doc's funeral—even a reporter or two—and I was still amazed by how many lives he had touched in his time in Colorado.

My brother took my arm, and we made our way to the street and then the hotel, where my trunk was ready to load into his wagon. I was going to Penny Hot Springs to stay with Alexander and Eva for a time and to figure out what I was going to do from here. Doc and Alex had talked about this, I learned, and at first, my instincts rebelled from anyone trying to arrange my life. In time, I found comfort in the fact that these two men who both loved me were looking out for my welfare. I had no desire to return to Arizona, and being close to Doc, even if he was under the earth instead of on it, was comforting. I felt as though the foundation of my life, or at least the most important part of it, had crumbled beneath my feet, and I was bereft, both at Doc's absence and my own inability to accept that this time he was gone forever. I didn't want to live without Doc, but I didn't want to die, either. I felt as though the rest of my life would forever be a gray world without passion, joy, or excitement because it would be one without Doc.

We rode out of town, into the teeth of a sleeting mist, and after a time, I leaned on Alexander's shoulder and he put his arm around me.

"It'll be all right, Kate," he said. "Not today, or even tomorrow, but eventually. We're here for you."

Tears ran down my face—it was the first time I'd really let myself grieve—and I let them come, mingling with the harsh touch of icy rain. I was grateful to Alexander for all he'd done, but he didn't really understand. I loved Doc Holliday with every fiber of my being, and I had since the first time I'd laid eyes on him back in Texas, sitting at that piano playing Chopin in Shaughnessey's saloon. I would love him until the day I, too, was laid down in the grave.

Doc was right. We were just like those snowflakes, and there would never be anyone quite like us ever again.

POSTSCRIPT

Mary Katherine Haroney Melvin Elder Cummings was born in Pest, Hungary, on November 7, 1850, and died in Prescott, Arizona on November 2, 1940, just days short of her ninetieth birthday.

After Doc Holliday's death on November 8, 1887, she lived for a time in Colorado, and in 1890, she married a blacksmith named George Cummings in Aspen, Colorado. It seemed to be a marriage of economic necessity, and the two set up domiciles in various mining towns in Colorado and Arizona, Cummings blacksmithing and Kate working as a cook. Things did not go especially well, and by 1899 she left her husband, reputed to be an abusive alcoholic, and took a job at a hotel in Cochise, Arizona, as a housekeeper for Mr. John Rath.

On June 2, 1900, she left there, having found employment as a housekeeper with one John J. Howard, a miner from Dos Cabezos, a small town in southeastern Arizona. For more than thirty years she remained there. On Howard's death, even though he left her his property and all he had, she arranged for his inheritance to go to his daughter. Destitute, she petitioned then-Governor George W. Hunt, a friend from her days in Globe, to be admitted to the Arizona Pioneers Home in Prescott. Although Kate was not technically an Arizona native, having been born in Hungary, Governor Hunt allowed her to take up residence in the Arizona Pioneers Home in Prescott, Arizona, in 1931, and she lived there until her death nine years later. She is buried in Prescott.

They say she was not particularly well liked during her years in Prescott, and if Kate's earlier years are considered along with her distinctive personality, it seems likely that was true. God only knows how she existed for thirty years in Dos Cabezos, now mostly a ghost town, especially when she was living with John Howard, a man history says was extremely unlikeable. Then again, Howard was a maverick himself, a ne'er-do-well miner and likely a bootlegger, an occupation Kate may have been only too happy to assist with, and possibly a man whose quirky personality matched her own. I think Kate found a haven of sorts in Dos Cabezos, a place she never planned to leave and one where she would be unlikely to run into anyone from her old life. There are stories about her reclusiveness, many from children who would occasionally see her through the window, clad always in black, smoking cheroots and drinking coffee.

Historians, both legitimate and not so much, have attempted to interview her and tell her story, but she was both guarded and confused, and little viable information has come from those efforts during her years in Prescott.

From the first moment I learned about Kate, she intrigued me, and I instinctively felt she had been wrongly portrayed, or at least one-sidedly portrayed, in all the movies and books about Tombstone, the Earps, and Doc Holliday. Much of what has been written about her is untrue and sensationalized. While the Haroney family's entry into North America likely began in New York with other European immigrants, rather than as a sojourn in Mexico with the Emperor Maxilimilian, her father was a medical doctor to the royal family, and I decided to use the Mexico story regardless, as it helps illustrate her background and her character. I have used language and quotes from letters and histories for Kate, Doc, and the Earps in this story. For the rest, I have attempted, sticking with the known facts of her past and filling in the large blank spots with a fiction writer's prerogative, to tell Kate's story in a way that I hope she would approve and appreciate.

Rest in peace, Kate. You were, indeed, one of a kind.

ABOUT THE AUTHOR

Kathleen Morris lives in Arizona and graduated from Prescott College in Prescott, Arizona. She has an editorial business and teaches writing. Kathleen has traveled extensively throughout the West, particularly interested in western frontier and Native American history, researching and becoming familiar with many of the locales described in this book. After discovering Kate's final resting place in Prescott, she wanted to find out more about her and tell the real story of this fascinating woman, her life, and loves. *The Lily of the West* is the result.

The employees of Five Star Publishing hope you have enjoyed this book.

Our Five Star novels explore little-known chapters from America's history, stories told from unique perspectives that will entertain a broad range of readers.

Other Five Star books are available at your local library, bookstore, all major book distributors, and directly from Five Star/Gale.

Connect with Five Star Publishing

Visit us on Facebook:
  https://www.facebook.com/FiveStarCengage

Email:
  FiveStar@cengage.com

For information about titles and placing orders:
  (800) 223-1244
  gale.orders@cengage.com

To share your comments, write to us:
  Five Star Publishing
  Attn: Publisher
  10 Water St., Suite 310
  Waterville, ME 04901